That Time I Accidentally Killed the Wrong Guy

Rebekah Sinclair

An Accidental Series
Stand-Alone

Triggers

⚠ This book contains:

High levels of violence, dark humor, explicit content, and a truly irresponsible body count. It includes assassins, betrayal, morally questionable problem-solving, and a series of events that spiral wildly out of control due to one very unfortunate misunderstanding. Reader discretion is advised. Or ignored. That's on you.

Side effects of reading may include:

- A long-standing inability to look at hot dogs the same way ever again.
- Uncontrollable laughter at moments that would make a normal person seek therapy.
- Elevated heart rate due to high-speed chases, collapsing buildings, and the persistent feeling that everything is about to go very wrong.
- Intense distrust of anyone who decorates with a nipple-clad lampshade.
- Mild to severe confusion about whether this is a rom-com, an action movie, or a cautionary tale. (It's all three.)

- Lingering thoughts of *"that could have gone worse"* immediately followed by *"holy shit."*

Trigger warnings include:

- Excessive exposure to killing. Not symbolic. Not restrained. A fuck-ton of it.
- Grave desecration and a complete disregard for the dignity of the deceased, including but not limited to corpse mishandling, misplacement, transportation, and general disrespect.
- A deeply upsetting scenario involving a three-day-old corpse and an industrial hot dog grinder.
- Graphic violence and death of an unusual and creative variety, including but not limited to:
    - Beheadings
    - De-eyeing
    - Boiling
    - Hanging
    - Suffocation
    - Broken necks
    - Death via 150 mph Airplane
    - Egg-drop–related violence (we're not explaining this)
- High-octane, action-packed sequences featuring car chases, building collapses, rooftop escapes, and stunts Tom Cruise would absolutely approve of.
- Cannibalism and one deeply offensive lampshade.

- Blood. So much blood. An amount that should raise questions.
- Strong language used creatively, aggressively, and sometimes just because.
- Explicit sexual content intertwined with violence, betrayal, and morally gray decision-making.
- Use of nearly every weapon imaginable, including firearms, blades, blunt objects, and a processed meat rocket launcher (standard issue).
- Eternal resting places that include, but are not limited to, a pile of camel shit.
- Unapologetic female rage, poor life choices, and a protagonist who solves problems permanently.

If you're easily offended, like your hot dogs innocent, or are deeply committed to nonviolent conflict resolution—this book may not be for you.

But if John Wick feels like a perfectly reasonable life coach?

You're in the right place.

For @HotDogLadyReads
Jess:

We mustard-mit, the Distracted Inklings are glad you stick with us through thick and thin buns. Book signings would be the wurst without you, and above all—we relish your friendship.

You're one in a kielbasa million.

1

Saint

The world's newest tallest building is groaning under its own ego, one bad wire away from folding in on itself. I'm at least fifty floors above sane altitude, hands shaking as I reach for the junction box welded into the steel beam.

Blood slicks my fingers. Some of it mine. Most of it not.

A shadow moves behind me.

I spin just as an assassin lunges, blade flashing. He gets a single breath of triumph before I slam my fist into his jaw and wrench his arm sideways, keeping his hand wrapped around his own gun. His trigger finger spasms. The bullet tears through his neck, then the forehead of the man charging up behind him.

One shot. Two corpses. It's just another day at the office.

The gun is mine before either body hits the industrial carpeted floor.

A third assassin bursts through the half-collapsed doorway, swinging a machete like subtlety is beneath him. I fire once and he drops. The machete clatters across the entrance tile, spinning toward the wall.

Another blade whistles past my ear. Close enough to shear a strand of hair. That one actually pisses me off.

I snatch a knife from my boot and fling it without breaking stride. It buries itself in the thrower's throat, pinning him to the wall like a very poorly placed art installation.

My lungs burn. My shoulder is bleeding where someone grazed me a few floors down. My white tank is a crime scene.

None of that matters.

Not with the junction box gaping open, two final wires dangling like a dare. Twist them, and this 184-story vanity project drops into the desert like a felled titan. I get thirty seconds to escape if I'm lucky.

Twenty, if the building decides it's had enough of me.

I reach for the wires and twist once, twice before cold metal presses to my temple.

A long-range sniper rifle. Up close.

It's like a cold fingertip against my skin, steady despite the wind threading through the shattered framework of the floors I've just come from. I can feel my heartbeat in the raw cut along my shoulder, but the pain has settled into something clean and usable. A reminder, not a distraction.

And then that voice I hate rolls in behind me, low, delighted, smug enough to make my pulse stumble.

"Well, well," he murmurs behind me, tone smug and intimate. "If it isn't Saint James…"

I breathe out through the side of my mouth. "I know. I'm just as disappointed to see you here too."

My fingers twitch toward the last two wires dangling from the gutted junction box. The entire skyscraper hums beneath my feet, its spine vibrating with the tension of a structure seconds from collapse. I've rigged charges down its throat, floor after floor, a stitched line of destruction waiting for this final pulse.

The barrel presses harder into my skin. "Don't even think about it."

"You're late to the party," I tell him. "I've been thinking about it since the elevator shaft."

He shifts his weight, boots scraping against the metal grate—a subtle adjustment, the kind you make when you want a cleaner angle at the kill. Wind gusts against the windows like a phantom drum. Somewhere below, alarms wail through the stairwells like distant sirens in a sinking ship.

"It's over, Saint," he says, as if the words have any power over me. "You've run out of luck and floors."

I let a faint, humorless smile pull at my swollen lip. "The trail of bodies I left on the way up suggests I'm just getting started."

His breath brushes my cheek—too close, too familiar. "I've waited years to watch one of my bullets go through your skull."

"Mmm, I know." My voice drops to a soft rasp. "But I do enjoy putting a damper on your plans. It's practically a personality trait at this point."

"You think you're so fucking funny?" That draws the crack in his composure I've been waiting for. His tone sharpens, no longer amused. "This all started because *you* killed the *wrong* man."

A slow burn ignites behind my ribs. Not rage—rage is loud. This is quieter, colder, the kind of anger that steadies my hands instead of shaking them.

"We both know this started long before that body hit its shallow grave."

"Even now," he counters, "with a gun to your head and every assassin in the world climbing this tower to claim your bounty, you still can't admit you made a mistake."

I huff out a soft laugh, the kind that tastes like blood and defiance. "That's what happens when your balls are bigger than your brain. You forget one simple little detail."

My fingers tighten around the exposed wire—subtle, deliberate, the shift of someone choosing a moment instead of reacting to one. He feels it. The pressure of the rifle increases, firm enough to bruise.

"And what's that?" His voice lowers, the coil before a strike.

"That I'm Saint motherfucking James."

I tilt my head just enough to let the moonlight catch my grin.

"And I don't make mistakes."

I slam the wire against the beam.

A burst of bright, violent sparks leaps across the space between us, catching him full in the eyes. His scream rips through the chamber, raw and ragged, as he twists away. The rifle jerks in his grip, and I shove the barrel off my temple a heartbeat before he fires. The shot goes off beside my ear— too close, too loud. Pain detonates through my skull like someone drove an ice pick into my eardrum, the sound collapsing into a high, vicious ringing that swallows every- thing else.

For a moment my vision swims. My knees threaten to buckle. The metallic taste of adrenaline floods my tongue.

The bullet tears sideways, shattering the nearest pane of

glass. A violent burst of night air slams into the room, freezing and hungry, whipping my afro back and dragging smoke toward the open void three thousand feet below.

I grit my teeth and shake off the disorientation. No time to cradle a blown-out ear.

I twist the wire again, once, twice—the practiced motion of someone who's done this more than she'll ever admit—and press it to the ignition plate.

A single spark jumps.

The skyscraper shudders, a low, resentful groan echoing through the vertical labyrinth beneath us. Then, far below, the first bomb erupts like a muffled thunderclap. One floor. Then the next. Then the next. A chain of detonation rising through the building like the heartbeat of a dying giant.

Every assassin still clawing their way upward realizes at the same moment:

they're not racing to catch me.

They're racing to outrun death. And it's already winning.

I turn back to him.

Smoke curls around us. The floor vibrates with the approaching destruction. The air tastes electric.

Thirty seconds to escape.

Maybe less.

But killing this bastard?

Yeah, I can spare a few.

Saint

5 DAYS AGO

The moon is entirely too pleased with itself tonight.

Full, bright, and shining directly on me like it's judging my life choices while I dig a grave with a shovel better suited for a kindergarten sandbox. Sweat rolls down the back of my neck despite the cool night air, and the dirt here is packed so tight it feels like I'm trying to carve through concrete with a salad spoon.

"This is what I get," I mutter, levering out another miserable scoop of earth. "One week. One damn week of vacation, and I couldn't keep my homicidal little hands to myself."

The corpse lying a few feet away doesn't answer, naturally. He just stares up at the moon with those glassy dark eyes, looking far too peaceful for a man who'd been stupid enough to land himself on the Guild's hit list. Stupid enough that I said yes even with a suitcase half-packed and a beach reservation already paid for.

A low rush of movement whispers across the landscape

—the distant thunder of one of Japan's high-speed trains slicing through the night. It rises, swells, then fades again, leaving the silence thicker than before.

No witnesses.

No civilians.

Just me, this body, and my terminal inability to take a damn break.

"Easy job," I grumble to the grave that still isn't deep enough. "In the middle of nowhere. Quick in, quick out. Doesn't even interfere with my flight. Genius move, Saint."

I jam the shovel back down. The handle vibrates in my palms. My shoulders ache. The moon slides out from behind a drifting cloud, brighter now, throwing silver across the clearing...and straight across the corpse's face.

His eyes catch the light.

Staring.

Silent.

Judgy.

I stop digging, sweat stinging my eyes as I glare back at him.

"What are you looking at, anyways?"

I grab another fistful of dirt and throw it out of the hole just to make a point.

He still doesn't answer.

Which somehow annoys me even more.

I should've stayed my ass in the hotel.

One night. Just one night to relax before my flight to Hong Kong in two days. Then Singapore. Then Bali. A whole string of places where no one expects me to kill anyone, and I fully intended to keep it that way. But no— apparently I can't be trusted alone with a hotel bathrobe and a minibar without sniffing out a contract and convincing myself it's "just one quick job."

I blame the renovations happening in my apartment. The noise. The dust. The lack of hot water. I've been cooped up for weeks, and I haven't taken a real vacation in years. I travel constantly, but it's always recon over ramen, assassinations between espresso shots, one neat little murder followed by a red-eye home. That is not vacation. That is homicide with extra steps.

So this time, I treated myself. Booked flights. Packed outfits that don't double as tactical gear. And my first stop had to be Japan.

I lived here for years—back when the ink on my Guild initiation papers was still drying and I was the clueless little New Yorker dropped into a world that felt bigger, brighter, sharper. Everything about Japan cracked me open. The food. The language. The impossible quiet of rural nights. Even the discipline.

Especially the discipline.

Master Kenji—Takahashi Kenji, legend of the Guild— took me in when I was barely more than a street rat with a decent punch and terrible impulse control. His training was strict. Brutal. No distractions. No indulgences. No softness. For months, I wasn't allowed off his property. Just drills, meditation, sparring, more drills. A life carved down to bone.

But as I proved myself, he let me explore farther. First the nearby villages. Then the small towns. Then the cities, neon and alive, teeming with people and noise and possibility. I fell in love with all of it.

It's been too long since I came back.

I make a mental note—call Master Kenji. If he's still here, he'd get a kick out of seeing me again. The old man always did have a soft spot for his most stubborn student. And I feel like an ungrateful brat for not visiting sooner.

A rush of a bullet train cuts through the night again, pulling me out of my wandering thoughts. The sound fades as the quiet settles back over the clearing, and with it comes the reminder that I'm not alone.

I look at the body.

Still sprawled where I dropped him. Still staring at the sky like he's contemplating the moon. Still dead as the dirt I'm shoveling.

I study his face, squinting as if that might tell me what crime got him a slot on the Guild's list. Embezzler? No—he has soft-office-hands. Maybe a smuggler. Or a trafficker. Or someone who pissed off the wrong executive in the wrong backroom.

I shake my head. None of it fits.

"Well, it doesn't really matter now, does it?" I mutter.

Another shovel-full of dirt hits the pile.

The hole is finally taking shape. Not pretty, not deep enough for Guild standards, but I'm sweaty, my tiny shovel is an insult to Earth-moving tools everywhere, and he isn't in a position to file a complaint.

"Good enough," I say, brushing the hair out of my face with the back of my wrist.

I jab the shovel into the earth one last time and lean on it, breathing hard under the moon's bright, nosy glare. My heartbeat is steady. My muscles ache in the good way. For a fleeting second, it actually feels peaceful.

Me, a grave, and a mark that better not be more trouble than he's worth.

I climb out of the grave and straighten, brushing dirt from my hands until my palms sting. The night air is cooler up here, untouched by sweat and exertion, and for a moment I just breathe it in before circling the body.

Time to make it official.

I pull out my phone, tap the Guild's secure app, and the kill-log interface opens with its usual cold efficiency. I crouch, grab his wrist, and press his thumb to the screen. The scanner flashes once, blinks red, and throws an error.

Of course.

I try again, angling his thumb differently, wiping away the smear of blood with the edge of my sleeve. Another red flash. No signature. No print. Nothing.

A low groan escapes me. "You have *got* to be kidding."

I lift both his hands and finally see the problem: shredded palms, skin torn open from when I hurled him through the third-floor window of that empty office building. Clean kill. Minimal noise. No witnesses, no security, no alarms.

Convenient then.

Infuriating now.

"Couldn't have just landed on your back, huh?" I mutter. Fine. If the thumbprint's useless, there's always the backup.

I tilt his head, pull his eyelid open, and bring my phone close. The retinal scanner hums softly. One beat, two—then the app flashes bright green.

Kill confirmed.

Funds transferred.

Vacation back on track.

"About damn time."

I stand and nudge him lightly with the toe of my boot. The body rolls into the grave, landing on its back with a soft thud. Moonlight hits his face just right, and that crooked little smirk he died wearing seems even more obnoxious now. It'll probably still be there when he starts to rot.

"Enjoy your new home," I tell him, voice low. "No neighbors. No noise complaints. Perfect retirement plan."

I kneel at the edge of the hole, mini-shovel dangling from one hand while I rest my forearms on my knees. My breath eases. My pulse slows. The night settles again, empty and wide, the wind carrying only distant train noise and the faint hum of insects. No one is going to wander out here. No one is going to find him.

The job is done.

The promise of real rest is finally within reach.

I take one last look at him and sigh. "Goodbye, unlucky bastard. And I swear—no more kills. At least not until my vacation is over."

With the solemnity of someone who doesn't have much faith in that statement, I scoop the first shovel-full of dirt and toss it onto his chest.

The first layer of dirt settles over him, soft as dust. The night is still again, save for the faint hum of a train far in the distance. For a moment, it almost feels peaceful.

Almost.

As much peace as a woman can get while standing over a half-dug grave with a dead man staring up at her.

I set my jaw, raise the shovel, and get back to work.

3

Saint

I wake to a wall of sunlight stabbing directly into my skull.

Hotel rooms always do this.

All that pristine, expensive blackout technology...and somehow the light still finds one microscopic gap in the curtains and aims for my face like it holds a grudge.

I groan, roll to the side, and pat the nightstand until my fingers find the crystal tumbler I never bothered to wash. There's still a swallow of whiskey at the bottom. With one eye squeezed shut against the glare, I tip it back.

The burn kicks straight down my throat.

"That'll pep you up," I croak.

I flop onto my stomach, arms wrapped loosely around the pillow, letting out a long breath that sinks into the mattress. My eyes fall shut almost immediately. Sleep drags at me in warm, heavy waves, whispering that a few more minutes won't hurt anyone.

My shoulders ache—a dull, satisfying throb from hacking at packed earth with a shovel the size of a toddler's toy—but last night's hot shower and the bowl of tofu tempura ramen I ordered from room service worked miracles. Nothing knocks me out faster than salt, heat, and fermented soybeans. I'm soft like that.

Master Kenji lives only a couple hours' drive from here. Plenty of time to rest before I see him. He'll probably scold me for letting my form get sloppy, then feed me until I can't breathe. The man only knows discipline and hospitality.

I let myself drift.

Almost asleep again.

Then the buzzing starts.

One vibration.

Then another.

Then another.

A relentless, mosquito-like drone coming from the phone beside my head—each buzz sharpening into a tiny spike of irritation. If this keeps up, my "no murders" vow from last night is going straight into the trash.

I grope blindly for the phone, intending to silence it, but the screen lights up before I can swipe.

A whole string of notifications. All from the Guild app.

That wakes me up faster than the whiskey.

I blink the sleep from my eyes and scroll through them. Looks like the message boards are losing their collective minds about something—reacting in real time, half chaos, half enthusiasm, exactly like assassins on the internet always are.

"Damn, they're not playing."

"Biggest bounty I've seen in years."

"Biggest bounty in Guild history, numb nuts."

"Worth the risk?"

"For this payout? Hell yes."

"Wanna buddy up on this one? 50/50?"

"Fuck yes, brother."

"Someone's about to get smoked."

I snort under my breath. Vultures. Give them a juicy contract and they salivate like it's treat time at the zoo. The Guild tries to pretend we're professionals, but the message boards always expose the truth.

Curious now, I scroll upward.

The comments keep getting wilder.

"That's not a bounty, that's a retirement plan."

"I knew that bitch would piss off the wrong people."

"I'm calling it now: contract will be claimed by breakfast."

"If anybody else gets here first, I'm gonna lose my mind."

"This is gonna be fun."

I frown, half amused, half confused. They don't usually gossip this hard unless it's political. Or personal.

Another notification pops up—bounty listing finalized.

My thumb hesitates.

Then I tap it.

The screen loads and I shoot upright in bed, blankets falling around my waist, the cold AC licking across every inch of exposed skin and leaving goosebumps in its wake.

My throat goes tight.

The bounty is not on some dignitary.

Not on a crime boss.

Not on a traitor.

It's on me.

My face.

My file.

My kill history.

A price on my fucking head.

My heartbeat stumbles.

"What the hell...?"

The details sharpen as the app registers the full posting:

Saint James has broken the Guild's #1 law and is sentenced to death.

Payout unrestricted.

Open to all active and former operatives.

My stomach knots.

That law isn't just written. It's sacred.

No kill without contract.

No exceptions. No bending. No excuses. You break it, you're done. Most assassins would rather die than cross that line.

Most.

A sharp sting rises in my chest, something old and unwelcome, and I force it back down before the name attached to it can break through.

I focus on the screen instead, scanning for the mistake.

There has to be one.

The contract from last night should be here. I logged the hit. Accepted it through the official channel. Claimed it within the window. Retinal verification, clean execution. Nothing sloppy, nothing suspicious.

I open my kill history and it's fucking empty.

Not partially. Not corrupted.

Gone.

As if I never accepted the contract. Never confirmed it. Never touched the man who's currently six feet under the dirt outside town.

My chest tightens.

"How the hell did—"

My phone vibrates in my hand again, harder this time, as if the Guild app itself is frantic. The message boards are exploding—notifications piling faster than I can swipe.

Assassins planning meetups.

Calling dibs.

Splitting travel routes.

Placing bets on top of the bounty like this is some kind of sick tournament.

And the number... the bounty itself is obscene.

A figure so big it feels like an insult to the entire industry. Designed to tempt every hunter alive. Designed to make them sprint.

The kill needs to be confirmed within two days.

A guarantee the pursuit will be immediate and vicious.

My mouth goes dry.

"Fuck."

The posting time catches my eye.

One hour ago.

Which means the hunters are already moving.

Already packing.

Already tracking.

And I've been unconscious in a hotel bed, drooling on the pillow while the world geared up to put me in the ground.

Before I can think, the screen refreshes. Everything freezes for a moment—then collapses outward, dumping me unceremoniously back at the login page.

I try my username.

Access denied.

User not found.

My stomach drops.

That's the moment it hits—really hits—like a blade settling between my ribs.

My identity is gone.

My history erased.

My status burned out of existence.

I am no longer Guild. No longer protected.

I'm the world's most wanted mark.

Every assassin across every continent now has my name glowing on their screen.

And they've all had a one-hour head start.

I'm already moving before the thought finishes forming.

Time to fucking go.

4

Saint

I'm dressed in seconds.

Jeans. Shirt. Boots. All black. Nothing fancy, nothing memorable. My backpack hits the bed and I start throwing essentials inside with the efficiency of someone who's had to flee more than one country in her lifetime.

IDs. Cash. Passport.

Brass knuckles.

Throwing knives.

Burner phones.

My fingers find my Swiss army knife on the nightstand. My favorite one. The multi-purpose, multi-problem-solver that's bailed me out of more situations than I care to count. That goes straight into my back pocket.

Two more blades slide into the holsters strapped around my ankles. Familiar weight. Familiar comfort.

I snap open a magazine, check the bullets and I slam it back into place. One gun goes into the shoulder holster under my arm; the other into the waistband against my spine, shirt pulled over it to hide the outline.

Next problem: my hair.

My afro is a whole personality, as she should be, but right now she's a liability. Every photo, every dossier, every file the Guild ever kept on me features it. An easy beacon in a crowd.

The fact I can't take care of her this morning pisses me off more than I already am. The fact I have to tame my baby down—murderous rage.

I slide a thick elastic headband into place, pulling it back until my curls are cinched tight and contained. It'll buy me a few seconds of anonymity. Maybe

I grab the pack of gum from the nightstand, unwrap one piece, pop it into my mouth. Then another. The familiar artificial strawberry hits my tongue and steadies me. Always has.

I've got to get a fucking move on, so I sling my leather jacket on.

Backpack is snug over both shoulders and my mirrored aviators are the finishing touch.

I turn once, scanning the room—every corner, every shadow, every surface that might hold something I need—but there's nothing, and I can't afford to spend another second here.

I ease the door open and slip into the hallway.

Two doors down, an older man sits slouched in a chair like he's guarding the wallpaper. Hat pulled low. Chin on his chest. Completely zonked the hell out. The bottle of wine in his hand is more air than liquid; the neck of it rests precariously on his thigh.

Not a threat. Just drunk and inconveniently present.

I scan the hall anyway, tracing the corners, the vents, the ceiling fixtures—every obvious nest an assassin would stake out if the roles were reversed. I've done it myself. Twice I've watched someone go rogue, watched the Guild hunt their own like wolves tearing at a stray. One of those times hit too close to home; the memory tries to claw upward, but I push it down before it takes shape.

The contract on me is open.

Guild members, independents, exiles.

Anyone with a pulse and a gun and with *this* bounty, plus to notoriety of taking down the Guild's top killer, ghosts from all corners of the globe will be turning up.

In three long strides, I'm at the stairwell. I shove the door open and slip inside, boots hitting concrete as I take the steps two at a time, the echo of my own descent chasing me. Elevators are a death trap. Stairwells at least give me corners, angles, options.

My breathing stays measured. Controlled. No panic—panic gets people killed faster than bullets.

The fake ID I used to check in should buy me time. I have several aliases; some I've never even deployed and won't be in the Guild cache. They'll know I'm in Japan because of last night's hit, but that only narrows it to a few cities.

The morning rush is already rolling through the streets —commuters pouring into stations, bakeries opening, shops unlocking their doors.

Crowds are good cover.

Crowds are also collateral waiting to happen.

I don't like the tradeoff, but I don't have a choice.

I hit the ground floor, slip into the lobby without slowing, and blend into the morning foot traffic. The building's glass doors slide open, and a wave of city noise slams into me—train horns, bicycle bells, chatter, the soft hum of life moving normally while mine is seconds from detonation.

But it's fine. I'll move fast and keep my head down.

All I need is the bullet train. Once I'm on it, I can disappear for an hour or two.

But before I even think about Kenji's place, there's another stop I have to make. A necessary one. I'm under no illusion he can save me—interfering with a Guild bounty would be suicide for him too. He follows the old rules. Neutrality. Observation. Intervene in nothing unless the Guild commands it.

But his estate is neutral ground.

And he has resources—gear, weapons, tools—that I can restock with.

I can disappear properly once I'm off this island and find out who the fuck called a hit out on me. Because someone is certainly going to die over this.

It's just not going to be me.

The train station is only a few blocks away—straight shot through morning foot traffic, down a vendor-lined street, across a plaza where businessmen cluster around convenience-store coffee. Easy enough under normal circumstances.

Not today.

I'm half a block from the station entrance when I see a familiar face.

Old guard.

One of the long-timers who's been killing professionally since before I learned to tie my shoes. He's leaning against a newspaper stand pretending to read a paper.

My pulse doesn't jump.

My stride doesn't change.

I keep walking like I didn't clock him from fifty feet out but internally, every instinct wakes the hell up.

Fine. One assassin is manageable. Let's see who else is here though.

I catch another across the street.

Young, twitchy, watching the crowd instead of blending with it, trying too hard not to stare in my direction. His jacket hangs too heavy on one side—gun weight. Fucking rookies. Bringing a god damn cannon to a knife fight.

I don't look directly at either of them.

I don't need to.

I keep moving, sliding through the pedestrian flow, letting the shifting bodies cloak me. The scent of grilled skewers and fresh bread blows through the air—normal, comforting. The kind of morning that should've been peaceful.

Instead, every step feels like nudging closer to a tripwire.

The station is one long block away now.

My fingers drift casually toward my jacket zipper—not to open it, but to feel for the shoulder holster beneath. The market street narrows up ahead. Vendors call out deals in rapid-fire Japanese. Bells chime softly from a passing bicycle.

Behind me, footsteps quicken.

Ahead, someone shifts position.

I feel it before I see him—the third assassin stepping just slightly out of place. He's by a kiosk selling tourist trinkets: keychains, phone charms, tiny fans. Too still. Too centered. Waiting for me to walk straight into range.

Shit.

I keep walking.

Three more steps.

Four.

I wait as long as I can.

Longer than I should.

Then he steps into my path.

A polite little move.

A soft smile.

A click of readiness behind his eyes and all bets are off.

He steps out—too confident, too certain he's read my approach. He expects me to hesitate. Maybe veer. Maybe widen my path so he can corner me cleanly.

I don't give him any of that.

My pace shifts—not a stop, not a flinch. Just a slight quickening of the last two steps that throws his timing off. His hand twitches toward his jacket and that's all I need.

I move twice at once.

My right hand flashes up, the thin blade of my multi-tool snapping open with a whisper. I jab it into the soft triangle of his neck—fast, deep, precise—right through the artery. No flourish. No wasted motion.

His breath catches wetly.

At the exact same moment, my left hand clamps around his gun hand. Four fingers snap in a clean, efficient sequence, each break sharp enough to make his knees buckle. He can't shoot. Can't scream. He's too busy choking on his own blood, eyes going wide as he tries to process what just happened.

I catch him before he falls.

To everyone else on the street, it looks like I'm helping a drunk. An unsteady man. A boyfriend who had one drink too many before breakfast. My arm settles around him, supporting his collapsing weight.

"Easy," I murmur, guiding him as his legs fold.

I turn sharply, slipping us both into the indoor market entrance just beside us. Fluorescent lights flicker overhead, humming softly. A handful of early vendors unpack crates, too focused on their own tasks to notice anything out of place.

I sit him in the nearest empty chair, angle his body so it slumps naturally, head down like he's simply nodding off.

He won't be moving again.

I wipe the blade against the inside of my jacket as I walk away, sliding it back into my pocket without looking down.

Then I cut down a row of stalls—quiet, quick, slipping between racks of produce and shelves of dried fish—before taking another sharp turn into the maze of the market.

No one stops me.

No one calls out.

No one notices a thing.

Exactly the way I like it.

The indoor market swallows me whole—steam hissing from griddles, vendors shouting orders, customers bumping into each other with polite, muttered apologies. The noise alone is enough cover to take down an army.

I head for the side door midway through the building, weaving through the crowd.

Right on cue, Mr. Twitchy barrels in behind me—the idiot with the cannon stuffed in his jacket. I don't need to turn to confirm; I can feel the ripple of space around him as people instinctively give him a wider berth. Subtle as a car alarm.

I roll my eyes. *Of course he followed.*

I pivot left before he gets a chance to spot me, slipping between a couple browsing pickled daikon. The air reeks of frying oil, miso, and sweat. Perfect.

Then I see her.

Unlike the obvious dogs outside, this one is actually dangerous: an older woman, pushing a metal cart piled with vegetables. Quiet. Unassuming. But the sleeve tugged too far down her wrist is a tell—all that overeager fabric hiding whatever spring-loaded blade she's got waiting under there.

She brushes past a stall, and I pluck a mushroom right off the vendor's heap without breaking stride.

Kenji taught me that one.

A harmless little thing when sautéed.

Deadly in seconds when raw.

I don't slow. I don't look at her. I simply reach out, seize her throat, and shove the mushroom past her lips so hard my knuckles brush her uvula. Her eyes bulge. She tries to inhale. Bad choice—she has to swallow or choke.

She swallows.

She recognizes the taste before the bite even hits her stomach. Her pupils blow wide. She staggers, claws at her throat, and runs—searching for a bathroom, a sink, anything to reverse the inevitable.

She won't make it five steps before her gut lining liquefies.

"Thanks, Kenji," I mutter, slipping through a narrow path between two ramen stalls.

I'm three strides away from the side door when I freeze.

Because standing dead center in the aisle—tall enough to

see over the shoppers' heads, turning slowly as he searches—
is a ghost.

Alejandro Cruz.

Sombra.

The Shadow.

He shouldn't be here.

He shouldn't be anywhere.

He was exiled two years ago, stricken from every record, declared kill-on-sight. The manhunt was vicious; the rumors even more so. Some said he died. Some said he vanished into the mountains. Some said he took out half the hunters sent after him before evaporating like smoke.

But here he is.

Alive.

And hunting *me*.

He looks exactly the same.

Six-six, maybe six-seven, shoulders broad enough to eclipse the aisle. That strong, sculpted face—molten dark eyes, jaw sharp enough to cut glass, the effortless elegance he always carried wrapped in expensive leather and a tailored coat meant for someone who makes death look fashionable.

No sniper rifle, which is...wrong.

He's never without a long-range kill option.

Never.

The fact that he's on foot means he came in close.

For me.

He turns—and locks eyes with me.

My steps halt without permission.

The market blurs.

The noise drops to a muffled hum.

For one suspended second, it's just us and memory hits like a blade to the ribs.

The beach and breeze. Salt clinging to our skin. His hand sliding down my thigh and my fingers tangled in his soft hair.

His mouth at my ear whispering, *I'll be right back. Promise.*

Then he walked away and betrayed the Guild. Two days later, his exile notice hit the boards.

Open contract.

Kill on sight.

And then he disappeared like fog in sunlight, yet here he stands.

And as if he knows *exactly* what I'm remembering, the motherfucker has the audacity to grin.

Hardly a smile—just the faintest tug at one corner of his mouth.

Almost not there but I see it.

And I'm going to cut it off him.

Saint

The world snaps back into motion the moment I hear him.

"I said fucking move!"

Twitchy's voice tears through the market, a dozen yards behind me.

Yeah—he definitely saw me.

I pivot just enough to catch his expression. That murderous glare blazing with the fury of a thousand pissed-off devils. Honestly? It's almost funny.

I swing my gaze back to Alejandro, lift an eyebrow, give him a tiny nod.

Then I run.

He does too.

I shove through the last cluster of shoppers and hit the door at full speed, bursting out into the street. The cold air smacks my face, but I don't slow. My legs take over—trained muscle memory, long strides, razor focus.

Behind me, the old-timer drops his newspaper. His sprint isn't what it used to be, but he's still fast enough to be annoying.

I keep going.

Head down and arms pumping.

Dodging commuters already spilling into the sidewalks.

A gunshot cracks behind me.

The bullet slams into a wooden stall so close to my head I can feel the splinters kiss my cheek. Guess the old man's not in the mood for cardio.

Screams erupt and the street explodes into chaos.

People scatter, running in every direction—and I use the mess to duck down an extra block.

I plan to double back toward the station, but a sharp, cold feeling tightens in my gut.

Eyes.

On me.

Alejandro.

He went high.

Probably staring at me through a scope right now, finger hovering over a trigger that's ended more lives than famine.

I veer hard, turning down an aisle I nearly miss. Bright umbrellas stretch overhead like a canopy, shielding the alley from any aerial viewpoint. Perfect.

I slip through them, adjusting my route every few steps in case a high-caliber round is tracking my skull.

My hand dives into my pocket. Fingers close around a coin.

I hit the end of the alley at a sprint, vault over a low gate, then another, ignoring the guards shouting behind me as I clear the barriers surrounding the station plaza.

I *should* have checked train schedules yesterday.

If I had been here working, I would have every train and flight schedule down in case I needed a quick exit. But I was acting like a person on vacation instead of a burnout assassin trying to detox from murder.

The time is going to cost me precious seconds.

Lucky me—I spot the departure board over the heads of a rushing crowd. One line jumps out:

Platform 4 – Departure in 2 minutes. And headed in just the direction I need.

Perfect.

Until Twitchy steps right into my path, dragging out the oversized cannon he brought to this little party. Bold. Mostly stupid. But bold.

He doesn't get a shot off because I slam the heel of my hand into the muzzle, smashing it back into his face. His nose breaks with a wet crunch. Before he can scream, I twist, grab his chin, and snap his neck. His body drops—and so does the ridiculous gun, clattering across the polished tile like a fallen anchor.

I'm already moving and within seconds, I slide into the ticket kiosk, jam the coin into the slot, and pound the button for Platform 4. The machine whirs, slow as molasses, counting down the longest five heartbeats of my life.

I scan the station entrance.

The old man arrives—sweating, winded, furious.

But no Alejandro.

Doesn't matter.

He's somewhere. I know he is.

The ticket drops and I snatch it, sprinting for the stairs.

Now I just look like any other commuter running late— except my pulse is a live wire and someone will absolutely die if they touch me right now.

I take the stairs two at a time.

Three when the gap's small enough.

People complain as I shoulder past; I don't look back for pleasantries.

The turnstile slows me again.

I mutter every curse I know while fighting with the ticket and the reader.

At last, the gate opens—right as a calm female voice announces in Japanese:

"Stand clear. The doors are closing."

I am definitely not standing clear.

I push off the floor, hit a dead sprint, and launch myself forward. The train doors begin to slide shut—

I slip inside a heartbeat before they seal.

Breath ragged.

Hands shaking.

Heart pounding.

The train glides forward, smoother than butter, barely a vibration beneath my boots. I stay near the front of the car for a beat, watching the right side for movement. Nothing suspicious catches my eye.

I start walking left, slow enough to blend, fast enough to keep my lead. My eyes never stop moving—every face, every hand, every shift in posture.

Doors slide open when I approach, then seal quietly behind me.

The next car smells like coffee—rich, dark, comforting. My stomach twists. I could kill for caffeine. Maybe a breakfast sandwich. Normally I'd have something in my bag—a protein bar, fruit jerky, something quick.

But I wasn't supposed to be running for my life today.

I was going to all-inclusive resorts. Beach lounges. Umbrella drinks.

My backpack is barebones and it's my own fault.

I pass through two cars without issue.

Halfway down the third, adrenaline spikes—sharp, electric—half a second before a hand whips out toward me.

I drop my weight and he misses, fingers slicing through empty air.

My knife is already in my hand, the pointed blade flicking open with a quiet snap. I thrust directly toward his face—

He twists, fast, and I drive the blade into the seat just behind him instead. Foam hisses. Fabric tears.

He uses the opening to grab my wrist, wrenching me sideways. My body whips across, slamming into the seat beside him. I hit the cushion hard, shoulder jarring.

I throw an elbow—sharp, tight—but he blocks easily, angling me back. I twist under his arm, slide across the space, and hook myself onto the seat opposite him. Both my hands grip the armrests as I lift my body fully off the ground and kick.

Both boots slam into his chest—hard.

His breath leaves him in an undignified "oof."

His pistol clatters to the floor.

I don't think—I draw my gun on instinct, bringing it up—

But he's already reaching down. He grabs the fallen gun, and I stomp my heel onto his hand, pinning both his wrist and the weapon to the floor.

He snarls and reaches up with his free hand, grabbing my wrist to shove my aim off-line before I can fire.

And in a second we're locked in a perfect stalemate.

Alejandro's dark brown eyes burn into mine.

Exactly as intense as he's always been.

The entire fight was silent. Violent, yes. But contained. Focused. Not a single passenger at the far end of the car turns our way.

We breathe hard in sync, sweat pearling at our hairlines.

"I'm not here to kill you, Saint." He whispers. His voice is deeper than I remember. Richer. Maybe it's the adrenaline. The close quarters. Or maybe it was always like this, and two years was enough to dull my memory.

His Spanish accent slides through me like it always did, tracing down my spine, but I keep my face blank.

"Excuse me if I don't believe you," I mutter back, tone sharp enough to cut.

"What other choice do you have?" he asks quietly.

"I could kill you at least a dozen ways without leaving my seat."

The soft thrum of noise comes from the next doorway behind him.

A train attendant greeting passengers in Japanese, stepping car to car, checking tickets, taking coffee orders.

Alejandro and I stay frozen.

My foot still pins his gun hand.

His fingers still clamp around my wrist, keeping my weapon angled toward the wall.

Two seconds until the attendant looks our way.

One.

We break apart at the same instant—guns vanishing into holsters, postures resetting as if we've been here, calm and harmless, all along.

By the time the attendant reaches us, Alejandro is leaning back with an easy smile—one of those disarming, devastating ones that makes strangers trust him and enemies hesitate.

She switches to English the moment she sees us. "May I get you anything from the café?"

Alejandro begins to answer he's already ordered when another attendant arrives behind her, pushing a cart.

Two coffees.

Two breakfast croissants.

Ham, egg, and cheese for him.

Egg and cheese for me.

He smiles politely as he takes the coffees.

Then he glances at me—and the smile turns wicked, like he sees the "eat shit and die" written all over my face.

Fuck him.

I take the coffee anyway.

He pulls a small folding table from the armrest and sets his down neatly, then reaches back for the two plates. He slides his onto the table, then holds mine toward me like a peace offering.

"Five minutes," he says softly. "That's it."

I study him, looking for anything—tension around the eyes, tightness in the jaw, the tiny muscle that used to twitch when he lied. I used to be able to read him effortlessly. I thought I could.

I had no clue that the day he kissed me goodbye on that beach, he planned to go rogue. To kill without sanction. To ignite a powder keg between two volatile nations. To disappear.

He waits.

Alejandro has always been more patient than I am.

"Five minutes," he repeats, "and you have my permission to slit my throat if I say anything you don't like."

"What if I didn't like that?" I say in a quiet threat.

His smile widens.

Not mocking. Not cruel.

Certain.

He leans back, knowing damn well I'm going to take the deal. And the breakfast.

I grab the plate and he savors his small victory with a sip of the hot coffee before he says, "Well, well. If it isn't Saint James."

Alejandro

Saint sits across from me, eyes still bright from the chase. She hasn't touched the sandwich. The coffee sits untouched too. No surprise. She probably thinks both are poisoned.

I wouldn't blame her. If our roles were reversed, I be suspicious.

Forty-eight hours. That's all the time I had.

Two days since my broker whispered that the Guild planned to sacrifice her the way they tried to sacrifice me. And in those two days, I had to find her—never easy, especially when she doesn't want to be found—shadow her through the job that would mark her as an exile, and slip a tracker onto the bumper of the car she stole so I'd know where she dumped last night's corpse.

Then came the waiting.

Sitting in the hotel room across from hers while the Guild put a hit out on their golden girl. Five assassins came for her; five ended up in my room instead. My broker's switch in the reservation system worked perfectly. Busy night at my door. Bloody, too. The double queen beds are buried under bodies now, stacked neatly.

When her Guild app finally woke her up and betrayed her, my broker's device was already planted in her room, piggybacking off her network access. The text came seconds later: She's up.

I left two minutes before she did. Had to deal with one last assassin in the hallway. No time to hide the body, so I propped the old man in a chair like any other drunk who'd passed out where he stood. The cleaning staff is in for a memorable morning.

Now she's here. In front of me. All fire and heat, exactly as she's always been. That soft floral scent mixed with worn leather hits me like a ghost of a life I used to be a part of.

She hasn't changed.

Except she has—she's better at hiding her tells.

I don't even see the shift in her expression before her fist cracks into my nose.

"Fucking Christ, Saint," I growl, grabbing a napkin and pressing it to my face before blood gets everywhere.

She finally picks up the coffee depositing her pink gum to the edge of her plate. She takes a slow sip. A bite of the sandwich. Apparently she's decided I'm not here to kill her.

Her gaze lifts, sharp and bored at the same time.

"You've wasted a minute staring at me," she says. "You're down to four now, so I'd get to the point."

Mi Pícarita*. Always impatient.

And I do have a point.

Just not one she's ready to hear.

I lean back in the seat, napkin still pressed to my nose, and watch her eyes. Hungry. Suspicious. Running on instinct and caffeine fumes.

"I'm here to propose a truce. To be partners."

---

* **my little troublemaker**

She snorts. "In what universe?"

"In this one," I say. "The only one we get."

Her jaw ticks. She hates when I talk like that—quiet, certain, as if the truth is something I decide.

"I don't partner with traitors," she says.

"And I apparently don't exist anymore," I counter. "Yet here we are."

Her gaze flickers, a crack in the mask. She doesn't want to think about the day two years ago that is so eerily similar to her reality today.

It's still too new for her to feel real yet.

"You're an exile, Alejandro. The Guild burned your file and salted the earth."

I let out a soft huff. "And now they're doing the same to you. Welcome to the other side."

Her fingers curl around the coffee cup like she's imagining strangling it. Or me.

"You expect me to believe you?" she asks, taking another bite. "After the stunt you pulled two years ago? After you vanished?"

Vanished. That's one word for it.

Exiled is the one the Guild prefers.

Framed is the one that ruined us.

I study her face—the tightness around her eyes, the grief she refuses to look at. She isn't asking for truth. She's asking if she's a fool for still wanting it.

"Believe what you want," I say quietly. "But the reason I disappeared is the same reason you're sitting across from me now."

She tries to hide the flinch. Fails.

"Don't," she whispers. "Don't pretend we're the same."

"We are the same," I murmur. "We were framed. Both of us. Different jobs. Same architect."

She goes still. No breath, no blink.

There it is.

The shock. The cut. The crack. She can't deny there could be truth to it.

But she recovers fast—always faster than I expect.

"If you know who set me up," she says, "say it."

"I will," I tell her. "When you agree to work with me."

She scoffs. "You're unbelievable."

"I know." I drop the napkin, test my nose and it's not bleeding anymore. "But I'm also right."

She narrows her eyes. "You're stalling."

"I'm negotiating."

"You're hiding something."

"So are you," I say. "But it doesn't matter. We have a common enemy. The Guild wants us both dead."

Her laugh is humorless. "You think that earns you trust?"

"No." I lean forward, lowering my voice. "But it earns me five minutes of your time. And I plan to use them well."

"I don't believe the Guild did this." Her gaze is a wildfire held behind glass. Dangerous. Beautiful.

Exactly as I remember.

"Then you are naive, Saint James. And naivety won't survive a single night."

I wait for the refusal. The insult. The knife.

Instead, she stands up and walks away. "You have two minutes left."

Same old Saint. Always making me work for it.

I follow her down the length of the train, and, as always,

the world moves for her. People take one look and part like tide around rock. When I come through, they suddenly forget how to step aside. I shoulder past a businessman who huffs. Pathetic.

Saint doesn't slow. Her hand lifts occasionally as she sips the coffee I brought—tiny, cautious tastes, like she's still debating whether I poisoned it. Eventually, she drops the rest in a trash can.

"So what is this?" she calls, not bothering to face me. "You hovering behind me until I get sentimental?"

"It worked once."

"It didn't."

"A little," I say.

She reaches the final car, the one that houses the secondary conductor cabin. Dark. Locked. And absolutely not meant for passengers.

Saint inspects the lock as she pulls out that ridiculous pocket knife she refuses to stop carrying. Stainless steel, worn handle, multi-purpose attachment she sharpened herself. I lean against the opposite wall, arms folded.

"You are still using that?" I ask, letting the disbelief coat every syllable. "You know they make real tools now."

She doesn't look up as the lock clicks open. "Some of us don't have to overcompensate with a sniper rifle the length of a small car."

I step behind her, close enough for my shadow to swallow hers. "You know damn well I don't overcompensate for anything, Pícarita."

She gives an eye roll so exaggerated it might qualify as choreography. "Everything with a Y chromosome says that."

She slips into the conductor cabin. Wind hums faintly

around the sealed window as she starts working the rubber lining free—methodical, efficient, silent. I stay close, because I know she'll let me talk as long as my words don't evoke my earlier agreement to having my throat slit.

"We can work together," I say.

"No," she says immediately.

"You didn't even hear the offer."

"You didn't give one."

"Yet."

She tightens a strap on her pack. Another around her waist. Another across her chest. All silent preparations for a plan she clearly finalized long before I sat across from her with breakfast she didn't trust.

I try again. "We share an enemy."

"We share nothing."

"You're an exile now," I say softly. "Just like me."

She goes still for half a second. Then: "Who set you up?"

Direct. Precise. The same way she kills.

I say nothing, keeping my eyes fixed on hers and the silence becomes heavier around us.

She nods once, resigned. "Yeah. That's what I thought."

Her hands flex around the window frame. "Well… time's up."

Her heel snaps back like a piston.

Saint's kick hits the exact pressure point along the frame, and the entire reinforced pane rips free in a single slab. It tears out of the housing with a deafening metallic crack and gets sucked backward into the slipstream.

Wind detonates through the cabin, slamming into me hard enough to steal my breath. The pane hits the tracks behind us—barely visible before it disintegrates under the train's speed, pulverized into sparkling debris the wheels chew to dust.

Sensors scream. The brakes seize in rapid, angry pulses as the system registers the catastrophic breach.

I throw an arm up to shield my face but Saint doesn't flinch.

She gives me a casual little salute—the kind that says she's enjoying this more than she should—steps to the edge and grabs the cord hiding within the panel of her backpack.

"Hasta luego*, Alejandro."

The parachute deploys instantly, ripping her out of the train in a blur of black fabric, wild hair, and absolute refusal to stay anywhere I want her to.

"Fuck—"

Two years without a trace, and now I've had her within arm's reach for less than five minutes before she hurls herself back into the void.

She hasn't changed.

Not the danger or the audacity.

The train begins to slow, hazard alarms pulsing through the cabin, but it won't matter. I know exactly where she's going. I knew the second she headed for the train station.

My pulse steadies. The hit from seeing her—alive, furious, close enough to touch—is still there, vibrating under my skin, but I clamp down on it. Later.

Right now, there's work to do.

I pull out my phone and dial.

My broker answers on the first ring. "Did it go well?"

"Blow the tracks in ten seconds," I say.

---

* **See you later**

On the other end of the line there is a half a huff disguising an amused chuckle. "Guess not."

Saint

The chute hits the ground before I do.

I land hard—knees bending, breath punching out of me—and immediately yank the parachute toward me, rolling the fabric into something that vaguely resembles a bundle instead of a death trap. I don't have time to fold it properly. I'll do that later. Right now, I barely have time to breathe.

Not when the Guild scrubbed last night's contract clean.

Not when I woke up framed for killing a man *they* told me to kill.

Not when the only clue I have is the corpse I buried six hours ago.

I sling the half-stuffed chute into my bag and tighten the straps across my chest. The forest around me is quiet—Nagano foothills, just beyond the high-speed line. Remote enough to bury someone without a hiker tripping over their foot in the morning. Close enough to civilization for last night's escapade to be little more than a detour on my schedule.

Instead, I'd muttered at him, cursed the flimsy shovel,

cursed the rock-hard soil, and thrown him into the ground like a pissed-off raccoon.

Great job, Saint.

Really professional.

I push through the trees, boots sinking into damp earth, irritation simmering hotter with every step. I was supposed to be on a beach today. Or asleep. Or literally anywhere but hiking back to a half-assed grave because the Guild's collective brain cell had a malfunction.

His burial mound comes into view—just a slight rise in the soil, messy, rushed. And right now, I hate past-me with a passion usually reserved for assholes who don't tip.

"Should've minded my damn business," I mutter as I kneel. "Should've stayed on vacation. Should've bought a bigger shovel."

I push away the top layer of dirt with my gloved hands, feeling for the stupid little shovel I threw in with him out of spite. My fingers scrape metal. Found it.

"You and I are in a toxic relationship," I tell the shovel as I yank it free.

I start digging—quick movements, controlled, pushing aside the soil I packed down in a fury last night. My heart thrums faster. Not from exertion.

From dread.

If the Guild erased his contract...

If they framed me...

Then whoever this guy is, he matters.

Not as a target.

As a message.

I shovel faster. Dirt loosens. A smear of gray cloth appears underneath, right where I left him.

I toss the shovel aside and switch to my hands, digging until my fingers brush the fabric stretched across his chest.

"Okay," I breathe, leaning in. "Let's see what the hell you were worth dying for."

His face comes into view first.

Of course it does.

And the expression is exactly as stupid as I remember it —eyes wide, mouth slack, like he died confused and mildly disappointed in himself. If he weren't covered in dirt and currently being exhumed by a woman he unintentionally ruined, it might almost be funny.

But the eyes ruin it.

Wide open. Packed full of soil.

Just... gritty little horror marbles.

"Nope," I mutter, grimacing. "Absolutely not."

I pull the sunglasses off my head—my favorite pair, the ones I stole from that French arms dealer I slept with once— and shove them onto his face.

Much better. Creepy, but better.

I search his jacket pockets first, patting down fabric still damp from burial. Nothing in the left. Nothing in the right —until my fingertip catches on a slip of paper. A crumpled receipt.

I smooth it open.

A small restaurant logo in Little China, New York.

A timestamp from two days ago and a menu order I can't pronounce.

"Perfect," I say, pocketing it. "Exactly what I wanted—a scavenger hunt."

I dig through the remaining pockets. More nothing. My irritation spikes so fast it almost warms me. I yank my backpack off with a huff and shove more dirt aside, checking his front pants pockets.

Empty.

I need to roll him over so I can check the back. Maybe the waistband or his boots. Something.

I stand, brushing dirt off my thighs, shifting my stance—

A blade whistles past my cheek and buries itself in the earth next to my head.

Instinct hits before thought.

I spin, gun already drawn from the back of my waistband.

The assassin charging me doesn't even get a full second of recognition before I put two bullets in his chest and one between his eyes. He collapses mid-stride, momentum skidding his body into the dirt like a sack of grain. Judging by the direction he came from, he approached along the tracks.

I move fast. Drag him by the collar, roll his body to the edge of the shallow grave I'm kneeling in, and position him in a crude shield—a barrier of dead weight between me and the open approach.

Then I listen.

Nothing but wind, faint tremors from the tracks, and the pounding of my own pulse.

But it won't stay quiet.

I know that.

A lone assassin means more are coming.

My jaw clenches and I take the blade from the dirt with a little more force than necessary. "How the hell did someone find me this fast?" It joins my small arsenal, sliding into the sheath at me ankle.

Could've been someone on the train.

Someone who jumped off after I did.

Or someone who didn't need to jump—someone who never boarded.

Doesn't matter. Not now.

They know where I am.

Which means I have seconds—maybe a minute—before the next one arrives.

I crouch again beside the corpse, fingers already searching for anything I missed.

"I swear," I mutter to him, "if you don't have something useful on you, I'm going to kill you again."

I grunt as I grab the corpse by the collar and haul him toward the opposite ledge, dragging his dead weight out of the grave. He thuds against the dirt beside today's freshly made friend, and I waste no time dropping to my knees.

I need to check the soil.

If he dropped anything—key card, burner, chip—this is my only shot to find it.

My hands sweep through the loose earth, digging, feeling textures: leaves, roots, a few stones, damp grit. My heart hammers so loud it's almost all I hear.

I start counting in my head.

Twenty-nine, thirty, thirty-one...

If I hit sixty, I leave. No matter how unfinished this is.

The forest behind me shifts—no, *stops.*

Birds go silent.

Leaves freeze mid-sway.

Even the breeze forgets how to move as every instinct in my body goes rigid.

I freeze too. Hands buried in dirt.

Thirty-eight. Thirty-nine. Forty.

A soft metallic click ripples through the tree line. Barely audible—like whoever did it tried not to make a sound at all —but it echoes twice off the trunks.

A rifle.

A sniper settling into position.

Cold blooms under my skin. I'm crouched in a grave— bad angle, bad cover, bad everything. If he's got a clear line, I'm done.

The Guild has no shortage of sharpshooters. But Alejandro was the best.

Below me, sure.

But still the best.

I'm not a sniper. Never pretended to be. I like my work up close, personal, firsthand.

Long-range? That was always his playground.

Which means whoever is in those trees isn't him.

The forest that was silent suddenly fills with distant noise. Engines. Several of them. And tires crunching over gravel and roots—closing in.

Fantastic.

A fucking welcoming committee.

The two corpses flanking me are the only reason I'm not already dead; they block most sight-lines except straight over- head. I risk a glance sideways through a carved gap between their bodies and see headlights.

One vehicle leads the pack, faster, cutting through the trees like it owns the road. Window down. Arm hanging out. Driver too relaxed for someone charging into a gunfight.

Alejandro.

Driving like he's cruising down Santa Monica Boulevard

instead of barreling through the Japanese wilderness with a kill squad behind him.

His car skids toward me, flinging a wave of dirt at me. The rear passenger door swings open before the tires even settle.

"Need a lift?" he calls out.

Perfect.

At least now I know he's not the sniper waiting to ventilate my skull.

My odds improve by a spectacular two percent.

I toss my pack into the back seat first. Then I climb halfway in—

"Hold on," I snap, making sure he doesn't decide to be helpful by flooring it.

I grab a fistful of the dead man's collar and heave.

"He's coming with us."

The corpse drops onto me as I scramble inside. The momentum sends his limp body right on top of me.

A sharp thump reverberates through him and his torso jerks.

Sniper round misses me and hits him.

"Thanks, buddy," I mutter, pushing his face off mine.

Alejandro stomps the accelerator. The wheels spin, spit dirt into the air, and the car fishtails once before catching traction.

Then we're gone—ripping down the forest road with assassins behind us and a corpse riding shotgun.

Alejandro

"Saint, what the hell—" I snap the moment the fresh corpse hits the back seat.

She doesn't answer. Doesn't even look at me. She just climbs over the bench seat with the grace of a cat burglar and slides into the passenger side as if we aren't being hunted through the forest.

Seatbelt on.

Posture relaxed.

Expression bored.

"What? You've never seen a dead body before?"

She opens two pieces of pink gum and pops them both in her mouth with a sly grin. And yes, I fucking look at that mouth before turning back to the... lack of road.

A sniper round punches into the trunk, reminding me we're not.

"Puta madre*..." I mutter, jerking the wheel as the car fishtails across uneven terrain. Roots, rocks, dips—this forest hates cars almost as much as it hates assassins. "Me cago en todo lo que se mueve..."†

But we're close.

---

* **Motherfucker**

† "I swear to God, everything is fucked."

Just ahead is a narrow maintenance road, and beyond that, a highway entrance where I can lose the riffraff behind us.

The car bucks hard as we hit a patch of exposed roots. Saint barely reacts—just reaches up to adjust the elastic band around her hair like the force of impact personally offended her styling choices.

I'm weaving between trees, scanning for the road, when a second vehicle barrels up beside us, matching our speed. I risk a quick glance.

"Ah, hijo de puta*... you've got to be kidding me."

La Cucaracha†.

The Guild's most irritatingly persistent assassin. You could drop a building on him, and he'd crawl out asking for a raise.

His window rolls down.

He grins at me—big, stupid, toothy grin—like we're old buddies catching up at a reunion.

His gun rises.

I shout over the engine, "Long time no see, Cucarach—"

A silver blur slices past me.

Saint's dagger.

It buries itself dead-center between his eyes. His grin freezes, drops. The gun slips from his hand. His foot slams down on the accelerator as his head snaps back.

The entire car veers left—straight into a tree.

Full speed.

---

* You son of a bitch
† The Cockroach

Metal crunches. Glass shatters. The impact echoes through the canopy.

I blink once. "Rude much? I didn't even get to say hello."

Saint pops a big pink bubble of gum, lets it snap loud enough to sting my pride, and says, "Pretty sure his last thought was relief he didn't have to hear your voice again."

I open my mouth. Close it.

She does that to me—drops a casual insult like a grenade and strolls away from the explosion.

The passenger side smacks into a dip, and she's yanked halfway out of her seat before bouncing back in. She doesn't swear. Doesn't gasp. Just adjusts a curl behind her ear.

"Driving like this... must be exhausting for you," she says. "All that effort. Just to stay average."

I choke on air. "Average? ¿Qué coño estás diciendo?*"

I slide us onto the maintenance road, tires spraying gravel. As soon as I try to form a rebuttal bullet punches into the rear windshield. Both of us duck.

She's out her window a heartbeat later, balanced like a gymnast in a gunfight. One clean shot and she hits the front tire of the nearest car.

It fishtails, spins sideways, and rolls—slamming into two others in a spectacular pileup.

A fireball shoots up like the forest is competing in an action-movie audition.

"Subtle," I mutter.

"My specialty," she boasts, settling back into her seat like she isn't a menace.

---

* What the hell are you saying?

The highway appears ahead, a concrete salvation. I put the pedal down, engine snarling as we rocket toward it. I check the mirror every other second, watching for followers, while Saint props her foot on the dash and twirls a piece of her curly hair like we're out for Sunday brunch.

I hate how good she looks doing that.

A break in the median appears. I angle toward it. Just as we pass, I slam the brakes. Saint lurches forward, hands slapping the dash to brace herself.

The dead guy in the back rolls off the seat with a thud.

"Hold on tight," I warn.

I shift into reverse, throw an arm across the back of her seat to brace myself, and gun it backward through the median and onto the opposite side of the highway.

"You threw my friend on the floor," she says flatly.

I grin. "Somehow, I think he'd be more pissed about you throwing him out a window than me tossing him onto the floorboard of our getaway car."

Her eyes narrow and my smirk widens.

Now she knows that I tailed her last night.

Dios*, I love irritating her. It lights her up in ways bullets never could.

"You're driving the wrong direction," she says.

Like I don't fucking know I'm reversing at top speed, dodging confused commuters who have no idea an international kill squad is right behind us.

Once I clear the densest pack of cars, I slam the brakes again and yank the wheel. We spin. Fast. Clean. A perfect arc.

---

* God, I love irritating her.

At the exact moment the nose of the car swings forward, I hit the gas.

We lurch, straighten, and tear down the highway—now pointed in the right direction and leaving a chorus of honking cars and bewildered drivers behind us.

I keep the pace up until the last shadow drops off the mirror. No headlights. No engines. No crawl of movement along the tree line.

Finally, I ease off the gas.

"I think we lost them," I say, letting the car settle out of its fight-or-die tension. The engine's growl softens into something like normal.

Saint immediately adjusts her foot on the dash and starts flipping through radio stations like we didn't just outrun a firing squad. Static, more static, then some over-sweet pop song she leaves on purely to annoy me. Probably succeeding.

I let her have five seconds of quiet before I ask:

"So. My proposal."

Her head tilts. Barely. A predator's disinterest.

"What do you think? A truce? Partners? At least until we stop being target practice?"

She flicks the radio volume down a notch.

"Details."

Of course. She'd ask for the one thing I can't just hand over. I filter what I can give her through what I refuse to— sorting truths, half-truths, and the pieces that will get both of us killed if I say them out loud.

"If you think you were set up," she says, "you must have a theory."

I snort. "*If?* Like it's optional? Like I should consider the possibility I tripped and fell face-first into treason?"

She gives the smallest shrug. "Stranger things have happened."

"No," I say. "This wasn't an accident. I was there as a favor to a friend. A guard. Nothing more. I'm the reason he's still alive today. I certainly didn't try to kill him."

"Convenient." Her tone cuts the air like a wire.

"I don't poison people," I snap. "It's too close for me. I like distance."

She doesn't respond—not verbally.

Instead, her head turns toward the window.

That tiny movement lands like a knife under my ribs.

Distance.

Her specialty.

Her shield.

And the exact thing that destroyed us.

Once, we were lovers.

Or something just shy of admitting it.

Neither of us willing to name it.

Neither of us willing to say what it was turning into.

Until it ended with one night that broke everything.

She exhales slowly. "Or maybe your plan didn't work, so you stayed close to salvage it. Finish the job later."

Of course she'd twist the blade.

"It was a politician," I say. "Up for re-election. A state dinner. On the ride home, he started suffocating. Lips blackening. Collapsing in his limo." I shake my head. "I almost didn't save him. Shouldn't have. He was touch and go all night, but the bastard refused to die."

A humorless laugh escapes me.

"And the next day he stands in front of cameras and

blames his opponent for trying to kill him. It worked. He won."

Saint's silence sharpens the air.

"If I wanted him dead," I continue, "he would be. You know that. We both do. This was something else. Something coordinated. Something bigger." I glance at her. "Two countries were on the brink of war. He stopped it. But imagine if they'd succeeded in killing him that night."

Her eyes narrow. "War would've been immediate."

"Yes." My fingers tighten on the wheel. "Lots of profit in selling wars."

She shifts slightly, posture still relaxed but attention razor-edged. "So, you think someone was orchestrating conflict. Placing politicians where they need them. Manipulating global pressure points."

"Not someone," I say.

My throat works once.

"*The* one."

She stiffens like she's daring me not to say it.

I say it anyway.

"The Guildmaster."

Saint

We drive for hours with nothing but the engine, the road, and the ghost of everything unsaid between us.

Alejandro handles the wheel like he owns the whole damn mountain range, broad shoulders relaxed, one hand draped over the top of the steering wheel. Every time we hit a curve—and there are a hundred winding turns on the way into Kenji's territory—the car shifts, and I'm too aware of him beside me. His heat. His presence. The way he takes up space without trying.

I focus out the window, watching the shadows deepen as we get farther from the city and closer to where I grew up. Or as close to "grew up" as an orphan ever gets.

Kenji's homestead appears only in fragments at first—a flash of a ridge, the glint of a far-off roof, the silver thread of the mountain stream cutting through the valley. Several buildings tucked into the slope. Gardens terraced by hand. And the training yard where some of the deadliest people in the world were carved into their final shapes.

Where I was carved.

Dropped on the steps of a New York orphanage at three days old. Unclaimed and raised by no one, I aged out and fought the world tooth and nail… until someone offered me a different kind of life. A profitable one.

Until the Guild.

Until the initiation night where I stood in a room full of killers-to-be. Kenji saw me and claimed me as his student. His only one before. His only one after.

I tell myself I'm going home.

But it's the closest thing to home I've ever had, and that's its own kind of sting.

"Turnoff's ahead," I say quietly.

Alejandro shifts gears. Takes it slow. He knows better than to blast into a Guild master's land at full speed unless he wants a hidden arrow through his throat.

"Pull off here," I add. "Kill the lights. Engine too. We walk from here."

He turns both off without arguing.

I open the door, slipping into my leather jacket and breathing in the cold mountain air. The moon paints the path in silver.

"Grab Skippy," I tell him.

He stares at me. "Who?"

I jerk my chin toward the corpse slumped in the back-seat. "Your new best friend."

"Por el amor de Dios…*" he mutters, rubbing a hand down his face. "We are not dragging a dead man through a forest."

---

* For God's sake…

"We are," I say, already stepping away from the car. "I'm not leaving him. Not until I know who he is."

"That is a terrible plan," he grumbles. "A ridiculous, impossible, stupid—"

I glance back at him, deadpan.

"Is it because you've lost so much muscle mass?"

He looks down at himself so fast I nearly laugh. Hands patting his arms, chest, like he's checking for missing parts.

"Lost—? I have not lost muscle." He flexes his arm as if the mountain fog needs convincing. "I've actually put on muscle."

"Oh, I'm sure," I say, dripping sarcasm. "If you can't lift him, just say—"

He grabs the corpse by the collar so violently the body jerks upright like a marionette.

"I can lift him," Alejandro snaps. "Por supuesto que puedo. *Watch."

He hauls Skippy out of the car, muttering Spanish curses under his breath the entire time—something about saints, demons, and poor life choices—while dragging the dead weight through the gravel.

"See?" he grumbles. "Perfectly capable."

"Congratulations," I say. "Your ego lives to fight another day."

"Barely," he mutters, adjusting his grip as the corpse's arm flops across his knee. "This is still ridiculous."

"And yet," I call over my shoulder as I head toward the path into Kenji's land, "you're doing it."

---

*   Of course I can. Watch.

His answering sigh is loud, dramatic, and deeply offended.

"Fantástico," he says dryly. "I always dreamed of being promoted to pack mule."

"You know, have big dreams," I say, already heading up the faint dirt path toward the dark outline of Kenji's compound.

Alejandro grunts behind me as Skippy's body thumps over another root.

We make it down the ridge, to the point where the trees thin enough that Kenji's territory begins. I kneel, raising a hand.

"Stay here," I whisper. "I'll only be a moment."

Alejandro shifts Skippy to one arm. "And if he kills you?"

"Then I'll be longer than a moment."

I don't wait for the next complaint. I trot up the slope, toward the narrow cart path that leads to the main gates— old wooden beams with iron nails driven by hand. Opening them is easy. Kenji never bothered with locks. Locks aren't challenges. Locks don't separate the worthy from the dead.

No, the real challenge is knowing where he'll strike from.

I slip through, eyes scanning everything. Shadows stretch long over the courtyard. The gardens he tends are quiet, still. The stream murmurs behind the main building. The air smells like pine, stone, and memory.

For a moment—just one—I feel that old whisper of nostalgia. This place made me. Broke me. Built me again. Maybe he doesn't know I'm here. Maybe he's away. Maybe—

The thought dies as something snaps past my cheek, so close the wind of it stings my skin.

It hits the wooden post behind me with a loud *ping*, burying itself into the beam.

One of Kenji's infamous glass beads.

I pivot, already dropping into a crouch—

A blur of white flashes to my left and there he is.

He moves like lightning and living steel—faster than anyone his age has any right to. His white gi flickers in the moonlight as he closes the distance, silent as snowfall.

I only avoid the first strike because I trained under him.

He aims a palm strike at my sternum. I twist sideways, grab his wrist, go for a sweep—

He's gone before my leg even commits to the arc.

He counters with a hooking kick that whistles past my jaw. I duck, roll, come up in a fighting stance. He doesn't wait. He never waits.

He leaps, spinning—heel aimed at my temple.

I block with both forearms, the impact jolting down to my spine.

"Still slow," he says calmly, landing light as a feather.

"Still short," I shoot back.

He narrows his eyes—amused, insulted, both.

He lunges again, this time grabbing for my collar. I let him get close, palm the back of his hand, twist with my whole shoulder—

He redirects my leverage like water slipping around a rock and sends me skidding back three steps with a flick.

I grit my teeth and launch forward, snapping a kick toward his ribs. He blocks with his elbow, catches my ankle, and flips me—except I catch myself mid-fall, palms hitting the ground, legs sweeping around in a low spinning kick meant to knock him off balance.

He jumps over it.

Jumps.

At sixty-something.

He lands, grabs my wrist, tries to leverage my weight forward—

But I'm taller and stronger than the girl he trained years ago.

I anchor my stance. He doesn't move me.

"Better," he murmurs.

"Older," I counter.

He smiles.

And that's worse.

A smiling Kenji usually means he's about to try to break something.

Before I can fully reset my stance, he moves.

A blur—faster than my eyes want to track.

First move:

He snaps forward with a knife-hand feint toward my throat. I parry—he wanted me to. Because the second I commit—

Second move:

He pivots inside my guard, hooks his foot behind my ankle, and slams his elbow lightly—*precisely*—into the pressure point beneath my collarbone. Pain sparks down my arm. My balance breaks.

Third move:

He grabs my wrist, uses my own forward momentum, and sweeps my other leg clean out from under me.

I hit the ground flat on my back, breath punched from my lungs, the stars above me blurring for half a second.

The fight's over.

I don't need him to say it.

Every nerve in my body already knows.

Kenji steps into my vision, hands clasped neatly behind his back, breathing steady, not a single hair out of place. He tilts his head, assessing me the way he always has—like a craftsman checking his handiwork.

"It is good to see you, Saint," he says softly before he turns and walks toward his house.

The endearment lands exactly where his elbow did— deep, precise, and impossible to ignore.

I suck in a breath, roll to my side, and try not to look as wrecked as I feel.

Kenji turns without a word and walks toward the main house.

Traditional wooden beams. Sliding shōji doors. Lantern light glowing soft and warm against the night.

I follow, boots quiet on the porch out of habit—because running or not, this place has rules.

Inside, the air smells like cedar and green tea.

He moves with his usual unhurried precision, pouring hot tea into two small cups. One is set in front of me. The other, he takes for himself. He sits.

"Your face is bruised," he observes.

"My pride is bruised," I mutter, raising the cup to my lips for a small sip.

His mouth twitches the barest fraction. "You are hunted."

I exhale through my nose. "The world knows."

"Yes." He lifts his tea. "A dramatic way to announce one's retirement."

"Not my choice." My voice goes tight. "I need help."

"As a master," he says calmly, "I can offer none."

The words hit harder than his throw.

My jaw clenches. "Are you going to turn me in? Take the hit yourself?"

He doesn't even blink. "You would not have come here if that were a concern."

I look away. He's right. I hate that he's right.

"Besides," he adds, blowing the steam gently, "masters are not obligated to report the sighting of an exile."

That word.

Exile.

I flinch before I can school it. A tiny betrayal of control.

Kenji, of course, sees everything.

His voice softens—not gentle, exactly, but close enough for him.

"You were set up, Saint. Anyone who knows you understands this. You would never betray your Guild."

I take a bigger sip and swallow hard. For a moment, I'm eight years old again, staring at the man who promised to forge me into something the world could never break.

"I need a way off Japan. And weapons." My tone is steady, but I'm shaking inside.

He sets his cup down. I wrap both hands around mine letting the heat ground me.

"I thank you," he says, "for visiting an old man. I only wish you would come when you are not running for your life."

"Well," I say dryly, "I'll put it on my calendar."

He stands.

Just... stands.

Like the conversation is over. I stare at the floorboards at his feet. Still wearing his split-toe boots from working in his gardens.

He walks toward the back door, speaking as he goes—his voice shifting into that drifting, absentminded tone he uses when he's saying something he technically isn't saying.

A plane roars overhead—low, loud enough to rattle the shōji screens. Kenji glances up at the ceiling as if the noise personally offends him.

"These local airstrips," he mutters. "Always sending out cargo shipments at ridiculous hours. Every hour, it seems. Impossible for an old man to sleep."

My eyes narrow.

There it is.

Hidden in the mundane. A hint.

He slides open the back door, letting in a slice of cool night air.

"And," he says lightly, almost to himself, "I must remember to fix the lock on the barn. It keeps slipping. Wouldn't want it swinging open all night."

He steps outside, still not looking back.

"Best if I sleep early," he adds. "Will need to be up at dawn so I can fix it."

Then he vanishes into the darkness.

No goodbye.

No good luck.

Just riddles wrapped in small talk—pointing me toward escape... and weapons.

Just Kenji.

Helping the only way he's allowed.

And leaving me to decide what kind of exile I'm going to be.

Alejandro

The forest floor is softer than it has any right to be. Moss, pine needles, the faint smell of cold dirt. I'm stretched out on my back, hands behind my head, staring up at the stars like some romantic fool waiting for inspiration to strike.

Next to me:

my dead companion, Skippy.

Saint's emotional support corpse.

"So," I say, glancing over at him, "what's your real name?"

Silence.

"Not much of a talker, huh? That's fine, mi amigo. I can talk enough for both of us."

Still nothing.

He's a terrible conversationalist.

I inhale deeply, stretch my arms behind my head, and sit up—but the moment I do, something in my chest tightens. The openness bothers me. Too much sky. Too much exposure.

I should be up in the trees looking through a scope. Seeing the world from the angle where I'm the threat, not the target.

With a sigh, I stand.

Time to relocate.

I grab Skippy by the collar and haul him upright, feet dangling a little off the ground. Tonight's fashion choice—Saint's donated sunglasses—is sitting crooked on his dirt-smeared face, giving him a grim parody of a smile. Like he knows the punchline to a joke no one's told.

I adjust the glasses, tugging the frame straight and then realize...

he's not sagging.

The corpse is holding its own weight.

"Well," I murmur, yanking him slightly back and forth, "son of a bitch."

I lower my hand off his shirt very slowly, shifting my weight to him inch by inch. The dead man sways once. Twice. I catch his shoulder to stabilize him—

And there he is.

Standing upright.

All on his own.

"Look at you." I let out a sharp laugh and pat his chest. "Well done."

It is, objectively, ridiculous.

His sunglasses slip again. I pull them off and instantly regret it.

He's been dead about twenty-four hours. Dirt clings to his eyeballs. His lids are half open. His expression hasn't softened with time—it's gotten worse. Sunken. Smeared. Grim.

"Dios..." I grimace. "Put those back on."

I slide the shades onto his face, adjusting them until he looks... well. Not good. But better.

Much better.

I scan the forest floor to make sure I haven't dropped

anything—weapon, phone, dignity—then look uphill for somewhere I can relocate to. Somewhere elevated. Hidden. With a clear view of the path where Saint will come back through.

Skippy's sunglasses gleam faintly under the moon as I glance down.

And that's when I notice a bush beside him, heavy with berries such an unnaturally bright blue they look like they've been Photoshopped into the forest.

I pluck one, roll it between my fingers, and squeeze. It collapses instantly, bleeding a darker blue smear across my thumb.

Interesting.

A twig snaps just before a bullet zips past my head.

I dive sideways as Skippy tips over like a felled tree to the ground behind me.

"¡Joder, para ya!"* I bark. "It's just us!"

From the trees, Saint's voice cuts through the night.

"Who the fuck is *us*?"

I gesture at the corpse like it should be obvious. "Me and Skippy. Who the fuck else would it be?"

She steps into view, expression sharp, eyes scanning the scene—me kneeling in the dirt, the blue smear on my thumb, Skippy eating a bullet chest-first like a loyal shield.

"Why," she asks slowly, "was he standing like you were about to start a witch séance in the woods?"

I toss the crushed berry down and wipe my hand on my pants. "I was experimenting."

"Unless you want to shit yourself to death," she says,

---

* "Damn it, stop it already!"

pointing at my hand, "you should wash that off. Those berries are insanely toxic."

I lift my hand to smell it. "It's very sweet-smelling."

"Never mind the Oregon Trail cosplay," she says. "Why were you foraging and playing with dead people?"

"I was *not* playing."

I grab Skippy by the collar again and haul him upright. "But look—"

I balance him. Let go.

He stays standing, swaying slightly.

"Ta da! He stands."

Saint stares like this is somehow the worst thing she's ever seen—and keep in mind, she's buried more bodies than most cemeteries.

"Good for him," she says flatly. "We need to go. We've got a plane to catch."

She turns and starts back toward the car.

Which, of course, is when I give Skippy the slightest nudge on his shoulder.

He wobbles.

Left side. Right side. Left again.

A listing, drunken shuffle down the slope.

"Look!" I call after her. "He can walk!"

Saint turns with a look that's a cocktail of disbelief, horror, and pure, exhausted judgment. Like she's trying to decide if she should shoot Skippy again or me or both.

I pat the corpse's shoulder. "Don't worry amigo. She's always like this."

"I can hear you," she snaps.

"I know," I say, and Skippy tips forward like he agrees with me, face-planting in the dirt again. "Ah, fuck me."

We ditch the car half a mile from the freight strip—no lights, no signs, just a sprawl of warehouses and cargo bays pretending to be too boring to bother with.

Perfect place to smuggle two assassins and a dead man.

I pop the trunk and pull back the side panel, revealing my rifle case nestled where the spare tire should be. Long-range precision. My actual comfort blanket.

I sling it over my shoulder and reach into the back seat for Skippy.

He flops into my arms like a sandbag wearing sunglasses. Only slightly stiff.

I hoist him across my shoulders and wait while Saint arms herself.

She's checking her ankle sheath, sliding in an extra knife.

Reloading her gun with a fresh magazine.

Adjusting the strap of her harness like she's preparing for a triathlon, not a felony.

I should not find this as attractive as I do.

Minutes later, we're crouched behind a patch of tall grass near a chain-link fence that surrounds the airfield. A few truck headlights sweep the gravel beyond. Workers wander between loading docks, bored and oblivious.

I whisper, "Where exactly are we going?"

"New York," she says without looking at me.

I raise a brow. "And what is in New York?"

She reaches into her back pocket and pulls out a crumpled slip of paper.

"Takeout."

She hands it to me.

It's a receipt for Chinese food.

Printed with an address in Little China, New York.

"From Skippy's pocket?"

She rolls her eyes hard enough I hear it.

"Yeah. The only thing he had on him."

I pat the corpse's shoulder. "You're more useful than you look, amigo."

Saint kicks me lightly in the shin.

That's her way of saying *focus*.

A warehouse bay door grinds open across the yard, spilling yellow light onto the pavement. A forklift buzzes past. The workers don't look back.

"Now," she whispers.

We cut through the fence—her little pocket tool does the job in a few clean clips—and slip across the open ground in the forklift's wake. Inside the warehouse, no one notices us. Too many crates. Too little supervision. Too much noise.

A bulletin board near the office doorway holds stacks of documents and several clipboards. Saint taps one with her finger.

Flight manifests, cargo loads, destinations, and times.

And there it is.

A cargo jet departing directly to JFK International.

Last cargo load already signed off.

We exchange a look, and she nods once.

Outside, through the warehouse's high windows, I spot the plane sitting on the tarmac—its bay doors open, last crates strapped in. A group of workers loiter by a fuel truck for a smoke break, backs turned. No one is watching.

"Go," she says.

We sprint across the tarmac—me with Skippy bouncing

on my shoulders like some morbid backpack—and slide up the cargo ramp just as the workers start arguing about whose turn it is to buy cigarettes.

Inside, the compartment is cavernous, dim, and humming with the low vibration of running engines. We duck behind a tall stack of produce crates, squeezing into the narrow pocket of space between pallets and the wall.

Saint settles in first, guns secured, jaw clenched in concentration.

I wedge myself beside her, Skippy propped in the corner like he's supervising.

The cargo door begins to close, and the lights dim.

The engines rise to a hungry roar and Saint exhales once.

We're in.

On a plane to New York with no seats and one dead man dressed like he's ready for a tax audit.

I look sideways at Saint.

"Romantic, no?"

She elbows me in the ribs, but it was worth it.

The moment the plane levels off—engines roaring loud enough to rattle bones—Saint moves like she's allergic to staying still.

We've got twelve hours in a flying metal box. She could at least pretend to relax for five minutes.

But no.

Of course not.

She shrugs off her leather jacket and lowers Skippy to the floor between us. Then she starts unbuttoning his shirt with clinical precision.

"Wow," I say. "Didn't know you were into that."

She ignores me—an impressive talent she's honed to art form.

The shirt comes off. Two bullet holes stare back at us—both courtesy of today's festivities, not part of his original death. Poor Skippy. What a way to start your afterlife.

Saint examines him for tattoos, scars, anything. I'm watching her face when something catches my eye.

A thin incision, fresh and running along the inside of his forearm.

"Here," I say, pointing.

She leans in, presses her thumb gently around the wound. Something solid shifts under the skin.

"There's something in here," she murmurs.

"A chip?" I guess.

"Maybe. It's hard."

I pull out my pocketknife, flicking it open with a satisfying click. "Let's cut it open and see."

Saint's hand is instantly on my wrist. "No. What if it's a deadman's switch?"

"He's already dead," I remind her.

"No, you idiot—rigged to destroy itself if we try to remove it." Her eyes narrow. "It could have information we need, and we could fry it."

I tilt my head. "It could also be a tracking device. The Guild wanted him gone for something."

She exhales slowly, thinking fast. "We'll have to risk it eventually. But not up here. Besides—what are they going to do? Blow us out of the sky?"

"I wouldn't put it past anyone."

She smirks. "They need my body to claim the kill. So, we've got that on our side."

She re-buttons Skippy's shirt, smooths it down, and props him upright facing us, like he's part of the conversation.

"I've got a guy in New York who can help," she says. "He's not Guild. I can trust him."

Something sharp twists in my chest.

A guy she can trust.

Not me.

I don't show it—haven't survived this long by bleeding in public—but the jealousy slides under my skin like a blade.

She tosses her jacket against a stack of crates, pulls her backpack under her head like a pillow, and closes her eyes— completely, maddeningly relaxed.

I wait a moment, then another.

"Who is it?" My tone is too forced to sound innocent, and she fucking knows it.

Her lips curve, just slightly. "You'll see."

I hate that answer.

I hate the smile more.

And I hate that Skippy is still sitting there across from us, wearing sunglasses, and looking like he's enjoying the fucking show.

Saint

The car has been idling for maybe thirty seconds when the smell finally creeps in. Not sudden. Not dramatic. Just a slow, sour-sweet curl of something wrong threading through the air vents like it's clocking in for a shift.

I catch it the same moment Alejandro does.

We both go still.

Then, very slowly, we turn our heads toward each other.

His nose wrinkles.

My stomach drops.

Neither of us wants to look behind us but we do anyway.

Skippy sits upright in the center of the backseat, seatbelt fastened like he cares about road safety, head tipped at a disturbingly jaunty angle. His grin—once stupid, now sinister—looks even worse with his lips turning that grayish-purple shade you only see on corpses and bad Halloween makeup.

But that's not the worst part.

Our gazes drift down to his shirt.

The white button-down isn't white anymore. First it

was dirt-stained from the grave, and now... now it's wet. Two bullet holes bloom dark across his chest, leaking a dark liquid that I'm going to try really hard not to think about.

"Oh, for fuck's sake," I mutter.

Alejandro lets out a strangled sigh. "He's leaking."

"He wasn't leaking on the plane."

"It was pretty cold though. He's been dead over twenty-four hours," he says, like that's supposed to comfort me. "Bodies do things."

I drag a hand down my face, trying not to gag. The smell is stronger now, mixing with the heat of the car, the Brooklyn air, and whatever died in the sewer last winter. Great. Perfect ambiance.

"Let's hurry this up," I say, pushing out the door before I start dry-heaving.

"Agreed."

Alejandro heads for the trunk. I trail after him because I need to get away from this smell. He lifts the lid and stares into the mess like he's hoping the universe packed us a solution.

Then his shoulders sag in relief.

He pulls out a puffy jacket—oversized, violently blue, and ugly enough to be a hate crime.

"Thank God," he breathes, already shaking it out.

I blink at him. "That's your plan? Put the corpse in a winter coat?"

He shrugs, absolutely serious. "Better than walking in with... that."

I look back at Skippy's leaking shirt, then at the blinding jacket.

"True," I mutter. "Let's wrap him before he stains the seat."

That is how I find myself, two minutes later, wrestling a dead man's swelling arm into a sleeve while Alejandro tries to zip the front. The jacket bunches. Skippy's neck gives a soft crunch when his head flops forward. I hiss under my breath and shove Alejandro's hand aside.

"You're doing it wrong."

"You're making it worse."

"*You're* making it worse."

Skippy slides sideways.

We both grab him before he face-plants into the parking lot.

It turns into whisper-yelling that absolutely no one wins.

By the time we drag him to the elevator, I'm sweating and one bad moment away from homicide number two.

The elevator shudders as it climbs, old cables groaning like they resent our existence. Alejandro props Skippy upright, holding him by the jacket collar like he's escorting a very drunk friend home. I stand beside them, arms crossed, panting hard and profoundly irritated with everything, especially Alejandro's breathing.

He glances at me, earnest and exhausted.

"Let's not fight in front of the kid, okay?"

The "kid" tilts sideways, head thumping against the elevator wall in some macabre show of solidarity.

I stare at both of them in silence. The smell of death, old elevator grease, and my own patience burning out fills the tiny metal box.

The doors ding open, and I step out without looking back.

"If you don't shut up," I say, perfectly calm, "I'm going to punch you in the nuts."

Behind me, Alejandro mutters, "I love it when your mama is feisty," while dragging Skippy out of the elevator like this is all somehow normal.

The hallway hits us like a punch of noise and heat the second we step out. A baby screams somewhere behind a thin apartment door. Two people are tearing each other apart in Spanish behind another, the argument so fast I only catch the rhythm, not the words. An old woman with white hair sits in a hallway chair shucking peas into a metal bowl like she's monitoring the whole building.

I nod at her. She nods back.

Alejandro gives her a too-charming "hola," because he can't help himself even while hauling a leaking corpse.

"So," he says, breathing hard, "who is this very trust-worthy guy you're dragging us to?"

I savor the irritation simmering off him. "A friend."

"That's descriptive. This *friend* have a name? Or are we playing twenty questions in a hallway full of witnesses?"

We reach the end of the hall where a single door sits under a flickering light, cigarette smoke leaking from other apartments creates an odd haze near the ceiling.

I stop. "Oh, I'm sure you've heard of him."

Alejandro opens his mouth, probably to bitch at me again, but the door cracks open first. A short Mexican woman in her mid-thirties eyes us with suspicion.

Before she can speak, I slip into Spanish. "¿Está Grim?"*

Her whole demeanor shifts when she recognizes me. She

---

* "Is Grim here?"

smiles, shuts the door, and I hear the rattle of multiple chains being undone. All of them. It sounds like Fort Knox.

Alejandro sucks in a breath beside me. "Grim?" Shock, awe, a hint of terror. "As in... the Grim Reaper?"

"The very one."

He props Skippy against the wall and immediately starts grooming himself. He smooths his hair, tugs his shirt straight, checks his reflection in the plexiglass of a bulletin board fixed to the cinderblock wall—like showing up rumpled to meet the most notorious hacker alive would be a cardinal sin.

"Why didn't you tell me you know the world's most prolific hacker that has ever lived?" he hisses. Then, panicked, "Do I smell like dead guy?"

He lifts his arm, sniffs, winces. "Fuck."

The door swings open and the woman steps aside.

The apartment is a riot of sound and scent. The kitchen is immediately to the right, a second woman standing over a pot of tamales. She nods at me, then at Alejandro, then at the corpse. No reaction beyond mild acknowledgment.

I push through a curtain of hanging beads and step into the living room. It's a chaos collage of thrift-store furniture: mismatched couch, battered recliner, a giant TV that looks like it cost ten times more than everything else combined.

Two teenage boys are parked on the coffee table, yelling at each other over a video game. The older one curses so loud the woman in the kitchen snaps,

"¡Oye! ¡Mira tu boca, chamaco!"*

---

* "Hey! Watch your mouth, kid!"

"Sorry mama." he yells back without even glancing away from the screen.

He lands the winning blow in the game, throws his hands up—then finally notices me standing in the doorway.

His face cracks into a grin.

"Ayo, Saint. What's good?"

I lean against the wall, arms crossed, one foot hooked over the other. "Same old shit."

He stands, offering a dab. I return it.

Then he notices Alejandro. And Skippy.

His face scrunches. "Who's the nerd?"

I don't bother hiding the smirk. Alejandro looks between me, the kid, and the corpse like he's walked into a fever dream.

"Alejandro..." I gesture lazily. "Meet the Grim Reaper."

There's a full beat where his brain just... stalls.

Then he sputters, "The Grim Reaper is a *fucking child*?!"

Alejandro

The kid blinks at me like I've insulted his entire bloodline.

"I'm nearly a man," he insists, lifting his chin. "I have a mustache."

Before I can respond, the other boy hops off the coffee table and barrels toward us. "Same. Look."

He tilts his face up proudly, presenting the faintest whisper of fuzz above his lip like it's proof he fought in a war.

"Who are you?" I ask, because reality is bending in ways I'm not prepared for.

"I'm his cousin. Theo." He keeps pointing at the fluff, waiting for validation.

"That's peach fuzz," I say.

Both boys look gutted—like I've denied them their rites of passage. They start talking over each other, arguing about growth patterns and hormones and how *some* people mature later but still count as men, which is apparently directed at me.

While they defend their tragic lip hair, the two women— definitely sisters, same sharp cheekbones and efficient energy —start clearing the long dining table. They move with the kind of wordless coordination shared by women who've survived several children, three jobs, and a hundred emergencies before breakfast. Masa tubs, notebooks, a cracked vase, a pile of laundry—gone in seconds.

Then they unroll a giant plastic sheet and gesture at the corpse like they're inviting us to set down groceries.

This entire apartment is its own brand of insane.

Saint doesn't miss a beat. "We need help identifying him."

A notification chimes from a computer in the corner. Grim walks toward it without looking away from Saint, fingers already flying across the keys.

He grins like Christmas came early. "Yeah, I heard about your little predicament."

Lines of code cascade across the screen. A digital swoosh flashes across the display, followed by the Grim Reapers infamous ASCII skull—the one that has tanked firewalls on four continents.

The one who rerouted a mercenary convoy in Syria by hacking their GPS and sending them in circles until they ran out of fuel.

The pixels dissolve, and the screen settles back into its idle pattern of a screensaver.

"Holy shit," I feel the weight of it settle in my chest. "It's really him," I murmur, the words slipping out before I can stop them.

Saint glances sideways at me, the edge of a smile tugging at her mouth. She's enjoying this—watching me process the Grim Reaper in the form of a sixteen-year-old with a headset, a curfew, and opinions about algebra.

"We've gotta be quick," she says, voice low but certain.

"I'm being framed for his murder, and I don't want the world's assassins tracking us here."

Grim nods, already rising from his chair. "I got you, señora apocalíptica."

He steps up to the table and—God help me—takes a selfie with the corpse.

Theo darts in, flashing peace signs like this is a vacation photo for social media.

Then Grim angles his phone over Skippy's face for a close-up. He reaches for the sunglasses.

"I wouldn't take those off," I warn, too late, my hand reaching out.

He lifts them and both boys' recoil instantly, faces twisting.

"Oooh!" Theo steps back, holding a closed fist over his mouth.

"Dude—gross," Grim mutters, keeping his arms locked straight and taking another picture. "The scans will get a better hit without the glasses."

The images upload in seconds. Screens bloom across the monitor—surveillance archives, DMV records, social feeds, blurred crowd shots—everything flashing past too quickly to absorb.

I drift a little closer to her, voice low. "He's a kid. And you just... trust him?"

Her mouth curves, subtle and sharp. "Not all of us have trust issues."

"Oh, that's fucking rich from you," I mutter.

She tilts her head, finally looking at me. "Only with some people."

The implication stings more than I want to admit. "Grim has never failed me."

As if waiting for its cue, the computer chimes—a bright, decisive ping that slices through the room.

Grim leans back in his chair, grinning like he just solved world hunger. "Got him."

The monitors flare to life, every screen in the room vomiting images, files, and clipped bits of security footage. Our dead man appears in a dozen angles—walking through lobbies, tapping on his phone at train stations, sipping coffee in an elevator. He looked a hell of a lot healthier in those than he does on the plastic-lined table behind us.

Grim starts typing again, fast enough that the keys blur. More windows open. Then more. Every new one stacks over the last as he drills deeper.

"There we go..." he mutters, eyes sharp behind his glasses. "Name: Owen Liang."

I squint at the picture—nerdy, stiff posture, wire-rim glasses. The kind of guy who apologizes when someone else bumps into him.

Grim keeps going, narrating like a sports commentator.

"Accountant. And not the fun kind. He does numbers for the Guild and a few freelance merc groups on the side." His lips twist. "Neutral territory, gray-market stuff. Paperwork for people who hate paperwork."

Saint leans in a little. "So why does he matter?"

Grim shrugs, pulling up another file. "Pretty low profile. No socials. Pays taxes on time. Owns a sad little one-bedroom in Chicago. Office is there too." He gestures vaguely. "The human equivalent of a beige cardigan."

He clicks into another thread—some kind of encrypted message chain—and frowns.

"Okay... here's something," he says. "Chatter on a dark net board. Looks like he was trying to trade information."

My interest sharpens. "What kind of information?"

"Not sure," Grim says, eyes scanning rapidly. "The posts are vague. But he was asking around. Looking for someone."

"Who?"

Grim sits back, expression flattening into something more serious than I've seen from him so far.

"He was looking for a ghost," he says quietly.

Then, after a beat:

"Literally. *El Fantasma*.*"

He scrolls. Scrolls again.

"Nothing past that. The trail stops. Last activity was a few days ago."

Grim says the name like it's a bomb he's dropping on the table.

El Fantasma.

The word hits hard enough that I almost forget how to breathe. Not visibly. Not outwardly. Just the quiet, controlled clench behind my ribs that I've mastered over a lifetime.

Saint stiffens beside me. Not fear—recognition.

Theo turns toward her. "What's the big deal? Who's that supposed to be?"

Grim swivels lazily in his chair, tapping his fingers against the armrest. "Untraceable," he says, shrugging. "Which is saying something, considering I can find everyone.

---

* The Ghost

But this one? Nothing. No chatter, no footprint. Could be a guy. Could be a woman. Could be a fifty year old. Could be no one."

Theo whistles low, impressed.

Saint speaks without taking her eyes off the dead man. "Most assassins like leaving a mark—something flashy. A tell. But this one doesn't. No calling card. The absence is the signature." Her voice drops. "A ghost."

Grim adds, "Whoever it is made an impossible shot once. One-in-a-billion physics-defying shit. People still argue about whether it was luck."

I swallow that. Don't react. Don't show even a flicker.

"So what about the takeout receipt in his pocket?" I ask, steady, neutral. "Anything from that?"

Grim spins back to the screen. "Looks like he got intel Fantasma was in Japan. Liang must've come here first, flown out, and then—well." He glances at Saint. "Had the misfortune of running into *her*."

She ignores the jab, frowning down at the body. "He's got something under his skin."

She pushes up his dirty sleeve. His forearm is swollen— fat, tight, mottled purple-green.

"Gross," she mutters.

She presses lightly, and the skin gives beneath her thumb. Grim steps in and pokes it too.

"Wicked," he says. "Theo—come feel this."

Theo rushes over, poking the swelling like it's a science fair project.

I snap. "Focus. Can you get it out without damaging whatever it is? It was probably implanted a few days before he died."

Grim opens his mouth—but doesn't answer.

Because every alarm in the apartment detonates at once.

Sirens. Buzzers. Harsh digital shrieks.

All the monitors flicker, Owen Liang's files evaporating in a blink and reforming into grids of security feeds—dozens of angles from around the building.

Figures move across several screens. Shadows. Shapes. Too coordinated to be random.

Assassins.

"Shit," Grim mutters.

"¡Niño!" his mother snaps.

"Sorry, Ma!" He's already typing, screens flashing, windows stacking. He brings up motion trackers, heat signatures—every tool in his arsenal lighting up at once.

Saint steps forward, steady as ever, her eyes scanning the images. "Does the body have a tracer on it?"

Grim shakes his head, fingers still flying. "If he did, I'd see it. Or at least get interference." He clicks through three diagnostic windows, all clean. "If there's anything, it's running on such a low frequency it slipped under my baseline filters." A beat. "So probably not."

"Fuck," Saint says.

He looks up sharply at her, something hard and older flickering through his face that makes him look much older than sixteen. "You need to go. Now."

No argument. No questions.

Saint moves first. "Get Skippy."

Grim yanks open a desk drawer, digs through tech clutter, and pulls out a cheap burner phone. He presses it into Saint's hand. "Use this if you need me again."

She nods, tucking it into her jacket while I lift the corpse carefully—his dead weight more noticeable now that urgency is eating through the room.

One of the women—Grim's mother—already has the apartment door open, her body blocking as much of the hallway as she can.

Another alarm screeches.

One of the security feeds on the monitor jumps to the forefront—enlarging automatically.

Grim sees it first. His face goes tight.

"Go now," he says. "They're here."

Saint

Gun drawn, I sweep the hallway first. Left. Right. Empty—at least for the next three seconds. Alejandro stands behind me with Skippy slung over one shoulder like a grotesque gym bag. I don't need to look at him to know exactly where he is. I feel him at my back, radiating tension.

"Let's go," I whisper.

We move fast, quiet, practiced. The stairwell is a death trap with a body—too many blind corners, too many angles for ambush. The elevator is the lesser evil.

I hit the call button. The hallway hums with old fluorescent lights, buzzing like they're nervous for us. Alejandro shifts behind me, adjusting Skippy's dead weight.

Then I notice it.

He's also holding a fucking taco.

In his other hand. Wrapped in a napkin. And he's eating it. Actively. Taking a big, satisfied bite.

"Are you fucking kidding me?"

I smack it right out of his hand. The taco splats to the floor as the elevator dings open.

He yelps, offended. "What? Mama Grim gave it to me as we left. Am I supposed to say no?"

"Yes," I snap, stepping inside. I clear the corners, then jerk my chin. "Move."

He follows, wiping his hand on the back of Skippy's arm as the doors slide shut around us. The elevator rattles downward, ancient cables groaning. Every floor feels like an eternity. We reach the ground, slip out into the alley, and sprint to the car.

We dump Skippy into the backseat—no seatbelt, no dignity, no time.

"I'm driving," I say. "You shoot."

Alejandro doesn't argue. He tosses me the keys, rounds the hood, and jumps into the passenger seat, gun already coming free of its holster.

I fire up the engine, slam the gearshift into reverse, and tear backward out of the narrow parking space—

Only to hit the brakes hard.

Two cars block the mouth of the alley. Engines idling. Blacked-out windows roll down exposing faces we recognize all too well—assassins we've crossed paths with before. Their eyes gleam with the kind of hungry purpose that says they didn't come to talk.

"Well," I murmur, pulse steadying into something cold and sharp, "looks like this just became a high-speed chase."

I rev the engine once—sharp, taunting—then drop my foot to the floor.

The car surges forward like it's been waiting its whole life for this moment. I aim not for the front bumper, but the exposed flank of the first assassin car. We slam into it with a violent crunch, metal screaming as my fender bites deep into their door.

I don't stop.

I keep pushing, grinding them sideways across the street. The assassin inside fumbles for his gun, eyes wide, mouth forming curses I don't bother reading. The tires catch at the curb, the whole frame tilts, and then the car flips onto its side with a hollow, bone-rattling thud.

I keep pushing—shoving them the last few feet until we hit the brick storefront across the street. Glass bursts. Metal folds.

"One down," I mutter.

I don't waste a breath. I throw the car into reverse, swing the wheel hard, spin us in a tight arc, and floor it straight into the second car before they can react.

We plow into their front end and shove them backward —out of the alley, into the open intersection behind us.

A horn blares.

A massive garbage truck appears from the right, going way too fast for city limits. It slams into the assassin car with enough force to lift it off the ground before crushing it beneath its tires like a tin can.

I wince. "Two down."

I drop us back into drive and peel away, tires screaming against asphalt. A hard right, then another. The city becomes a blur of neon and brick and pissed-off taxi drivers.

Three cars swing into the street behind us—coordinated, hungry, closing fast.

Alejandro twists, window down, gun already up.

"I've got these."

Alejandro leans out the window and fires. The first

bullet punches straight into the front tire of the nearest car. The rubber explodes, the vehicle skidding sideways into its partner. Both fishtail at once, slamming into a street sign with a twisted metallic shriek.

Two taken out in one motion.

He pivots to the third car, fires twice, metal sparking off the hood.

"Damn it," he growls. "This one's armored. Get me on the driver's side."

I weave around a minivan, slide us into the opposite lane, and ease off the gas just enough to give him a clean angle. Traffic blurs past us, horns blaring, but he's already shifting—bracing his foot against the door, fingers locking onto the window frame.

Then he goes still.

Completely still.

The chaos outside, the ricochet of bullets, the screaming city—all of it falls away from him. I can feel it. That quiet, cold recalibration of a predator aligning with the kill.

He exhales.

One shot.

It threads perfectly through the metal slats of the assassin's front grill, slips past the engine block, and finds the tiny exposed gap between the armored plates for the air vents.

The driver jerks, blood splattering the inside of the windshield before the car veers sharply to the right and slams into a row of parked vehicles.

I let out a breath. My shoulder slumping as I let the tension go.

"Nice shot," I say.

His mouth twitches. Not a smile. Just the shadow of one.

It feels like the number of assassins chasing us doubles in an instant. I take another corner hard, tires screaming, and the rear end swings just wide enough to give me a clean count.

Four cars.

Two motorcycles weaving between them like sharks in shallow water.

Alejandro leans across me without warning, rolling down my window. His arm brushes my chest, and—for one ridiculous second—I register that he smells good. Clean. Warm. Something sharp under it, like cedar.

"Sorry—excuse me—coming through—"

Then he fires twice.

One of the motorcycles jerks violently, the rider skidding across asphalt in a shower of sparks.

The second bike is still bearing down on us when I wrench the wheel right. The sudden force throws him closer —his shoulder pressing into mine as he mutters a quiet, vicious, "*Joder**..."

The curse slips out like a reflex, rough and annoyed.

It pulls a tiny, involuntary smirk from me.

Then I clip the second rider cleanly, sending him and the bike flying down the subway stairs in a blooming fireball of orange flame.

Alejandro and I share a look—one beat, sharp and wordless. Appreciation without admission. Gratitude neither of us is petty enough to say out loud.

----

* Fuck

The back windshield explodes behind us, glass blasting forward like shrapnel. Alejandro ducks, twists, and returns fire through the shattered frame. His bullet finds the driver between the eyes. Their car swerves, plows into the one beside it, and both spin out in a roaring metal tangle.

"We need to lose them," he says, already reloading. "Or we'll be doing this all fucking night."

"Yeah," I mutter. "No shit."

I cut left—hard enough that the tires give a high-pitched squeal—and shoot straight toward a parking garage entrance.

The flimsy gate arm tries to rise, pathetically slow. I hit it at full speed. It snaps clean off and whips across the hood like a thrown stick.

One of the assassin cars behind us overshoots the turn, skidding past the entrance and slamming into a parked sedan. But three more surge after us, headlights flooding the garage shadows.

Alejandro tenses. "What is your plan exactly?"

I barrel deeper into the structure, concrete pillars strobing past us as I throw the wheel hard left.

"Just shoot."

Gunfire echoes behind us, ricocheting off cement like angry hornets. Our tires scream around another tight turn, rubber smearing across the floor. Alejandro doesn't waste bullets—he waits. Patient. Taut. A predator riding out the chaos.

Then he fires.

The round slices through the narrow gap between two pillars and punches straight into the driver of the last pursuing car. Their headlights swerve, slam into a column, and go dark.

Two left.

We spiral higher. Up one level, then the next. The structure hums with gunshots, engines, and our shared pulse drumming in the air between us. When we break onto the top deck, open night yawns above us—nothing but sky, cold wind, and a drop that would turn us into confetti.

Alejandro's irritation finally slips through. "There is literally nothing up here except gravity. Tell me you're not—"

"Hang on."

"Saint—"

But I'm already flooring it, shooting us toward the far edge of the roof.

At the last second, I jerk the wheel. Hard.

The car whips around in a brutal pivot, fishtailing as momentum drags us sideways before straightening. We swing past the two cars chasing us in the opposite direction —close enough to feel their exhaust against my skin.

I extend my arm out the window, elbow locked, gun steady.

For a breath, time slows.

We pass the first car, our windows lining up perfectly. The driver faces me—smug smirk, cowboy jawline, eyes that think they've already won.

Motherfucking Colt Harrington.

The Texan.

Sharpshooter.

Asshole extraordinaire.

I pull the trigger and the bullet shatters his window in an

exploding starburst of glass. He jerks, flinching—reaction ruining the precision he prides himself on.

He tries to mimic my turn, but he doesn't have the timing. He slams the front of his car into the concrete barrier of the deck. The impact forces him to back up, curse, reposition.

Time is money, and he just overspent.

By the time he's realigned his car, we're already tearing toward the opposite edge of the roof. Alejandro sees it now —the plan that didn't exist thirty seconds ago but apparently exists now.

The end of the deck.

A tow truck parked there, its bed tilted down at a perfect angle.

His eyes widen.

He braces, grabbing the oh-shit handle with both hands.

I slam the accelerator.

"Oh *shit*!" He yells out.

We hit the ramp hard—metal clanging, the chassis protesting—but the truck does its job. The angled bed launches us upward, momentum catching like a fist under the ribs.

The car lifts.

Airborne.

We leave the building behind entirely, carried in an arc across open sky. Another rooftop rushes toward us—fast, too fast—

And for a heartbeat, we're weightless. Just four spinning wheels, a dead man, a furious man, and me, hurling through the night between two concrete worlds.

Saint

Alejandro is having a deeply spiritual moment of panic.

"¡Mierda! Carajo! Maldita sea—joder—puta madre—NO!"

Rough translation:

- ¡Mierda! — "Shit
- Carajo! — "Fuck!" but angrier
- Maldita sea! — "Goddammit!"
- Joder! — "Fuck!" (with more Spanish flavor)
- Puta madre! — "Motherfucker!" (intense frustration)
- NO! — Self-explanatory panic cherry on top

Put together? "Shit! Fuck! Goddammit—fuck—motherfucker—NO!"

In layman's terms?: I realize what you're about to do and I hate everything about it.

And unfortunately for him, we're already midair.

And weightless.

My ass lifts off the seat.

Alejandro's ass lifts off the seat.

Skippy's entire corpse drifts upward from the back like some grotesque astronaut on a zero-gravity joy ride, limbs floating as gracefully as rigor mortis allows.

Alejandro releases one long, beautifully tortured, "Shiiii-iiiiiiiiiiit."

I keep both hands firm on the wheel, eyes locked on the trajectory ahead—

or close enough to ahead.

Because the rooftop we thought we were landing on is actually a glass dome.

We hit it with a thundercrack of shattering crystal.

Light explodes around us—white, blinding, raining shards.

Then the car slams downward, crashing through the opening and hitting a marble floor with bone-jarring violence.

The world resolves into white stone walls. Pedestals. Paintings. Sculptures.

A museum.

Of course it's a museum.

The impact sends Skippy tumbling into the footwell behind us, but I don't give him a second glance. I jam the accelerator again. The wheels scream and we drift into the spiral walkway that winds down the interior like a stone helix.

Down we go.

Sideways.

Screeching.

Sculptures blurring past.

Tourists screaming and diving for cover.

Miraculously—insanely—I don't hit a single thing.

At the bottom, the spiral spits us out toward a pair of giant double doors thrown open to a portico decked out for a gala. Yellow lights twinkle overhead. Guests in tuxedos and gowns stroll with champagne flutes.

"Hold tight!" I shout, my hand laying on the horn.

We launch through the doors, blasting into the party like the world's least welcome fireworks display. People scream and scatter as we bounce down a wide staircase. We obliterate a buffet table, sending towers of fruit, pyramids of pastries, and floral arrangements exploding across the lawn. Waiters dive behind hedges that don't stand a chance.

Finally, we hit street level and I straighten the wheel, checking my mirrors for shadows. It's all clear. For now.

Then I glance back at Skippy sprawled in the floorboard like a dropped mannequin.

I look at Alejandro.

He has an entire sampling platter in his lap—quiche squares, melon balls, a profiterole, half a crab puff—and he calmly plucks up a mini quiche, pops it into his mouth, and chews like this is Sunday brunch.

I stare at him. "I can't believe you."

He shrugs, brushing pastry off his shirt.

"What? I didn't get to finish my taco."

We ditch the mangled, glass-filled, fruit-splattered stolen car outside the train station. The moment the doors slam shut, Alejandro goes straight for Skippy—grabbing the corpse's swollen arm and tugging it toward him like he's about to start a field autopsy right there on the sidewalk.

Then he reaches for my knife.

I smack his hand before he can touch the hilt. "Absolutely not."

"We need the chip," he argues, already nudging Skippy's arm again. "It's right here. The swelling means it's close to the surface. One slice—"

"You have your *own* knife," I remind him.

He shrugs. "Yeah, but yours is sharper."

"And you're not slicing open the body in the middle of a train station," I snap. "One wrong move and you toast the chip. We didn't survive a car launch through a museum ceiling to fry the only lead we have."

He grits his teeth. "So what? We carry him forever? He smells."

"No. We find somewhere with an X-ray before we cut him open."

Alejandro stops, looks around. The train station is bustling—announcements echoing, luggage wheels rattling, commuters speed-walking like they're being chased by their own bad decisions.

Then he gets a look in his eyes.

An idea.

A stupid one. I can already tell.

"Oh no," I mutter. "Whatever's happening in your brain right now? Stop it."

He grins and goddamn him, those dark brown eyes have a fucking twinkle in them. "I know where we can go. And we can ditch Skippy there too. No questions asked."

I roll my eyes. "Inspiring confidence, truly."

For a moment, I let the idea spin in my head—not because I trust him, but because time is hunting us and options are bleeding out fast. If he actually has a contact who won't blink at the sight of a corpse with a mystery implant, I can't afford to dismiss it. My Guild resources will be stripped, even neutral vendors have to step back during the manhunt.

Or, womanhunt, I suppose.

I stare at him, doubtful as hell but the idea is slowly growing on me, and he knows it. He goes around to the trunk and retrieves his broken down sniper riffle, slipping the strap over his head and fixing it between his shoulder blades. "Owen *is* from Chicago."

Alejandro makes a face. "Who the fuck is Owen?"

I blink. "Owen Liang. Our dead accountant."

He shakes his head dramatically. "No. Absolutely not. He is now and forever Skippy. Owen is ridiculous."

I pinch the bridge of my nose. "Skippy is not better."

"It's too late. It stuck."

I let it go. We have bigger problems. And unfortunately, that includes the fact that Alejandro's "source" could be anyone from a disgraced medic to a smuggler with a questionable digestive tract.

"You're an exile," I remind him. "Meaning you can't use Guild assets. So, whatever 'sources' you have left are firmly in the bottom-feeding section of the black market."

He shrugs. "You have your contacts. I have mine."

"Yeah. Mine aren't wanted in three countries."

"Four," he corrects, smug. "But who's counting? And don't forget—you're an exile now too, mi Pícarita."

I stare him down. He stares back. Annoyingly confident.

And he's right—we don't have time.

He jerks his chin toward the display board. "Chicago. Overnight line. Boarding in ten."

Lucky us.

"Let's go."

I exhale, long and resigned. "Fine. But if your source is a guy who works out of a basement with a pet ferret named Hannibal, I'm stabbing you in the thigh."

Alejandro grins like he'd enjoy being stabbed in the thigh. "Deal."

Which, frankly, is the exact moment I know something is going to go wrong. The universe hates us too much for anything else.

We find a wheelchair abandoned near the parking garage elevators—rusty, one wheel squeaking like it's begging for death. Perfect. We plop Skippy—*Owen*—into it. His head lolls to the side in a way that looks disturbingly natural, like an overworked commuter taking a sad nap.

We push into the terminal. Alejandro uses a kiosk, pays cash he lifted from some poor bastard's pocket thirty seconds earlier, and somehow also pockets a pack of pink bubble gum from the snack rack.

He hands it to me with a wink and a devil's grin.

It's my flavor.

I pretend the flip in my stomach doesn't exist as I pop two pieces.

We keep moving. Snatching what we need as we go.

A woman about my height stands staring up at the departures board, her rolling suitcase parked directly behind her.

A rookie mistake.

As we pass, I grab the handle and keep walking. The suitcase glides neatly behind me like it's always belonged to me.

Alejandro spots a duffel bag at a man's feet—the guy too busy on his phone to notice the world burning around him. Alejandro swoops down and grabs the handles, plopping squarely in Skippy's lap.

"Hold this for me, amigo."

Skippy does not object.

We find our platform just as boarding begins. The private sleeper cars are still locked—they won't open them until we're already moving. Which means we're trapped with the general population for a bit with a smelly corpse and I think is getting puffier by the minute.

Fucking terrific.

We maneuver Skippy into the common car, slotting him into a seat by the window. Alejandro angles his head just right so he looks like a guy who had one too many glasses of merlot and passed out before the train even left the station.

People barely glance at him.

Just another tired traveler.

Alejandro sits beside him. I take the seat across just as the train rumbles beneath us, engines humming to life.

For the first time in hours, we're not being shot at, chased, or launched off rooftops.

It doesn't feel like relief.

It feels like the deep breath before the next explosion.

The dining car smells like overcooked meat and stale coffee, which—unfortunately—only makes my stomach growl louder. Alejandro hears it, smirks, and pushes out of his seat.

"I'll be right back," he says, already weaving toward the food counter.

Great.

Now it's just me and Dead Skippy.

His lips have gone an impressive shade of dead-man blue, and his skin has that waxy sheen that says we're officially entering the "clock is ticking" portion of corpse transportation.

Across the aisle, a kid keeps making faces at him—crossing his eyes, sticking out his tongue, trying to get a reaction. The dad is oblivious, glued to his phone. The mom, baby strapped to her chest, shushes the kid half-heartedly.

I shake my head.

You couldn't pay me enough for that job.

I try focusing on Grim's intel—Owen's swelling arm, the implant we can't risk slicing open, the dark web chatter—but Alejandro returns before I can get far, balancing a plate piled with hot dogs like he's catering a children's birthday party. He drops two bottles of water and some random snacks onto the table.

I stare at the hot dogs, scandalized.

"That's disgusting."

He grins, taking off his rifle case and propping it between him and Skippy.

Fuck. Owen.

"You and your aversion to eating land meat is a crime against good Spanish cuisine."

"Hot dogs are hardly good cuisine or Spanish." I can't help the sour expression on my face. "They barely count as food as is. You have no idea what is in those things."

He smirks. "Please, you eat like a woodland creature with trust issues. Let the adults enjoy their food."

"And you look like a man who eats hot dogs for the shape, not the taste." I snip back.

He pauses, considers the hot dog in his hand, shrugs, and takes a massive bite. I grimace as he chews with commitment.

I push the hot dog trauma aside. "Let's talk about the accountant."

Alejandro gives an exaggerated chew like he's savoring my suffering. "Okay, what have you got?"

"You think that hit makes sense? Skippy was sniffing around for Fantasma?" I ask. "That he was actually looking to hand off intel?"

"Wouldn't be the first idiot with a death wish." He wipes his mouth with a napkin. "But yeah. He if was asking the wrong questions on the wrong boards. Someone was going to notice."

There's something he's not saying though.

"You think it was something else?" I push.

"You know what I think." Alejandro doesn't miss a beat. "I always think the Guildmaster's behind shit. It's never a bad bet."

I lean in, elbows on the tiny table, voice lower. "They're both phantoms, you know. The Guildmaster. El Fantasma. Nobody knows what either one looks like. No photos. No sightings. Not even rumor-level descriptions."

He lifts a brow, waiting.

"So what if they're not two people?" I say. "What if they're the same person?"

Alejandro's eyes flick to mine—quiet, unreadable. He

doesn't confirm. Doesn't deny. Just lets the thought hang between us like a suspended blade before he looks away for a moment.

Then I notice he isn't really listening.

His attention is drifting past me.

I follow his line of sight.

A woman across the aisle is making eyes at him. Overtly. Hair toss, lip bite, smolder—the whole ridiculous package. My jaw tightens. "Does that shit actually ever work?"

Alejandro catches my tone instantly and a slow grin cuts across his mouth.

"Oh? Is the infamous Saint James jealous?"

I scoff. "Please. Jealous of what? You? Absolutely not."

"Uh-huh." He laughs under his breath. "Keep watching, Picarita."

He stands. Walks several tables back, past the woman, to take a plate from a train attendant, thanking them in Spanish.

And the woman across the aisle keeps staring.

Only... she isn't staring at him.

She's making eyes at Skippy.

The corpse.

My mouth falls open. "Oh, you've got to be fucking kidding me."

Alejandro turns back, holding a plate absolutely devoid of anything with legs. Fruit, a cheese quesadilla, a cup of yogurt. He sets it in front of me like he planned it all along.

"For you," he says. "They didn't have a large selection."

I look from him, to the plate, to the woman flirting with a dead man.

"You know what?" I mutter. "I take back everything I said. People are fucking insane."

15

Alejandro

The sleeping-car doors hiss open, dumping us into a narrow hallway that feels about three inches too tight for two people and one dead man. We take the very last compartment on the far end. Smart choice. If we need a fast exit or Saint's coworkers decide to start a fight, at least we won't snap this train in half.

The walk is a nightmare. Our very dead, very bloated travel companion slumps between us, feet dragging, shirt leaking through the spare jacket we shoved on him back at Grim's. The jacket hides most of the mess and keeps innocent commuters from screaming about the smell of—well—death marinated in high-speed chases.

I lower him to the carpeted floor of our compartment, mutter something that might be a prayer or a curse, and go hunting for supplies. Anything. A few feet down the hall I check over my shoulder to be sure Saint didn't follow me and pull out my phone.

Still no message from my broker.

Maybe less communication right now is better. I text the Chicago business name and Skippy's real name.

Vincenzi Tower and Owen Liang.

My broker responds with a single thumbs-up emoji,

because apparently my life has been reduced to cartoon hieroglyphics.

I shove the phone away and keep searching. The gods finally take pity on me. In an open luggage cubby outside a family's room, I find a rolled-up sleeping bag. I whisper a thank-you to whatever deity oversees petty theft and corpse management.

By the time I get back, Saint's kneeling beside the stolen suitcase she "liberated" earlier, rifling through it like a raccoon.

She eyes the sleeping bag. "What's that for?"

"Finally," I say, dropping it on the floor, "a body bag for our pulse-less friend."

I unroll it, unzip it, and gesture at her. "Arms or legs?"

She takes the arms without complaint. I lift his ankles.

His body makes a "U" shape, and we make it halfway to the bag before the corpse lets out an enormous, wet burp.

A straight-up belch of the fumes collecting inside our puffy friend.

The smell hits first—sulfur, rot, and something that suggests eternal punishment.

I drop his legs so fast his heels thud against the carpet. "No. No. Saint, absolutely not. That came from hell. I am not—"

"Lock the fuck in, Alejandro." She swears at me, snapping her fingers once. I wave my hands like I'm clearing a smoke bomb.

"You try holding this end next time," I choke out, "and we'll see how much you like getting a dead man's burp to the face."

"I'll pass, thank you," she mutters, pinching her nose.

We finally maneuver him onto the sleeping bag. She stands, grabs a handful of supplies from the suitcase, and heads toward the little en-suite bathroom.

"Open a window," She nods her head toward them. "I'm going to shower."

"Shower?" I ask, leaning against the doorframe, slightly winded and definitely smelling like a mortician. "Need company?"

She doesn't even look back. "You gave me permission to slit your throat. Remember?"

I grin. "That was on the other train."

She shuts the bathroom door in my face.

The shower is trash. Water pressure like a dying faucet. A drain that gurgles like it's protesting my existence. But right now? It feels perfect. Heat, steam, and the rare moment where I'm not hauling a leaking corpse or dodging someone trying to kill us.

My stolen suitcase came with a few blessings: a pair of jeans that actually fit, a clean T-shirt, even socks. Miracle-level stuff.

The bathroom, however, is roughly the size of a coffin. I can't turn without elbowing the wall or knocking my head into the mirror. So, I towel off just enough to avoid soaking the carpet, wrap the towel around my waist, and step back into the cabin.

Saint looks up.

Her eyes drag down my still-wet chest, lingering on the drops sliding down my stomach, and land squarely on my crotch. She tries to mask it. Fails. The flash of surprise, the flicker of admiration, the reluctant appreciation... I catch it all.

I know exactly what kind of body I'm working with. And I know she remembers what it felt like against hers. The way we moved together. How well we fit.

And now she's staring directly at my dick.

Danger. For both of us.

I turn away, keeping the towel tight around my hips as I slide into a pair of boxer briefs. Her gaze stays glued to me, and I can practically feel it like a hand.

"Shall I leave them off for you, Saint?" I ask, still facing away.

A pillow hits my back.

"You wish."

"You were the one staring."

I don't bother hiding my grin as I pull on jeans, shirt, socks. The borrowed deodorant smells like cedar and questionable decisions, but it beats eau de corpse. I even find a travel-size cologne that doesn't smell like someone's dad.

I give Skippy a couple sprays for charity.

He still stinks. Even with the window cracked, the AC blasting arctic air, and the body zipped tight in a sleeping bag, the cabin has a distinct kick. The kind of scent that says *yes, someone here is dead* but tries to be polite about it.

Saint's already stretched out on her bed, eyes on the ceiling, fingers laced behind her head. Fresh from her shower, she ditched the headband and let her hair spread wild. I've always liked her hair. One of those details you don't forget about Saint James.

Among other things.

I climb onto the bed across from hers, sit with my ankles crossed and my arms folded. Guard mode. Comfortable enough to pretend this is normal.

"Get some sleep," I tell her. "I'll stay up and keep an eye on the kid."

She scoffs and rolls over, giving me her back.

"Good night, Saint."

She lifts a hand and flips me off without looking.

I laugh under my breath. "Good night, Skippy."

Then I dim the lights, settle in, and let the rhythm of the tracks carry us forward while I keep watch over a corpse, a woman who might kill me in my sleep, and whatever the hell waits for us in Chicago.

I absolutely fell asleep.

I know I did because Saint kicks the hell out of my boot and my whole spine tries to escape my body.

"What the—"

"Something's wrong, Sleeping Beauty." she snaps.

She yanks open the cabin curtains. The dawning light outside crawls past us—too slow. Train-creeping-through-a-haunted-rail-yard slow.

Weapons are in our hands before either of us consciously reaches for them. Muscle memory. Kill first, ask questions never.

I crack the cabin door open and peek out.

Nothing.

Not good nothing.

Wrong nothing.

The hallway is empty. Silent. No passengers, no hushed conversations, no snoring tourists. Just the hum of the slowing train and the distant clack of metal on metal.

I check the window. We're rolling through some kind of industrial graveyard—giant warehouses, shipping containers stacked like metal tombstones, floodlights still on despite the rising sun.

Every instinct I have lights up.

"We need to go," I say.

"No shit."

We both grab for Skippy. The second I unzip the sleeping bag, I instantly regret existing.

A thin rivulet of... something... slides out and trickles across the carpet toward the bathroom.

"Oh come on."

Skippy's abdomen is round and tight like he swallowed a beach ball. His shirt buttons strain, one hanging by a thread. His neck's swollen. He's seconds from popping like a goddamn piñata.

Saint gags. "I'm going to vomit."

"You're the one who wouldn't let me cut his arm off. Fucking deal with it."

I sling my rifle case over my shoulder while Saint throws open the cabin door, weapon up, sweeping left, then right. No threats.

She storms off anyway, shouting over her shoulder, "Get him upright and in the hall!"

I mutter curses in three languages and grab a dry corner of the sleeping bag. I'm dragging a human soup pouch into the hallway when Saint marches back toward me pushing—a goddamn baby stroller.

She parks it beside me like this is normal transportation for corpses.

I stare at it. "You're kidding."

"It's better than carrying him," she says. "He's wet."

"Fucking fantastic. Let's get this over with."

We wrangle his soggy body onto the stroller seat. His head lolls. His belly bulges. The stroller wheels give a sad squeak. Saint cinches a bungee cord across his chest. I test the rig by rocking the stroller hard.

It holds. "Huh, not bad." I hate how impressed I am.

Saint heads toward the back of the car, gun up. "No assassins," she calls. "For now."

I move to the front to check the connection between our car and the others—and get my answer.

"We've been separated from the rest of the train," I call back.

We're drifting alone, slowing, until the tracks drag us to a final, inevitable stop.

Saint stomps back down the hall, pushing Skippy's stroller like she's taking him for a polite afternoon walk. "What a great lookout you turned out to be," she snipes, parking Skippy off to the side.

She kicks open the rear door and steps onto the platform, staying back from the edge.

"Oh, it just gets better and better," she mutters.

"What?"

"It's a fucking hot dog factory." She's furious. Almost offended. Then she looks back at me, deadpan. "You'll be thrilled."

I pull back on my gun and check the round chambered. "Let's just find another car to steal and get the fuck out of here."

Saint

RED RIBBON PROVISION CO.
Quality Meats Since 1949
Family Owned & Operated

A goddamn hot dog factory.

Just my fucking luck.

Of all the places on earth we could've been dumped... this. A monument to liquefied mystery meat. I gave up most land animals years ago, but apparently fate decided today was the day to surround me with the worst form of meat imaginable.

My throat actually tightens just thinking about it. Between Skippy's corpse cologne and the smell of industrial processed... whatever... I might legitimately puke for the first time in a decade.

I scan the lot for exits, but there's nothing. No cars. No guards. Just a line of eighteen-wheelers backed against the loading docks. This must be the rear of the factory. Parking lot will be on the other side, of course. Figures.

I'm about to call back to Alejandro—tell him we split, I

go high, he goes low—when a bright *ping* snaps off the metal shell of our train car.

A heartbeat later I hear the gunshot.

Well. So much for planning.

"Incoming!" I bark.

I grab Skippy's janky stroller and shove it hard, wheels squealing as it rattles back down the train car toward Alejandro.

"Get him off the other side!" I shout. "I'll draw fire!"

Alejandro immediately argues, because of course he does.

"I'm faster," I snap. "Shut up and move!"

I've already got both guns out, loaded, warm, familiar. My heartbeat steadies. My breathing evens. Combat mode drops over me like a second skin.

I bounce once on my heels. Twice. A few fast breaths.

Then I jump.

I hit the ground in a roll, gravel scraping my shoulder, momentum snapping me upright. The second I'm vertical, I'm running. Hard. Fast. Zigzagging across open pavement as another bullet whines past my ear.

The eighteen-wheelers near the back doc—one of them is running—that's my mark.

I sprint low, cut across open asphalt, and slide under the nearest abandoned trailer. Metal slams above me. The world narrows to shadow, grease, and the staccato echo of distant gunfire.

There's movement on one of the rooftops near the north side. I don't hesitate to allow him a chance to relocate. I ease out from behind the large tires and take one shot.

He drops without a scream—dead a second after he bullet left my gun.

I roll to the opposite side of the trailer, eyes scanning. Another shooter crouches on the roof of an adjacent warehouse. Amateur camouflage. Sloppy posture. Easy pickings.

Before I fire, I check Alejandro's position. He's at the far end of the drifting train car, the one we got sabotaged into. It's still creeping along the track like a drunk snake, inching us deeper into this mess.

He sees me watching and coils back like a spring.

I match him for one heartbeat.

Two.

Then, we launch.

I burst into the open, firing twice. The rooftop shooter jerks, tumbles, vanishes. But more shots ring out. Three. Four. Maybe six of them circling the yard.

A little ambush party. Probably planning to split the bounty. Cute.

Probably why they rigged the train car instead of taking the hit inside it because they wanted the work to feel earned.

Well. Congratulations.

Saint James will make them fucking earn it.

Alejandro is running full sprint, stroller wheels screaming behind him. Skippy's corpse lurches around like a wet, sagging puppet.

Alejandro fires without breaking stride. His target drops from a rooftop. I track the fall but don't slow down, heading straight for the open loading-dock doors. Inside means cover. Narrow walkways. Equipment. Places to bottleneck the idiots who think they can corner me.

I'm ten feet from the door when I hear a different shot blast across the factory yard.

Deeper. Sharper. High-caliber.

A sniper.

The bullet whispers just past my afro. The dirt several feet to my right explodes in a tight puff. I feel the singed ends of my hair, feel the heat of the bullet that rushed through it.

Oh. Hell. No.

I turn, scanning, hunting—and then I see it. A glint on metal. A silhouette on top of the old water tower at the edge of the factory yard.

Cowboy hat tipped back so it doesn't interfere with his scope.

The Texan.

Of course.

Colt Harrington. Little bitch baby.

My least favorite mosquito with a superiority complex.

I knew he wouldn't let New York go. Not after I bested him on that rooftop. He's been my rival since day one—a competition he invented because he couldn't stand being anything but the best.

We shared the same initiation ring. Thirteen rounds. Neither of us managing to put the other down. That was the day Kenji stepped in, pulled me out and claimed me as his student.

The whole room gasped almost drowning out Colt's muttered "mother fucker".

And he has never, ever let it go.

Always number two.

Always in my shadow.

Always furious about it.

Of course he'd chase this job. Of course he'd risk everyone else's bullets just for a chance to take me out and crown himself king.

Well, asshole. Not if I can help it.

He gives me a one-finger salute from the tower, and I hear the metallic click of him chambering another round.

I step backward until I'm inside the loading dock, out of his line of fire. Alejandro climbs into one of the platforms, hauls Skippy's stroller up after him, the whole contraption rattling like a dying shopping cart.

"What's the plan now?" he asks.

My eyes stay on the tower.

"I need to blow up that water tower."

I'm on a mission.

Alejandro's behind me wrestling Skippy's busted stroller like it's a cursed shopping cart from hell, wheels locking, frame wobbling, dead guy sloshing. It's pathetic. And loud. And slowing us down.

I don't wait for him.

I shove through the next set of double doors and instantly regret it.

The smell hits like a wall of bricks. Hot meat. Hot, *wet* meat, to be exact.

I'd almost rather smell Skippy.

Almost.

The factory floor is chaos. Stainless-steel tables. Giant vats churning. Steam vents hissing. Plastic-wrapped towers of meat product waiting to be processed. The constant buzz of machinery and conveyor belts grinding mystery protein into shapes that should not legally exist. This is hell for vegetarians and assassins alike.

Shots ping off metal behind us. Footsteps. Yelling.

"Move!" I shout at Alejandro.

"I'm trying!" he barks, kicking one of the stroller's wheels until it limps forward. "Skippy's leaking again!"

"Then stop pushing him like a toddler and pick up the whole damn thing!"

"I'm not carrying a corpse like a baby, Saint!"

I ignore him. I'm scanning for parts. Tools. Anything long, hollow, and structurally stupid enough to become a makeshift weapon.

Bingo.

A thick, stainless-steel sanitation tube—twelve inches in diameter, maybe four feet long—leaning against a wall near a maintenance station. Perfect rocket-launcher body.

I snatch it up, the weight solid and promising, and jog deeper into the factory. Alejandro curses behind me, fighting off an attacker who leaps from behind a bin of raw pork slurry.

There's a grunt, a smack, and a wet *thud*.

Alejandro yells out, "I think he landed in the meat!"

"Then he's finally contributing to society."

An attacker rounds the corner at me. I don't slow. I palm my knife thrusting fast into his abdomen six times before he even registers the first cut. He folds over with a wheeze. I kick him backward into a vat of boiling water. The churn blooms dark red in an instant.

I keep going, my mind already assembling the weapon.

Propellant. Stabilizer. Ammunition.

This place has all three.

Unfortunately.

I move fast, weaving between conveyor lines and towering racks of boxed product, Alejandro swearing somewhere behind me as he clatters over equipment with Skippy's stroller.

I cut behind a massive metal cabinet and freeze.

Someone's already there.

A factory worker, curled into himself like a human shrimp. Hairnet trembling. Safety goggles fogged. Apron speckled with meat dust. He looks at me like I'm a hallucination brought on by inhaling too much steam-processed protein.

I keep my gun raised out of habit. He flinches.

"Name?" I ask, clipped.

He mumbles something unintelligible. My ears catch only the tail end: "–ark."

"Speak up."

He swallows hard. "Mark. With a K."

"Perfect, Kark." I hook a fist in the front of his apron and haul him upright. "I need something flammable. Now."

His whole head bobs like it's on a spring. He points one trembling finger toward a side hallway. "C-cleaning station. Big red canisters. Very, um... very not approved for... anything."

"Excellent. You're coming with me Clark."

Gunfire cracks somewhere behind me. Alejandro yells something dramatically unhelpful.

I pull the guy by the collar into a crouched sprint. He scuttles beside me like a terrified crab trying to keep up.

We duck around a row of stainless-steel mixers. An attacker leaps out, barreling straight at us.

I don't hesitate.

One shot and he drops hard onto the concrete.

Dude-man squeaks. Actually squeaks.

"Relax," I mutter. "You're not on the menu."

He makes a broken noise that suggests he isn't convinced.

Across the factory, Alejandro is fighting off two thugs at once—one hand throwing punches, the other trying to keep Skippy's stroller from collapsing under its own structural despair.

"Saint!" Alejandro shouts. "A little help?! Emotional support?! Anything besides whatever the fuck you are doing!"

"I'm busy building a weapon of mass inconvenience!" I call back.

"Son of a— Of *course* you are!"

I drag What's-His-Face around a stack of sealed boxes and slip us into the cleaning station. Rows of industrial degreaser canisters line the wall—huge, red, sloshing containers covered in warning labels that basically read *Don't you fucking dare.*

Perfect propellant.

I shove the steel tube I stole earlier into my new friend's arms. He nearly collapses under the weight.

"Hold that, Clint." I say.

He nods like a bobblehead seconds from a nervous breakdown. "Mark."

Whatever.

Time to build a rocket launcher out of degreaser, stainless steel, and the world's least heroic sidekick.

And soon?

Frozen hot dogs.

God help the idiots who think they're taking me down today.

17

Alejandro

Saint is somewhere below me, sprinting through the factory with a nerd who looks like he's about to piss himself. A real catch. Meanwhile I'm up here dragging Skippy's corpse-on-wheels through a battlefield.

Helpful.

So helpful.

The factory layout is a goddamn maze—machines, conveyor belts, metal railings, blind corners. I get funneled up a ramp and onto a set of catwalks high over the factory floor, the stroller rattling like it's trying to shake itself apart.

Gunfire cracks behind me.

Perfect.

They're coming from everywhere.

And Skippy is... well... Skippy.

"We're going this way," I mutter to him like he's capable of caring, swerving left along a narrow catwalk.

The frame wobbles. One wheel locks. Another squeals. The whole stroller shimmies like it's seconds from spontaneous combustion.

"Hold it together," I hiss. "We're almost—"

A shot hits the railing behind me, sparks spitting. I duck, push forward, but something catches—the stroller jerks sideways, tips, and Skippy's body slumps halfway over the railing.

"Shit."

I drop my rifle to one hand and lunge.

I catch him by the wrist. Barely. A swollen, waterlogged, unholy wrist that feels like it's made of gelatinous doom.

He dangles there.

Dead weight.

Literally.

The skin around his elbow begins to stretch.

Then tear.

"Oh you've got to be kidding me!"

Another attacker barrels toward me on the catwalk. I kick him square in the chest, send him smashing into a rail pillar. My gun fires once—center mass—but I can't spare a second to watch him fall.

I'm holding Skippy.

I'm fighting.

I'm slipping.

And Skippy's goddamn arm is coming apart.

"SAINT!" I bellow. "A little help! Preferably now!"

The fight below stutters—the chaos freezing for a split second—as everyone looks up.

Saint spots me.

Eyes widen in absolute horror.

Because Skippy...

lets go.

Or more accurately—

his arm detaches at the elbow. His body drops like a sandbag straight into a massive open tank of meat chunks on the factory floor.

There's a bone-rattling splash.

A ripple of silence.

Then—

BZZZT

A factory buzzer blares.

The grinder kicks on.

The tank churns.

The blades spin.

Skippy's body is dragged under, sucked into the machinery like a sacrifice to the gods of processed sausages.

We watch—

all of us, enemies, and allies and Nerdy McNerdykins—

as the tank grinds him into a bubbling pink slurry.

Shoes.

Suit.

Rotting flesh.

Bits of swollen anatomy I refuse to identify.

And—just to make this the worst possible reality—Saint's sunglasses go in too.

The mix funnels down a chute and slides through a quality-inspection scanner.

A cheerful *ping* sounds.

A green light flashes as a sign lights up:

PASSED.

I look down at Saint.

She looks up at me.

Shared disgust.

Shared trauma.

Shared what-the-actual-fuck.

We don't even get a chance to breathe.

Because the world snaps back into motion—

attackers screaming, weapons firing—

and the fight explodes into full throttle all over again.

All I've got left in my hand is Skippy's forearm—fat, swollen, hand still attached.

Perfect.

It's the one with the chip, too. Maybe Chicago's shadiest gremlin can salvage something before everything goes straight to hell.

An attacker charges me, screaming like he's the main character.

I don't have patience for main characters.

I swing Skippy's disembodied arm and bitch slap him across the face. Hard.

Something wet and disturbingly chunky splatters onto him, but I absolutely do not investigate.

He recoils, gagging. I pull my knife, and drive the blade straight into his skull. His eyes cross like a broken cartoon before he topples off the catwalk.

I don't watch him fall because two more men and a woman rush me next, thinking numbers will help.

They won't.

I grab Skippy's empty stroller by the twisted frame, spin once, and hurl it with everything I've got.

It becomes a projectile.

A metal rocket of Walmart engineering.

It slams into all three of them. One man flies backward over the railing—

—straight into a conveyor belt lined with chopping blades.

The machine doesn't even break rhythm. Knife-like

teeth shred through whatever hits them, including the guy who made the mistake of fighting me today.

I don't slow.

Saint is somewhere ahead, yelling and firing shots like the battlefield owes her rent. She takes on one hand-to-hand before pulling her blade and jabbing lightning fast into his throat. I run full sprint toward her.

"We need to go!" I shout.

"I KNOW THAT!" she screams back.

I reach her just in time to see a shooter raise their weapon and instinct takes over.

I grab Saint, yank her into my chest, and pivot so my back faces the threat.

The shot cracks.

White-hot pain rips through my shoulder, burning deep, dropping fire along my nerves. I grit my teeth and refuse to let go.

Saint looks up at me from the circle of my arms.

Her green eyes are wide—bright, furious, alive with the adrenaline of battle. Her breath comes fast against my throat. Sweat beads on her brow. She's still gripping her gun, ready to kill the next idiot who tries us.

"Thanks," she breathes.

My gaze drops to her mouth.

She licks her lips.

And my stomach does something irritating and warm.

I force myself to meet her eyes again. "Anytime."

Her chest rises and falls against mine.

The gunfire around us fades for half a second before we both come to our senses.

"Now... can we get the fuck out of here?" I mutter, gripping my shoulder with my good hand. "Before anything else leaks, pops, or tries to kill us."

Saint clocks the severed arm in my hand and grimaces, but there's nothing to be done about it now.

We crouch beside her newest recruit—the trembling factory worker. He nods at me like we're old comrades in war.

"I'm Mark," he squeaks, holding out a hand.

"Alejandro," I reply—and hand him Skippy's detached limb, palm-first.

He shakes it before he realizes what he's holding.

The sound he makes is... not flattering.

I grab a clear plastic bag off the floor, shake the dust from it, and hold it open. "Put it in here."

Mark drops the arm inside like it's radioactive. Saint joins as I tie the bag tight, cinching the knot hard.

"I just need one clear shot once we get outside," she announces, adjusting the last component on her improvised launcher.

"What the fuck do you need that for?"

"Tex is here," she snaps. "The hemorrhoid of the Guild."

"You haven't killed him yet?"

"Rule number one. No kill without contract."

"Such a rule follower," I mutter. "And look where that got you."

She ignores me and turns to the factory worker.

"Kevin—"

Mark blinks. I blink.

Who the fuck is Kevin?

She doesn't break stride. "When I say the word—"

"It's Mark." I correct her and at the same time Mark says, "It's Mark."

Saint actually gets pissed like we're the ones that are wrong. "It's whatever the fuck I say it is. When I say the word, I want you to run as fast as your little legs can go and get the fuck out of here."

Mark nods furiously. "Okay. Which way—"

"Go!"

He bolts, scrambling between machinery, his terrified scurrying echoing behind us. Hopefully he makes it out. And not in the form of a hot dog.

Rest in peace, Skippy.

Saint and I move together, fluid and synced, sprinting toward the loading-bay exit. We're ten feet from the doors when they explode inward and five attackers' storm in, guns raised.

I fire first—drop one clean and hear the dreaded hollow click of an empty magazine.

Saint steps up beside me.

She lifts her absurd, stainless-steel, OSHA-violating rocket launcher to her shoulder, sights down the length of the tube, and says—

"I'm about tired of these fuckers."

Then she pulls the trigger.

Saint

I've never seen hot dogs do this.

They tear through bodies like shrapnel.

One slams into a woman's eye socket and stays there, buried deep enough to hit brain. She drops instantly.

Another punches straight through a man's neck—clean entry, clean exit, arterial spray painting the loading bay in a lovely shade of *fuck-you-red*.

They all go down.

Alejandro stares at me, impressed despite himself. "Well... that was a lot more effective than I expected."

Always doubting me.

I reload fast—my last shot, the final hit of propellant, and a bundle of rock-hard frozen hot dogs from the bag clipped to my side.

On our way out the door, I lay out the plan.

"Just distract him long enough for me to line up my shot. Then get the fuck out of the way. We're riding out on that eighteen-wheeler."

A lone assassin bursts out from behind a truck and hurls a knife at my chest.

It barely misses—grazes my arm on the way past, hot pain blooming as blood rolls down my skin.

Alejandro doesn't even break stride.

He hurls his own knife, and his aim is better.

The blade sinks into the attacker's eye with a wet, meaty thunk.

"Hijo de puta." Alejandro mutters, stomping over to retrieve his knife.

The man collapses. Alejandro yanks his blade free, snags a discarded pistol off the ground, and surveys the carnage. It looks like a few assassins took *each other* out—good. Less work for us.

He checks the gun's load, satisfied, then adjusts the heavy rifle strapped across his back. Skippy's severed arm is tucked under his like a grotesque baguette.

His gaze flicks to my bleeding bicep. "You good?"

"You know I've had worse. Let's move."

We fall into step like we never stopped.

We always worked well together. Could read each other before a single motion was made. And it looks like nothing's changed.

Alejandro lifts the gun and strides forward, firing steady bursts—keeping Colt Harrington busy in the tower's perch. Long legs, sure aim, rounds ringing off rusted metal.

I follow close, adding more accelerant to the tube, dropping to one knee as I shoulder the launcher. My sight line aligns perfectly.

Right over the top of Alejandro's head.

"Now."

The second I say it, he drops flat and rolls. I fire.

One second later, a barrage of frozen hot dogs—accelerated by degreaser, vengeance, and spite—slams into the water tower.

The old metal groans and buckles.

Then erupts, the whole structure shattering in a rusted bloom.

I spot Tex diving off the opposite side, avoiding death by about half a heartbeat. I missed him, but the tower goes— and the water follows.

"Let's go!" Alejandro shouts, grabbing my good arm, hauling me up.

We sprint back across the loading docks just as forty thousand gallons of water explode outward, a flash flood sweeping the trucks and machinery into chaos. Eighteen-wheelers slam into one another, smashing cargo and metal with violent crunches.

We race to the one truck not overturned yet, clamber onto the trailer as it's lifted and carried by the flood.

We run—unsteady, slipping—toward the cab, drop down, wrench open the doors, and dive inside.

Alejandro tosses the bagged arm behind the seats, slams the truck into gear, and floors it.

The tires spin on soaked concrete, struggling for purchase.

The truck fishtails once—twice—

Then lurches forward.

We blast through the factory gates, bounce over a set of rails carrying freight carts, and finally surge onto the open road.

Only when the truck stabilizes do I glance into the side mirror.

All I see is thousands of hot dogs drifting across the

flooded yard, bobbing like tiny pink corpses in an ocean of chaos.

Have I mentioned how much I fucking hate hot dogs?

The drive to Chicago is quiet. Bouncy as hell, every pothole rattling my teeth, but quiet. Neither of us feels like talking, not after the day we've had. I'm starving, I need a shower that could double as an exorcism, and for once in my life I'm actually grateful not to be babysitting a decomposing corpse in the backseat anymore.

Close enough.

The severed arm jiggles on the metal floor with each bump. It's gross, but I find myself watching it anyway as Alejandro navigates the truck deeper into the city. The streets get narrower block by block, buildings closing in like they want something from us.

If the chip in that arm is fried, we're screwed. Back to square one, except this time we'll be exhausted, half-feral, and probably hunted by every trigger-happy idiot from Tokyo to JFK.

Alejandro breaks the silence. "First forty-eight hours on your contract are nearly up."

Yeah. I know. My whole body knows. By morning, the initial bounty expires, and then there are only two options.

He glances at me. "You think they're going to raise it?"

"Yup."

Normally, for an exile, the price dips after the first window closes. Then it goes open-ended—set reward, no expiration, whoever brings in the body wins the prize. Exiles are long games. Slow hunts.

But sometimes, not often, the price goes up.

"They blew the bank on the first contract because they wanted a response," I say. "Since they're going to fail—and we both know I'm not dying tonight—they'll raise it. Bigger reward, bigger swarm."

I lean my head against the vibrating window. "It's only going to get crazier from here. If you're backing out, now's the time."

"I'm not going anywhere." Alejandro doesn't even pretend to consider it. "Not until it's done."

He doesn't elaborate on what "it" is, and I don't ask. Whatever vendetta he's nursing is running parallel to mine, and for now, that's enough.

He pulls the truck into a parking lot before the road tightens into the kind of street you only drive down if you're begging to get stuck. The engine idles, then cuts off.

"Let's stick the arm in your backpack," he says. "Take a taxi the rest of the way to my contact. Buses have cameras. The sooner we get underground, the better."

Alejandro handles the eighteen-wheeler like it's his personal ballet. Watching him work the clutch and spin that oversized wheel is almost indecent. Jaw locked, brow pulled tight, the muscles in his forearms flex every time he shifts. There's something about watching a man command machinery the size of a small apartment building that shouldn't be doing it for me.

Maybe it's the forearm porn. Maybe it's knowing exactly what those hands can do.

Either way, the truck rolls to a stop and I flick my gaze up.

Of course he's looking at me.

He's wearing that stupid smirk, the dangerous one, made worse by the single curl of dark hair hanging over his eye. "Anything you'd like to share with the class?"

I take my time dragging my gaze down, then back up again. "You have small wrists."

I hop out before he can respond.

From the pavement, I watch him through the open door. He's staring at his own wrists like they just betrayed him. "Small what?" he mutters. "No."

I pretend not to hear, grabbing my pack and unzipping it. The arm goes inside, thank every deity for heavy-duty plastic and blessed scent containment. Even the juice stays put.

Alejandro climbs out once he's reassembled whatever's left of his ego. He slings his rifle case over his shoulder with practiced ease.

"Who's your contact?" I ask.

He smiles. I don't trust it. "You'll see."

Yeah. I'll see, all right.

Thirty minutes later, I'm following him into a shady-ass alley and down a set of concrete steps. Above us: a ramen shop. Beneath us: the kind of place where people get murdered for fun.

Alejandro must sense my lack of enthusiasm because he throws a "trust me" over his shoulder.

Fat chance.

He knocks twice on a rusted metal door. The place looks diseased.

No one answers. For a long, agonizing stretch, all I hear is the distant hum of the ramen shop. Then—movement. The sound of someone stomping through a sea of empty bottles. Cursing. A crash. Something rolling.

Then comes the real wait: no fewer than ten thousand locks clacking and sliding open. Someone takes their home security very seriously.

The door cracks open. Two enormous eyes blink at us behind glasses so thick they could magnify a star. The living embodiment of a mole squints up at Alejandro, then at me, then past us, checking for threats.

"Is she the body?" he asks, inspecting me like a lab specimen.

"Do I look dead, motherfucker?" My multitool is in my hand before he finishes blinking. The blade flicks open with that satisfying snap.

Alejandro laughs. "No, old friend. Our cadaver made its way into sausage casings. We do have an arm, though. But I fear it's a bit too rank, even for your tastes."

The mole-man grumbles and swings the door wider.

The inside is... not much. Trash everywhere. Takeout containers from upstairs. Metal surgical trays stacked in corners. It's cold enough to bite bone, but a fireplace roars in the corner, embers glowing hot enough to liquefy steel. Several lamps cast sickly yellow light, each shade made from some stretched hide I can't immediately identify.

The mole—whoever he is—scurries away, muttering like he's tunneling through the earth.

"Who the fuck is this guy?" I whisper.

Alejandro hesitates. Actually hesitates. "Uh... you can call him Frank."

There's something he's withholding. I can feel it.

"That it? Just Frank?"

"In some of the darker pits of hell, he's known as Dr. Frankenstein," Alejandro says lightly. "He has a thing for the dead."

"Do I want to know?"

Then it hits me like a brick to the temple.

"You said Skippy was 'too rank, even for your tastes.'" My gaze sweeps the room again. Heat rises up my neck. Then I look at the lampshades—and the heat drops to ice.

"Does he eat them?"

Shock. Revulsion. And a sudden existential fear that I might end up as part of a Chicago ramen bowl.

Alejandro chuckles, unslinging his rifle and pulling the strap of my backpack off my shoulder. "Always a quick study."

"Well, it's not hard when the lampshade has a fucking nipple on it."

He squints. "Oh. So, it does."

He opens the pack, pulls the arm out, and plops it onto the metal table in the middle of the room just as "Frank" returns, holding some kind of wand.

"First things first..." Frank mutters. "Gotta check for bugs."

Alejandro

I f I could've taken a picture of Saint's face when I told her Frank was a cannibal, I would've framed it. Hung it somewhere classy. Maybe above a fireplace in a home I'll never own. Her green eyes went dinner-plate wide, her mouth forming a perfect O of horror and profanity waiting to happen.

Worth it.

I roll my shoulder again, wincing. The bullet graze keeps pulling every time I move. I probably need stitches. Definitely need a shower. Preferably without a corpse nearby, but I'm a realist.

Frank starts with the arm, thank every saint in the sky he leaves it sealed in the plastic. Then he turns that oversized wand on me. I lift my arms like I'm at airport security, let him wave the device around until it gives a clear tone.

Then it's Saint's turn.

I expect nothing. She expects nothing.

So, when the wand emits the faintest beep, my head snaps toward her.

Frank waves again, zeroing in. Saint frowns. I frown harder.

Her Guild sigil.

A tattoo. The one every assassin gets after initiation.

Their master key. Unlocks weapons caches, medical rooms, safe lodgings, transport hubs. All the places neutral or allied to the Guild. I had one too. Mine was burned off the day I became an exile.

"How is there a tracker in my sigil?" she asks.

"I've never heard of them doing this," I tell her. And I haven't. Not in all my years. Not even in the darkest corners of the Guild's history.

"Explains why assassins showed up everywhere we were," she mutters.

Frank starts backing away like she pulled a grenade out of her pocket. He sputters, waving his hands, yelling at her to get out of his basement lab.

"Cut it out or burn it off," he shrieks. "Or leave. The Guild will keep tracking you. Then the assassins come. They'll swarm this whole block. And if they find me—"

Yeah. We all know what happens.

He might have Pentagon level security on this place, but the Guild tracking us this close? The vultures will circle the entire neighborhood until they find her. And by extension, him, and me. We've both got an open contracts on our heads.

She stands there, thinking. Too quiet.

Then she puts her switchblade straight into the fire.

"Saint," I say immediately. "Think about what you're doing."

"I have," she says.

She's right. Every assassin in the Guild is after her. Her contract expires in hours, and instead of dropping, it'll spike. They all turned on her. Even if she clears her name... someone set her up. Someone high enough to get her contract past the inner circle. Get it to the Guildmaster's desk.

If he approved the hit, there is no level of the Guild she can ever return to again.

Frank thrusts a bottle of whiskey at her like it's first aid.

She takes it without blinking, pours some on her wrist then takes a long swallow. There is no hesitation when she presses the glowing blade to her wrist.

The smell hits first. Burnt skin. Burnt ink. Burnt identity.

Her jaw tightens. She doesn't scream. She doesn't flinch. She holds the blade steady until her own sigil sears away in a dead-black line.

When she's done, she holds her wounded wrist out and I catch the faint tremor she's hiding. Frank nervously scans her again.

Nothing.

He lets out a long, shaky breath, slumping into a chair like he just survived a natural disaster. Grabs the closest bottle beside him—God knows what's in it—and drinks deep.

"You can stay," he says. "Shower. You stink."

That's rich, coming from a man who decorates with human-skin lampshades and ramen containers, but I'll take the win.

"You got everything I asked for?" I say when Saint excuses herself to one of the showers.

Frank glances around like the walls are listening. "Yes, but you need to pay double. You shorted me a body."

"The broker will cover it."

He sniffs, clearly unconvinced, then waddles off through a side door. A second later, the unmistakable smell of noodles and broth seeps in. Must lead straight into the ramen shop's kitchen.

I hope to God he'll come back with something edible, instead of the usual... whatever he eats.

I finished my shower first. Hot water stings the bullet-wound at my shoulder, but it does what it needs to—rinses off two days of blood, sweat, and cross-country corpse transport. As soon as I knew we were coming here, I had my broker send over a care package. Fresh clothes, boots, a new shirt that doesn't smell like the inside of a body bag. I requested one for Saint too—figured she'd either appreciate it or stay in hotdog scented leather. Which I highly doubt.

When I stepped back into the main room, I grab a trash bag from under the sink and start clearing off the table. Takeout containers, rusted tools, a handful of things that definitely used to hold something that previously had a pulse.

The arm is gone—hopefully Frank put it in his fridge. Hopefully.

Saint emerges minutes later in clean clothes, hair damp, skin flushed from the hot water. She looks... lighter. Human, almost.

"Thanks for the clothes," she says.

I nod. No point making a thing of it.

Frank returns—praise whatever deity handles miracles—carrying stacked to-go containers of ramen wrapped in plastic, steam fogging the inside. Behind him shuffles an old woman with a hunched back and a red apron, like she's been cooking noodles since the Industrial Revolution. She sets down a bag of sides, a carrier with a tokkuri of warm sake, and several chilled bottles of Kirin.

Then she's gives a polite nod and smile, backing away and leaving through the same door.

Saint's eyes go feral with hunger. She's already moving toward the table, apparently willing to forget the nipple-clad lampshades if there's soup involved.

I scan the containers: tofu, pork, chicken. I slide the tofu her way. Frank grabs the pork like a dragon claiming treasure and disappears back into his cave.

That leaves the two of us.

There are cups inside the bag. I pour us each a serving of warm sake. She clinks her cup lightly against mine.

"To not being dead yet," I say.

She smirks. "Or a lampshade."

We drink.

We eat. Talk. Laugh a little too easily considering the last forty-eight hours. We trade stories—mostly old ones, a few new ones we'll pretend aren't trauma in disguise. She sits on one side of the long bench table, I sit on the other.

"Yeah, Puerto Rico was fun," she says, her laugh fading as she takes another pull from her Kirin.

She's looking around the room. I'm looking at her.

The flames from Frank's eternal fireplace flicker in her eyes. And for a second, it's not this basement-lab-trash-pit. It's the beach the night before I left—her back pressed to my chest, my arms around her, both of us staring up at the sky like we weren't about to destroy each other.

She catches me looking. Holds my stare while she drinks, slow and deliberate.

"It's good to see you, Saint," I say.

A ghost of a grin touches her mouth, but she doesn't give me anything back. Instead, she reaches into her bag and pulls out a medic kit.

"You need stitches," she says.

I take another drink of beer. There she is—same woman as always. Never says the thing that matters, but she'll fix you before she buries you.

"Shirt off," she adds. "Turn around."

I climb onto the bench, facing away from her. She settles on the table behind me. I hear her wash her hands, metal tools clicking, the quiet rhythm she's always had when she works.

She inspects the bullet wound carefully.

Her hands are gentler than they have any right to be. For someone who kills for a living, her touch is soft.

Coolant mist hits my shoulder. "Feel that?" she asks.

"No."

"Good."

The needle goes in. Clean, efficient, no hesitation.

"You were always good at this," I say.

She gives a small chuckle—focused but amused. "You were always getting wounded."

I sip my beer. "Yeah, but you should've seen the other guys."

She shakes her head. A few faint tugs later, the needle hits metal and gets tossed aside. She tapes gauze over the stitches.

I swing one leg over the bench to face her. "Your turn."

She rolls her eyes but sits next to me. I check the knife wound on her arm and dig in the kit for wound-closing strips and skin seal.

"You should've let me stitch you first," I say. "You used your kit on me."

"I'll be fine." She shrugs. "Can't have you walking around with holes in you."

"It was just a scratch."

"That bullet said otherwise."

I pull the wound together with the strips. She winces and I mutter an apology. She lets it pass.

I keep stealing glances at her and it doesn't feel like a choice. My eyes go to her without even trying.

"You seeing anyone?" I ask, trying for casual but it lands like a grenade between us.

"Who has time for that when there are contracts to collect?" She takes a sip of beer, hiding in the motion.

I finish the bandage. "Turn around."

She obeys without biting my head off. That alone says too much.

I take her wrist and she faces me. Her eyes lock onto mine as I clean the burn from her newly ruined sigil. Her skin is warm and I want to press my lips to the softness here.

My own scarred-over sigil sits opposite hers, the perfect mirror of everything we used to be.

She looks at it. Then at me.

I wrap her wrist in gauze, eyes never leaving hers. The pressure in the room shifts—heavy, close, charged.

"All set," I say, my voice rougher than I meant.

She takes a slow breath. "Thanks."

She stands, closes the kit, slides it back into her bag.

I stand too, and I catch her wrist—the unbandaged one.

I don't even know what I meant to say. I just know that if she walks away, this moment goes with her, and I can't let that happen.

She looks at me.

I look at her.

"I meant it that night," I say finally. "I was coming back."

Her eyes flicker—hurt, sharp, quickly swallowed.

"But you didn't."

Everything inside me tightens, heat surging up like a pressure bomb finally going off.

"And I've hated that night ever since," I say.

I pull her into me and my mouth collides with hers—two years of restraint obliterated. It's not gentle. Not careful. It's what happens when you starve and finally get fed.

One hand cups her jaw. The other drags her against me as I spin her, pushing her back into the table.

She braces with one hand behind her. Her other hand threads into my hair at the nape of my neck, and she moans when I kiss her harder, tongue sliding against hers with the kind of abandon I've been denying since the moment she walked back into my life.

I'm starving.

And she's the only thing that's ever filled me.

Saint

This is a bad idea. I know it in the marrow of my bones, the kind of certainty you get right before the trigger pull. It doesn't matter. Not when Alejandro's mouth is on mine, rough and hungry, not when his hands are skating up my thigh and the friction from his jeans is exactly where I want it. Maybe I want to punish myself. Maybe I just want to forget the last two years—every single moment I kept running from one contract to the next. Either way, I'm not stopping.

He pulls back, just enough that our breaths tangle in the small space between us. "Tell me to stop."

I bite his lower lip—hard enough to remind him who he's dealing with. "If you stop, I'm stabbing you."

His laugh is low, dangerous, and so goddamn familiar I want to crawl inside it. He lifts me like I weigh nothing, my legs locking around his hips as he carries me through the clutter, past the table with its godawful lampshades and half-burnt ramen boxes, straight to the room we'll be sharing.

Every step is a silent dare, his arms solid beneath me, my fingers digging into his hair like I can anchor myself to something that's already half-gone. His mouth never leaves my neck.

He lays me down—gentler than I expect. I pull him down, kissing him hard, as his body covers mine, heat sinking into all the places I've been cold for too long.

He pulls back again, searching my eyes. "Last chance. If you don't want to do this—"

I let my grin sharpen, even as my pulse hammers. "If you don't fuck me right now, I'm going to open up that bullet hole and shoot you again."

He laughs—dark and hoarse—and that's it. The last line gone.

He strips his shirt off in one smooth motion, and I pull mine over my head, fingers finding the zipper on my sports bra. The fabric parts down the center, and I watch his eyes track the motion as it slips off my shoulders.

His gaze drops straight to my breasts, dark nipples tightening in the cool air. The hunger on his face hits me like a live current.

He drops to his knees on the mattress, sitting back on his heels as he unbuckles his belt. I rise up to mirror him, sliding my fingers over the button of his jeans, down the zipper, pushing denim and boxers just low enough to free his cock.

God, he's beautiful like this. Tan skin. Dark hair dusting his chest. Muscles tightening with every breath like he's trying not to break.

I sink onto my hands and knees in front of him. Grip him at the base. Keep my eyes locked on his as I drag my tongue up the length of him, slow enough to make him curse under his breath, before sealing my mouth around the head and sucking.

His head tips back, eyes closing, a deep groan spilling out of him.

"Mierda, nena... así."*

Then, rougher, "Dios... tu boca es un pecado."†

His compliments go straight to my core. The man has an incredible cock, but better than that, he knows how to use every part of him—hands, mouth, body—like he was born to wring pleasure out of a woman.

But right now, I want to make him lose control.

I hollow my cheeks, take him deeper, stroke him with one hand while my tongue works the underside. His breathing slips into ragged territory. His hands slide into my hair, fingers winding at the base of my skull as his hips pulse up, not forcing, just meeting me. Matching me.

Another minute of this and he'll come. We both know it.

And neither of us wants it to end yet.

He groans down at me. "Ven aquí, Pícarita."‡

A single finger hooks beneath my chin, lifting my face to his. He kisses me, deep and slow this time, tasting himself on my tongue, breathing like he's relearning it.

"I don't want to come down your throat," he murmurs against my mouth. "Not right now, at least."

His hands slide down my hips, under the waistband of my tights, fingers slipping between my legs. The second he feels how wet I am, he lets out a low, satisfied rumble.

---

* "Damn, baby... like that."
† "God... your mouth is a sin."
‡ "Come here, little troublemaker."

"Quiero comerme este coño,"* he says, voice wrecked with intent.

His finger slides inside me. My breath stutters.

"Y luego quiero enterrarme dentro de ti."†

His hands are everywhere, reverent and greedy, as he peels my leggings and panties away, baring me to the cold air and his hungry gaze. I watch his face as he takes me in—dark eyes heavy with heat, tongue darting out to wet his lips. "So fucking beautiful," he murmurs, voice low enough it scrapes across my skin.

He kisses the inside of my knee, teeth scraping, lips dragging heat up the inside of my thigh. When he reaches my hip, he doesn't stop—just keeps moving, mouth teasing a slow, torturous path, never quite where I want him. My hands fist in his hair, but he's in control now. His lips close around my nipple, sucking until I arch, then biting until I gasp.

He smirks against my skin, then trails kisses down, down, over my stomach, my hips, pausing at the mound above my clit. His breath is hot, making me twitch, and then finally—finally—his mouth is on me.

He licks me slow, savoring every moan, every shiver. When he fixes his mouth around my clit, it's not gentle; it's filthy, practiced, like he's staking a claim. "Joder, eres perfecta...";‡ His tongue circles, then flicks, then plunges deep, and my hips jerk up into his mouth.

"Fuck, Alejandro—don't stop," I gasp, my voice raw. I

---

* "I want to eat this pussy,"
† "And then I want to bury myself inside you."
‡ "Damn, you're perfect..."

grab at his hair, but he just growls, hands gripping my thighs, holding me open for him. He works me over, relentless, switching from slow, lazy laps to fast, ruthless flicks that have me teetering on the edge.

He pulls back for just a second, glancing up at me, lips slick, stubbled chin shining. "Mírame, Pícarita."* His voice is dark velvet, all command. "Quiero verte venir."† I force my eyes open, holding his stare, letting him see what he's doing to me.

He grins, then sucks my clit hard, fingers sliding inside me, curling until I break—arching, cursing, clawing at his shoulders as I shatter on his tongue.

"Fuck—Alejandro—don't stop, don't fucking stop—"

He doesn't, not until I'm limp and boneless, my pulse thundering in my ears, breath coming in ragged gasps. I'm ruined, but I want more.

He drags his mouth up my body, slow only because he likes to watch me squirm. I'm shaking, skin fever-hot, barely catching my breath before he's on top of me again—bigger, heavier, hunger in his eyes. His cock is hard and leaking, pressed between us, leaving a hot smear across my stomach as he grabs my wrists, pinning them above my head with one hand.

We both know there is no risk of a pregnancy. Guild initiation requires it. And producing little fuck-trophies is never something I wanted.

He doesn't ask if I want this. He knows the answer. My

---

* "Look at me, you little troublemaker."
† "I want to see you come."

thighs open for him automatically, my hips arching up, desperate.

Alejandro grins, teeth sharp in the low light. "Look at you. Always pretending you're in control." He shifts, lining himself up. "But you want to be ruined, don't you, Saint?"

I bite his shoulder, hard, just to prove I can. "Shut up and fuck me."

He laughs, dark and savage, and pushes inside in one rough thrust that knocks the air out of my lungs. He's thick, stretching me so good it hurts, and for a second I think I might actually fall apart.

He moves hard, relentless, hips slamming into mine, the mattress beneath us rattling with every thrust. He fucks me like he's angry—at me, at himself, at the years lost between us. Every sound he makes is a growl, every word in Spanish, dirty and reverent all at once.

"Así, Pícarita, así—mira cómo me tomas, how you squeeze me—joder, you feel so fucking good—"*

I drag my nails down his back, clawing, daring him to go harder, rougher, to give me everything he's got. He pins my wrists tighter, driving in deeper, making me cry out. It's too much. It's not enough.

"Is this what you wanted?" he rasps, his voice rough with need. "To be fucked like you're nothing but mine?"

I bare my teeth, daring him. "Prove it."

He does. He fucks me through another orgasm, not letting up, not giving me a second to recover. I shatter, legs shaking, gasping his name and curses and nothing at all.

---

* "Like that, little troublemaker, like that... look how you take me... damn, you feel so good."

He barely gives me time to breathe before he's moving again—hands rough as he drags me up, spins me, and pushes between my shoulders until I'm bent over the edge of the mattress, ass in the air. My pulse thunders. I don't ask for mercy. I want none.

"Stay there," he growls, and I do. My hair tangles in his fist as he lines up behind me, and when he drives back inside, I bite my forearm to keep from screaming. He's deeper like this—harder, hips slamming into me, each thrust making my legs quake. The slap of skin, the obscene wet sounds, the dim light of a single bulb in the ceiling. It's all chaos. All heat.

"Play with yourself," he orders, voice low and fraying, Spanish curses threading through every word. "Quiero verte venir otra vez, Pícarita. Hazlo."*

I reach down, fingers working my clit, still so fucking sensitive I almost can't stand it. But I want more. Need more. He yanks my head back, forcing my spine to arch. My eyes roll, every nerve ending burning as he pounds into me, dragging pleasure and pain tight together until I'm begging —swearing, pleading, grinding back to take all of him.

"Fucking—harder, Alejandro—don't you dare stop—"

He slaps my ass, handprint blooming hot across my skin. "Look at you, taking everything, so goddamn greedy—" His words are a growl in my ear as he fucks me deeper, rougher, like he's trying to erase the years and the guilt and every goddamn thing that came between us.

The pressure builds—hot, violent, inescapable. I rub my

---

* "I want to see you come again, little troublemaker. Come for me."

clit harder, moaning his name as I come again, body shaking so hard my arms nearly give out.

He follows with a guttural moan, hips jerking as he empties inside me, hands gripping my hips hard enough to bruise. For a second, neither of us moves. Just gasping, shaking, strung out and ruined.

He finally lets go of my hair, his breath heavy at my back. I straighten, shoving my wild hair out of my face, refusing to look at him. My legs are barely holding me up. My heart's still trying to claw its way out of my chest.

I taste blood on my tongue from biting down too hard and grin. No regret. No apology.

Let the world come for us tomorrow. Tonight, I'm alive. And starving.

Alejandro

Waking up next to Saint always felt good—her hair in my face, her knee in my ribs, that familiar weight pressed up against me. But waking up to the slick heat of her mouth wrapped around my cock? That's fucking paradise.

I open my eyes to the sight of her between my legs, dark hair tangled around her face, eyes locked on mine. Her mouth is heaven—hot, wet, greedy, taking me deep before pulling back slow, tongue tracing the head, teasing every nerve ending raw. My hand fists in the sheets, hips bucking helplessly as she drags her tongue along my shaft, lazy as a cat, like she's got all the time in the world.

"Fuck, Saint—don't stop, you know what that does to me—"

"Good morning." She hums, lips curving into a smirk, and the vibration nearly undoes me. Just when I'm right on the edge, she pulls off, stroking me slow with her hand, watching me fight for control. I growl her name, nearly begging, and she just licks the tip, lazy as hell.

"You like making me suffer, Pícarita?" I rasp, voice half-broken.

She doesn't answer. Just goes back down on me, sucking harder, tongue working the underside, building me up again

—faster this time, like she wants to break me. I'm close, too fucking close, and then she pulls back again, letting my cock slip free with a pop. My body aches for her, balls tight, the ache almost painful now.

"Goddamn it, Saint—" My hands tangle in her hair, trying to guide her, but she just grins, wicked and sure, and ignores me.

"So impatient, Alejandro."

The third time, I'm a mess—sweating, shaking, desperate. She lets me get right to the brink, my cock throbbing against her tongue, and then stops again, mouth trailing down my thigh, watching me squirm. I curse in Spanish, every muscle tight.

"Please, fuck—Saint, please—"

The fourth time, she finally shows mercy, swallowing me down until I hit the back of her throat, moaning as she takes everything I give her. I'm already gasping, barely holding on. "God damn—Saint, just like that, don't stop—please—" I choke out, voice breaking as she sucks harder, her grip bruising my thigh. "God, you're going to kill me—mierda, Saint, I'm—"

I come hard, hips jerking, a raw groan tearing out of me. "Saint—that's it, fuck, that's so good—" My words tumble out half-Spanish, half-begging, lost in the wet heat of her mouth as she drinks it all, slow and deliberate, swallowing like she wants to savor the taste of me.

I collapse back, boneless, chest heaving, a wreck beneath her. There's nothing left in me but gratitude and a low, guttural laugh.

She wipes her mouth with the back of her hand and flashes me that savage grin. I'm ruined, and I fucking love it.

She grabs her clothes off the floor and heads for the door, tossing a look over her shoulder. "Your cock was about to bore a hole in my back, so I thought I'd help you out a little."

I push up on my elbows, managing a half-smirk. "I appreciate your dedication to the cause."

She just snorts and disappears out the door, turning toward the bathroom.

I flop back, scrubbing my hands over my face, still catching my breath. I'm half-tempted to follow her, haul her up onto the sink, and bury my mouth between her legs—but then my phone starts buzzing from somewhere in the tangle of last night's clothes.

I sit up, keeping the sheet over my lap, and dig through my pants until I find it. One glance at the encrypted message, and my stomach sinks.

Fuck. The bounty on Saint hasn't just gone up—it's quadrupled. It was already the highest contract on the books—ten million, dead or alive, collectable by any Guild or free-lancer willing to try. Now? Five hundred million. Enough to make every desperate rat in the underworld start sniffing for blood. No expiration. No mercy.

This changes everything. Makes our next move damn near suicidal.

Before I can even process it, Frank pokes his head in, the mole-man's coke-bottle glasses catching the light. "The car I secured is here. You can blow it up if you need to."

I snort, shaking my head. "Thanks, Frank. Can't make any promises."

He disappears as fast as he came, muttering something about explosives and ramen.

I stare at the phone. Half a billion fucking dollars on Saint's head. Every hour we're aboveground is a risk.

I type out a reply back to my broker. "We need a new plan. Fast."

Vincenzi Tower rises like a glass blade in the heart of downtown Chicago, all steel, mirrored panels, and money. The kind of place that pretends not to notice the blood in its own drains. Saint and I walk in like we belong, eyes up, reading everyone and everything. The security guard at the desk gives us a glance, but nothing more. Another Tuesday.

We stop in front of the polished granite directory and Saint adjusts her backpack straps while we scour the board. There it is, sandwiched between a law firm and an "innovation startup" that's probably just a shell: Morley & Brandt LLP – Certified Public Accountants. Floor 32.

Boring. Perfect.

We weigh our options fast, low-voiced—book it as a walk-in and risk a desk jockey looking us up? Pull the fire alarm and draw every security goon in a ten-block radius? Neither is good, not with this many eyes.

Saint nudges my arm before I can decide. "There," she murmurs. Two janitors and a supervisor, pushing big rolling carts stacked with trash bags and cleaning supplies, vanish through a set of double doors that someone left propped open.

We lock eyes. No words needed. In less than a minute,

we're inside, moving like ghosts—Saint is already digging through a laundry bag for uniforms, and I lift a ring of keys off a too-trusting supervisor. She raises an eyebrow at me, smirking as she pulls her hair into a knot and snaps on a pair of blue gloves.

Within minutes, we're janitors. Disposable, invisible, everywhere and nowhere. I shove a trash cart in front of us for cover, Saint takes the clipboard, and together we move through a side corridor toward the service elevator.

Nobody notices the help.

I scan the key ring—sure enough, one is labeled "32." As we step into the elevator, Saint leans close, voice barely audible: "Let's keep this quiet. In and out."

I hit the button for floor thirty-two. The doors close with a hush, and we start to climb, all the pressure and risk bearing down as we move higher, closer to the wolves.

Floor thirty-two. We slip out of the elevator and hit the rear entrance—one quick turn with the key, but Saint's already picking it, multitool flashing in her hand. No rush. Nothing draws attention like a janitor sprinting. We move slow, emptying a few bins, eyes scanning the maze of nameplates.

Then I see it. "Thank fuck, he's got a private office," I mutter, nodding at a door at the end. Saint's on it, popping the lock faster than I can blink. Inside—dark, blinds drawn, the only light from the city outside.

She's already flipping open the burner Grim gave her, hitting speaker before it rings. Grim picks up on the first buzz—voice all teenage cockiness, no business being this deep in assassin shit.

"We're in the dead guy's office," Saint says. "I need every-thing you can pull, fast."

I'm elbow-deep in the file cabinet, rifling through ghosts. All standard for a dirty accounting firm—aliases, payouts, shell companies, contracts for jobs that never happened. Caleb Thatcher, "The Houseguest." Low-level stuff. Stamped deceased. Nothing new, nothing worth dying over.

Saint's wrangling Grim like always—bossy, sharp, not actually related but they spar like family. He texts her a link, tells her to stick the phone near the computer.

"It's not even on," she gripes.

"So turn it on," Grim fires back, pure attitude.

Saint boots it. Password screen blinks and dies—Grim's already inside. Code flashes, progress bars crawl, windows flicker as he rips the guts out of the drive. Saint leans in, watching. She's not interested in chatter, only what got this guy dead.

Grim's running his mouth. "Jesus, this guy was a nerd. Chewbacca wallpaper, Chewbacca memes—does anyone over thirty even—wait."

He goes silent. Suddenly, a wave of documents opens—fake news headlines, dozens at once, flooding the screen.

Headline: Presidential Candidate Assassinated at World Energy Summit

Sub headline: *Rogue mercenary Saint James assassinated Presidential hopeful at World Energy Summit. After an extensive manhunt, the assassin opened fire on law enforce-ment and was killed. Three officers were injured, no fatalities.*

It hits. Saint goes rigid. Grim is dead quiet. I stare at the screens—her obituary, set to auto-publish.

Saint reads it again, voice flat: "Assassin opened fire on law enforcement and was killed."

Silence, thick as blood.

I clear my throat. "Well, at least they had the decency to make you go out guns blazing. Beats death by food poisoning."

Saint

The voices stop right outside the door. I jab the speaker button, cutting Grim off mid-ramble. Alejandro and I both drop behind the desk, knees bumping as we hit the carpet. The laptop screen is still up—progress bar at one hundred percent. Fucking finally.

I whisper, barely audible, "I'm taking this laptop with me. Make sure no one can trace it."

Grim's answer is quick, cocky. "I got you, S."

I snap the phone shut, kill the laptop, and shove it into my bag. "Let's get the fuck out of here."

When we hear silence outside, I ease the door open a crack, watching for movement. The hallway's empty. I nod at Alejandro, and we slip out, silent, closing the door behind us. I lock it with the multitool—muscle memory by now.

Then the radio static hits. Somewhere close. A voice—male, tense, half a floor away: "Be advised, possible suspect matching description. Female, five-nine, dark skin, big hair. Security sweep in progress. Do not approach—repeat, do not approach alone."

My blood goes cold. I catch Alejandro's eye. We both know who they're talking about.

He mouths, *Dumpster.*

I mouth back, *No. Rear door.*

We have the argument—no words, just a battle of wills and hand signals. He wins, probably because I can't risk us both getting caught, and because I'm pissed but not stupid.

I climb into the dumpster, as quietly as possible. It smells like cleaning chemicals, burnt coffee, and corporate rot. Alejandro yanks a pair of headphones out of his uniform pocket, pops them in, and starts humming off-key like he hasn't got a care in the world. I glare at him. He grins and winks.

He grabs a big wastebasket from under the shredder—full of freshly destroyed paper—and dumps it right on top of me. I shoot him a look that says I will kill you, but he only shrugs and keeps moving.

The guard comes around the corner. I hear the wheels slow, the little squeak as Alejandro stops. The guard's voice is clipped, suspicious. "Hey. You see a woman back here? Five nine, five ten—"

Alejandro pulls out one earbud and gives a blank look. "Lo siento, no hablo nada inglés."*

He rattles off something fast in Spanish like *I just work here*, shrugs, then slides the earbud back in and keeps pushing the cart, whistling something out-of-tune.

The guard mutters, then moves on, shoes squeaking down the hall.

I don't breathe until I hear Alejandro's footsteps again,

---

* "I'm sorry, I don't speak any English."

pushing the cart away from trouble. Goddamn. I'm making him pay for the paper shreds. I'll be picking confetti out of my hair for days.

I'm cramped. Hot. There's paper in my bra. I text Grim while Alejandro wheels us down a side hall.

> SAINT: can you hack the security system of the building we're in?

> GRIM: that question offends me

> SAINT: we need to be invisible

> GRIM: give me 30 seconds

Alejandro pulls the dumpster into a dead corner, out of the line of sight. "Coast is clear." He offers his hand and I glare at him. Not mad just, *really*? He's watched me scale a nine-foot fence with broken ribs. Doesn't matter. He still offers, because sometimes the killer steps back and the gentleman shows up. I take it, just to speed this up.

The flip phone vibrates.

> GRIM: you're a ghost.

Perfect.

I shoulder my bag and nod at Alejandro. "Let's go. We'll take the main elevator—Grim's watching." He nods, falls into step, head down like he's just another night shift nobody.

As we walk, he glances over. "How'd you end up with the Grim Reaper on speed dial, anyway?"

I just smirk, firing back the line he gave me yesterday: "You have your contacts. I have mine."

I punch the elevator button. It dings open, empty, and we step inside. I hit the lobby and as the doors close, I exhale.

Two floors down, three business suits step in—one yammering about stocks, another texting, the third pretending to ignore us. The next stop, two delivery women wedge themselves in looking at Alejandro first, then me. Red insulated bag clutched in hand, cheap perfume, the scent of burritos overlaying the day's sweat. Alejandro and I exchange a look—neither of us like where this is headed.

Floor nineteen the mother fucking doors open again. And we all stare. Seconds pass and it's not until the doors start to slide shut that anyone moves. Everyone gives way for a goddamn clown to join us. Full makeup, rainbow wig, shoes that squeak like an old mattress, and a bunch of balloons. He grins at us all, then stares ahead, blank-faced. The doors slide shut, trapping us with our own personal horror show.

Two floors go by. No one breathes. I can't take it anymore. I sigh, long and heavy. "Oh, for Christ's sake. Let's get this over with."

I snap out and kick the ever loving shit out of the nearest delivery lady right in the back. She goes flying into the panel, elbow mashing the emergency stop. Elevator jerks to a halt and all hell breaks loose.

One delivery girl is down, but her friend lunges—spring-loaded blade popping from her sleeve. I catch her wrist, snap the bone, and she screams. I rip the knife from her hand and drive it into her windpipe—twice, fast, no hesitation. Like two bites from a snake and she drops.

But there's no time to savor it. I fling the knife across the box, and it buries itself in a businessman's hand—gun and all—pinning it to the elevator wall. He squeezes off a round that barely misses Alejandro's head. It blows out the corner light, glass raining down.

Alejandro moves like he was born for this. He yanks the blade free and, without pause, stabs it straight into the top of the guy's skull. The man drops, eyes wide, blood painting the wall.

He's barely clear before the clown barrels into him—the painted-on smile is no longer happy. It's all rage and desperation crammed into five square feet. Alejandro takes the hit, back slamming into metal, but buries elbows in the clown's back until the guy stumbles. Then he drives a boot into the clown's nose, snapping his head back, making him stumble into the opposite wall.

The second businessman, greed in his eyes, tries to take out the clown for the bounty—brass knuckles flashing. The clown ducks, and the man's fist shatters against the wall with a sick crunch.

I've got the first delivery woman—she's recovered, wild-eyed, blood on her teeth. She leaps off her dead partner's back, using the wall for height, but I duck and let her fly over me. She crashes, rolls. I catch her by the neck, drag her down, and break it with a grunt.

A gun comes up—the third businessman, finger trembling on the trigger and aimed at my chest. I grab his wrist, twist, and slam him into the wall. My hand closes over his and I make him fire until the clip's empty—holes in the paneled ceiling, nowhere that matters. He's shaking. I smash his nose with the butt, then bring it down on his temple. He slumps. I grab his chin, shove the barrel into his eye, and push. I hear the squish of his brain around the gun's barrel as much as I feel it. He convulses once, then goes slack jawed. One remaining eye rolling back.

Alejandro's still at it with the clown—blows flying, both bleeding. Alejandro takes two to the ribs, then grabs the clown's head and drives his face into his knee, hard enough I hear teeth shatter. He grabs the clown's balloons, wraps the strings tight around his neck, and starts choking him out.

I straighten my back, hands on my hips, breathing hard and take in the final show.

"You just going to watch?" he grunts, not looking at me.

"Pretty much," I say, letting him finish his work.

The clown goes limp, slides to the floor like a sack of rotten potatoes. Alejandro waits a beat, then lets him fall.

"Maldito gilipollas,"* he mutters before spitting on the clown's crooked wig. He starts shoving bodies out of the way, working his jaw.

"Looking for some souvenir teeth?" I pant, leaning against the bloody panel as my phone vibrates in my back pocket. Miraculously not shattered. "They don't make 'em like they used to," I mutter, eyeing the carnage as I flip the screen. Grim, of course.

> GRIM: Maybe find a new elevator.

I huff a laugh, stuffing the phone away. "We need to find a new ride down."

Alejandro, ever the opportunist, snags the gun the first

---

* "You fucking idot,"

businessman dropped and tucks it behind his belt. Then he stretches up—tall bastard—and pops a ceiling tile, exposing the guts of the elevator shaft. Cool air, a ladder, and freedom.

He leaps, grabs hold, and hauls himself out with barely a strain. He turns and leans down, hand extended.

I sling my backpack over my shoulders and step up, not even eyeing his grip, just taking it.

"Oh, now you have no fuss to make when I offer my assistance?"

We lock wrists and he pulls me up with barely a grunt, muscle flexing. In an instant I'm beside him, peering into the black maw above.

"You know," I pause for dramatic effect. "You talk with the confidence of a much taller man," I say, fighting the smirk.

He gives me a look like I've lost it. "Are you fucking kidding me?" He stands up to full height, arms out. "I'm six-six. You want a measuring tape, baby? I'll let you measure something else while you're at it. See how small I am."

I roll my eyes and head for the ladder bolted into the wall. He follows, grumbling under his breath about "short people slander." I climb, hands sure, blood still drying on my knuckles. Below, he pauses just long enough to draw the gun, aims, and fires a single round into the elevator cable. The cable snaps, shrieking, and the box full of corpses plummets into darkness with a grinding roar.

"Overkill, much?" I say, still climbing.

"Cleanup," he calls back.

At the next floor, I wedge my multitool into the crack between the elevator doors. It takes some force, but the lock gives and they open just enough. He gets his fingers in and pries them wide. "Could a short man do that?"

"Mm, probably." My nonchalance is killing him.

We slip into a deserted hallway, cool tile underfoot, fluorescent lights humming.

I hit the button for another elevator, just two battered assassins waiting politely for the next ride.

"Hey." I nudge his shoulder. "Think we'll get a mime next?"

He snorts, wiping a bloody knuckle on his jeans. "Fuck you, Saint."

Alejandro

I slam my door so hard the window rattles. She does the same—always has to match me, beat for fucking beat. My hands are still shaking. Adrenaline's jacked too high, won't drain. Too many bodies, too much blood, too fucking soon after the last fight. We can't even make it to noon without someone in a mask trying to carve us open.

I shove the gearshift, throw my arm over her headrest, and reverse hard enough the tires scream. Don't care who hears it. Let the whole city know we're pissed.

Saint's not saying a word, just breathing heavy, eyes wild. Her hair's stuck to her cheek—someone else's blood in the strands. I barely check the street before I cut left; an oncoming car honks, skids, nearly clips the bumper. I don't even blink.

She finally cracks, voice edged and sharp: "Next time, don't bother missing. Could use more fucking obstacles."

It gets under my skin—everything does right now. The fucking clown. The idiots who thought they had a chance. The fact that it doesn't matter what we burn, what we hide, who we kill—they always find us. Rage doesn't bleed off; it just boils, looking for something to break.

My knuckles ache from clenching the wheel. I can smell her—sex, sweat, adrenaline, a hint of copper that shouldn't turn me on but does. She glances at my mouth. My dick's already half hard and all I want is to pin her down until neither of us is thinking about the last hour.

She looks at me like she'd let me. Maybe wants it as much as I do. I almost miss the turn.

Fuck.

"How were we found so fast?" The question is an itch I can't scratch, another wound that won't heal.

She doesn't even look at me. "Don't ask me. I'm new to this exile shit... you're the veteran."

She'll never let it fucking drop. I grit my teeth. "I told you—I was framed. Just like you. Unless the Washington Post started hiring psychics and sent one to the future to catch you gutting that politician two days from now."

She fires back instantly, "Like you've been honest." She tries to make it sound bored, but she wants it to land like a blade.

"And you have?" I snap. "Why does the Grim Reaper jump when you say? You whisper and the little asshole comes running."

Her jaw tightens. "I don't owe you a fucking thing. Not to a coward who walks away and disappears for two years like a scared dog."

That's the one that cracks something in me. Not the accusation. The *tone.* Like she's daring me to do something about it.

That's when I whip the wheel, hard enough the tires scream.

I cut a savage U-turn, car sliding, bumper nearly catching the curb. Another horn, another missed collision I almost wished happened. I've not had enough spilled blood today.

I whip the car down an alley, slam it into reverse, and pin it until we nearly hit the back wall. The car jerks. Her seatbelt snatches her hard. Her hands go to the dash, and then she shoots me a look that could curdle paint.

"That little stunt supposed to scare me or just make your dick feel bigger?"

Her mouth always gets her in trouble. "I'm fucking tired of hearing you."

I unbuckle, the click of the belt lost in the sound of her doing the same. She's climbing into my lap the second the metal's free, hands in my hair, mouth crashing into mine. It's not a kiss, it's a collision. All tongue and teeth, her nails raking my jaw, her hips grinding down on me like she wants to ride me through the goddamn seat.

I bite her lip until she hisses, and she just bites back. I grab her ass, hard enough to leave a mark. Her breath is hot against my ear.

"Fucking brat," I growl, squeezing harder.

She just laughs, low and cruel. "Like you're going to fucking do something about it."

She's all over me before I can even think, mouth on mine, biting, sucking, her hands in my hair and yanking like she wants to rip something out. I meet her, kiss for kiss, teeth clashing, tongues fighting for dominance. Every sound is a dare. I can feel the sweat on her skin, the scent of her mixed with leather and blood. I want to mark her. I want to leave something she'll still feel tomorrow.

My hand slides under her shirt, under her bra—she gasps when my fingers find her nipple, rolling it, pinching just enough to make her jolt. She moans, grinding harder against my cock, her whole body vibrating with need.

"Harder," she demands, voice raw.

I pinch and tug, pulling her head back with my other hand, mouth closing on her neck, sucking until I feel her pulse jump under my tongue. She grinds down, rocking against me with a little noise that goes straight to my dick.

"Yeah, I know how you fucking like it," I growl, grinding up to meet her, hips moving rough and insistent.

"You pretend you want control," I say, squeezing her breast until she hisses, "but I know what you want, Saint."

She glares at me, eyes flashing. "You don't know anything about me anymore."

Before I can answer, she kisses me again, bruising and desperate, riding me like she's chasing a high she refuses to ask for. She's soaking me through her pants, rubbing harder and harder.

"You haven't changed," I mutter against her mouth, voice breaking from want. "You want to be fucked the same way you want everything else. Hard. Fast. You want to win, even when you're losing."

She digs her nails into my shoulder, scraping across the bullet wound from yesterday, and I grunt, pain and pleasure tangled. "But don't act like I don't know you. You're only lying to yourself. You want to fight, and you want to fuck, so let's do it."

I pinch her nipple again, vicious, and she cries out—half pain, half pleasure—her hips stuttering against mine. Her nails rake me again, and our pace goes wild, grinding against each other until she's trembling.

"Come on, Saint. I know you're close. You always are

after a fight. Fucking admit it—this is what you want. You want me to ruin you, right here in this fucking alley, where anyone could see. Take it. Come for me, right now."

She whimpers, legs shaking, breath ragged. I press harder, rolling her nipple and grinding up until she finally breaks—body locked, eyes rolling back as she comes, soaking me through both our clothes.

I let her ride it out, then shove her back with one hand, breath still ragged. "Get in the back seat."

She's gone, scrambling over the console, already tugging at her pants. I pull off her boots. Watch her working her pants down those long legs. I grab the ankles and pull them off the rest of the way and toss them into the passenger seat, voice low and sharp:

"Put your feet up on the seats, Saint."

She does, nothing left on her but a shirt, panties, and socks. She's panting, thighs shining. The wet patch on her panties nearly makes me lose it.

"Fucking soaked," I mutter, unbuckling my belt.

I twist around in the front seat, can't take my eyes off her —shirt riding up, panties clinging to everything, legs spread across the cracked leather. She's breathless, flushed, wild. Looking like something I want to own.

"Pull your panties to the side," I order, voice guttural.

She doesn't hesitate. Hooks a finger in the damp fabric and drags it aside, exposing her cunt—glistening, lips swollen from grinding on me, begging for more. I lick my lips, grip my cock through my jeans just to keep from losing it.

"Let me see you," I rasp. "Wider."

She opens her legs further, feet still on the headrests. I

can see everything—the way she's still trembling, the slick on her thighs, the way her pussy clenches at nothing.

"Touch your clit, Saint. Nice and slow."

She obeys, fingers finding her clit and circling, hips twitching as she lets out a moan. I watch, mesmerized. My hand drops, unzips, takes out my cock—already leaking. I stroke myself, slow and rough, eyes never leaving her.

"Yeah, that's it," I breathe. "Look at me while you do it."

Her gaze meets mine, pupils blown. She's biting her lip, fighting a moan, dragging her fingers over her clit just the way she likes it. Her hips lift off the seat, greedy for it.

"Open wider," I snap. "I want to see you throb when you come."

She groans, fingers moving faster, and my hand matches her pace. The car smells like sex and sweat and her.

"Fucking perfect," I tell her, voice a low growl. "Show me how filthy you are. I want you coming on your own fingers before I touch you."

She gasps, legs shaking, her body all tension and hunger, wet and exposed for me and no one else.

"Now, Saint. Come for me again. Let me fucking watch you." She's so fucking close. I know it.

She spasms, hips bucking, fingers slick and glistening, her pussy pulsing and desperate. I squeeze my cock, biting back a curse as I watch her orgasm.

She slumps back, panting, hips twitching every time she circles her clit, trying to drag herself down from that edge. I shove open the driver's door, zipper already down, cock hanging heavy, thick with need. I want her taste in my mouth, want to ruin her completely.

"Don't stop yet, Pícarita."

The door slams behind me. I'm at the back door in a heartbeat, reaching in, grabbing her ankle and dragging her to me. My dick jumps just seeing her—wet and pink, a clear drip of slick running down her slit. I groan, low and rough, because that's mine.

"Let me taste," I growl—not a request. I grip her thighs and yank her closer, bury my face between her legs. My tongue slides up her cunt, licking up that drip, moaning into her because fuck, she tastes like everything I want and nothing I deserve. "Now turn around."

I climb in after her, shut the door, stroking my cock—so fucking hard it hurts—watching her get on her knees, hands on the door, looking over her shoulder at me, ass pushed out, ready.

"Look at you," I sneer, stroking myself. "So desperate for it you'd let me fuck you in a filthy alley, like the cock-hungry little slut you are."

I palm her cheeks, kissing one, then the other before I peel her panties down and get a view of her gorgeous pussy. 'Beautiful." I say, tilting my head and watching her.

She arches her back more, spreading for me. She wants this as much as I do.

"You just going to look all day or fuck me?"

She's drunk on sex and thirsty for more.

"Don't worry baby, you know what I'm going to give you."

I don't make her wait. I can't. I line myself up, stroke the head of my cock up and down her slit, spreading her wetness, dragging it over her clit just to hear her whine, just to make her want it that much more. Then I push in, one long, brutal stroke, bottoming out, my hand tight on her shoulder, dragging her back onto me.

Fucking heaven.

Her pussy grips me, pulsing in waves that drag another broken groan out of my chest. I grab her hips, driving her back onto me with each thrust—hard, relentless, everything inside me focused on the next slick, brutal slide.

The car rocks. The glass fogs. Her ass slaps against my hips, every smack echoing in the tight space. I catch her hair, fingers tangling in her curls, dragging her head back so she can't miss the way I watch her come apart. She claws at the seat, breathless and wild, her moans growing louder—too loud.

I spot a cop car across the street. The bastard makes a U-turn, coasting past the mouth of the alley, slowing. Creeping past and I can't tell if he's scouting us out or not. Saint sees him too.

But I don't fucking care. I'm not stopping. Not for him, not for anyone.

"Let him try," I growl, dragging her hair back until she's arching, still taking every inch. "He comes over here and I'll put a bullet in his head while my cock stays buried in you, baby."

She laughs, breathless and raw, her hand working between her thighs. I tell her to rub her clit—watch her obey, fingers fast and needy. Her cunt tightens. My hips stutter. The sound she makes is enough to finish me off.

"That's it, Saint."

We come together, hard enough I see stars, her body clenching around me as I empty inside her, my jaw clenched so tight it aches. "So fucking good."

I don't move. I rub my hands along her back, kneading her hips, riding out the last aftershocks until my cock stops pulsing. Only then do I lean in, press two quick, hungry kisses to her spine. "Fuck, Saint."

I pull out, slow, watching as my cock slides free—soaked. No shame in it. She sits up and turns to me as I grab the half-used roll of paper towels from the back, tear off a wad, and slide my hand between her legs. The touch is gentler now. She shivers, but meets my eyes with a smirk that promises I'm not done with her, not by a long shot.

"Well, that was cathartic," I say, cleaning us up with clinical efficiency.

She snorts. "You may not be good for much, but you can fuck."

I let my other hand wander down the curve of her ass, squeezing, my nose brushing hers. "Are you flirting with me, Saint James?" I catch her mouth in a soft, claiming kiss before she can answer.

When I pull away, I murmur, "Because I'll happily fuck you again if you've not had enough."

She slides her panties on—deliberately slow, letting me watch. "I doubt you'd be able to get it up again," she says coolly, but her eyes flick down. She knows exactly how long I can go.

Her pants come next. "Besides, I want to get back to Dr. Creepy's and see what's on that laptop."

I finish wiping off, toss the used paper towels behind me, and watch her lace up her boots. We climb out, the cold air biting at our skin.

I tuck my cock back into my pants as she rounds the SUV, her eyes on me the whole time.

"But I'm driving this time."

24

Saint

Alejandro bangs on Doctor Disgusting's door for five minutes, fist aching by the time the locks start rattling. Inside, he's probably tripping over his own filth. He finally gets it open—twelve different bolts sliding, scraping, protesting. The place doesn't smell any better than usual. If anything, it's worse. There's a tang that sticks to your teeth, like copper left out in the rain. Once you know he eats people, you can't smell anything else.

I'd rather take my chances outside. Let the world's assassins try their luck. At least then I know what I'm up against.

Alejandro pushes inside, eyes scanning the room, always on edge. "Boot up the laptop. I'm getting lunch."

I'm not going to argue it. I'm fucking starving. I rummage under the counter, surprised when I actually find a bottle of cleaner—miracle. I give the table a scrub and wash my hands. There's no point dying of infection before someone manages to shoot me.

I power up the laptop and text Grim. *I'll need you—soon.* He answers before I even put the phone down. Typical. Always waiting for the next mess I'm about to drag him into.

For a second, I glance over my shoulder—like Alejandro's going to be standing there, demanding to know why I trust Grim. He can't know. No one can. That's not a risk I'll ever take.

I'm dying for something to drink so I pull the fridge door open and instantly regret it. It's like Jeffrey Dahmer got a membership at Sam's Club.

Naturally there would be a severed fucking head sitting on a dinner plate. Yellowed skin, milky eyes rolled up, mouth slightly sagging. My mouth curves down in a frown.

There's a jar of fingers floating in brine—like the world's worst pickles—next to a half-gallon of OJ and a takeout box slick with oil. The "beef medallions" on the bottom shelf don't look like anything that ever mooed.

I slam the fridge shut before I puke. I don't even like meat. Definitely not pickled fingers or an ear sandwich-bagged like leftovers. My skin crawls and a shiver grabs hold of my spine.

The lock clicks again, and Alejandro returns, arms full—two white paper bags bulging with containers, another stuffed with water bottles. Thank fuck. I'm dry as dust.

He sets the bags on the table. "I wouldn't go looking for food here if I were you," he warns, a beat too late.

I ignore him, tearing into the bags. He's gone out of his way—not a scrap of meat in sight. Not even for him. I catch his eye, chopsticks pausing over a piece of tofu dripping in chili oil. He acts like it's nothing, but I see him watching me scan the spread—crispy tofu, lo mien, spring rolls, vegan kimbap, a pile of bean sprouts and mushrooms. All of it safe.

He shrugs, nonchalant. "Figured you wouldn't be able to stomach much here."

I grin, mouth already full. "The pickled fingers were looking tempting, but this is better."

He just smirks and digs in, and for the first time since we got away, the air between us isn't poison.

We're sitting so close our thighs touch, laptop balanced between us, the table still smelling faintly of bleach and whatever the hell Dr. Disgusting was chopping up earlier. I steer with one hand—opening folders, swiping through files —while Alejandro eats beside me, always half-watching the door. Grim's on speaker, his voice low and precise, the hum of his servers in the background.

"You're safe," Grim says, matter-of-fact. "The laptop's cold. No signal, no ping. They'd need God himself to trace you now."

"Comforting," I mutter, not entirely convinced.

Alejandro pops a spring roll in his mouth, nodding at the screen. "Find anything that explains why the Guild swarmed in five minutes flat?"

I flick open another folder—bank statements, fake invoices, pages of numbers coded in a way only an accountant or a criminal could love. "Looks like he did the books for Vincenzi Consulting."

Alejandro arches a brow. "That's not consulting. That's an Italian mob family. Well—makes sense why the place was crawling with the Guild so fast."

"Everyone's got their hands dirty," I say, clicking deeper, scrolling past wire transfers that jump from New York to Tokyo to Switzerland and back. "Mob bosses, Guilds, state contracts. Gold bars disguised as fertilizer shipments. Enough to build a RICO case against half the planet."

Alejandro leans in, voice low. "The accountant—he was more than just a numbers guy."

"Yeah," I say. "He was collecting. Stockpiling evidence, blackmail, leverage—every dirty secret he could get his hands on. He covered his ass six ways from Sunday and he was a hell of a lot better with a computer than his job demanded."

Grim whistles over the line. "I'm impressed. This is insurance of the nuclear variety."

I click faster, nerves humming. "Anything in here could've been what got him killed. We need to find the thread he pulled—what made him panic, reach out to El Fantasma, and end up hot dog meat."

Alejandro grabs another container, leaning in closer, his knee pressed to mine. "It's got to be something? He was sitting on this for years—why the hell blow his cover now?"

"Grim, take over," I say, pushing the laptop closer to the mic. "Pull up those articles—the ones set to drop in two days. The ones where I apparently murder a politician."

He's silent for a second. Then windows flicker across the screen, popping open and snapping shut so fast I can barely keep up. The mouse moves on its own—Grim's in control now, hands flying somewhere in a windowless room full of cold monitors and empty coffee cups.

Code runs. Folders scroll. Lines of text blur by. Then— headlines, in rapid succession, stacking up like a bad hand of cards:

ASSASSIN SAINT JAMES STRIKES AGAIN— SENATOR CHARLES HARTLEY DEAD IN CHICAGO SHOOTING

NOTORIOUS KILLER SAINT JAMES BEHIND POLITICAL ASSASSINATION, SAYS FBI SOURCE

SHOCKING: FRONT-RUNNER HARTLEY MURDERED DAYS BEFORE ELECTION—IS ANYONE SAFE?

Every article has a different spin, but the narrative is locked. I'm the villain. The evidence is airtight, the details grotesquely specific—time, place, my face pulled from a thousand surveillance feeds, all of it orchestrated to make sure the world knows Saint James is public enemy number one.

Grim's voice is flat in my ear. "They want you burned before you ever get close."

He opens a new window. More headlines, this time focused on the target: Senator Charles Hartley. The perfect American politician—sharp suit, white smile, born for the debate stage. He's the top candidate for president, projected to sweep the election. Voting starts in two months, and every news feed has him shaking hands, kissing babies, standing in front of flags.

Hartley's campaign is all blue-sky, middle-America dreams: lower taxes for working families, real education reform, increased teacher pay, free community college. He's promised affordable healthcare—no "Medicare for All" fairytale, just lower premiums, and drug costs. He talks about criminal justice reform, actually puts numbers behind it. No war drums, no talk of enemies—he's selling peace for the first time in a generation, and the country's eating it up.

Alejandro leans closer, reading over my shoulder. "They're making you the next Lee Harvey Oswald."

"Yeah," I say, throat dry. "Except this time, the body's still breathing."

I stare at my own name, bolded in black and red. The

trap's set. They're not just coming for me—they're coming for anyone who stands in the way.

Grim's voice is cold now. "You're not just getting framed, Saint. They want a public execution. By the time those stories go live, it won't matter what you did or didn't do."

More articles flicker across the screen. Grim's voice is steady, clinical, like he's dissecting my obituary.

"Global manhunt," he mutters. "Every outlet's got a version. Saint James killed in a high-speed chase through the Loop. Saint James gunned down by police in a South Side shootout. Saint James found dead in a tunnel pile-up. Take your pick."

I watch my own deaths play out in pixels, each one messier than the last. None of them real—yet. But all of them plausible enough to pass for truth with a body to pin them on.

Alejandro leans back, arms crossed, jaw tight. "Whoever staged this knows you won't go down easy. That's why they set you up. Make it look like you broke Guild law, paint you as a traitor—give themselves a reason to put every hitter on your trail, make you desperate, keep you moving."

Make it look like you broke Guild law.

I don't let anything show. There are rules and there are lines you don't cross—lines that, once crossed, put you in the ground. I keep my expression carved from stone, eyes on the screen, mouth set. Let them think I'm unfazed.

If anyone ever figures out what I've actually done, it won't just be my blood on the line.

Grim's voice cuts in. "Doesn't matter who kills you now.

They just need a body. That's why they sent the whole world—figure someone will get lucky."

I give a thin smile, cold. "That, and they know it'd take all of them to actually kill me."

Alejandro nods, gaze never leaving mine. "If you're supposed to be dead, that means someone else is going to take out Senator Hartley."

I tap the desk, thinking fast. "We need to know why he's the target. What's to gain with his death?"

The answer's staring us in the face. Hartley's selling peace, and there's too much money in war. Every file the accountant collected—every shell company, every bribe and contract, every nation buying blood and calling it law. Wars are for sale. So are presidents.

"Someone wants to be the one pulling the strings. Someone wants the money to keep flowing."

Alejandro and I lock eyes. The answer's too obvious now, almost cliché if it weren't so fucking deadly.

At the same time, we both speak:

"El Fantasma," I say.

"The Guildmaster," Alejandro echoes.

25

Saint

"El Fantasma," I say.

Alejandro scoffs. "No. The Guildmaster."

I flick a crumb off the keyboard, jaw set. "They could be the same person, you know. No one's ever seen either of them. For all we know, the Guildmaster is just El Fantasma in a different suit."

He shakes his head, dismissive. "That's fantasy, Saint. The Guildmaster runs an empire. El Fantasma's a story you tell when you can't find the real problem. You're chasing shadows."

"Funny for you to say, Sombra*." I narrow my eyes using his old name. He narrows his back, both of us knowing that name is dead. "Shadows get people killed. Every piece of shit that's ever come after me in the last two years has dropped Fantasma's name. You think that's an accident?"

"Yeah, I do." His voice is flat. "It's a smokescreen. Guildmaster's the power. The rest is noise. You keep looking for ghosts, you'll miss the shot right in front of you."

---

* Shadow

I snap the laptop shut just to break the rhythm of his smug certainty. "You really believe that? You think all these threads—contracts, hits, the money, the politics—they're all run by some middle manager behind a desk, while the world whispers about a ghost for fun?"

He matches my glare, knuckles white on the table. "You want there to be a ghost," he says, voice tight. "Because then it's not your precious Guild turning on you. It's just some phantom out to get us all."

"That's rich, coming from you." I shoot back, unable to keep the edge from my voice. "How many jobs have you run for them? How many times has your info come from nowhere, like someone's feeding you the answers?"

He bristles, jaw ticking. "I get my intel from the same places you do. The difference is, I know which leads are worth chasing."

"Do you?" I lean in. "Or is it just easier not to ask who signs the contracts? Not to think about what happens when the Guild's done with you?"

He's in my space now, leaning forward until there's nothing between us but heat and old scars. "You really want to go there? The only people who survive this job are the ones who understand they're disposable. The Guild would burn every one of us if it came down to it—and you know it."

I flinch, just barely, because he's not wrong. But he's not right either. "Don't mistake cynicism for insight, Alejandro. You act like I'm naïve, like I don't know what this life is. But you're just pissed because they exiled you. Maybe the Guild betrayed you, but that doesn't make every answer a conspiracy."

He laughs—cold, bitter. "You still want to believe in something, Saint. Even if it's just a myth. That's your problem."

"And yours is that you want to believe in nothing. That's how you end up a ghost yourself."

For a second, I want to hit him. Or drag him onto the table and let all this violence bleed out the other way.

I take a breath, force my voice steady. "There's always something in the shadows. And sooner or later, we're going to find out who's really pulling the strings."

"Yeah." He doesn't blink. "Just make sure you don't get yourself killed chasing ghosts first."

The tension's a live wire, stretched to snapping—until Grim's voice crackles through the speaker. "Hate to break up your little lovers' quarrel, but I think I can solve this one for you."

I roll my eyes. "Enlighten us, Grim."

"Found something. A file buried so deep it may as well be in hell."

He move the mouse and shows us. It's called "El Fantasma". I shake my head seeing the words. Not understanding how Alejandro can really keep preaching the ghost is not real.

Grim keeps going. "There's a voice file—five days old. It's just labeled Phone call 174 but it's the only one in here."

"Play it," I say, voice flat.

A burst of static. Then two voices—both run through heavy distortion, genderless, originless, every syllable blurred by tech. Impossible to pin which one is which. They speak in measured, professional tones—every word cold, calculated.

The room stills. Alejandro and I both lean in, all that argument collapsing into a single, focused silence.

Grim presses play.

Two voices, both warped by distortion—neither is identifiable, but both are calm, deliberate. The first speaks, a hint of command beneath the tech filter.

"...Everything's in place. We proceed as discussed."

A pause, then the second voice. "Where do we meet, once it's done?"

A cold beat, then: "Kurohana Palace. Main garden entrance. Neutral territory—no weapons. You'll get your confirmation."

The file ends. Just like that, the temperature in the room drops.

Alejandro stares at the screen, stone-faced. I keep my breathing steady, but my mind is spinning.

The Kurohana Palace—a garden, a casino, a fortress for the syndicates and Guilds. It's neutral ground in name only; the kind of place where no one dares bleed unless they're ready to spark a war. Whoever picked it knew exactly what they were doing.

I piece it together in my head, cold and methodical. The accountant found the plot—maybe even before it was set in motion. He knew where they were meeting, and when. He was desperate to reach El Fantasma. It was practically screaming from his files, the panic, the urgency, the last-ditch messages to every burner account he could find.

And now he's dead and I'm framed for it. But it doesn't end there. I'm not just collateral—they're setting me up as the trigger for the next kill. I'm supposed to take the blame for assassinating the golden boy senator. They aren't building an alibi—they're constructing an entire narrative, brick by bloody brick. The kind that will outlast my corpse.

The accountant had a file on the ghost—just like everyone else. Only this one was buried deeper, harder to crack. Paranoia or survival instinct, hard to say.

One of those voices has to be El Fantasma. I just don't know which.

Grim's voice cuts through my thoughts, harried now. "Gotta go—Mamá's screaming at me. I'll keep digging, text if I find anything." In the background, a woman's voice rattles off a list of sins and groceries, rapid-fire Spanish. Grim curses, then disconnects. The cursor goes still.

The laptop's mine again. I click around, restless, half hoping for some magic bullet. There's a folder—*Pictures*. I open it.

Nothing. Black and white images, out of focus, as if the camera was shaking or the photographer was moving fast, too fast. One is blurry, like whoever took it had to duck away.

Based on the count in the corner of the folder there are forty six pictures like that, all the same. Fragments. Ghosts of a bigger picture, and nobody has all the pieces.

It's almost funny. This is what the world's deadliest men look like up close—blurs, shadows, a single foot on a helicopter rail. No faces. No names. Only proof that someone was close enough to take the shot, but never close enough to see the whole thing.

That's the point, isn't it? None of us ever see the whole thing. Not until it's too late.

I shut the laptop, turn to Alejandro. "We need to get to

Dubai. Kurohana Palace. Scope out the senator. Watch for whoever's sent to take the shot."

He nods, eyes narrowed. "And if we can't stop it?"

"We kill the assassin ourselves. Take the body, take the story, take the last move away from the ghosts who think they can script every ending."

He cocks his head, studying me. "You sure you're up for this?"

I meet his gaze, unflinching. "What other choice do we have?"

He grins, sharp and mean. "None at all."

That's settled. The plan is ugly, but it's ours.

And it's the only way to burn down a lie this big.

I need air. Real air—not the iron-thick stench of rot and bleach that passes for oxygen in this flesh-eating basement. I shove the laptop away and mutter to Alejandro, "Bathroom." He doesn't argue, just gives me that unreadable look as I slip out.

Inside, I close the door and lean hard against it. I turn the tap, splash cool water over my face, letting it drip down my neck. The mirror is cracked at the corner, but I can still see my own eyes—tired, wired, too alive. I study the reflection, searching for cracks.

Where does Alejandro fit in all this? What's his angle, really? He says he came back because the bounty on my head was too high to ignore, but I know him. There's always more than one reason. Always another layer. He's in deeper than he admits, and I'm going to make him tell me what the hell he's after.

I towel my face dry, steady my breath, and step back into the main room.

He's gone.

Alejandro—gone. Just vanished, no sound, no shadow on the wall. The absence slams into me harder than it should. Instead, Dr. Doom is hunched at the stove, flicking a kettle on, lost in his own world with headphones jammed deep.

I scan the space, heart racing. My eyes dart to the table. The laptop.

Relief cools me down when it's there. Right where I left it. Still closed.

I force myself not to run, not to look like prey. "Frank," I call, but he doesn't even flinch, too lost in whatever carnage he's brewing. "Do you know where Alejandro—"

The kettle hisses. Dr. Doom shuffles away, deeper into his lair. I don't follow. There's no fucking way I'm walking back there to end up stuffed into a barrel of acid or something.

Instead, I grab the laptop and retreat down the hall to my room, shutting the door with a snap.

Sitting on the bed, I flip the laptop open. The screen wakes up in the same folder—pictures, blurred, black and white. My gaze drifts to the corner. My chest goes tight.

There were forty-six files when I left.

Now—there are only forty-four.

Alejandro is gone. And so are two pictures.

Alejandro

Saint's in the bathroom when Frank scurries in—eyes wide, coke-bottle glasses magnifying the panic. He looks like a rodent who just saw the trap shut on his tail.

"Guildmembers sniffing around up top," Frank whispers, voice shaky. "Two blocks north. They know she's around here somewhere."

I nod, already moving. There's no time for questions. I slide open the closet by the door and pull out my long-range rifle case. Frank hovers behind me, twitchy as hell. "I'll take care of it."

He nods and unlocks the million latches on the basement door, his fingers a blur. The locks clack and rattle like bones. He glances over his shoulder, but I'm already moving.

My eyes land on the laptop—the lifeline holding our next move together. "Close that for me, amigo."

Frank nods, headphones slipping back over his ears as he sinks into the static of a hundred radio frequencies, whispers, and whatever the hell else keeps him anchored to this hole.

Talking to his back, I say, "Tell Saint I went out to find a nest."

She'll know what that means.

I close the door behind me, and before I've taken two

steps I hear the bolts sliding home, chains drawn tight. Frank's paranoia is the only thing keeping this place from getting raided twice a day. And why it's one of the few places safe enough to bring Saint.

I sling the rifle case across my chest, hands in my pockets. Not rushing. Just another predator on the street, following the scent of trouble.

I head two blocks south—not north, they'd be expecting a fight if I came looking for them so directly. I find a fire escape, climb high, cross a roof slick with old rain and pigeon shit. The city's open below me, loud and oblivious. This is the part I like best—height, distance, the illusion of safety.

I set the rifle down, lock the bipod, stretch out on the tar paper, and let my heartbeat settle. The metal's cold, the city's loud, but through the scope, everything gets quiet. Every detail sharpens. This is where patience matters—where the first shadow is never the right one, and the real threats are the ones who know how not to look like threats at all.

I pan the crowd slowly, scanning for tells. Guildmembers are predators in plainclothes—always a little too relaxed or a little too tense. The eyes don't linger; they sweep. Hands never stray far from pockets or bags. They never cluster unless they're about to move. They don't check their phones—they check reflections. Not the sort of people who get lost in a city—they're the ones who come here to hunt.

I spot a man standing in the shade of a closed bodega, not smoking, not really waiting. He's not watching the street—he's watching for what crosses it. Another perched at a bus stop, reading a newspaper nobody reads anymore, shoes too nice for the neighborhood. One more, pretending to argue with someone over Bluetooth, but the conversation is dead air, all for show. His eyes are always on the reflections, never on the street.

It takes a certain paranoia to spot them—exile sharpens it, turns it into instinct. Anyone could cash in an open contract on an exile. Anywhere but neutral ground, like the Kurohana Palace. In two days, Saint and I will be there, where the only law is the one that keeps bodies off the floor. Until then, it's just open season.

I breathe steady, finger loose beside the trigger, letting my pulse sync with the city's. I watch. I wait. That's how you stay alive: see everything, move only when it matters, and never blink first.

I don't stop at street level. Any fool can watch a sidewalk. Guildmembers love the high ground—snipers especially. You can't survive exile without learning to think above the city. I scan the rooftops, the windows, every line of sight I'd choose myself.

Most snipers want open lines, clear sight, nothing in the way. Me? I like the places nobody else would bother with— the ones that look impossible, the ones that would ruin an average man's shot. That's why no one ever finds me. While the rest take predictable perches, I settle where no one thinks to look. I've always been good at making the impossible shot.

I scan the city from my blind, eyes tracking rooftops, windows, fire escapes—anywhere a hunter would nest. If there's another rifle out here, I'll find it.

I search the upper stories with my own eyes first—never give your position away with a glint of glass. The first rooftop I check is clean, empty HVAC units and gull droppings. The next—just a sun-bleached lawn chair, nobody home.

The third place, though—a set of office windows in a half-abandoned brick building across the avenue. Fourth floor, corner suite. Shades drawn, except one, left just high enough for a barrel.

Colt Harrington. The Texan. Looks like he crawled out of the mess Saint dropped on him at the hot dog factory— barely a scratch.

He's set up in the corner, profile taut, back pressed against the frame so nothing of him shows but the barest sliver of shoulder and cheek. Rifle braced, scope to his eye, everything about him coiled and efficient. No wasted move- ment. The hat's pulled low, not for style but to cut reflec- tion, his mouth set in a thin, humorless line.

He sweeps the street with slow, methodical passes, pausing just long enough on each potential mark. Even from here, I can see the calculation—every twitch, every shift. He's not sightseeing. He's hunting. Tracking the same suspects I am, maybe waiting for Saint to show, definitely holding a grudge.

Colt Harrington: every inch the pro. Swagger buried under discipline, but make no mistake—it's still there, simmering. Just waiting for a reason to show itself.

Let's see if we can tone that down a little.

I settle the scope on him for a beat, smirk curling at my mouth. I could put one through his left eye, watch him slouch right out of that chair. But I can't kill him yet. Not until it matters.

Instead, I make a tiny adjustment—slide the crosshairs down to the street, dialing in for wind, timing, and distance.

Colt won't see me, but he'll know someone's close. Sometimes you have to remind a rival you're still in the game.

I wait, patient as stone. When the perfect moment comes, I'll take the shot. Not to kill—just to say hello. Let the rats know there's a bigger snake in the grass tonight.

I watch the street. Three men who'd be predators on any other day, any other block. This afternoon, under my eye, they're just meat waiting for gravity.

The sun is starting to slip behind the buildings, shadows stretching out long and merciful. That's good. It'll help. I wait, patient, tracking their lazy circles. Two start moving, trying hard to look natural and failing—sweat in their posture, nerves in their step. The third sits, just as I predicted, the perfect mark. The other two adjust without meaning to, drawn into the geometry only a sniper sees.

I adjust my aim, let my breath slow. Wait... and wait... wait a little more... The city hushes for a beat.

Then—with one squeeze a single bullet punches through all three skulls—clean, sharp, blood misting the summer air—and slams into the red brick behind them. It's art. Art that I don't bother to admire it.

Already, my rifle swings up, sight snapping back to Colt. He's frozen, just for a second, caught as his mind catches up with what just happened.

I steady, inhale, fire.

Second shot, clean as a promise—right through Tex's beloved Stetson. The hat flips twice, carried by the shockwave, landing on the far side of his perch. A warning.

I'm moving before the first scream slices the street. Rifle half broken down, kit tight against my chest. I don't run. There's no need. By the time anyone realizes what's happened, I'm gone—already a ghost, already halfway back to Frank's, the only echo my kill shot and Colt's ego bleeding out on the fourth floor perch.

Frank's locking everything down, chains rattling, grumbling about under appreciation. Saint leans against the wall, arms crossed, legs bare beneath a dress that begs for trouble—hits just above the knee, bright against all this gray. It's begging for tequila and to be spun across a dance floor.

"You have a date tonight, Pícarita?" I ask, voice low.

She cuts me a look. "I could ask you the same thing."

I glance at Frank, fire off in Spanish, "You didn't tell her I left?"

Frank spits and sputters, "Didn't hear any damn message —got the Guild up top, can't listen to everything." He lurches back to his hole, still muttering.

I set my rifle case in the cabinet, lock it up. "Sorry mi amigo didn't tell you. Had to deal with some uninvited guests—fast."

Saint eases, just a fraction. "See anything good with that today?"

I grin, grabbing a bottle of water, draining half before I answer. She's watching. I notice her watching and she knows it. She rolls her eyes and looks away with a huff.

"Gave our regards to the Texan."

That gets her attention. "Kill him?"

I shake my head, savoring the tease. "Just said hello."

"Well, that's unfortunate." She uncrosses her arms and

puts her hands on her hips. "Well, I'm not eating another crumb of food from this cesspool, so..." She lets the sentence hang. I get it. She wants out as badly as I do.

Saint James in a dress is a sight I could savor without complaint. Not here, not in this hole, but outside under real lights, music in the air, my arm around her waist where everyone can see. She deserves more than rot and shadow.

"Care for any company?" I step in close, voice dropping, finger tracing the dip of her top where it threatens to slip toward her breast. My head lowers, drawn in, almost brushing her mouth with mine. I want her out there—dancing, smiling, lit up by more than bare bulbs and bad memories. Even if it's just for a few hours.

She turns away, and I pull back, swallowing the sting. "We're not a good idea," she says. "We had an itch. We scratched it. We can't let it happen again."

An itch.

I nod, hiding what I feel. "As you wish, Pícarita. But I must ask... Are you ever going to trust me, Saint?"

She holds my gaze, unblinking. "Not sure if that's possible."

I force a shrug, glance around, act like it doesn't stab. "Well, can you at least tolerate me for a meal? I know a place we can go."

She crosses her arms again, chin high. "Do they serve anything other than noodles or pickled fingers?"

I let a real laugh slip through. "Much better. You'll see."

She nods. That's as close as I'll get to yes. "Okay then. Give me ten minutes." I disappear into the bathroom, the rush of the shower drowning out whatever else she might say.

27

Saint

W e wade through a sea of bodies, pressed tight by the crush of the covered market. Everything smells like cumin, roasted meat, sweat, and perfume—no inch of air unclaimed. Alejandro leads, moving with the kind of confidence only someone raised on chaos can pull off. He turns sideways, slipping between two women arguing over oranges, then glances back at me with a smirk, a wink. He holds his hand out.

I take it. His palm is warm—steady. I catch the sharp bite of his cologne, some expensive blend undercut with sweat and gun oil, all tangled up in the heat of his skin. He pulls me through the crowd with practiced ease, never hesitating, never letting go.

The market is a maze, but he navigates like he was born in it, weaving us through stalls and tight alleys until we duck through a plain metal door. On the other side, the world shifts: we cut through a kitchen, the staff hardly looking up. One guy on the grill gives Alejandro a nod, grease-slicked spatula tapping the counter. Alejandro returns it with the ghost of a smile.

A second door swings open and we're somewhere else entirely. Overhead, strings of yellow lights web the air, casting everything in a forgiving glow. Music thumps, layered with laughter and the rise and fall of voices. Bodies press and twist on a makeshift dance floor in the center; a bar glows at the far corner, crowded with regulars and newcomers alike. Tables dot the shadows, high and low, everyone draped in the easy pleasure of a night unburdened by consequence.

Alejandro leans in, voice pitched low for my ears only. "We'll be safe here. Try to enjoy yourself tonight."

I arch a brow. "I've got a knife strapped to my thigh."

His smile is all sin, white teeth and promise. The devil himself would fall to his knees right there.

He leads me to the bar, orders two shots of tequila, sliding one toward me. "To not being dead yet."

I raise one eyebrow, glass to my lips. "Yet."

We eat. We talk. We drink. The table fills with little plates —gambas al ajillo, pulpo a la gallega, crispy patacones on the side. The best paella de mariscos I've ever had in my life. Alejandro orders everything in rapid Spanish, laughing with the bartender. I stick to seafood and vegetables; no land meat, but I'm not above devouring half the shrimp on the table. He keeps the plates coming and refills my glass whenever it's empty.

"How do you know this place is Guild-free?" I ask, spearing a grilled octopus tentacle, pretending it's not the best thing I've tasted in months.

He grins. "My cousin's back in the kitchen. There are little pockets everywhere the Guild doesn't know exist. This —" He gestures at the strung lights, the crowd, the music—

"this little piece of paradise, hidden behind three buildings, is one of them."

I blink. "Didn't realize you had family."

He laughs, soft and dangerous. "What, you think I was born one day from a sniper's scope? Just—" He makes a gun with his fingers, "—appeared, fully grown, ready to piss off the world?"

I shrug, taking another bite, then chase it with cold beer. "Just figured you were an orphan. Like me."

He goes still, smile fading a notch. "I didn't know that."

I wave him off. "Don't sweat it. Kenji's the only other person who does."

He turns thoughtful. "Your old teacher—Kenji Takahashi, right? Never had the fortune to meet the man."

A smile tugs at my mouth. "Kenji was...relentless. Hard. Never gave up on me, not once. First person who ever came into my life and stayed there."

We let the conversation drift, both of us eating slower, talking around old wounds. The music swells, the crowd shifts, and for a moment the world is just the two of us at a battered wooden table, sharing plates and memories.

I break the spell. "Guess as close as we were, we didn't really know anything about each other."

He looks at me then—really looks. His eyes darken, slow and intent. He reaches over, callused thumb brushing my cheek, palm warm. "I suppose we didn't."

The silence hums, loaded with everything we've never said. He holds it a second longer, then breaks away, rising with a sudden breath. "We're dancing."

He drains his beer, nods to the bartender for two more, then pulls my chair back, hand outstretched.

"No, we're not," I protest, but the words are hollow. There's no bite to it. He knows it.

"We are. There's no way we're leaving before I see that dress move around the dance floor, mi Picarita."

I sigh, making a show of irritation, but I take his hand all the same. He pulls me up, spins me straight into the current of dancers, and suddenly, I'm not thinking about knives or death or anything but the music and the heat of his hand in mine.

Alejandro dances like he fucks—precise, confident, hands in exactly the right place at exactly the right time. The way he moves makes it easy to let go, to let him lead, and that's exactly why he's dangerous. I should be thinking about Guild contracts, assassins, escape routes. But he's like gravity, and I'm all iron filings.

The music swells and the lights blur, and it's just us in the center, pressed close, heat rolling off him in waves. His eyes never leave mine, not for a second. He steps in, slow and deliberate, so close our faces almost touch.

"Have you seen anyone...since me?" he asks, voice pitched for me alone. There's something almost desperate in the way he says it, like he needs the answer to be what he hopes.

I could lie. It'd be easy, would save us both from where this is going. But I don't. "No," I say, honest as sin. It makes the air go thick, charged.

His arms slide all the way around my waist, pulling me flush against him. I loop my arms over his shoulders, feeling the tension wind tighter. His mouth hovers over mine—so close I can feel the heat, the promise, but he doesn't touch.

"Why?" he breathes, voice rough.

There's that look again. He's waiting for a truth that will either cut him or set him on fire. I don't look away. "I didn't want anyone else." The words are barely there, but he hears them.

He doesn't wait another second. He closes the distance, taking my mouth in a kiss that's slow and deep, one hand sliding down to grip the back of my thigh, pulling me hard against the evidence of just how much he wants me.

I'm breathless when I break the kiss, our bodies still swaying, tangled in the beat. "We said we weren't itching any more scratches."

A tray of tequila sweeps past. I grab a shot, tilting my head as Alejandro's tongue traces the column of my throat, tasting sweat and salt and promise.

"You said that. Not me." His mouth works up my neck and I tip back, half the tequila burning its way down.

I offer him the rest, holding the glass up. "Want some?"

He nods, mouth brushing mine, tongue sweeping into my mouth as he tastes the tequila straight from my lips. "Delicious," he murmurs, breath ghosting across my skin.

I push him back with a wicked grin, finish the shot, never breaking eye contact. I step away, slow—one step, then another. "I need the little girls' room."

I walk toward the stairs, his eyes tracking every move and I glance back just as I reach the top. There's a clear moment when he makes a decision, throwing back a shot of his own as I disappear through the bathroom door, heart thundering, already knowing he's coming after me.

The bathroom is empty, the hum of the dance floor muffled by the thick door. I slip off my panties and tuck them behind my back, settling against the sink. The anticipation crackles—every second is a dare.

Alejandro enters a moment later, eyes locked on mine, and shuts the door with a decisive *click*. His gaze drops, taking me in and the way I'm waiting for him, hands hidden.

He closes the distance, grabbing my jaw and kissing me hard—hungry, devouring, his tongue staking its claim. His hand drops to my thigh, fingers skimming up to my holster. He slides my knife free, and drags the flat of the blade along the curve of my hip, barely touching.

"Looking for these?" I murmur, and flash him my panties—taunting, challenging.

He growls, dark and low, and drives the knife into the metal stall wall beside us. The handle vibrates. "You're a dirty girl, Saint James."

He kisses me again, rougher, and grabs my hips, spinning me so my back's pressed to the stall. "Hold on," he commands.

I barely have time to reach up, grabbing the knife's handle overhead, when he drops to his knees. He lifts my dress, spreads me open, and drags his tongue over me, slow and deliberate.

He hooks my leg over his shoulder, angle perfect for him to feast. The first stroke of his tongue has me gasping, hips stuttering, my hand gripping his hair as I tip my head back, mouth open for the sounds I don't care who hears.

He pulls back just enough to speak, breath hot on my skin. "Tell me how good I make you feel."

He wants praise—needs it, craves it—and I'm happy to give. "So fucking good, Alejandro. You know exactly how to ruin me—don't stop," I release a sigh, "just like that."

He hums, tongue working deeper, lapping, sucking, his hands holding me steady when my legs threaten to give out. My hips roll, chasing every pulse of pleasure, every flicker of his tongue. I shudder, thighs trembling as the orgasm hits—sharp, consuming, white-hot.

I cry out, body arching against him, and he rides it out, mouth relentless until I have to push him away, spent and shaking.

He stands, face slick, eyes bright with triumph and hunger. He wipes his mouth with the back of his hand, leans in close, mouth grazing my ear.

"Now," he whispers, voice rough, "ask me, Saint."

He kisses me as his fingers fumble with his belt—one arm around my waist. I hear the rasp of the zipper, the heavy drag of denim.

"Ask what?" I manage, voice thick.

His mouth barely leaves mine as he frees his cock, pressing in close, like he's starving for me. "Ask me who I've been with."

I meet his eyes, lips brushing. "Who?"

He hooks my leg over his arm, balances me on one foot —my grip tight on the sink, the other on his shoulder. He holds my gaze, voice guttural: "No one." The word cracks like a whip as he drives into me with one hard, deep stroke. He doesn't give me a second to breathe, to answer, to do anything but gasp as he starts to fuck me like he's got some-thing to prove.

He's pounding into me, hard enough my teeth rattle, sweat running down both our bodies.

I dig my nails into his back, locked onto his wild eyes.

"You could fuck half of Chicago and still come crawling back for my dick."

"You wish." I bite out before I take his mouth in a claiming kiss.

He grins, savage. "You're a fucking liar—listen to you, soaking wet, dripping down my cock. That's for me, Saint. Always has been."

He picks me up, barely breaking rhythm, slamming me back against the stall, fucking me deeper. "Don't pretend you haven't thought about me these two years. I know you have. Every goddamn night."

I try to sneer, defiant. "Don't flatter yourself."

He sets me on the sink, opens me wide, starts driving in harder—ruthless, demanding. "Admit it. You touch yourself thinking about me. Every fucking time. Say it."

His hand finds my throat, squeezes just enough to make the world spin. His voice is a growl in my ear. "I think about you every time I make myself come, Saint. Every fucking time."

"Oh my God." I groan out, head falling back as my orgasm tightens.

"Admit it baby while you come on my fat cock."

I fall apart around him, hips slamming up to meet every brutal thrust. "Yes—fuck—yes, I do. Harder, Alejandro— fuck me harder—"

The last few pulses rip through me, and that's when the sink gives, snapping off the wall. Water explodes everywhere. He shifts quickly, holding my weight. His hand on the mirror to steady himself for the last few thrusts, making sure I finish coming. That his dick pulses one last time deep inside me.

He slides out, steadying me back on my feet and grabbing paper towels. Fisting his cock and wiping himself clean, we both look around the demolished bathroom and burst out laughing.

He tosses the used towels and kisses me, still rough, still hungry, before finally letting me go to zip himself up.

I pick my ruined panties out of a puddle. "You think the restaurant's gonna know we've been fucking when we walk out of the bathroom dripping wet?"

He snatches the panties from my hand and tosses them in the trash. "I don't fucking care. You won't need these, Picarita."

He swipes two fingers through the mess between my thighs, gathering cum and slick, then sucks them clean, eyes locked on mine.

"Because I'm nowhere near done with this pussy tonight."

28

Alejandro

I come awake in a full-body jolt, convinced I'm about to die.

Like, actual death. Heart-explodes, soul-leaves-my-body, obituary-mentions-Irony death.

Because I open my eyes and Frank's face is two inches from mine.

I used to think "scared to death" was dramatic. Turns out it's a very reasonable medical condition when a cannibal hovers over you at dawn breathing like a haunted moose.

He jerks back. "You're gonna miss your flight."

"Yeah? And you almost made sure I never take another one." I bark at him in an angry whisper. My pulse is doing cardio on its own. "You ever wake someone up like a normal human, or is jump-scaring people your spiritual calling?"

Frank squints. "Your dick is out."

I sigh. "That kind of thing happens when you give someone a heart attack, Frank."

Beside me, Saint shifts, her thigh brushing mine under the sheets. Last night flickers across my mind, and my mouth betrays me with a tiny, smug curve. God, she's trouble.

Frank, because he has zero sense of privacy, lifts a plastic bag. "Your broker delivered the IDs and tickets."

Then he pulls out something worse. A wig.

A long, braided wig.

"Also sent this."

I stare at it.

Oh, she is going to hate that.

Gloriously, violently hate it.

Saint opens one eye, sees the braids, and lets out a noise that is ninety percent disbelief and ten percent plotting-a-murder.

"Don't," I warn her, already amused. "You know you have to wear it."

"I would rather tell Tex he's better than me."

"He may still be around if you'd like me to find him," I smirk.

She glares. I grin even more. Everything feels normal for half a breath.

Frank backs toward the door like he's escaping a bomb about to detonate. "Get dressed. You need to leave in ten."

Frank drives the kind of van people warn children about. Classic white. A dent the size of God's fist in the sliding door. Random patches where the paint has given up on life. If vans had rap sheets, this one would be on parole.

The interior is no better. Takeout containers, water bottles, and what might be a petrified french fry skid back and forth every time Frank takes a turn. There aren't even real seats in the back, just a turned-over milk crate that creaks with my every shift. My ass stopped having blood flow three blocks ago.

He pulls up to Departures and brakes like he's docking a submarine. He stops at the very beginning of the curb, the place normal people avoid because it pisses off airport security. Naturally, Frank is obtuse and incredibly paranoid.

Glancing around, his beady eyes blinking fast behind his ultra-thick glasses.

"You first," he says to Saint.

She meets my eyes. The braids transform her. She looks... average. Normal. Like any other traveler with a carry-on, a flight to catch, and absolutely no plans to commit felonies before lunch. It's disorienting.

And, yeah. I hate it.

She hoists her bag, says nothing, and steps out.

The van door slams behind her, cutting the sound of rolling luggage and airport chatter into a neat, muffled clip.

I shift forward, climbing to the passenger seat, gun case on the floor between us. Frank rolls down his window and coasts toward the far end of the terminal.

When he finally stops, he turns to me. No speeches. No macho farewell.

Frank just nods like he's sending me into mild inconvenience instead of potential death.

I take his hand, grip firm. "Thanks," I tell him. "For everything."

He nods again, eyes steady, then pulls away. That's about as much sentiment as you'll get from Frank. I watch him drive away only a second, wondering what he does with that van. But knowing his diet, it's best not to give these things too much thought.

I sling the gun case at my side and set off toward the sliding doors, merging into the current of unapologetically stressed-out travelers.

Up next: security.

My personal favorite place to test how much anxiety a human body can hold before spontaneous combustion.

Saint is about fifteen people ahead of me in the security line, already chewing one piece of pink gum and unwrapping a second.

Great.

Fantastic.

Phenomenal.

She only double-gums when she expects a fight.

Saint has this sixth sense, like an internal barometer that measures incoming chaos. And the gum? It's her meditation bead. Her rosary. The thing that centers her right before she unleashes absolute devastation with nothing more than a pocketknife and spite.

The line moves at a decent clip for airport security, but not fast enough to keep my skin from crawling. I know how to blend in. I've spent the last two years of exile doing exactly that, becoming wallpaper everywhere I go. But this is different.

Because it's not just me on this mission.

And blending in becomes a goddamn performance when your brain won't stop calculating every threat she might walk into.

I force myself into the mindset of a normal traveler. Irritated. Sleep-deprived. Mildly homicidal toward airline baggage fees.

Not someone scanning for a Guild of assassins crouched behind a stranger's carry-on.

Saint reaches the front. Her fake ID scans clean. She breezes through like she hasn't murdered a few hundred people.

She moves to the conveyor belts, dropping items into the bins with bored efficiency.

I peel off to a different guard several booths down, then a different scanner entirely.

I'm not worried about the carry-ons. Our tech's good enough that the scanners see whatever we want them to see. Cute little TSA-compliant silhouettes. Probably socks and a travel-sized shampoo bottle in Saint's backpack. Nothing fun.

Same goes for the body scanners. Every operative has a chip that keeps the machines blissfully ignorant. The scanner won't notice the gun tucked against my spine or the two knives Saint keeps in her ankle sheaths like jewelry.

Shoes off. Belt off. Gun case in a tray.

I step through, arms lifted.

The scanner clears me without a hiccup.

Now the case.

Always the case.

There's always some risk—a rogue guard doing their job too enthusiastically, a random inspection I can't talk my way out of. Even with the illusion tech disguising the contents, the case still needs to pass human hands.

Right now, the monitor sees a violin. The tech in the case will make sure the scanner gives it a green light. Not sent away for a random inspection.

The case rolls toward me.

I slip into my shoes, shove loose items back into my pockets, and reach for the handle—

A TSA agent steps into my personal space like he's leading national security.

"Excuse me, sir," he says. "I'll need to open the case."

My stomach drops into my ass.

And that wiggle of gum-chewing intuition Saint had?

Yeah.

I think it's about to pay out.

The TSA agent gestures at the case like he's asking permission to touch a newborn.

I press the release latch.

Not the real one—the secondary button that triggers the holograph.

I crack it, looking inside to make sure the perfect 3D illusion is cast: black velvet lining, a delicate violin nestled in its curves, an ornate bow beside it. It even reflects the overhead lights on the sheen of the wood.

The agent whistles. "Beautiful piece."

Then he reaches.

I snap my hand out. "Ah ah. Please don't touch."

I widen my eyes just enough to look like a panicked musician, not a man hiding the kind of weapon that dissolves governments.

"The wood is very delicate," I explain. "Oils from fingers, temperature shifts... it's temperamental."

I start closing the case, slow and reverent. "You understand."

The agent backs off immediately, hands raised. "I do. I played for ten years."

Of course he did.

We make the kind of small talk that edges right up against my gag reflex—what brand he used, how he misses it, how airport hours ruined practice time—but it smooths the moment. Staying calm and avoiding becoming memorable.

After a glance at my watch, he gets the point. And with the case strap over my shoulder, the weight settled between my shoulder blades, I walk away without being shot or detained.

A win.

I spot Saint in the tunnel that leads to the high-speed terminal shuttles. She's propped against the wall like she owns the corridor, arms crossed, wig still on, her jaw working a giant pink bubble like she's trying to intimidate it into submission.

She looks like a stranger.

A pissed-off, wig-wearing stranger with bubblegum confidence.

"Took you long enough," she says.

I shake my head, brushing past her. She pushes off the wall and falls into step beside me.

"You look good in the wig," I tell her. "You should keep it."

Her bubble pops in a violent snap.

"Fuck you."

Saint

We ride the escalator down toward the plane train like we belong here.

No scanning. No tension in our shoulders. No tells.

We stand side by side, bored travelers waiting for metal doors to slide open, eyes forward, minds empty. That's the trick. Looking is what gets you noticed.

The doors open.

One herd spills out, dragging roller bags and screaming children. Another herd funnels in. Alejandro and I move with them, swallowed by bodies and noise.

His back is to the platform. Mine isn't.

And that's when I see him.

Silas Crow.

If death had a frequent flyer account, Silas would be platinum status. Tall, lean, expensive jacket. Calm eyes that don't miss a thing. He's not rushing. He's hunting.

He scans the faces inside the car, slow and methodical, like he knows a contract is near.

The train doors are still open and his gaze is about to drift over us when I move.

I grab Alejandro by the front of his jacket and pull him down into a kiss.

It lands perfectly. Familiar. Convincing.

His hand comes to my hip without hesitation, like muscle memory never forgot me. Like his body knows mine better than his own. The contact is grounding and dangerous all at once.

But the kiss is actually serving another purpose. Holding hands or a peck on the cheek is no big deal but most people get uncomfortable seeing a couple kiss so intimately. They avoid looking too deeply. Not wanting to be a creep or a subconscious thing–maybe a little of both.

The doors slide shut and I pull away, glancing over Alejandro's shoulder and finding Silas still on the platform. Hands on his hips, still hunting the fresh wave of travelers off the escalator.

The train lurches forward and launches into speed, smooth and violent. Alejandro grabs a hanging strap to steady us.

"What was that for?"

The cabin is stuffy, recycled air thick with too many bodies and cheap cologne. The lights strobe past the windows, turning everyone into fragments. I rise onto my toes, mouth brushing his ear like I'm about to tell him I love him.

"We have company."

He doesn't tense. Doesn't swear. He just exhales.

And then he almost looks disappointed.

Like the kiss was supposed to mean something else.

That's the problem. Falling into him like this is dangerous. I know it. I've always known it. I told myself it had to stop, told myself last night was just muscle memory and bad judgment and proximity. One more fuck won't hurt, I said. The bathroom would be the end of it.

Then Frank's place happened. Hours of it. Like we'd never learned how to stop.

Now the train sways, and the movement pushes us together again. My shoulder presses into his chest. His hand is still at my hip, steadying me like it belongs there. The stupid wig itches under the cap, hot and wrong and not mine, and the urge to rip it off nearly makes me feral.

This time it actually has to end.

Because this doesn't end with tears or regret. It ends with a body bag. Caring is how you die in this line of work. Caring is the split second of hesitation before the blade goes in your ribs. Caring is trusting the wrong mouth, the wrong bed, the wrong promise. I've seen lovers turn on each other over contracts, over money, over survival.

Trust is a luxury. We don't get luxuries.

The train slows. Terminal F flashes overhead.

My pulse spikes anyway.

The doors open, and travelers pour out like nothing is wrong with the world. Like no one just scoped us on a platform. Alejandro looks down at me before we move.

"The plan stays the same."

I snort under my breath and step forward. Yeah right. He just jinxed us. The universe heard that and immediately started sharpening knives.

We move with the crowd, but my awareness sharpens, edges clicking into place. I scan reflections in glass. Watch hands. Count exits. If Silas Crow was here, others could be too. Chicago would be the place to catch me. Airport. Transit choke points. High density. Easy disappearances.

But only if they knew I was still here.

I burned my sigil two days ago. The second we reached Frank's, I was off the map. I could've left the city an hour later. Taken a train west. Gone underground. There was no tether left for them to follow.

And yet Silas Crow was on that platform, scanning faces like he wasn't guessing. Like he knew his mark hadn't gone far.

My bounty's open. Bigger than it's ever been.

That kind of money doesn't sit blind.

The realization slips in cold and unwelcome.

They didn't track me.

They were told.

I glance at Alejandro, his profile calm, unreadable. His broker handled the IDs. The tickets. The timing. All of it clean. Professional. Too clean.

If I misread him... if I misread who he trusted...

Then this isn't magic or luck or coincidence.

I adjust the strap of my bag and keep walking, jaw tight, gum popping once, sharp. We're off the train now, swallowed by the terminal.

Plan stays the same.

Sure.

For about thirty more seconds.

The escalator lifts us into the terminal, and the first thing waiting at the top is the flight board. Big. Bright. Impossible to ignore. I let my gaze hit it like I'm just another irritated traveler checking a delay.

Our flight isn't even boarding yet.

Twenty minutes.

That's a fucking problem.

Twenty minutes means standing around. Sitting at a gate. Being predictable. It means letting the Guild's patience outlast mine, and patience is their specialty. Airports are perfect for it. Bottlenecks. Crowds. Too many places to hide a blade and call it an accident.

I don't intend to die next to a charging station.

My eyes keep moving, sliding down the board with purpose now. If I'm still being hunted, then waiting is the worst possible plan. I need to be moving. Ahead of them. Somewhere they aren't expecting me to be yet.

Dubai is the destination either way. That part doesn't change.

Another Emirates flight catches my eye. Same city. Different timing. As I focus on it, the board updates.

Now boarding.

There it is.

That flight will be gone sooner. Doors closing. Pushback, then taxi. I could be airborne before anyone realizes they're searching the wrong gate. If I can get on it, I buy myself hours. Time to think. Time to figure out how they still know where I am. Time to work out who's feeding my location to the Guild and why my bounty just got juicier instead of going quiet.

Time to end this before someone gets lucky.

The catch is Alejandro.

Our gate is in the opposite direction. I can't peel off without him noticing. And if someone close to him is compromised, or if I read him wrong entirely—then keeping him with me is a liability I can't afford.

This plan doesn't include him.

I glance at him once, memorizing the angle of his jaw, the easy way he owns space like nothing could touch him. Then I turn back to the board, already mapping paths, crowd density, where I can lose him without raising alarms.

If I can slip away cleanly, I get ahead of this.

And if I don't?

Then I stand still for twenty minutes and wait for death to walk up behind me with a boarding pass.

Hard no.

"Our gates this way." Alejandro slides his hands into his pockets and turns to the right.

I keep my tone light, bored, normal. "Okay, I need to hit the bathroom," I say. "I'll meet you at the gate."

He nods looking across the sea of faces, already assuming I'll fall back in beside him in a minute like a well-behaved travel companion instead of a walking murder liability.

Perfect.

I slip into the women's bathroom and pray for a second exit on the opposite side. Something that will dump me out somewhere away from Alejandro.

But airport bathrooms hate escape routes apparently. It's all wide walkways, lines of mirror and sinks. On the other side is a valley with toilet stalls on each side.

No exit.

I stop in front of a mirror and wash my hands. The wig itches and I hope I get the chance to break someone's neck with it before this is all over with. I need to blend in. I need to look like someone about to complain about airport prices and still buy the water anyway.

Decision made.

I shrug out of my leather jacket, roll it tight, and shove it into my backpack before settling the straps back onto my shoulders. The weight is familiar. Reassuring. Hopefully Alejandro won't remember what color shirt I was wearing.

Heading back to the wide tunnel that will spit me back out in the crowded terminal, I spot a mom wrestling with a very squirmy toddler who is resisting the changing table mounted to the wall. The diaper bag hanging on the handle is not a thought in her mind right now. Neither is the ball cap shoved in it.

I lift the hat off the top without hesitation. Quick. Clean. I flip it on backward to add a little something more to my refreshed disguise.

I hover just inside the entrance, half-hidden by the bend in the wall, pretending to check my phone while I watch the concourse. I need to make sure Alejandro went to the gate before I make my move.

And because my brain hates peace, it pulls on the loose thread.

The laptop yesterday.

The two files missing from the Guildmaster x El Fantasma folder.

I slide Grim's flip phone out of my pocket and type fast.

> SAINT: Can you check the accountant's laptop. See if any files were deleted yesterday.

I hit send and the sound of Alejandro's deep voice hits

me. Not because he's speaking at regular volume. Because he's not. He's trying to be quiet.

I hit send, and the sound of Alejandro's voice reaches me.

Not because he's loud.

Because he's doing the opposite.

He's just on the other side of the bathroom entrance. I can picture him without seeing him. Back turned to me. One shoulder angled toward the wall like it might absorb secrets. Phone pressed to his ear. One finger plugging the other so he can hear better over the terminal noise.

Careful.

And he's speaking Spanish.

"Todo depende del momento oportuno."

"Everything hinges on the right timing."

My stomach tightens.

My brain scrambles for benign explanations because that's what brains do when the alternative gets you killed. Maybe he's talking to his broker. Maybe he's updating logistics. The summit. The timing. Maybe I'm paranoid.

But paranoia doesn't usually feel this specific.

The dread settles anyway, heavy and unwelcome, sinking into my chest like it knows the layout. I don't move. I don't breathe any louder. I don't let my reflection change.

Because this isn't about catching him in a lie.

It's about the possibility that I didn't read Alejandro wrong by accident.

It's about the possibility that I trusted the wrong person on purpose.

I slide the phone into my back pocket and let my shoulders relax like I'm done with it, like nothing just shifted under my feet.

I'm still in the bathroom tunnel, half-shadowed by tile and bad lighting, when I spot a killer across the concourse.

He's moving. Walking with purpose. Eyes scanning faces instead of stores. Another hunter that knows prey is near.

Then he sees Alejandro.

The reaction is tiny. A flinch that never quite becomes one. A split-second sharpening, like a blade catching light. He pivots smoothly, drifting toward a charging counter, posture melting into casual as a phone appears in his hand. Pretending to email.

He glances up again and confirms it. That I'm not paranoid. He's id'ed Alejandro and when his eyes flick sideways, he gives a sharp and deliberate nod.

It's not big. It's not dramatic. But it says everything anyway. Like he's telling someone:

It's him.

Alejandro has an open contract. Exile special. The kind the Guild leaves dangling because someone will always want the credit. But this isn't about collecting on him. Not really.

If they know he's here, in Chicago, then they know I'm close. Someone could've seen us leave that office building together. Someone could've spotted us last night at the restaurant.

If they're watching him, they're waiting for me.

I pull my phone back out and step forward, pretending I'm mid-text, turning as I go so Alejandro is behind me now. Out of sight. Out of reach.

I couldn't go back for him even if I wanted to. Even if I weren't already planning my exit. The second I move toward him, everything detonates. Too many civilians. Too many cameras. Too many people who didn't wake up today planning to bleed out next to a Pretzelmaker.

Alejandro can handle himself.

These people can't.

And if he gets tied up in a fight, eyes on him instead of me, that actually helps. Buys me time. Buys me space. Lets me slip toward the gate while he's still scanning the crowd for where I went.

I'm practically doing everyone a favor.

I keep my pace even, heart steady, and slide the phone back into my pocket just as someone walking the opposite direction clips my shoulder.

Not hard. Just enough.

"Excuse me," they say automatically.

I turn with the reflex, matching her movement for half a step, and I know her instantly.

Rook. Broker-turned-assassin. Made the jump three years ago and did well enough that people stopped asking why.

At first, her expression is automatic. Polite. Blank. A stranger who clipped another stranger in a crowded terminal and is apologizing.

Then it changes.

Not all at once. Just a flicker. Her eyes narrow a fraction and never leave mine. I can see the thought forming behind her stare as recognition tries to line itself up with memory.

Wait... could that be—

I don't give it oxygen.

I press my lips into a thin line and nod like I'm just another traveler who's never wrapped piano wire around anyone's throat and keep walking. My pace stays even. My posture loose. Nothing about me says *running*.

I make it a few feet. Enough to almost believe I slipped past her clean.

Then her voice cuts through the terminal noise, warm with familiarity and edged with certainty.

"That you, Saint?"

Alejandro

I hear her name before I register the voice that says it.

"Saint James?"

My head snaps left, eyes cutting through the terminal with practiced speed, cataloging movement instead of faces. Crowds blur together until one figure sharpens into focus—a woman in a backward baseball cap, plain black tank, the exact height and build my body recognizes before my brain does.

That's what Saint was wearing under her jacket.

It has to be her.

Two yards behind her, another woman moves with the same urgency, not chasing, not lagging, just close enough to matter. From the corner of my vision, a man near a charging station straightens a fraction too quickly, posture shifting from casual to ready in a way civilians never manage.

The pattern locks into place.

I don't pause to analyze it. I don't hesitate. My hand is already sliding back toward the gun holstered behind me, the motion small and controlled, invisible to anyone who doesn't know what violence looks like before it happens. I catch the charging-station guy's eye and know instantly that he's lethal, trained, waiting for the moment to move.

Unfortunate for him that I'm faster.

I keep the gun tight to my body, angled so it disappears into the geometry of my frame, the suppressor turning what comes next into something almost polite. I fire once, clean and precise, the round punching straight through his heart.

There's no spectacle. No spray. No sound worth mentioning. He simply folds, collapsing to the floor like a man whose body forgot what it was supposed to do next.

"Oh my God," a woman nearby cries, rushing toward him. "Sir? Are you okay?"

He isn't, and he never will be, but I'm already moving past them, tracking the direction Saint went as she slips deeper into the terminal.

My jaw tightens as I follow.

Was she leaving me?

Or did she see this coming and move first to draw the heat away?

I don't have time to decide which answer I like better.

Movement flares behind me, and I pivot just enough to see another man clock the body on the floor, his gaze snapping from the dead assassin to the space I occupied a second ago. Partner. Confirmed. He hesitates for half a breath, trying to find me in the noise.

That half breath costs him everything.

I walk backward with the flow of traffic, gun already pointed, my pace steady enough to look accidental. The second shot lands just as clean as the first, dropping him without ceremony before anyone can register what's happened.

Two bodies. No panic yet. Just confusion.

I turn forward again and pick up my pace, easing into a

light jog as I follow Saint's path through the terminal, weaving around screaming civilians and overturned luggage.

Whatever she saw, whatever she's running toward, I'm not letting her handle it alone.

Not now.

I almost miss it.

Saint redirects fast, slipping sideways into one of those privacy pods bolted along the wall, the kind meant for breastfeeding or pumping or whatever else airports pretend counts as dignity. The woman following her doesn't hesitate. She goes in after her like she thinks this ends one way and one way only.

Well. Nice knowing you. Whoever you were.

It takes less than ten seconds before Saint is walking back out, pace unchanged, expression bored enough to be insulting. I don't need to see inside the pod to know how that went. Anyone arrogant enough to think they could take Saint James alone deserved the outcome.

Behind me, the atmosphere finally starts to crack.

The two men I dropped are bleeding now. At first, someone probably thought they'd fainted. Heart attack, maybe. People like to assume the mundane before the horrifying. That illusion doesn't survive long once blood starts seeping through shirts and pooling on polished terminal floors.

A woman screams. Then another. Voices rise in sharp, overlapping bursts of confusion and fear. People behind me surge forward, trying to escape whatever they think is coming. People in front stretch and crane their necks, desperate to see it. Terminal employees' jog toward the noise, one already barking into a walkie like she's trying to outrun the inevitable.

By the time I reach the central hub of the terminal, the illusion of normalcy is dead.

This is the intersection, the wide-open food court where restaurants form a rough circle and nowhere feels safe. And that's when the Guild shows itself.

They arrive like they always do, without panic, without urgency. Escalators deliver them from below, sunglasses still on, expressions calm, eyes already hunting. Elevator doors slide open and release a few more, spreading outward instead of clustering. Some move in pairs, heads close, murmuring quick updates. Others peel off alone, loners by choice or reputation, scanning angles and exits like they're deciding where the bodies will fall.

They're surrounding us.

Then a voice cuts through the chaos, smooth and arrogant, soaked in a Texas drawl that makes Saint stop dead in her tracks.

"Saint James..."

Colt "The Texan" Herrington doesn't need to shout. He announces it instead, a declaration meant as much for the other assassins as for her.

"She's mine."

Something ugly twists in my chest, hot and sharp, and I realize I'm already unscrewing the suppressor from my gun without remembering deciding to do it. My hands move on instinct, fueled by a fury I don't bother interrogating.

My eyes stay locked on Saint as she slowly turns to face him, the space around her going unnaturally still. I can feel the tension ripple outward, killers pausing mid-step like animals waiting for the first crack of thunder.

I should've killed him yesterday.

But not yet. Not until he plays his part.

Colt smirks and raises his gun, confidence written all over him. He's good long range and more comfortable with heavy firepower. He likes distance and destruction. Likes feeling untouchable.

Unfortunately for him, my specialty is not sniping. I'm not exclusive to the long-range club. My specialty is simple. Hitting targets. With anything.

I could flick a bead at a penny and hit Abe Lincoln right on the nose. If I miss, it's because I wanted to. I know one other master of the Guild with the same specialty. Two marbles I keep in my pocket for that very reminder.

Saint's eyes find mine for half a heartbeat, and that's all it takes.

"Go," I call out.

I pull the trigger a fraction of a second later, the shot tearing through the air and taking Colt's trigger finger clean off just before he can fire. The report cracks loud and final, echoing through the terminal.

Travelers scream and dive for cover. Colt howls, clutching his hand as blood sprays and his gun clatters to the floor.

It's me that rings the fucking bell. And on my signal, all hell breaks loose.

Alejandro

Chaos erupts all at once, loud, and shapeless and impossible to outrun.

People scatter in every direction, screaming, dropping bags, slipping on polished floors as alarms begin to howl overhead, the shrill wail of something pulled too late. The terminal fractures into panic, and threaded through it are the assassins who came prepared for exactly this.

The first one makes the mistake of closing the distance with me.

I pivot into him, drive my knee hard into the small of his back, and feel his spine give with a wet, final sound that never gets old. He drops before he can scream. At the same time, I fire once over his shoulder, the shot clean and centered, and the man rushing me from the side folds instantly, skull snapping back as he hits the ground.

No time to admire the work.

Saint is already running, moving against the tide of fleeing civilians, drawing the hunters toward her like gravity. They want her dead, and they don't care how many people get trampled in the process.

One of them reaches her first.

I see her swing a food court chair like she was born with it in her hands, the metal frame cracking into his face hard enough to drop him, then she spins and hurls it at another assassin charging in from her flank. The chair connects and explodes apart, sending him sprawling.

She dives into a convenience store just as a gunshot cracks through the air, glass shattering where her head was a second ago. I angle toward her, firing as I move, dropping the shooter and never breaking stride.

She bursts back out of the store with a phone charger looped around an assassin's throat, yanking it tight and hauling the woman backward into her body. The assassin claws at her neck, choking, while another attacker launches a handful of ninja stars that thunk uselessly into the human shield's abdomen.

Saint doesn't flinch, just keeps pulling on that cord, her hold locked as the woman in her grip claws uselessly at it while Saint scopes out the next threat.

" Oh, hey, Derek," Saint says calmly.

He's already finishing someone else when he answers, blade stabbed into another assassin's ribs like this is just a messy office dispute.

The struggles from the assassin she's strangling turn sloppy, then weak, then stop altogether.

He glances at Saint as the body slumps. "Hey, Saint."

The woman hits the tile with a heavy, final sound.

He shrugs once, almost apologetic. "It's nothing personal, you know." Then he punches her.

The right hook lands clean and spins her halfway around, hard enough that I feel it in my own jaw.

She doesn't fall, just grabs.

Her hand closes around the meat cleaver sitting on the cutting block of the Chinese fast food counter, and she buries in Derek's head with a crack, dropping him mid-step like his strings got cut.

"Well, Derek," she says evenly, already turning away, "it feels personal."

She's talking to a corpse.

I still don't quite get to her.

Someone kicks my gun out of my hand, sending it skidding across the tile. We collide hard, bodies slamming together, fists flying. I take an elbow to the jaw and answer with the butt of the gun when I reclaim it, striking his skull again and again until he drops boneless at my feet. "Mother fucking asshole." I grit out.

I'm almost to her now, near the same Chinese fast food restaurant, when another shot rips through the space and blows out the glass. "Oh, shit."

Shards rain down, rice and meat and sauce splattering across the floor in a steaming mess.

I grab a massive pan of egg drop soup from the counter and fling it straight into an attacker's face. He screams as the scalding liquid blinds him, and I'm on him before the sound finishes, snapping his neck with both hands.

Saint sweeps low, knocking a woman off her feet, dodging the snap of nun chucks as they whistle past her head. She grabs the giant pan of fried rice, hefts it once, and brings the edge down with everything she has. "Wrong bitch."

She growls out as metal hits bone.

The pan clatters to the tile, and the woman's body goes slack, her head separated so cleanly it takes a moment for my brain to catch up. Steam curls around the corpse, rice scattered everywhere, her eyes staring lifelessly at the ceiling. Saint's face was probably the last thing she saw.

Saint doesn't notice the next assassin, gun raised and aimed square at her.

But I do. "Watch it." I call out. Lunging and ripping the pan back up, angling it just in time as bullets slam into the metal. Sparks fly while I brace us both behind it, my eyes searching her face. "What's the plan, Saint?"

The clip empties, the gun clicks, and I rise in one motion, hurling the pan like a discus.

It slams into his throat with a sickening crunch, collapsing his windpipe. He drops instantly, hands clawing uselessly at his neck.

I snatch his gun and the spare clip from his belt.

"You'll see." Saint is already moving again, cleaver yanked free from Derek's skull, blood dripping from the blade. She throws it barely looking, end over end, and it passes so close to my shoulder I have to shift to avoid it.

A wet sound lands behind me.

A woman collapses, the cleaver buried in her chest. I step forward and finish it, driving my boot down until it punches through bone and into her heart.

"Let's go," I shout.

Saint doesn't slow. She was already turning, already sprinting deeper into the terminal.

A gunshot cracks behind us, followed by Tex's furious voice, thick with pain and promise, but we don't stop. "You should've taken the head shot, Alejandro!" We duck instinctively and keep running, weaving through smoke, alarms, and bodies.

I turn on occasion, sending a bullet or two behind us.

One shot hits a fire extinguisher and blasts an assassin in the face. The next shot kills them.

I'm trying to figure out what her plan is when I see it.

Red lettering, bright and unmissable at one of the gates ahead.

It's another Emirates flight to Dubai and the plane is already pulling away from the gate.

I bark a laugh I can't stop, breath burning in my lungs.

Fucking genius woman.

She found us a faster way out.

Now all we have to do is catch a plane...

and leave a small army of very angry assassins behind. Preferably dead.

The terminal is almost empty now, the chaos having burned itself out into echoes and alarms. A few unlucky souls are still hiding behind rows of bolted-together chairs near the gates, peeking out like prairie dogs deciding whether the world is safe again. Every other door is slamming shut, metal shutters dropping, the airport finally realizing this is not, in fact, a customer service issue.

Lockdown is starting.

Saint cuts right, eyes already locked on the gate for the Emirates flight to Dubai. The plane is there, nose angled, already turning away from the terminal like it's had enough of America for one day. If it starts its taxi, we're done.

And Saint knows it too.

She hits the closed gate door at full speed, shoulder-first, and it bursts open with a sound like a gunshot. She's through instantly. I'm right behind her. I wrench the door shut again, fire once into the locking mechanism, and hear the satisfying grind of metal jamming metal before I take off after her down the jet bridge.

Minutes ago, people were rolling suitcases down this tunnel, arguing about overhead bin space and seat assignments. Now it's empty, echoing, the hum of the plane vibrating through the floor beneath our feet.

At the far end, the door to the stairs explodes open.

A bald biker charges straight at Saint, face twisted with rage, fists clenched like he thinks this is a bar fight instead of a suicide note. Black leather vest flaps open over a chest webbed with tattoos. A leather studded collar sits tight around his thick neck.

"This is for my dog!" he roars, like that explains anything.

Saint doesn't give him a syllable.

She jumps, grabs the metal bar overhead, and swings herself clean off the ground. Both feet slam into his chest with brutal force, and I don't think he was prepared for just how hard it lands.

It's a deadly mistake to underestimate Saint James. One he's finding out right now.

He goes flying backward, smashes into the door he just came through, arms windmilling as gravity finishes the job. Twenty feet down, he hits concrete with a sound that tells me there's nothing left to argue about.

Saint is already turning for the stairs.

I reach the end of the tunnel, raise my gun, and put two bullets through what's left of his skull for good measure.

"What did you do to his dog, Picarita?" I call after her as she starts down.

"Not a damn thing!" she shouts back over her shoulder,

already jogging toward a Harley idling on the tarmac below. "That snaggletooth cotton ball ran away on its own."

Seeing the bike, I let out a sharp, heartfelt "Hijo de la chingada."*

It's big. Loud. Angry. And very much a one-seat situation.

Except for the sidecar.

Of course there's a fucking sidecar like this is the goddamn motorcycle outlaw version of the Wild West.

"I'm driving," I say flatly.

She swings her leg over the bike and settles into the seat like she was born there. "The fuck you are." She pops open a saddlebag, pulls out two silver revolvers, and tosses them to me. "Hop in, sweetheart." She nods toward the sidecar, grinning. "If he's here, his club is too."

Right on cue, the sound hits us. Engines. Deep, rolling, unmistakable. A dozen bikes at least, growling somewhere beyond the terminal, closing fast.

I climb into the sidecar with another curse, folding myself into it with all the grace of a man being punished by the universe.

"I feel like a fucking empanada," I half yell, half growl.

Saint laughs, wild and bright, and guns the engine.

We tear off across the tarmac, alarms screaming, engines roaring, and behind us, a pack of hunters finally realize their prey has stolen their leader's bike. And it seems they are quite pissed about it.

---

* "Son of a bitch."

32
Saint

Finding a specific plane on an active runway turns out to be a real scavenger hunt when the airport is the size of a small city and apparently no one told ground control that there was just a bloodbath involving fried rice in Terminal F. Jets are still taxiing like everything is fine, like today's crisis is a delayed latte instead of multiple bodies and a motorcycle gang with artillery.

I gun the Harley anyway.

The tires squeal, the tail slides and I nearly lose control. *Huh, not bad.*

This bike is definitely not stock. Seems baldy did some upgrades that may come in handy for our escape. Hopefully this bike is faster than the gang coming for us.

The motorcycle club comes in hot behind us, engines snarling, spreading out like they've done this before, which is not surprising. I weave us through service lanes and fuel trucks, eyes scanning tails and numbers, counting under my breath until I spot it. There. The Emirates bird, already rolling, plane number stamped clean and pretty on the tail like it isn't about to become my problem.

Gunshots crack behind us, sharp and angry, and I lean hard into the turn, swinging the bike around a plane being pushed back by a tractor just as something heavy whistles past my ear.

The stupid braids of this annoying wig flicking in my face as I move.

"Holy shit," Alejandro yells from the sidecar, bracing himself. "They've got some pretty big firepower!"

Something detonates behind us, close enough that I feel it in my teeth. The tractor driver dives clear just in time before the blast hits, fire blooming outward as the vehicle explodes into a spectacular mess of metal and flame.

"Do they have a fucking cannon?" I shout.

"Pretty much," he yells back.

He twists in the sidecar and fires, controlled and calm despite the chaos, and I catch a glimpse of one of the bikes lying flat as it skids across the tarmac in a spray of sparks. The rider doesn't move.

The unmanned plane keeps rolling, unguided now, until glass shatters and metal screams as it plows straight into the terminal windows. The sound is catastrophic. Shouting erupts instantly, and like ants to sugar, assassins swarm the breach, smashing out the remaining glass with chairs and trash cans, clawing their way out of the building to get their piece of the bounty. One gets shoved too hard and lands wrong, leg snapping with a sound I feel rather than hear.

I don't spare them another glance.

The terminal can eat itself alive for all I care.

I only need one thing and it's to get on that fucking plane.

Runways blur together when you're moving this fast,

white lines and blinking lights streaking past as I push the Harley harder. The Emirates plane is still ahead of us, lumbering and massive, beginning its slow, arrogant turn like it has all the time in the world.

We do not. And I need to figure out how the fuck we're getting on it.

Behind us, the motorcycle club fans out, engines howling, the sound vibrating up my spine. They're good. Aggressive. Sloppy in that confident way that comes from numbers and testosterone. I weave anyway, cutting sharp around ground vehicles and painted markers, trusting instinct more than sight.

Alejandro shifts in the sidecar, all six-foot-six of him wedged into a space meant for maybe a golden retriever and a dream.

"This is undignified," he shouts over the wind.

"You look adorable," I call back. "Really sells the exile sniper vibe."

Gunfire snaps past us. One round pings off metal close enough that I feel it through the handlebars. I jerk the bike sideways and clip a rider who got too close, my saddlebag slamming into his front tire. He goes down hard, bike flipping end over end before skidding across the runway in a shower of sparks.

Alejandro twists around, braced awkwardly, and fires with maddening calm. One biker drops. Then another. Precision work, even from a sidecar, which honestly feels unfair.

I think, fleetingly, about my original plan. About slipping away. About leaving him behind so I could get ahead of this, think, breathe, survive.

Yeah. That's not happening.

I don't know how I'm supposed to get onto this plane with a six-foot-plus assassin and a sidecar's worth of baggage, but I know one thing for sure. I'm not leaving him on the tarmac.

A bike surges up alongside us, too close, the rider grinning like this is the highlight of his week. He lunges and grabs the edge of the sidecar, hauling himself halfway in.

Great.

Now we're doing this.

Alejandro snarls something in Spanish and they grapple, all elbows and knees and absolutely zero grace. The sidecar wobbles. I keep us straight by sheer spite.

"Can you not?" I yell. "I'm driving!"

"I'm trying," Alejandro grunts, shoving the man's face away as a fist swings wildly between them.

The biker lands a punch. Alejandro answers with two, then three, efficient and brutal.

"Incoming." I warn, as casual as if warning we're about to run a red light.

He grabs the man by the vest, hauls him up, and for one ridiculous second they lock eyes.

"Tu madre es una perra," *Alejandro says growls, and dumps him out.

The biker hits the runway and rolls, tumbling directly into the path of another plane already accelerating for take-off. There is no dramatic impact. No heroic sacrifice. Just physics doing what physics does.

Bodies lose. Planes win.

---

* "Your mother is a bitch,"

The Emirates jet finishes its turn and lines up, engines whining higher, angrier. It's about to go.

"Saint," Alejandro says, urgency cutting through the sarcasm, "we are running out of runway."

"I know," I snap, gunning the engine harder. "I can see the plane."

Another bike surges up on my left. I lean into it without hesitation, shoulder, and steel meeting in a violent shriek as I ram him sideways. He loses balance, curses lost to the wind, and disappears in a tumble of chrome and bad decisions.

Then I do something insane.

I cut across the runway.

Hard turn. Full lean. The Harley fishtails, tires screaming as I bring us around in a brutal arc until the plane is no longer ahead of us.

It's behind us.

Lined up. Engines spooling. A wall of sound and intent.

Alejandro goes very still in the sidecar.

The Emirates jet roars louder, deeper, the kind of noise you feel in your bones. It's about to take the runway, and when it does, it will not care that we exist. In thirty seconds, it will be moving at a hundred and fifty miles an hour, and we will be a rounding error.

I roll the throttle and launch us forward.

We're on the takeoff runway now, racing away from the plane that is absolutely going to catch us.

Alejandro looks back once, then forward again. "Saint," he says carefully, like he's trying not to spook a wild animal, "I would love to know what the plan is."

"Get ready to jump."

A look of disbelief makes his pause a beat.

"...I'm sorry?"

"Stand up. Stay low."

The engines scream higher. The plane starts its run.

Alejandro swears, then does exactly what I tell him. He plants his feet in the sidecar, crouched, bracing himself with one hand, the other gripping the corner of his gun's case fixed on his back. The wind is savage now, tearing at us, trying to rip him free.

I keep my hands steady on the bars, my body loose but controlled, eyes flicking between the runway and the monster behind us. The plane is coming in hot and heavy, nose down, unstoppable.

"You get one shot," I shout over the roar. "Don't miss."

"Oh, Picarita," He laughs, sharp and feral. "I never miss."

I hold us steady as long as I can, then angle just enough to line him up.

"Now!"

Alejandro launches.

He clears the gap clean, slams into the landing gear housing, and locks on, body swinging violently, gun case banging against the housing before he finds purchase. The plane is still grounded, wheels pounding the runway, engines screaming as it eats distance.

He looks back at me, one arm already outstretched.

I gun the bike harder, chasing him, balancing on instinct alone as the Harley screams at its absolute limit. My eyes flick between him and the plane's nose.

Not yet... not yet.

I rise, feet coming up onto the seat, body centered,

patient, the bike steady beneath me despite the wind tearing at my clothes and the wig fixed to my head.

The runway is disappearing fast but I've got to hit this perfect.

Alejandro's brown eyes are locked onto me with an intensity I've rarely seen, and he gives me one nod. He's ready.

The nose lifts and that's the moment. My body coils back, all muscles tense and I jump.

The plane surges upward as I launch, the ground falling away beneath me in a dizzying drop. Alejandro catches me mid-air, forearm to forearm, the impact ripping a grunt from both of us.

"Got you."

The pressure is brutal now, wind screaming past, the aircraft climbing hard as I dangle beneath it, legs kicking uselessly.

Alejandro growls, face contorted with effort as he holds me, and I swing my free arm again and again until my fingers finally lock around his wrist with both hands.

He shifts, finds leverage, then lets go with one hand long enough to grab me properly. With a raw shout, he hauls me up as the landing gear begins to retract, massive machinery folding inward around us.

We scramble, half climbing, half dragging each other into the belly of the plane just as the doors close.

The noise drops to a muffled roar. The chaos is gone.

I toss my backpack and collapse onto my back. Arms spread, chest heaving, staring up at nothing, and alive in a way that feels almost offensive.

I laugh first. I can't help it.

"That," I say between breaths, "was fun."

Alejandro, sitting back on his heels, hands on his thighs and panting just as heavy as I am, turns his head, wild disbelief pinching his face. "I'm never traveling with you again."

Saint

This is the nicest fucking cargo hold I've ever been in.

I find a place to kneel, plant my weight, and finally let myself catch my breath. My lungs still burn from the climb, from the drop, from the sheer audacity of riding a plane into the sky like we had a death wish and something to prove. The first thing I do, the thing I've been thinking about since I shoved that wig onto my head this morning, is reach for my backpack.

My hair kit comes out as Alejandro opens his rifle case behind me, inspecting the weapon with something bordering on reverence. His breathing is steady now, controlled again, as if we didn't just gamble our lives on timing and grip strength.

My multitool slides back into my pocket, warm and familiar. My most trusted companion. While the plane climbed in altitude and banked hard to settle into its course, I was wedged into the landing gear compartment, prying open a service panel with that same tool, fingers numb and shaking as I broke us into the cargo hold reserved for Dubai's ritziest commercial travelers.

We made it inside just before the compartment sealed, breathless and bruised, tumbling into luxury.

We both took a moment to assess the space once we were in. It's tall enough for Alejandro to stand comfortably without ducking, which tells me everything I need to know about the kind of money involved here. The air is clean, pressurized, carefully filtered. The temperature is controlled down to the degree. Crates are strapped down with military neatness, and stacks of sealed food cases wait to be lifted to the passenger deck above, their labels pristine and absurdly elegant.

There are even a few spare bunks tucked along one wall, narrow but functional, and a small bathroom clearly meant for stewards stealing a few precious minutes away from constant demands for peanuts and pillows.

I jam the door that leads toward the passenger areas before anyone can get curious, then turn back to what matters.

I mist my hair until it's damp enough to wake it back up, fingers working conditioner through curls flattened by hours under that fucking wig. My breathing finally starts to slow as my hair does what it always does, springing back into itself, reclaiming space.

As I work, my mind keeps drifting backward, replaying the terminal in sharp, violent flashes.

The plan had been simple. Clean. Alejandro was supposed to be left thousands of feet below me, stranded among the rolling carryon's and screaming kids. I would disappear into the clouds and move on alone, the way I always do when things start to rot.

Instead, a bloodbath rewrote everything.

Now he's here, breathing the same recycled air, close enough that I can feel his presence at my back like pressure. Too close.

I reassess without emotion. That plan is dead and a new one will have to take its place.

That's when I slide Grim's flip phone from my back pocket, keeping my movements casual, buried in the cover of my hair routine. The phone looks absurdly small in my hand, scratched but intact.

I huff a quiet laugh. Really. The little phone that could.

The screen lights up immediately.

> GRIM: Just turn the laptop on. I'll find it.

The files.

The two missing photos I texted him about just before the airport erupted into violence. Proof of something. Or the absence of it.

"Fuck," I grit out to myself.

There's no service. No way to reply.

After deleting the messages, I close the phone and slide it back into my pocket, sealing the information away for later. I don't confront on instinct. I confront on proof. Until I have that, the knowledge of these missing files stays mine.

And that means the man I suspect might be working against me stays exactly where he is.

Behind me.

I cap the bottle, tuck my mirror and hair kit away, and that's when Alejandro finally says something.

"So," Already I can tell he's trying too hard. "How'd you know about this flight as a backup?"

The words are easy. Casual. The kind of question someone asks while cleaning a weapon, filling silence, making conversation.

But it's the tension underneath his words that lands like a blade in my back.

My hands still, not frozen, just quiet. I feel the shift in the air immediately, the way it tightens and sharpens. He's fishing, not for the answer, but for the tell. And he knows I know it, because we're both trained killers. And we're both still alive for the same reason.

We listen when something feels off. And his tone feels off.

I don't turn around. I don't answer.

The hum of the plane fills the space between us, metal vibrating, air rushing somewhere far above. I can feel him recalibrating behind me, reading the silence, adjusting his footing. He knows I'm hiding something.

I know he is too.

The quiet stretches, thick and charged, a fragile bubble swelling with everything we aren't saying. It presses in on my ears, my chest, until it feels like the wrong move will shatter it into something lethal.

Then we move.

Both of us rise at the same time, smooth and controlled, guns coming up in mirror-perfect synchronization. Mine clears my backpack without a sound. His is one of the biker's pistols, already an extension of his hand.

Straight arms. Steady aim.

No hesitation and no wasted motion.

I keep my face calm, my breathing even. I don't speak. I don't need to.

The one with something to cover up always does first.

Alejandro exhales slowly, measured, like he's the calmest man in the world.

"Saint," he says, level and deliberate. "Let's not get carried away."

I don't move.

My gun stays fixed on him, unwavering, the weight familiar in my hand. His remains trained on me, the space between us tight and humming, like the plane itself is holding its breath along with us.

Seconds pass. Maybe more. Time gets strange when the stakes are this high.

He speaks again, slower this time, like he's learned something from my silence.

"Why did you know about this second flight to Dubai?"

I don't answer. I don't give him anything more than a blink.

So I let him do what men like him always do when faced with a void.

He fills it.

"You were going to ditch me, weren't you?"

Silence.

"Was that the plan before the airport?"

Still nothing. I watch his throat work as he swallows, his eyes narrowing just slightly as he turns the question over in his head. I can see the calculation happening in real time, gears grinding as he tries to reverse engineer the moment everything shifted.

"Something changed at the airport," he says finally.

It's framed like a statement, but it's a probe. Less

guessing than walking himself through an interrogation he didn't plan on conducting.

His gaze sharpens. "What changed, Saint?"

I consider my answer carefully. We're locked in a standoff thirty thousand feet in the air, tucked into the underbelly of a plane we shouldn't exist on, surrounded by fuel, metal, and the very real possibility of mutual destruction. This isn't the place for truths that can't be controlled.

So, I give him one that can.

"You know how these things are," I say lightly, my tone almost casual, if you don't know what to listen for.

He does.

"Everything hinges on the right timing."

His eyes lock onto mine, and he knows exactly what I'm referring to. Half a conversation overheard, but damning enough to fracture trust clean down the middle.

He holds his aim for another long moment, thinking. I see the minute adjustment of his grip, the faint sheen of sweat at his temple, the way his breath shifts as he recalibrates.

Then, slowly, deliberately, he lifts his gun away from me and raises his hands in surrender.

I don't move. My gun stays right where it is.

"Who were you talking to?" I ask.

It's a simple question. Reasonable. Practical. Half the deadliest killers on the planet are hunting me, after all. And yet it lands between us like something far more personal, sharp with an edge I don't entirely recognize.

He steps toward me carefully, bends, and places his revolver on top of his rifle. Both weapons abandoned in plain sight. When he straightens, his hands are empty as he takes another slow step closer.

"My broker," he says.

"And what timing is so important, Alejandro?" I ask.

He takes another step. Too close.

"I haven't stayed out of the Guild's sights for two years by running headfirst into traps."

It's an answer shaped like wisdom. Vague. Defensive. Not actually an answer at all. The actual question is still unanswered.

Another step, and the barrel of my gun presses into his chest.

I can't mention the missing files. I can't risk tipping my hand before I know what they mean, before Grim confirms whether this is coincidence or something far uglier. If Alejandro is feeding my location to someone, he'll deny it without blinking. Worse, he'll keep me alive just long enough to walk me exactly where he wants me.

No. I have to be smarter than that.

I can feel him using proximity as a weapon, leaning into the space between us, testing whether my resolve will crack under familiarity.

Fine.

I soften.

Just enough.

My shoulders relax. My grip loosens a fraction. The tension leaves my brow, not completely, but enough to suggest hesitation instead of intent.

It works.

I see it in the way his posture eases, the tilt of his head as his expression shifts from guarded to something dangerously gentle.

He raises one hand slowly and brushes a finger down my cheek, the touch light, reverent, like he's reminding me of something I'd rather forget.

"We have too many secrets between us, Saint James," he murmurs.

His gaze flickers between my eyes, searching.

"If your price is a truth," he continues quietly, "then I will give it to you."

He pauses, and I can almost see the internal negotiation playing out. What he wants to keep buried. What he's willing to surface instead.

This is nothing more than a game I have to play to see this through. And I have no choice but to play it.

I lower my gun and he releases a breath. Takes the final step to close the gap between us. Our chests nearly touching. His hands slide along my arms, warm and steady, grounding in a way that feels practiced. Familiar. Dangerous.

He rests his forehead against mine and closes his eyes, breathing me in like the moment matters.

"I just held you from a commercial liner with one hand, Saint," he says softly. "You trusted me enough to jump."

He pulls back just enough to look at me, his thumbs brushing my cheeks.

"Trust me enough to fight this with you."

He watches me for another beat, then leans in slowly and kisses me.

I let him.

I tilt my head with his, close my eyes, soften my mouth against his, even as every instinct in my body stays awake and watching. When he pulls back, his voice is barely above a whisper.

"If I have to earn your trust one truth at a time," he says, "then I'll start with this one. My broker..."

I hold my breath. Because there are secrets assassins take to their grave. Would rather die than reveal. Their broker is one of them.

He looks at me steadily. Like he wants me to know how much this moment costs.

"My sister," he says. "My broker is my sister."

34

Alejandro

I watch it land.

The way her stillness sharpens. The way her eyes don't widen, don't flinch, but go distant for half a heartbeat as the information reorganizes itself in her head. Saint doesn't react the way other people do. She recalculates.

Family changes the math.

A broker is one thing. A sister is another entirely. It means loyalty layered on obligation; blood tangled up with survival. It means there are pieces of my life she never knew existed, let alone fit together.

I let her sit with it for a moment. Let the cost show on my face because it's real. There are secrets assassins take to their grave. I've buried men for less.

"She's been my broker since I was exiled," I say quietly. "I didn't know she was one before that night."

Saint's gaze snaps back to me, sharp now, focused.

"Everyone heard about my exile," I say. "The Guild made sure of it."

Saint stays quiet, watching me the way she always does when she's deciding whether the truth is being offered or negotiated.

"They said I poisoned a politician for a backdoor deal," I continue. "That I sold my loyalty for leverage."

I let the words hang there, ugly, and familiar.

"My sister knew better."

That gets her. Just a flicker, but it's there.

"Not because she trusted the Guild," I add. "She never has. She knew better because she knows me."

I pause, feeling the weight of what I'm not saying yet, what I'm about to drag into the light.

"And because the politician I was accused of killing was my brother-in-law."

I see it hit her then, a second shock folding into the first. Too many fragments scattered across the table at once. Too many truths arriving without warning. She doesn't speak, but her jaw tightens, eyes narrowing as she tries to build a picture from pieces that refuse to line up neatly.

Before she can say anything, a mechanical click sounds behind us.

Something slides into place with a soft, final sound, like a small door locking.

I turn, craning my head toward the source just as another muted hum kicks on. A panel along the wall lights faintly, heat indicators blinking to life.

Looks like dinner.

"Come sit," I say, nodding toward the cases stacked nearby. "I'll tell you what happened."

My stomach chooses that moment to growl, low and traitorous. I ignore it, but Saint doesn't miss anything.

"I need water," she says flatly. "Or things are going to get real ugly real fast."

She moves before I can respond, slipping between pallets with purpose, eyes scanning labels meant for the service deck above. She finds what she's looking for quickly, hauling out two large bottles and tossing one to me while I shift a few cases into something resembling seats.

We drink in silence, the kind that doesn't press but waits. Cold water burns its way down, settling my nerves, grounding me back in my body.

When we're done, I cap the bottle and rest my forearms on my knees.

"That night," I say, then pause, recalibrating even now. "It wasn't a job. It was a favor."

Saint doesn't interrupt. She rarely does when she senses something buried under the words.

"Mateo Serrano called me," I continue. "He was a politician by then. Ambitious. Careful. To him, I was former military. Special forces. The kind you're not allowed to name or admit exist."

I let out a breath through my nose, the memory settling into place.

"I never had to correct him. All he knew was that I wasn't allowed to talk about my work. That part was true. He didn't need to know I'd traded orders and shitty pay for contracts and blood."

Mateo had called because he was scared. Not theatrically. Not dramatically. The way men get scared when the rumors are solid and coming from the wrong mouths. He'd heard there would be an attempt on his life. He wanted someone he trusted nearby. Someone invisible.

"A plus-one," I say quietly. "That was how he framed it. Security for a night."

My sister, Lucía, had been too pregnant to travel. The rumors made it worse. Mateo wouldn't risk her, not then. So, I went instead. It wasn't Guild-sanctioned. No handlers.

No backup. Just family doing what family does when things start circling.

"A dinner party," I say. "Eighteen guests. No obvious enemies. No raised voices. No political opponents or tense silences."

The night had been almost boring.

They ate. They talked. People laughed. Nothing happened.

Mateo apologized afterward, embarrassed by his own paranoia. He joked about wasting my evening, said he'd over-reacted. I told him it was fine. That it was what family was for.

We were riding in the back of the limo when he asked me if he'd pulled me away from anything important.

I remember smirking.

"As a matter of fact," I'd told him, "you had."

I'd been thinking of Saint then. Of the island. Imagined the way she would be asleep waiting for me, one leg kicked out from under the sheet, her body turned just enough that it felt like an invitation. Like a beacon saying *come back alive*.

I never finished the thought.

Mateo started coughing. Then gasping. His breath hitched, sharp and wrong. His lips went blue fast, veins in his neck darkening like ink spreading under skin.

I shouted at the driver to get to the nearest hospital and hauled him down onto the seat, already moving. This wasn't a seizure. I knew that the moment I saw his eyes.

There was a medical kit in the compartment. I tore through it, hands steady, heart pounding. Activated charcoal. Antihistamines. An EpiPen.

I didn't hesitate. I injected him. Forced the pills down

with water. Rolled him onto his side and shoved my fingers into his throat until he vomited, violent and uncontrolled.

Then he stopped breathing.

I started CPR.

Every compression drove the air out of his lungs, and every time it did, I smelled it.

Sweet. Sickeningly so.

It's the kind of thing you never forget. The kind of detail that brands itself into your soul whether you want it to or not.

"That's why he lived," Saint says quietly.

I look at her and nod once. "Yes."

Mateo was already in office by then. Popular enough to be dangerous. Close enough to re-election that the timing mattered more than the method. Someone wanted his opponent to win without a fight, and the cleanest way to do that was a dead man just before voting opened. Sympathy shifts fast. Power shifts faster.

"They wanted him to die quietly," I say. "At dinner. In a limo. No witnesses who mattered."

Saint's eyes don't leave my face.

"But he didn't," I continue. "Because I was there."

Mateo clawed his way out of that hospital bed the next morning looking like hell, still pale, still shaking, still half dead. And then he did the worst possible thing for the people who tried to kill him.

He went on television.

He told them someone had poisoned him. Told them it was political. Told them he was still alive in spite of it. The country ate it up. Outrage does wonders for voter turnout. He won in a landslide.

That should have been the end of it.

Instead, it was the beginning.

"The hit failed," I say. "So, they needed someone to blame."

Security footage surfaced. Carefully edited. Just enough to show me entering the building. Just enough to put me in the limo. The story wrote itself. Assassin turned on his own. Poisoned a politician for leverage. Betrayed the Guild.

"They set the contract on me," I say quietly. "And they made it look righteous."

Saint's jaw tightens, the faintest tell.

"That's when my sister found me."

Lucía reached me before the hunters did. Before the whispers turned into knives. She came in the middle of the night, eyes too sharp, voice too calm, and asked me a question I didn't know how to answer.

She told me she was a broker.

Asked me if I worked for the Guild.

I almost laughed. Almost.

"It's a closed world," I say. "You don't know it exists unless you're already inside it. And suddenly she was standing there, telling me she'd been in it longer than I had."

I hadn't known. She hadn't known about me either. We stared at each other like strangers wearing familiar faces, both realizing the same thing at the same time.

That we'd been lying to each other our entire adult lives without meaning to.

"From that moment on," I say, "we worked together."

To keep me alive. To move me without patterns. To pull threads quietly and figure out who'd staged the betrayal and why. Lucía didn't just broker my contracts.

She rebuilt my existence from the ground up, piece by careful piece.

Saint is silent when I finish. Not distant. Focused. Like she's already mapping the parallels, lining my story up against her own and seeing how neatly they overlap.

Saint is silent when I finish. Not distant. Focused. Like she's already mapping the parallels, lining my story up against her own and seeing how neatly they overlap.

I lean in closer, lowering my voice even though no one can hear us over the hum of the plane. Old habits die hard. So does trust.

"Sound familiar?" I ask quietly. "Because it should."

Her eyes flick to mine, sharp and unreadable.

"They're setting you up to take a hit," I continue. "Not because you're in the way, but because you're useful as a body. Dead women don't argue. Dead women don't contradict the story."

I watch it land. The tension in her shoulder's shifts, subtle but real.

"They need someone else in power," I say. "Someone pliable. Someone already bought and paid for. And the timing matters, just like it did with Mateo."

I straighten slightly, just enough to look at her properly.

"This level of coordination doesn't come from the middle," I tell her. "Not from handlers or opportunists trying to make a name. It comes from the top."

Her jaw tightens. Good. She's listening.

"One person," I say. "One hand with a finger on every trigger, every contract, every rumor that turns into a knife in the dark."

I don't say the name. I don't need to. In our world, you

don't invoke monsters unless you're ready for them to look back.

"They tried to erase me because I survived," I add. "You're being hunted because you haven't died yet."

The plane hums on, steady and indifferent, carrying us across the sky like none of this matters.

Saint doesn't speak, but I can see the decision forming behind her eyes.

And I know, with the same certainty I had that night in the limo, that once this machine turns its attention fully on you, the only way out is through.

Together.

Whether she trusts me or not.

35
Saint

Alejandro is on his feet again, moving through the cargo hold with an ease that suggests he's already memorized the layout. The heating unit hums softly as trays begin to cycle toward some internal lift mechanism that will carry them up to the passenger deck above, where linen-draped tables and polished smiles wait.

He lifts a lid, peers inside, then another.

"Bingo," he says, pleased.

He pulls out two trays of hot food and sets them on the crate between us like an offering.

"No land meat," he adds, glancing at me with a wink.

"Open those," he says. "I'll find us dessert."

I watch him go, then peel back the foil. The smell hits me immediately, rich, and clean and wildly inappropriate for the place we're hiding. I eat slowly, methodically, because my body needs it even if my head isn't ready to rest.

While I chew, I let myself think.

I make peace, at least temporarily, with the things Alejandro didn't share.

Like what timing needs to be right.

Maybe it was the confession he just gave me. The truth of how he was set up two years ago. The story he's been carrying alone, carefully rationed, like ammunition.

Or maybe it's something else. Something that changed him after exile. Something that hardened into a new rule I don't know yet.

Maybe he blames me.

The thought slides in quietly and lodges there.

When the news broke, I reacted like the perfect Guild girl. I believed the lie. I didn't go after his contract, but I didn't question it either. I didn't dig. I didn't doubt publicly. I didn't reach out.

He would be dead if I had taken the job.

But I didn't save him either.

I was angry. Hurt. Offended that he would betray the Guild, the oaths we all take, the structure that keeps monsters like us pointed outward instead of inward.

Something twists in my chest when I think about his sister finding him immediately. Knowing without hesitation that he wouldn't do it.

She went to him.

I didn't.

The realization bites deeper than I want to admit, sharp and undeserved and mine to carry.

And still, there's something else. Something that doesn't fit.

Every time I open my fucking eyes, assassins find me. Perfect timing. Perfect placement. Like someone is moving pieces on a board I can't see. The missing files nag at me, an itch I can't scratch yet. They matter. I know they do. I just don't know how. Not until Grim tells me what was taken.

Alejandro returns before I can spiral too far, arms full like he's looted a five-star pantry instead of a plane's cargo hold. He sets down two salads, then two plates of dessert, each different. He adds a handful of miniature wine bottles and, impossibly, two actual wine glasses.

Not plastic.

I stare at them for a moment, then huff out a breath.

I shouldn't be surprised. Everything else on this plane has been excessive, curated, indulgent. Of course, even the emergency wine is high end.

Alejandro catches my look and smiles like he knows exactly what I'm thinking.

I take a sip, let the absurdity of it wash over me, and for just a moment, suspended between the hum of the engines and the weight of everything unspoken, I let myself exist in the quiet.

Not safe.

But fed.

An hour later, Alejandro watches me slide the Swiss knife back into my pocket after I twist open an actual bottle of wine. The little single-serve ones didn't survive dinner.

"Why in the fuck do you use that?" he asks, gesturing at my pocket.

I lift my glass. "Why not?"

He shakes his head, baffled in that way that's half amusement, half genuine disbelief. "The world is full of weapons, and you choose that."

"First of all," I lean back, full, and smug, legs stretched out as he tops off my glass. "I'm the weapon. Let's get that straight."

I take a slow sip.

"Everything else is just at my disposal."

His eyes linger on me a second longer than necessary before he looks around, scanning the cargo hold like he's searching for inspiration. He grabs a nearby weekend bag and starts pulling things out.

"What would you use this for?" he asks, holding something up.

"That's a spatula."

He tosses it to me, and I catch it easily.

"And what would the great Saint James do with a spatula?" he asks.

I twirl it between my fingers like a baton. "I don't know," I say thoughtfully. "Take over the mafia? What the fuck do you want me to say?"

I swat at him with it. He tries to dodge, but I still get him.

"Teach loud men a lesson," I add.

He laughs, digging back into the bag. "This?" he asks, lifting a rosary strung with black and red beads. There's a gleam in his eye now, trouble sharpening into something darker.

"Easy," I say. "Strangle you with it."

He laughs again and twirls it in a circle around his finger. "I was thinking some very naughty things in a confessional booth myself."

He shifts lower in his seat, legs spread, one dark eyebrow lifting. His posture is an invitation dressed up as arrogance.

"You're doing it again," I tell him.

He grins, all heat. "Doing what?"

I finish my wine, set the glass aside, and stand. I don't rush it. I step into his space, swing one leg over him, settling astride his lap like it's exactly where I belong. One hand braces on my thigh and slides up my hip. He drains the last swallow of his own wine before setting the glass on the floor.

Now both his hands are on my thighs, warm, possessive.

He looks up at me like he thinks he's won. But he was already half hard when I sat down.

"You think," I say softly, leaning in just enough to make it dangerous, "that you can keep me distracted with how well you fuck."

His hands tighten, my hips roll once, slow and deliberate pulling a groan from him.

"But you underestimate my ability to resist you."

He smiles like that's a challenge.

His hands move, teasing, coaxing, trying to pull a reaction out of me as my body betrays its interest. I let him think it's working for exactly three seconds.

Then I tilt my head, smile sweetly, and turn it back on him.

"How long do you think you can last," I ask quietly, "before you're the one who gives in?"

I settle onto his lap, thighs caging him, weight pressed deliberately where I know it'll drive him out of his mind. Alejandro's mouth quirks, but his hands stay right where I want them—palms open on my thighs, like he's learned not to test me when I'm in this mood.

"Planning to keep me here all night, Saint?" His voice is gravel, but there's a thread of challenge beneath it—one I'm happy to answer.

I press in close, lips grazing his jaw, letting my breath feather over the stubble on his throat. "If you're lucky." My hands slip beneath his shirt, feeling the play of muscle and old scars. "But you don't get to decide how this goes."

His pupils blow wide. He's used to being the one with the upper hand. Tonight, he'll learn just how good it can feel to let it go.

My fingers drag down, nails raking lightly over his chest. He shudders, hips bucking once beneath me. I pin him with my thighs, stilling his movement. "Don't rush. You're going to be good for me tonight, aren't you?"

He nods, almost involuntarily, tongue darting out to wet his bottom lip. "Yes, Saint." His voice is low—thick with the promise of obedience.

"Good." I trail my hands down his torso, tracing the line of his abs, stopping just above his belt. I unfasten it, slow and methodical, enjoying the tension stringing tight between us. He's watching me, every muscle straining for restraint, but his hands stay put.

"Lift." It's a single word, but he obeys, hips rising so I can push his pants and boxers down far enough for what I want. His cock is already hard—aching, heavy against his thigh. I wrap my hand around him, slow, teasing. He groans, head dropping back against the crate, exposing his throat.

"You want me to use you?" I whisper against his ear, hand working him in a steady rhythm. "Take what I want from your cock?"

"Yes." It's barely a sound. I press my lips to his throat, tasting sweat and skin, feeling the frantic beat of his pulse beneath my tongue. He's always been beautiful like this— untethered, desperate, trying to hold on and failing.

I slide down his body, kissing a line from his chest to his stomach, then lower still. His hands twitch, but I glare up at him and he freezes, understanding. I kneel between his legs, the soft glow of the cargo hold catching on my skin, painting us in shadows.

I take him in hand again, circling my tongue around the tip, tasting the salt and heat of him. He sucks in a sharp breath. "Fuck, Saint—" His hips jerk but I clamp my free hand on his thigh, forcing him still.

I tease him, lips, and tongue dancing, taking him deep and then letting him fall free, wet and aching. Every time he tries to thrust up, I stop, let him ache, let him beg.

"God, that's good," he rasps, voice gone rough. "Don't stop—"

I pull off with a slow, deliberate pop. "Not until I say, Alejandro. Hands behind your back. Now."

He does it—God, he does it instantly, gripping the edge of the crate behind him, knuckles white with the effort of holding back. I smirk, running my fingers along the sensitive underside of his cock, watching him strain before I take him deep.

I rise, letting his dick fall from my mouth, and he tries to follow my body with his hands. I catch his wrists, pinning them to the crate behind him. "Don't," I say, low and warning. "You just watch."

He does. He's learning.

I take my time, making a show of every movement. Boots first—black leather, scuffed from the abuse I put them through. I unzip them slow, toeing them off one at a time, letting them clatter to the floor. Socks next. I hook my thumbs, dragging them down, baring skin inch by inch. I'm not in a rush. I want him to ache.

His eyes burn into me, fixed and hungry. I smile, slow,

and mean, as I reach for the button on my leather pants. I keep my gaze locked with his, flicking the button open, drawing the zipper down so slow he actually groans. I peel them down my hips, shimmying them over my ass—no help from him, just the friction of tight leather and my own hands. I step out, stand over him in nothing but a black tank and panties.

He licks his lips, knuckles turning white where he's gripping the crate. "Take the rest off, Saint."

I shake my head, running my fingers over the hem of my shirt, teasing the fabric up, then letting it fall. "Not because you said so." I want him desperate. I want him to *need*.

He swears under his breath, but he waits. Good. I drag the tank off, slow, and steady, baring my breasts, my nipples already tight from anticipation. He leans forward, mouth parting, eyes gone half-wild. "Let me taste you," he rasps.

I palm my breasts, teasing my nipples with my thumbs, rolling them until I'm biting my lip, barely holding back a moan. His jaw clenches—he's dying to take over, but he doesn't. I won't let him.

"Not yet," I say, voice silk and smoke. "Hands there, mouth shut."

He shifts, cock jumping, thick and hard. But I'm not done with the show.

I slide my hand down, into the front of my panties. My fingers find my clit, circling, stroking, teasing myself just out of sight. He wants to see but I give him nothing but my heavy breathing and a wicked grin. "You don't get to look," I murmur. "That's for me."

He groans, fists clenching, sweat breaking at his hairline. "Saint—me estás matando*—"

I pull my hand free, shining with my own wetness. I bring my fingers to my lips, watching him watch me, and suck them clean, humming at the taste. "So fucking sweet," I whisper, licking every drop. "But you can't have any. Not yet."

His eyes are black now, pure hunger. He tries to take over again, but I silence him with a look. "You'll get what I give you. When I give it."

I drag my panties down, slow, kicking them aside. "Won't you, my good boy?"

He nods—wrecked, obedient and step back into his space, straddling him again, bare skin on his thick cock, heat meeting heat.

I'm wet—soaked and throbbing from holding the line of power. I line him up, sink down inch by inch, drawing out every second, every gasp. I don't let him move. Not yet.

"You feel that?" I whisper against his ear, grinding my hips in a slow circle. "That's mine, Alejandro. My cock to fuck." I lick his ear, rolling hard. "You don't come until I say so."

His breath is ragged. "Fuck—" The desperation in his voice is a goddamn symphony.

I ride him, slow at first, rolling my hips, chasing my own pleasure. He's shaking beneath me, jaw clenched so tight I can see the muscle jump. Every time he tries to thrust up, I tighten around him, clamp down, remind him whose game this is.

---

* You are killing me.

I reach down, circling my clit with my fingers as I move. It doesn't take long—he's thick inside me, stretching me just right, every movement pushing me closer. I let myself tip over the edge, riding the wave, never breaking eye contact. I want him to see what he does to me, what I'm willing to take for myself.

He groans, body shuddering, but I don't let him go. Not yet.

He tries to surge up, desperate for my mouth, but I catch his chin, forcing him to look at me. I don't soften. I keep my grip firm, my thighs pressing him deep inside me as I start to move—slow at first, then faster as his hands dig into the crate.

"If you betray me, Alejandro—" My voice is a velvet threat, dark and unyielding. I lean in until my mouth hovers over his, close enough to share a breath but not a kiss. "I'll put a bullet through you myself."

He grins, but it's strained. His whole body is shaking with the effort to hold back, to let me keep control. "You'd miss my cock too much to actually pull the trigger," he says, voice raw and teasing.

I laugh, a low dangerous sound, rolling my hips so his breath stutters. I tighten my grip on his chin, forcing his gaze to stay locked with mine. "Look at me." I ride him harder, the threat sharp as steel between us. "I will fuck you today and shoot you tomorrow if you cross me, Alejandro. Don't think for a second I won't."

That does something to him—his whole body tightens, a deep groan ripped from his chest as he tries to hold out, tries not to lose himself to the dangerous line we're walking.

He gasps, mouth nearly on mine, desperate and hungry. "Then I better not cross you, Saint."

The tension between us crackles—pain and pleasure, trust and threat, my hand at his throat, his pleasure entirely at my mercy.

"Joder, bebe," His eyes are closed, and his head is back. The grip of his hands on the crate behind his is nearly strong enough to break it. "Dios, quiero venir, Picarino."*

I ride him harder, savoring the way he trembles beneath me, obedient and desperate, completely mine.

Another orgasm tears through me, sharp and relentless. I ride it out, drawing it out, refusing to let up. He's sweating, shaking, face contorted with the effort of holding back. It's beautiful.

I lean in, kiss him hard, teeth catching on his lower lip. "You want it, then beg for it."

He does. He begs, desperate and filthy, the words tumbling out in Spanish and English, rough with need.

Only when I'm ready, when I've wrung every last drop of control from him, do I nod. "I'll let you have it." I ride him hard. Breasts brushing against the course hair on his chest. My hands on each side of his jaw as I bore my stare into his. "Come for me, Alejandro."

He does, hips thrusting up, finally losing himself. I ride him through it, feeling him pulse inside me, holding him there as he comes undone.

After, I rest my forehead against his, both of us breathing hard, bodies slick with sweat. For a moment,

---

* "God, I want to come, Trouble."

there's nothing but the sound of our breathing, the faint hum of the plane around us.

He looks up at me, still wrecked, still obedient, and I can't help but smile. "Good boy," I whisper, brushing a thumb across his cheek. "Now, come here."

I finally let him touch me, his hands roaming over my skin, hesitant at first, then greedy as if he needs to reassure himself I'm real. I lean in and kiss him, hard and deep, tasting sweat and victory.

"Lie down," I murmur against his mouth. "You've got a mess to clean up, and I've still got your mouth to ride."

We lie tangled together on a makeshift bed, old steward bunks dragged together and covered in spare blankets. My back is to him, the hush of the cargo hold lulling my body toward sleep but never quite pulling me under. I hear his breathing—slow, steady—but I know he isn't asleep.

I feel him shift, slow and careful, his movements practiced and quiet. I don't open my eyes and keep letting him think I'm asleep. I hear the faint click of a phone unlocking, see the weak glow behind me as he texts—thumbs moving with a silent urgency. The glow disappears. I listen as he slides the phone back under his clothes, every move calculated not to disturb me.

A moment later, his body curls against mine, his arm drapes across my waist, and he exhales like a man settling in for the night. "Forgive me, Picarino." It's barely a whisper against my neck but I let my body stay loose. Force my breath out even and stay awake.

He thinks I'm his. He thinks I trust him now.

But he's wrong.

36

Alejandro

The vibration drags me out of sleep—soft, insistent, a warning bell in the quiet belly of the plane. My senses snap awake, pulse quickening. I keep my breathing steady, careful not to shift too fast. Saint is behind me, her breathing slow, deep, oblivious. Still sleeping or faking it better than anyone I've ever met.

I move slow. Inch by inch, I lift my pants, fish out the phone buried beneath a layer of clothes. The message glows on the screen, stark and final:

> UNKNOWN: Landing in 1 hour. It happens tonight.

That's it. No signature, no trace. The moment I darken the screen, it'll erase itself. I slide it back, take a long breath, let it settle in my chest before I roll over to face her.

She's fucking gorgeous like this—face relaxed, freckles dark as cocoa against her skin. Her hair, usually big and wild and taking up all the space it wants, is flattened, and mussed from sleep, making her look softer, almost innocent. The sheet's slipped down, baring her back, the sweet curve of her waist. My gaze drifts lower—her breasts, the rise and fall with every breath, nipples dark and peaked, begging for my mouth.

My hand skims down her body, slow—along her waist, over her hip, tracing the line of her thigh. It's torture, having her here. Wanting her this bad. Knowing every touch is a lie, every soft moment a crack in the armor that's supposed to keep us both alive.

I wish it didn't have to be this way. Wish I didn't have to lie to her. But I do. She knows it, even if she hasn't put all the pieces together yet. That's probably the only reason I'm still breathing—because not knowing is killing her just as much as the truth would.

Still, I can't help the way my cock aches for her, the way my body wants her all over again. I tell myself I'm only going to wake her. That anything more is just begging for trouble —one of us will end up dead, and the odds are on me.

But hell if I can make myself care, not when she's this close. When I can still smell the taste of her on me.

I slide down her body, mouth pressed to her hip, letting my lips linger there. She makes a small sound, still deep in sleep, but it sends a jolt through me. Another kiss, closer to where I want to bury myself, and she shifts, just enough that it feels like invitation.

I press a kiss to the soft mound above her pussy, then lower, breathing her in. She smells like sweat and sex and Saint—undeniable, addictive. My hand glides down her thigh, finds her knee, and gently pulls, lifting her leg to rest on my shoulder. She's on her side, pliant in sleep, and I nestle in, taking my time. My tongue parts her, slow and savoring, tasting her, feeling her moan vibrate right through me. We're both needy, both starving, but I want to draw this out.

I work her with my mouth, steady, letting her stay wherever her dreams have taken her while I worship her body. I listen for the subtle change in her breathing, the way her hips start to rock, the small gasps as she melts under my tongue. She opens for me, wetter with every flick, her dream bleeding into something hotter, her moans coming quicker, hips pushing up to meet my mouth.

I want her to stay lost in that peace as long as she can, but I feel her starting to twitch, her thigh tensing around my head as I focus on her clit. My tongue moves faster, lips sealing around her, sucking gently. She's waking now, hips moving, hand tangling in my hair, pulling me closer, grinding her pussy into my mouth.

Her voice is wrecked, groggy and wild—

"Oh, Alejandro," she groans, her fingers tightening, nails biting into my scalp. "Fuck—my god—"

She's fucking my face, breath breaking into ragged, muffled noises as she tries to stifle herself in the pillow.

"Oh my god, Alejandro—fuck, just like that—just like that—" Her hips buck, thighs shaking around my head.

I don't let up, licking her through every pulse of her orgasm, refusing to stop even when she cries out, voice breaking, trying to shove me off, thighs trembling around my head.

Only then do I let her go. I push myself up, hands strong on her hips, turning her over onto her stomach. I want more —need more—of her, even if it destroys me.

I straddle her, my knees planted on either side of her thighs. She keeps her legs together—defiant, even now, making me work for every inch as I slide into her. She's still pulsing, slick and hot from the orgasm I just gave her. I fuck her slow at first, feeling her shudder around me, then pick up the pace, chasing my own edge. She's quiet, stubborn, her face turned away from me. I know she's not going to come like this. I want more from her—need her mouth, her eyes, her surrender when I break.

"Turn over," I murmur, voice thick. She does—mouth parted, face flushed, eyes wild with the afterglow. I hook her leg into the crook of my elbow, drive into her deep, my lips crashing into hers, swallowing her gasp.

I fuck her hard, steady, letting her ride the high. Forehead to forehead, I watch her—won't let her look away. "Eyes on me," I whisper. "Don't look away. Not now."

She holds my gaze as her pleasure builds, body tensing beneath me, the line between us burning bright and raw. I want her to see it—all the things I can't say. That I didn't want this, didn't choose it, but it's what we have now. It's all there is.

She comes, eyes locked with mine, and I let myself fall with her, hips stuttering, spilling into her as I press our foreheads together, never breaking the connection. For a moment, I almost believe in something softer—almost believe it's enough.

But I see it—the exact second she shuts herself off. The fire in her eyes snuffs out, replaced by cold calculation. Her hands, which a moment ago were clinging to my shoulders, go flat and hard, pushing at my chest.

I slide out of her, breathless and aching. She rolls away, stands up, and pulls on yesterday's panties and tank top without meeting my eyes.

"I'm going to find some fresh clothes before we land," she says, her voice steady, already halfway gone.

The luggage turns into our department store. Saint rifles

through a high-roller's roller bag, tossing me a disgusted look at a stack of monogrammed boxers, while I dig through garment bags for anything passably discreet. Its Saint who finds the motherlode—a cabinet packed with flight crew uniforms, pressed and ready, the airline's signature red hats and white scarves lined up like soldiers.

We both pause, catch each other's eye, and don't need to say a word. This is our ticket off the plane, and if we're lucky, through the airport without turning it into another Die Hard set.

She claims the bathroom first, carrying a stewardess uniform over her arm and her backpack at her hip. I hear the water start. I strip down, shower quick and brutal in the second stall—no time to linger. She finger-coils her hair in the mirror and I suit up in the captain's getup. Epaulettes. Gold stripes. Feels ridiculous, but if it gets us out, I'll wear a clown suit.

Saint emerges with her hair freshly twisted, the hat perched at a confident tilt, lips painted a vivid, fuck-you red. I look away, focusing on my gun case. The urge to see that lipstick smeared on my cock is not helpful right now.

She packs two water bottles, a few snacks, and her boots into her bag. Everything else gets left behind. We feel the plane drop lower, the pitch and whine of engines changing, the faint sense of pressure in our ears as we begin to descend.

We brace ourselves at the rails near the stairs—bags on our backs, knees flexed. Landing is a hell of a lot rougher when you're not buckled in like a good passenger, but we manage, knuckles white on steel, adrenaline settling in cold and steady.

I lean against the railing, arms crossed, eyes on the hatch

as the plane taxis to its terminal. Patience has never been Saint's strong suit, but right now, it's our only choice. She walks up the steps, pauses, listening. Looks at me—something in her eyes, sharp and alert. I join her, quiet.

The voices beyond the hatch are speaking French. I catch fragments—my French is serviceable, but not perfect.

She turns to me, voice pitched low. "They've been warned. Authorities are waiting at the gate for two passengers."

My stomach drops. She slides her bag off, sets it between her feet.

She continues, voice calm, "The captain told them the crew needs to transfer to another flight immediately after landing."

I breathe a little easier.

She nods toward the door. "Crew will exit through the rear. Every passenger's being id'ed before they can deplane."

I nod, grateful for the uniform, the hat, the cover. For once, being wrapped in polyester feels like a stroke of luck.

I make a last-minute rummage through the bags and snag two pair of aviator sunglasses.

Saint kneels, works her multitool to quietly unjam the maintenance hatch we rigged. We hear the main cabin doors open—voices, footsteps, the hush of orderly crew filing out.

She cracks the door, watches. Then, with a small gesture, she motions me forward, hand wrapped around her backpack's handle.

Time to go.

She opens the door like she owns the place, stride unhurried. I fall in behind her, matching her energy and sliding the glasses onto my face. We join the end of the crew, blending in behind a flight attendant with a pixie cut and the runway walk of a model.

The Emirates staff at the rear door—suits and official clipboards—nod at each crew member as they pass. Saint and I nod back, eyes forward, following the line through a separate gate and straight into the freedom of the Dubai airport.

I nudge her with the sunglasses, and she puts them. Eyes forward and shoulders back as looks like any other steward.

For now, at least, we've pulled off the impossible again. But if I know Saint, she's already plotting three moves ahead —and so am I.

Tonight is the night two years in exile have been leading toward.

Whatever happens next, there's no turning back.

37
Saint

Airports are built to dissolve people.

Too much glass, too many reflective surfaces, too many signs pointing in slightly different directions so that no one ever feels fully certain they're going the right way. Everyone moves fast while accomplishing very little, dragging roller bags and clutching coffee cups like talismans against panic. It's chaos disguised as order, and it works because no one wants to admit how lost they are.

Which makes it an excellent place to disappear.

As long as you're not wearing the uniform of an airline employee who just hijacked a plane.

"We need to change," Alejandro declares, already shepherding me toward a clothing store with his change in course.

"No shit," I mutter, eyes sweeping the open floor like I expect armed security to rappel through the skylight.

Everything is neutral and polished, racks arranged with military precision, lighting engineered to make you forget what time zone you're in. The red of my steward uniform looks obscene against it, loud and unmistakable. His captain's jacket is no better.

We may as well be wearing warning flares.

I don't bother being selective. Black jeans, a white tank, clean socks. Clothes meant to be forgettable. I scoop them into my arms and duck into a dressing room, kicking the door shut behind me before Alejandro even chooses between which fit of jeans he's going with.

My backpack hits the bench and the laptop comes out first.

I flip it open, connect to the store's network, and watch the indicators roll green. No lag. No interference. No digital hands reaching for me yet. My pulse doesn't slow anyway.

I text Grim.

> SAINT: It's on. We're moving.

Send.

The uniform comes off fast, practiced, rolled up and tossed in the corner. The heels are kicked off next. The mirror reflects a version of me that looks wrong without the hat, hair finger-coiled into place, lipstick still perfect like I didn't just help nearly turn an international flight into a crime scene.

I've got to get rid of that. Taking the uniform again, I wipe the lipstick off like it's offended me.

My phone stays stubbornly silent.

I pull the jeans on, tug the shirt over my head. My boots wait by the door. I glance at the phone again.

Nothing.

Alejandro finishes before I do. I hear his steps stop just outside the dressing room.

"Saint," he says quietly. "You good?"

"Almost."

I text Grim again.

> SAINT: Inside the terminal. Need to move.

Still nothing.

I run a quick network check again, more out of superstition than necessity. Everything remains clean, which somehow makes my skin crawl more. Silence is never neutral.

"You need help with your fucking zipper or something?" Alejandro asks. "Because we *really* should go."

"I'm fixing my hair."

"That is not a priority."

I yank open the door, hiding my body behind it like I'm still dressing. "The last man that fucked with my hair is dead. You wanna be next?" I shut the door before he can answer. All I get from the other side is a frustrated huff.

I stare at the laptop, my reflection ghosted in the dark screen, warped by the dim light of the dressing room. It has been useful. More than that. It's been my advantage, the thing that let me stay three steps ahead while everyone else chased shadows.

But Grim isn't answering.

That's the problem.

He should have answered by now. Even a single word. Even a curse. Silence from Grim is never neutral. It means he's busy, compromised, or cutting a line on purpose, and none of those options end well for the person still holding the data.

If this machine falls into the wrong hands, it won't just tell them what we know. It'll tell them who to burn.

And Alejandro won't wait forever out there.

I can already feel the clock tightening, the thin thread of patience he's holding snapping closer to the end. He'll come in if I take too long. He'll push. He'll force movement. And once that happens, this stops being my decision.

I glance at the flip phone on the bench, willing it to light up, to vibrate, to give me anything at all. A single message would be enough. One word to justify keeping this alive.

Still, nothing.

Fine.

I look back at the laptop. This thing has become a liability, not because it exists, but because I'm the only one still listening to it. Too traceable. Too valuable.

The decision lands clean and hard.

I wipe it.

Factory reset. Full overwrite. No shortcuts.

The progress bar appears, creeping forward like it has all the time in the world.

I send one more message to Grim.

SAINT: Wiping now. Leaving immediately.

The bar crawls past twenty percent, then thirty. I pull my boots on while it works, fingers moving faster than the machine ever will to fluff my hair out. Make it look like I've actually been doing something in here.

A knock hits the door. Sharp.

"Saint."

"Boots," I call back evenly. "One second."

Sixty percent.

Seventy.

Every nerve in my body hums. This is the danger zone, the space between action and consequence where everything can still go wrong.

"Fuck, Saint." Another knock, harder this time. "We need to leave."

"I know."

Ninety percent.

Ninety-five.

The bar stalls at ninety-nine.

Son of a goddamn bitch. Of course it does.

I stare at the sliver of empty space like I can will it to fill. One second passes. Then another. The laptop fan kicks up, whining in protest and I'm afraid he'll hear it.

"Saint," Alejandro says, his voice tight now.

"Almost."

"If you don't come out in five seconds, I'm coming in."

Four.

Three.

Two.

The progress bar completes.

I snap the laptop shut, yank the battery free, and shove both under the red pile of the stolen uniform. I straighten and pull my backpack on.

"Hold your fucking horses," I say, steady as stone, ripping the door open before Alejandro knocks again. I'm holding an armful of red fabric, bundled tight against my chest.

"Hold this," I say, shoving my bag into his hands. "I need to toss these."

He takes it automatically, eyes flicking down the corridor. "Make it fast."

I move to the trash can near the registers and dump the uniform. The laptop follows, wrapped but still making a heavier sound than fabric should when it hits plastic.

My shoulders tense.

Alejandro doesn't notice. He's too busy watching the exits.

"I need my jacket," I say, battery hidden behind my forearm.

I pull it from the bag, shrug into the leather, making sure the battery is concealed up my sleeve, cold and solid against my skin. We step out together, unhurried, blending into the current of travelers flowing past.

A few yards later, I shift the battery down into my pocket.

A guard stands in the middle of a cross-section, boots planted wide, eyes scanning. They land on me and linger.

One beat too long for me to be comfortable with.

I don't react. I don't rush. I don't look away quickly. Instead, I let my eyes lazily move to another face, like I'm people-watching during my trek through the airport.

Boots pound in front of us.

A squad of guards runs toward us, focused and fast. My shoulder tense and I hold my grip around the battery tighter. My hold on my backpack strap also tightening. But they rush past, not sparing us a glance.

Alejandro exhales through his nose. "Well, that'll wake you up in the morning."

But we may not be out of the clear yet. Not if someone reported a mysterious laptop thrown in a trashcan.

I glance back. The guards sprint past the store, past the trash, past my discarded problems. For now.

It takes a train and several moving sidewalks to reach baggage claim and the exits.

A surge of travelers' floods around us, rolling bags clipping ankles, shoulders bumping. Someone slams a suitcase into my heel and curses.

I use the moment.

"Watch it." The battery slips from my pocket into the nearest trash can, swallowed by paper cups and boarding passes.

Alejandro misses it, too busy glaring after the man who clipped his shoulder. "Asshole." He gives one more glare before putting his shades on as we walk through double sliding doors.

Outside, the air feels sharper, cleaner, like freedom pretending it doesn't have strings attached.

Alejandro scans the parking structure. "That one."

A dark sedan. Mid-size. Invisible.

I'm at the driver's door before he finishes speaking, multitool already out. The lock pops, and I'm at the steering wheel while Alejandro stands behind, blocking any passersby.

The engine turns over smoothly.

Alejandro pulls up a map on his phone. "I'll drive."

He slides into the driver's seat without asking and pulls his phone up on the console. The map is already open. A route already drawn.

I don't remember him entering a destination.

"Where are we going?" I ask.

He doesn't look at me. "Where Hartley will be."

I squint at the screen, then at him. "That's not the summit."

"It's the Atlas Complex," he says, glancing at his watch like the timing matters. "Keynote speakers have a brunch with contributors. He'll be there."

Something in my chest tightens.

"That wouldn't be public."

"The brunch was," he says easily, like he's been waiting for the question. "It was advertised. We're coming up on the window now."

He says it smoothly. Too smoothly.

Logical, on the surface. Public-facing event. Scheduled appearance. Reasonable assumption that Hartley would attend. It fits. It almost convinces me.

Almost.

Because the way he explains it carries more detail than people usually volunteer, especially when that detail involves where powerful men eat breakfast. Locations don't get broadcast. Attendee lists don't get confirmed. Not for safety. Not for men like Hartley.

I catalog it quietly and let my face go neutral.

"Fine," I say, opening the passenger door and getting in. "Let's go."

The engine turns over, and we pull into traffic.

I don't press him.

Not yet.

We pull away cleanly, merging into traffic like we belong there.

At the red light, my flip phone vibrates.

I pull it out low, hidden by my jacket, and read the single message.

GRIM: Got it.

I finally let myself breathe.

38

Alejandro

W e abandon the car four blocks out, which is close enough to matter and far enough to pretend it doesn't. Anything nearer would put us in range of cameras meant to catch plates, not people. The Atlas Building rises ahead of us, all glass and authority, the kind of place that pretends transparency while hiding everything that matters. We're still walking when we pass the back entrance, and that's when the plan finalizes itself.

Staff are arriving in plain clothes, jackets slung over shoulders, coffee cups in hand. A service door stands propped open with a five-gallon bucket, metal scuffed and dented, doing more work than any security checkpoint ever will. A few people linger off to the side, half-hidden by the building's shadow, cigarettes burning down between fingers as they kill the last minutes before clock-in.

No badges. No scrutiny. Just routine.

Saint slows half a step. I glance at her, and she glances back. Nothing passes between us that anyone else would recognize as communication, but the agreement lands cleanly.

That's the way in.

We pivot without breaking stride, turning toward the open door like it was always the destination. No hesitation.

No adjustment. We walk in the way people do when they belong somewhere, when they've done it a thousand times before and expect to do it a thousand more.

No one looks up.

No one asks a question.

We follow the sound of lockers slamming shut, metal on metal, the rhythm of people arriving for work. It leads us down a narrower corridor where the air smells faintly of detergent and stale coffee, to a window cut into the wall with UNIFORMS stenciled above it in peeling letters.

A small line has already formed.

The people ahead of us are familiar to the teller. Not friends, exactly, but known. One leans in with a half-smile and a comment about the shift. Another complains about the air conditioning like it's a shared joke. Names aren't exchanged, but recognition is enough. The teller slides folded fabric across the counter without breaking conversation.

The person directly in front of us hesitates. Too long. Gives their size, voice careful. The teller doesn't comment, doesn't smile. Just reaches back and pulls a bundle from the shelf.

New, then. Or at least not liked enough to be remembered.

When it's our turn, the teller's eyes lift to us, waiting. Expectant. Not suspicious. Just ready to be told what to do.

Saint doesn't pause. "Medium."

I follow immediately. "Large."

The words land like credentials.

The teller looks me up and down before turning away.

Fabric appears on the counter, still warm from being stacked.

"They run a little small, baby." She says to me, chewing a piece of gum that will likely be in her mouth all day.

Neutral jackets. Service shirts. Nothing with a name on it. Nothing that asks questions.

No ID or badge. No confirmation beyond the assumption that we wouldn't be standing there if we didn't belong.

I take note of it all.

The way systems rely on familiarity instead of verification. The way momentum replaces scrutiny. The way belonging is often just a matter of speaking first. It's the exact level of relaxation that will be scrutinized once an assassination takes place today.

"No one ever looks at staff," I murmur.

Saint doesn't look at me. "Not even the staff."

The locker room is crowded and loud, the kind of place where privacy is a suggestion at best. We don't even consider the open benches. Weapons change the rules.

We split without comment, each taking a stall.

Fabric rustles. Boots scuff tile. I change fast, movements economical, aware of every sound on the other side of the thin divider. When I step back out, Saint is still inside. I wait, eyes on the door, on the exits, on the people who aren't paying us any attention at all.

She emerges a moment later and crosses to a locker, opening it just wide enough to slide her backpack inside. She pushes it to the back, shuts the door, and spins the dial without flourish.

Then her gaze drops to the long black case in my hand.

She arches a brow. "You planning to balance that while passing caviar?"

I glance at the locker, then at the case. It doesn't even pretend to belong.

"I'll stash it," I say.

We move out together, falling into step as the corridor opens up and the noise thins. The plan surfaces naturally, the way it always does when there's motion to anchor it.

"I want eyes first," I say. "We observe. See who circles Hartley. Who's close without a reason. We don't move until something moves."

Saint is watching the flow of people, the way staff peel off toward kitchens and bars, the way security clusters without looking like clusters.

We pass an AV overflow room halfway down the hall, the door cracked open just enough to reveal stacked flight cases, coils of cable, a folding table pushed against the wall. Controlled chaos. Temporary. Unattended.

I slow without stopping. "Keep an eye out."

She does, automatically, scanning the corridor as I slip inside. The case disappears into the stack with everything else that no one wants to inventory. Black on black. Identical. Invisible.

When I step back out, she's already turned back toward me.

"This is wrong," she says. "We should warn him."

"No," I reply. "We don't tip the board unless we have to."

"If we force movement, the assassin adjusts," she counters. "That's when they make mistakes."

"Or they abort," I say. "Or they accelerate."

She stops walking. Just long enough to make the pause feel intentional. "Reaction reveals truth."

"Patience keeps people alive."

We're circling it now, the same argument dressed in different clothes. Saint believes pressure exposes shape. I believe stillness does. Neither of us is wrong. That's the problem.

She opens her mouth to respond—

—and then a cluster of staff in identical uniforms rounds the corner, moving fast and loose, talking quietly to one another. Trailing behind them is a short, plump woman with a clipboard and a permanent scowl, irritation radiating off her like heat.

She snaps her fingers. "You two. With the group."

We hesitate half a second too long.

She stops walking and fixes us with a look that suggests she has ended careers for less. "I said *move*. You're clocked in then you're working. Not standing out here. Go."

Saint falls into step without hesitation but she does give the woman a glare.

I don't doubt for a second that if she weren't currently prioritizing international stability, she would snap this woman in half and keep walking.

The woman follows for several paces, close enough to make sure we don't peel off, her presence a physical barrier to conversation.

The argument of our plan dies unfinished.

We're funneled through the kitchen doors into controlled chaos. Heat. Steam. The sharp clatter of trays. Someone presses a silver tray into my hands without looking at my face.

A chilled bottle of champagne is thrust into Saint's grip, condensation slick against glass.

"Careful," someone mutters. "Don't drop that."

We're pushed forward again, momentum doing the work of command. The manager's voice cuts through the noise as she strides past.

"Keynotes are arriving any minute. Eyes up. Smile. Keep moving."

The line of staff surges forward, carrying us with it.

Ahead, the banquet room opens like a stage.

And whatever plan we had is about to be tested by proximity.

Out on the floor, the brunch is already in motion. Linen-draped tables, polished silverware, soft music meant to suggest refinement without demanding attention. The kind of event designed to look harmless, like power doesn't eat croissants and drink mimosas.

Hartley arrives five minutes later.

He's smaller than he looks on screens, but tighter somehow, compressed into himself by the weight of expectation. His security detail is compact and disciplined, close enough to react without looking like a wall. I clock spacing first, then exits, then lines of sight. My brain runs the familiar calculations automatically.

My eyes do what they always do, sliding past faces and table settings to map the room the way a scope would. I mark distances without thinking, note elevations, sight lines, dead zones. It's muscle memory, not strategy.

There are no clean angles.

No balconies with uninterrupted views. No high ground that wouldn't immediately flag movement. The windows are decorative more than functional, glass broken up by structural beams that kill long shots before they start. Any elevated position here would be exposed, noisy, and slow.

A sniper would hate this room.

Close-range work is possible, technically. A blade in the crush of bodies. A syringe in a handshake. But that kind of kill sends a different message. Messy. Intimate. Improvised.

This won't be that.

Whoever is staging this kill this didn't intend subtlety or chaos.

Saint moves efficiently, distributing drinks, eyes always tracking Hartley's orbit. I can feel her impatience like static. When she speaks again, it's barely audible.

Saint drifts closer as we work, voice low enough to pass for idle commentary. "What do you think?" she asks. "If it were here, how would they do it?"

My attention doesn't leave the room. "It won't be today," I say. Then, because my mouth is ahead of my judgment, I finish it. "It'll be tonight."

The word lands wrong. I feel it as soon as it's out.

Saint goes still. Not frozen. Not startled. Just suddenly precise. She turns her head toward me, eyes sharp now, fully engaged.

"How do you know that?"

I release a sigh and my exasperation with it. "My broker... my sister texted earlier. Said it's definitely tonight."

"And you conveniently forgot to mention this," she says, tone flat.

"I was distracted," I say. Which is true. "A lot was happening."

The explanation sounds thinner the longer it sits in the air. Her expression doesn't harden. It sharpens.

Assessment, not anger.

I recognize the look immediately, and a cold weight settles in my chest. She doesn't believe me. Or rather, she believes the information but not the omission. Trust doesn't fracture loudly. It goes quiet. And hers is already gone for me.

I tell myself I'll explain later. That this isn't the place. That timing matters.

Saint hasn't taken her eyes off Hartley for a full minute. "I'm warning him anyway."

"No," I say. "Wait."

But she doesn't. She makes her way over. Not too fast but fast enough I can't rush over and stop her without drawing every eye in this room to me.

She adjusts her grip on the bottle she's holding, angling her body just enough to bring Hartley into reach. The choice is written in the tension of her shoulders, the way her weight shifts forward.

I know she's committing.

I should stop her.

I don't.

39

Saint

Fuck Alejandro and his selective honesty.

Fuck the pauses, the omissions, the way he talks like he's thinking three moves ahead while refusing to tell me which board we're playing on. I'm done letting him meter information like it's his to ration. Whatever happens after this brunch, I'm telling him to fuck off and meaning it.

I move with the line of staff, tray balanced, champagne bottle cold and sweating against my palm. My eyes never leave Hartley.

He's holding a flute. Still mostly full. He keeps lifting it, taking small distracted sips, the way men do when they're listening just enough to seem polite while scanning for their next conversation. He's relaxed. Comfortable. Untouched by the idea that someone, somewhere, has decided he's a message.

That flute is my opening.

I adjust my pace, angling toward him, already calculating the distance, the timing, the exact phrasing. Not a warning. Not a speech. Just enough to force movement. Enough to break pattern.

Someone steps directly into my path.

Another server. Too close. Too slow. I shift around them without a word, but the half-second costs me. A woman to my left catches my eye, lifts her empty glass with a hopeful tilt.

I stop.

I pour.

The champagne foams up obediently, bubbles racing to the surface like they have somewhere better to be. I keep my face neutral, my irritation buried deep and sharp. This is the job. This is the disguise. I finish the pour, nod once, and move on.

Hartley is alone now.

Not fully. Never fully. But the ring around him has loosened just enough. He takes another sip, glancing over the room like he's shopping for attention.

Now.

I step into his space, bottle angled over his glass, posture perfect.

"Mr. Hartley," I say quietly.

He looks at me, eyes flicking from the bottle to my face. He nods, already smiling, the kind of smile that assumes admiration is about to follow.

It doesn't.

The sound comes from my right. A sharp, violent clatter that doesn't belong in a room like this.

Glass shatters.

Someone shouts.

Security moves before the echo finishes bouncing off the walls. Hartley is yanked backward, his glass forgotten, his body shielded as men close ranks around him. The bubble compresses and hardens, impenetrable in less than a second.

My moment is gone.

I pivot instinctively, scanning for the source, and my stomach drops.

Alejandro is on the floor.

His tray lying half a foot away like it's been flung aside. Champagne and orange juice spread across the carpet in a bright, obscene spill. Another server stands frozen nearby, her tray of fresh mimosas tipped, two glasses shattered at her feet.

Alejandro looks up at me.

For a heartbeat, I can't read his expression.

Pain, maybe. Surprise. Or something else entirely. Something that looks uncomfortably like satisfaction. Like the quiet relief of someone who has successfully stopped something without having to say why.

Then it's gone, smoothed away behind his usual control.

Staff flood the space instantly, apologies already tumbling out of mouths that weren't involved. Someone kneels to help him up. Someone else is already blotting the carpet like this is a wine spill at a wedding and not a perfectly timed intervention.

I don't move.

I don't look at Hartley being hustled away.

I look at Alejandro.

This wasn't clumsy. It wasn't random. The timing is too perfect, the chaos too contained. He didn't just fall. He fell *there*. *Then*. Right as I was about to speak.

He didn't need to touch me to stop me.

That's the part that makes my blood go cold.

The manager barrels in, clipboard in hand, face tight with performative calm. Her voice cuts through the murmurs like a knife through silk.

"Apologies, ladies and gentlemen. Please," she says brightly, already gesturing toward the double doors at the far end of the room. They're opening wide, staff guiding guests with practiced efficiency. "Let's move into the brunch hall. You all look very hungry."

Laughter ripples, thin and polite.

The room obeys.

Hartley disappears through the doors, surrounded and protected, exactly where I didn't want him to go. Someone just got a clean read on response time and crowd control. And Alejandro made sure of it.

Staff usher me toward the kitchen with the rest, momentum doing the work of force. I let it carry me because resisting would only draw attention, and attention is a luxury I can't afford right now.

As I pass Alejandro, helping mop up the mess he created, he looks up at me.

His expression isn't pain or regret. It's calculation.

And in that instant, the question answers itself.

He didn't just stop me.

He's involved.

They don't ask.

Security doesn't argue. Management doesn't debate. I'm redirected with firm hands and polite urgency, steered away from linen and champagne and money like I'm a stain that needs to be scrubbed out before it sets.

"Back of house," someone says. "Please."

I let them push me.

The double doors swing shut behind me, cutting off the noise of the brunch, the clink of glass, the low murmur of powerful men pretending they aren't edible. The hallway is narrower here, colder, all concrete and stainless steel and utility lighting that doesn't flatter anyone.

My pulse is still ticking to the rhythm of breaking glass.

The sound replays on a loop. The timing. The precision. The way Alejandro just looked at me when it happened.

The flip phone buzzes in my pocket once. I pull it out without stopping, screen shielded against my palm.

GRIM: Deleted files incoming.

Of course it's now.

I close the phone and scan the corridor, already anticipating Alejandro's footsteps behind me. The inevitable attempt at damage control. The calm voice. The reasonable explanation designed to slow me down just enough for him to get ahead of me again.

Well, I'm not giving him the chance. I need to see what this is before anyone can shape the narrative around it.

The walk-in is in the middle of the kitchen's side wall, marked with a fading label and a dented handle. I grab it, slip inside, and pull the door shut behind me.

The cold hits instantly. Sharp and clean and absolute.

Metal shelves line the walls, stacked with produce, seafood, wrapped trays of things that once lived. The hum of the refrigeration unit is constant, steady, indifferent. The kind of sound that makes it easy to think.

I text Grim back with numb fingers.

SAINT: Send them.

The files load slowly, bars creeping across the screen like they're enjoying this.

Two images appear.

Both black and white.

Both grainy. Low resolution. They're security footage, not photographs. The kind of images that are never meant for anything except evidence or blackmail.

The first one settles into focus.

Alejandro.

He's in the left corner of the frame, half-captured, as if the camera wasn't meant to see him at all. The angle is wrong, tilted slightly, cutting off his face at the edge. You can see his posture, though. The line of his shoulders. The familiar way he stands when he thinks no one is watching.

The rest of the image is useless. Ornate carpet. Patterned. Expensive. In the opposite corner, the tip of another man's shoe intrudes into frame. Polished. Dark. That's it.

No faces. No context. Just placement.

The second image loads.

It's worse.

Another black-and-white still, higher angle this time. Rooftop security, judging by the perspective. Someone is climbing into a helicopter. You can see a bent knee. White pants. A dress shoe. The curved edge of the helicopter door. On a nearby handrail in the foreground is a hand. Someone else coming down to the helicopter maybe.

No faces.

No location markers.

Nothing that should matter.

I stare at the screen until my eyes start to ache.

Why these?

Why were *these* worth deleting?

They prove nothing. They don't even tell a story. Anyone could look at them and shrug.

I zoom in. Out. Tilt the phone. Study shadow and grain like meaning might bleed out if I stare hard enough. I commit the images to memory, every useless detail, every absence.

Then I text Grim again.

> SAINT: Anything else with these? Dates. Locations. Anything.

The response comes back fast this time.

> GRIM: First image: September 7, 2023.

> GRIM: Second: six months ago.

September 7.

Two years ago.

The night of the poisoning.

The night Alejandro became an exile.

The cold seems to sink deeper, pressing into my bones.

I exhale slowly, controlled, and look back at the first image. At the way he's positioned. At the fact that he's the only clearly identifiable person in the frame. The only one whose presence can't be explained away as coincidence.

My frustration tightens into something sharper.

Why delete these?

Why risk exposure? Why scrub files that don't incriminate, don't threaten, don't even clarify?

Unless the value isn't in what they show.

Unless the value is in *when* they were taken.

Alejandro is the anchor in the one photo and I still don't know what they mean yet.

I only know they mattered enough for him to erase.

That's not paranoia. That's priority.

I close the phone and slide it back into my pocket, the cold air biting at my skin. The hum of the cooler fills the silence, steady and unjudging.

I'm done waiting for explanations.

If Alejandro won't tell me the truth, I'll force it out of him myself.

And this time, I won't give him the chance to step in my way.

Alejandro

I send the text while walking as I drop the marble I picked up off the floor into my pocket.

> ALEJANDRO: Saint's in the wind.

The reply comes almost immediately.

> UNKNOWN: Not an option.

> UNKNOWN: Find her.

My jaw tightens. Of course there's no space for uncertainty, no room for complications. The plan doesn't bend because someone has feelings about it. It doesn't slow because Saint decided to think for herself.

Tonight is happening. No matter who resists it. No matter who tries to stop it.

And I need Saint next to me when it does.

There can be no other outcome than that.

> ALEJANDRO: I'll find her.

The AV overflow room is exactly where I left it. I pause at the corner, scan the corridor, let a pair of catering staff pass before slipping inside. The door swings shut quietly behind me.

The rifle case sits where it should, buried among identical black shells and tangled cables. I take a second longer than necessary to look at it, the weight of the choice settling in my chest.

Then I sling it over my shoulder and move.

If Saint's gone quiet, it's because she found something. Which means she's already moving. Saint never freezes. She pivots.

She's either half gone or already on her way to me.

The locker room is empty when I reach it but I check anyway, habit overriding trust.

I strip out of the service uniform in seconds. Jacket off. Shirt gone. Shoes kicked aside. I move with the speed of someone who has done this under worse conditions, with higher stakes. The rifle settles against my back like it belongs there, like it's been waiting.

I cross to Saint's locker.

The metal is cold under my fingers. The lock is still set. I test it once before I try a code that would have worked two years ago.

Nothing.

I exhale slowly and take out my blade. Stepping into the locker, using my body to hide the weapon, I slide the knife into the thin strip and pop the latch. The door swings open.

Just as my hand wraps around the handle and I pull it free, a shadow shifts behind me.

"Well, well," Saint says, voice smooth and sharp all at once. "If it isn't Alejandro Cruz."

I straighten slowly and turn.

She's leaning against the row of lockers, posture relaxed, eyes bright with a kind of focus I don't like seeing aimed at me. She looks calm. Too calm. Like the decision already landed and this is just the follow-through.

"Running away so soon?" she adds.

I don't answer.

Because there's no version of the truth she'd accept right now.

And because she already knows.

"Care to explain that little stunt back there?" Saint asks.

Her voice is level, almost casual, which tells me more than if she were shouting. She isn't looking for reassurance. She's measuring me.

I take a step back, then another, creating space without appearing to flee. As I do, I adjust my grip on her backpack, which feels a hundred pounds heavier than it should. The weight isn't physical. It's accusation.

"Someone bumped me," I say.

The lie barely survives the air between us.

Saint's mouth curves, slow and sharp, sarcasm bleeding into every syllable. "Oh, I bet."

She studies me for a moment, then exhales softly. "You know, I'm disappointed."

That lands harder than anger would have.

She steps away from the locker, arms loose at her sides, and that's when I notice the flip phone in her hand. Small. Ugly. Unremarkable.

Thank God it isn't a weapon.

"I thought you'd come better prepared," she continues. "Something cleaner. Like the real assassin setting off a chain reaction to keep me from warning Hartley." Her gaze flicks over me, unimpressed. "But someone bumped you. Okay."

She opens the phone, glances at the screen, and tosses it toward me.

"I'm more interested in these."

I catch it automatically. The images are already pulled up, grainy and monochrome and far too familiar.

My jaw tightens before I can stop it.

I tilt my head once. "Not sure."

I close the phone and hand it back.

She doesn't take it immediately. "You sure about that?" she asks. "That's your final answer?"

Her eyes sharpen, focus narrowing. "Because I'm giving you a chance here. After this, there aren't any more."

I hold her gaze. "Wish I could help."

She nods slowly. "I'm sorry to hear that."

The gun appears so smoothly it's almost graceful, drawn from behind her back and leveled at my chest in a single, controlled motion. Her arm is steady. Her grip flawless.

"I told you," she says quietly, "if you crossed me, this is what would happen."

I don't move. Any reaction would be read as weakness or guilt, and neither will help me now.

The flip phone rings.

Saint doesn't break eye contact as she answers and switches it to speaker. "You find it, Grim?"

"Yup," Grim replies. "Ready when you are."

I knew this was going badly. I hadn't realized how thoroughly I'd lost control of it.

"See?" Saint says, conversational now, almost gentle. "Grim was looking out for me. Didn't trust you, Alejandro."

She steps closer, the gun never wavering. "Kid's got good instincts."

She's taking her time. Letting the truth settle in layers.

I notice, distantly, that there's no suppressor on her weapon. In a locker room. In a building crawling with high-ranking officials.

The odds she fires here are low.

Which means I might still have a chance.

"Grim hacked your phone while we were at his house," Saint says.

My mind flashes back to that moment. Eight seconds. That's all he needed at the keyboard. Eight fucking seconds.

It almost makes me angry.

Almost.

If I weren't already thinking about my sister. About my family. About how exposed they are if this goes the wrong way.

"Play it, Grim," Saint says.

The recording starts, and I close my eyes before the first line finishes.

A woman's voice, calm and curious. "You deleted them?"

My voice answers, steady and unmistakable. "Yes."

Then the line that ends any remaining pretense.

"They're the only photographs that exist of the Guildmaster."

Saint tilts her head, studying me like a puzzle she's already solved.

"You're the only visible man in those photos," she says. "Aren't you, Alejandro?"

I say nothing.

"You deleted the evidence," she continues. "You controlled the narrative."

She isn't accusing me. She's stating fact.

Time compresses, options narrowing until there are only two left.

If I stay, she will shoot me.

If I run, I confirm everything she already believes.

The look in her eyes isn't anger or betrayal. It's judgment.

"You're the Guildmaster," she says.

She gestures wide with one arm, encompassing the lockers, the building, the entire situation, while the other remains trained on me. "All of this..."

Voices rise behind her. Too close. Too sudden.

Three women enter the locker room mid-conversation, and Saint pivots instinctively, hiding the gun.

It's the only opening I'll get.

I move.

I throw her backpack at her face and bolt.

I shoulder past the women hard enough to knock two of them off balance. They stumble into each other, blocking the doorway just long enough.

Seconds. A few precious seconds. That's all I need.

I break into the corridor, the rifle bouncing against my back as I run, my pulse loud in my ears.

For now, I'm out of Saint's crosshairs.

But one thought follows me with absolute certainty as I disappear into the maze of back halls.

Tonight, will change everything.

Saint

Night settles over the city like a held breath.

From up here, the summit looks less like an event and more like a ritual. Light spills outward in careful patterns. Music drifts up in soft, engineered waves. Below me, officials and press and world leaders gather in the desert to congratulate themselves on building the tallest thing yet, this one wrapped in the language of salvation. Clean. Renewable. A monument to the future, polished until it shines.

And I am above all of it, watching.

The ledge is wide, mercifully so. More than enough room for me to lie prone if I need to. Behind me, floor-to-ceiling windows reflect the last burn of the Dubai sun as it sinks into amber and then disappears entirely. The glass holds my silhouette for a moment before giving up and turning into nothing but night.

Below, the stage glows.

The auditorium is already filling, rows of seats swallowing bodies, anticipation humming like low voltage. Staff move with practiced ease. Security forms invisible lines that look casual until you know how to read them. Cameras perch everywhere, hungry and patient.

The stage is where it will happen.

It has to be.

Hartley is one of the first speakers. He always is. A known quantity. A safe opening act before the heavier hitters take the podium. He'll come out once everyone's settled, once the crowd has relaxed into its own importance. When they're comfortable. When they're paying attention.

That's when the shot would land.

A single, precise sound. A gunshot sharp enough to slice through applause and polite laughter. Enough to freeze the room. Enough to guarantee wall-to-wall coverage before the echo even dies.

That's the message.

I'm not here for Hartley.

I'm here to stop the person who plans to kill him.

I can't be framed for a murder that doesn't happen. And more importantly, I won't allow Alejandro to decide how this ends.

I shift my weight slightly and pull my backpack closer, movements economical, deliberate. The night air is warm, but up here there's a thin edge to it, just enough to keep me alert. I unzip the bag and begin laying out pieces on the ledge in front of me.

Methodical. Quiet.

My handgun comes apart in practiced motions, hands moving without hesitation. Components slot together with soft clicks, metal kissing metal. It converts cleanly, smoothly, until what rests in front of me is no longer a close-quarters weapon but something built for distance and intention.

My stand locks into place, anchoring the rifle when I need it steady. When the time comes, it won't shake. Neither will I.

Alejandro will be somewhere high.

I don't need proof to know that. It's instinct. Pattern recognition. He prefers elevation. Control. Distance. The ability to see everything before anyone else realizes they've been seen. If he's going to make a statement tonight, he'll want the cleanest line possible.

I scan the upper structures, the architectural flourishes that double as concealment. Catwalks. Service levels. Shadowed cutouts meant for maintenance crews and never meant to be noticed by guests sipping cocktails below.

To my left, a long stretch of windows runs along the upper wall. Beyond them, a pre-summit happy hour is in full swing. The space is bright and loud, all clinking glasses and curated laughter. People mingle like they're at a wedding instead of the opening of a global monument. Suits and dresses blur together, bodies leaning close in the universal language of networking.

I watch them through the glass, my reflection faintly superimposed over theirs. Two worlds occupying the same space and never touching.

I finish assembling the rifle and settle it into the stand, checking alignment, testing resistance. Everything feels right. Too right. The kind of calm that comes just before something breaks.

Below, movement catches my eye.

Hartley arrives.

Security tightens instantly, the shift subtle but unmistakable once you know what to look for. More bodies. Shorter distances between them. Hands closer to earpieces. Hartley himself looks unchanged, still wearing that relaxed confidence like armor. He moves through the space as if it belongs to him by default.

He reaches for a drink as a server passes, taking the last blue martini on the tray.

He snatches it without asking, nods at something someone says beside him, and takes a sip. His eyebrows lift slightly as he looks over the rim of the glass, already scanning the room for his next opportunity. Always looking for someone to bump elbows with. Always hunting advantage, even in moments meant to be ceremonial.

I track him, noting his position, his rhythm, the way his security rotates just enough to keep him covered without caging him in. He's comfortable. No clue his life could be over tonight.

I glance back to the audience below. The stage. Somewhere in this building, Alejandro is moving too. I can feel it in the way my focus sharpens, in the way the night seems to pull taut around me.

He thinks tonight belongs to him.

It doesn't.

I settle in, breath steady, eyes sweeping high to low, left to right, over and over again. I catalog everything. Angles. Distances. The places a person could hide and the places they couldn't. I am not looking for Hartley.

I am looking for the ghost who thinks he owns the ending.

When I find him, my heart stutters for a single, traitorous beat.

Not because he's here. I expected that.

Not because I found him. I've been hunting him since the moment I climbed up here.

It's where he is that stops me cold. And the look on his face. And the fact that he isn't moving at all.

Alejandro stands half-shadowed in a service doorway, dressed in a waiter's uniform that isn't the one from this morning. Different cut. Different venue. Same effect. He blends seamlessly into the architecture of the event, just another piece of staff framed by light and glass and bodies that never think to look twice.

His eyes are wide. Locked.

Not scanning. Not calculating.

Fixed on Hartley.

I flick my gaze down to the stage again. Hartley lifts the martini, what's left of it, and takes another sip. The glass is nearly empty now, probably more nerves than thirst driving him to drain it. He smiles at something said just out of frame, unaware that the room has begun to tilt.

I look back at Alejandro.

This is the part no one ever sees. The thing that makes men like him so dangerous. He doesn't look like a killer. He looks like the help. He moves the way they move. Stands where they stand. Exists inside the negative space of importance.

No one clocks him because no one ever thinks to.

Movement keeps you alive in rooms like this. Purposeful motion. Small adjustments. The illusion of task.

Alejandro isn't doing any of that.

He's too still.

The hairs along the back of my neck rise in warning, every instinct I have lighting up at once. Predators don't freeze unless something has gone wrong, unless the picture in their head no longer matches the one in front of them.

Then he blinks.

Once. Twice. Hard.

He shakes his head slightly, like he's trying to clear water from his ears, and whatever trance he was locked in breaks. His eyes start moving immediately. Fast. Sharp. He scans left, then right, then up.

He's checking elevation.

Vantage points.

He looks almost frantic now, searching the architecture instead of the man he was seconds away from burning into memory. His breathing changes. I can see it even from here, the way his chest lifts too quickly beneath the uniform.

Something is wrong.

Not later. Not hypothetically.

Now.

Plans don't unravel quietly. They fracture, and when they do, the people holding weapons adjust fast or they die. Alejandro is adjusting, which means the version of tonight he prepared for is already slipping out of reach.

And when plans change this close to execution, people get sloppy.

People get desperate.

I tighten my grip on the rifle, pulse steady despite the adrenaline flooding my system. Whatever he thought was going to happen is no longer under his control.

That makes him dangerous in a new way.

And it means I don't have much time left before everything goes very, very wrong.

42

Saint

The lights dim.

Not abruptly. Gradually, like the room is being eased into obedience. The constant, unfocused roar of hundreds of conversations softens, then thins, then fades into a low expectant hum. People turn toward the stage without realizing they've done it. Bodies orient. Attention collects.

Light begins to move.

Sweeping arcs of illumination skate across the stage as music swells, polished and hopeful. The announcer's voice rises over it all, practiced and warm, wrapping the crowd in language about innovation and vision and progress.

I search.

In two minutes, the mark will be on that stage. Alejandro knows that. Which means he has less than that to settle into position if he hasn't already. Less than that to decide how this ends.

The announcer builds momentum, praising the newest jewel of the desert, the miracle of sustainability, the promise of a future powered clean and bright. Applause blooms on cue. It sounds enormous from up here, like surf breaking against glass.

Then Hartley's name rings out.

My head snaps to the stage.

He walks out smiling, applause washing over him like he's earned it. He shakes hands with the woman who announced him, exchanges a brief word, then steps behind the podium. Confident. Comfortable. Centered in the cone of light.

I count automatically.

One minute. Maybe two if the introduction runs long.

I drag my gaze away and scan again, faster now, my eyes skipping between shadows and structural lines and dead spaces. I move too quickly at first, have to force myself to slow down, to look properly. I check the same locations twice because panic lies about certainty.

Then movement flickers at the edge of my vision.

Across the hall.

High. Recessed.

I find him.

He's positioned almost directly opposite me, tucked into a pocket of shadow where the architecture folds inward. The angle is clean. Too clean. He's no longer wearing the uniform from earlier but another waiter's jacket, tailored enough to disappear under stage lighting. From the floor, he would be invisible.

From here, he is unmistakable.

Alejandro looks up.

Not scanning. Not searching.

Looking directly at me.

We lock eyes across the distance, the moment stretching

thin and electric. The crowd below has no idea two rifles are about to decide the tone of history.

Then he breaks the stare and turns back to the stage.

His rifle is already assembled.

Still.

Leveled directly at Hartley.

I swivel my rifle toward him, the stand adjusting smoothly beneath my hands. I settle behind the scope, breath steady, movements precise. The crosshairs find him easily, frame his shoulder, then his head.

He shifts slightly, adjusting his stance. One eye closes. The other presses to the scope. He pulls back for a fraction of a second, checks the stage with his naked eye, then leans in again.

Professional.

Focused.

I stay on him, tracking every micro-movement. I adjust my aim higher, compensating instinctively. I don't want a body shot. I don't want time. I don't want chaos spilling outward in the wrong direction.

A clean headshot.

End it before it begins.

I draw in a slow breath and let it out just as slowly, settling myself into the pocket where the world narrows and nothing exists except distance and consequence. My finger rests against the trigger, pressure building but not breaking.

My heartbeat seems to pause.

Everything slows.

Alejandro inhales.

Hartley leans forward, hands braced on the podium, ready to speak.

And then—

There's a cough.

Not the polite kind. Not the clear-your-throat-before-you-speak kind. It's wet and tearing, like something has gone down the wrong pipe and clawed its way back up.

Alejandro leans back from his scope.

That's the first thing I notice.

He isn't aiming anymore. He's watching the stage with the same expression he had in the locker room. Calm. Almost curious. Like he's waiting for a clock to finish ticking.

I'm just starting to tighten my finger on the trigger when the cough comes again.

Harder.

Brutal.

Hartley bends at the waist, one hand gripping the podium as the other claws at his own chest. The microphone catches the sound this time, amplifies it, sends it rippling through the auditorium like a gunshot made of lungs and liquid.

Gasps ripple through the crowd.

I tear my eyes from Alejandro and lock onto the stage.

Hartley's face is already changing.

His lips are losing color, draining fast, turning an unnatural gray-blue as he sucks in air that isn't doing anything for him. His eyes are wide, whites stark, pupils blown like he's staring into something only he can see. He tries to speak, tries to inhale, but whatever is inside him has turned his throat into a closed fist.

He gags.

Black veins begin to spider up his neck, branching and

branching, crawling toward his jaw like ink dropped into water. His skin tightens, swelling subtly at first, then more obviously as his body panics and floods itself with every failed response it has.

Someone rushes the stage.

Then another.

Hands grab his shoulders, trying to hold him upright, as if posture will fix this. As if gravity is the problem. He retches violently, and thick, dark fluid spills from his mouth, splattering the podium, soaking his tie. It isn't vomit. It's blood, frothy and wrong, bubbling as if his lungs are trying to expel themselves through his throat.

The smell hits even from up here, sharp and metallic and unmistakably...sweet.

Hartley's body convulses.

His chest heaves in short, useless spasms. Each breath is worse than the last, a wet sucking sound that makes people in the front rows recoil. His hands clutch at nothing now, fingers curling and uncurling, nails scraping uselessly against the podium's polished surface.

His eyes roll back.

Someone screams.

The crowd surges forward and backward at the same time, a living thing breaking apart. People stand on their seats to see. Others turn away, hands clamped over mouths, faces folding in horror. A woman stumbles as she tries to flee, heels slipping on the carpet slicked with spilled drinks.

Hartley's legs give out.

They don't catch him in time.

He hits the stage hard, body slamming down like a dropped marionette. His back arches violently, a sound tearing out of him that isn't human anymore. His abdomen spasms, and his bowels give way, dark spreading beneath him, mixing with blood and bile in a grotesque stain that no one can look away from.

Security is shouting. Medics are shouting. Someone is crying prayers into a phone.

Hartley swells further, face bloating, tongue darkening as it protrudes slightly from between his teeth. Blood leaks from his nose now, thin and steady, while his mouth works soundlessly, trying to form a breath that will never come.

His body seizes one last time.

Then it goes slack.

The microphone squeals as it hits the stage, feedback shrieking over the silence that follows.

And then the silence breaks.

Screams. Wailing. Panic pouring through the auditorium as people push toward exits that suddenly feel very small. Security forms a perimeter too late, shouting orders no one listens to. The stage lights stay on, cruel and bright, illuminating the mess in perfect detail for every camera in the building.

Hartley doesn't move.

He never will again.

I lift my gaze back to Alejandro.

He's looking at me.

Not past me. Not through me. At me. The distance between us collapses into a thin, electric line, and for one suspended heartbeat it's just the two of us, framed against glass and light and catastrophe.

The second he realizes I'm watching him, he breaks eye contact.

He drops back into the scope.

And fires.

My head snaps to the stage so fast my neck protests, adrenaline spiking hard enough to blur the edges of my vision. I expect a body to fall. A secondary collapse. Someone else going down in a spray of panic and blood.

Nothing.

It's still Hartley, motionless and ruined, surrounded by the people who rushed in too late to matter. Hands hover uselessly over him. Medics kneel. Security shouts. No new victim. No fresh chaos.

I look back.

The doorway across the hall is empty.

Alejandro is gone.

No retreat. No scramble. No trace of movement. Just absence, like he was never there at all. A ghost that finished his work and evaporated.

Below, the conference center staff have switched to damage control mode, ushering people toward exits with firm voices and forced calm. Some attendees move readily, eager to escape the sight and smell of what just happened. Others can't stop looking back, faces twisted in disbelief, like Hartley might suddenly sit up and force them to watch it all again.

I scan the upper levels, the catwalks, the shadows.

Nothing.

My pulse pounds in my ears as my mind races ahead of my body. If he took a shot, it wasn't at Hartley. That means it was at something else. Or someone.

I pull the earpiece free from my collar, snap it into the port on the battered flip phone, and dial.

It rings once.

Then twice.

"Congratulations," Grim answers cheerfully. "You've reached Grim's personal hotline. If this is about murder, press one. If it's about betrayal, press two. If it's about your love life, hang up and rethink your choices."

"He's dead," I say. "And I need your help."

A pause. "Who? The boyfriend?"

I ignore that entirely. "Hartley. Poisoned."

"Fuck."

There's yelling in the background, a woman's voice sharp and indignant. Grim pulls the phone away and shouts, "Sorry, Mama," before coming back on the line. "Okay. That's bad. That's very bad."

I start breaking down my rifle as we speak, hands moving fast and precise, muscle memory taking over. Barrel off. Components separated. Everything stowed cleanly back into my bag. My eyes never stop moving, tracking the stage, the exits, the upper levels where he vanished.

Paranoia crawls up my spine.

"What the hell did he shoot at?" I murmur, more to myself than Grim.

"What?" Grim asks.

"I need you to hack the summit cameras," I say. "All of them. Every angle. Inside and out."

"Already doing it," he says around a crunching sound. He's eating something. Of course he is.

I stand, sling the backpack over my shoulder, and move along the wide ledge that had hidden me so well. I circle it carefully, staying low, until I reach the opposite side.

Alejandro's side.

The carpet is still warm where he was lying. The impression faint but there if you know how to look. I kneel, peer down at the stage from his vantage point, tracing the line of sight.

It's the same view I had.

No blind spots. No hidden figures. Nothing obvious that would justify a shot.

Which means the target wasn't obvious.

"I'm going down there," I say.

There's a beat of silence. Then, "Mmm," Grim replies thoughtfully. "That really a good idea?"

"It's the only one."

I move around the wall to the access ladder, its twin hidden in shadow just like the one I used. I descend quickly, controlled, sliding the last few feet down the rails and landing softly in the dark corridor that runs alongside the stage.

The noise from the auditorium is muffled here, panic turned into a distant roar. I slip along the back, staying in the shadows, my voice low as I speak into the earpiece.

"Tell me you've got eyes."

Another crunch. I glance to my right like he might be standing there, crumbs on his shirt.

"Yeah," Grim says. "I'm in. Every camera you could possibly want."

"Good," I reply. "Pull up Hartley's death. Alejandro took a shot. I need to know exactly when."

I pause, listening to my own breathing, already bracing for what the footage is about to tell me.

"At what—"

43

Saint

He's loaded onto a tarp.

Not a body bag. Not yet. Just a heavy sheet grabbed in a hurry, corners clenched in gloved fists as the medics lift together, awkward and strained, like they didn't expect him to weigh this much now that life has left him. The tarp bows in the middle as they raise him, the shape of his body obscene and wrong, fluids soaking through in dark, uneven patches.

For a split second, I think of Skippy.

The train.

The way Skippy burped corpse-breath straight into Alejandro's face, the sound almost comical if it hadn't been so wrong. So rancid it made his eyes water.

They maneuver Hartley onto the stretcher and wheel him away. The tarp goes with him, folded over what's left of his dignity.

Two staff members remain behind on the stage.

They just stand there, staring at the mess he left. Blood. Bile. Something darker. The air still holds it, a sickly-sweet stench hanging low and stubborn, coating the back of my throat.

And then I remember something else Alejandro said. A different night. A different body.

Sweet. Sickeningly so.

He told me that smell never leaves you. That it brands itself into your soul whether you want it to or not. That years later, it still crawls out of nowhere and reminds you exactly how close death really was.

Standing here now, breathing it in, I understand exactly what he meant.

"Okay," Grim says in my ear. "I've got it."

His voice shifts and he starts narrating what he sees, describing camera angles, timestamps, crowd movement. Then Hartley convulses on the feed, and Grim yelps.

"Oh—oh, Jesus, he's—he's vomiting. That's bad. That's really bad."

"Focus, Grim," I murmur. "Move past that."

"Okay. Okay," he says, a little breathless. Another crunch follows, loud in my ear, and I briefly consider committing a secondary murder just to make it stop.

Then, "Okay," he says again. "I've got it."

There's a pause.

Then a single, startled laugh.

"What a loser," Grim says. "He missed."

I shake my head slowly, scanning the floor around the stage. "No," I say. "He didn't. Alejandro never misses."

I move methodically, eyes tracing lines, angles, places a bullet could have gone without announcing itself. The shot had to land somewhere.

"Can you see where it hit?" I ask.

"Hold on," Grim replies.

I hear the faint sound of him squinting, the rustle of movement. In the background, someone speaks Spanish sharply, like an argument over a video game as he and his cousin must be watching the video together.

Then, "Yeah," Grim says. "I can see it. Let me pull the live feed."

Keys clack rapidly.

"Okay," he says. "I see you. Walk to center stage. Then stage right."

I do.

"Keep going."

I follow his voice.

"Almost," he says. "Almost... right there. Look down."

I stop.

I crouch.

There's a small impact mark in the flooring, easy to miss if you aren't looking for it. I rub my finger over it, feeling the roughness where something fast and violent kissed stone and kept going.

I straighten slowly, pulse steady despite the unease coiling tighter in my chest.

"He never misses a shot," I say. "This was on purpose. I need to know what was here. What he was shooting at."

"On it," Grim says. "Going back."

I keep looking anyway, circling, scanning, trusting my instincts more than the feeds. Grim rambles as he scrubs through footage, muttering about angles and shadows and compression artifacts.

Then my eye catches on something.

I can't tell what it is at first. Just a flash of color against neutral tones. Something out of place. I step closer.

Grim comes back on the line. "It's hard to tell," he says. "Really dark, but—"

I reach down.

"All I can see is a shoe," Grim continues.

My fingers close around something small and smooth. Polished. Cool against my skin.

Blue.

Familiar.

I lift my hand and let it rest in my palm, the weight insignificant and devastating all at once.

A marble.

"A shoe," I repeat quietly.

"Yeah," Grim says. "I'll send you a still frame."

Seconds later the phone vibrates in my hand. I open the file.

Grainy. Black and white. Security footage, compressed just enough to lose faces and keep shapes. And there it is, unmistakable now that I know how to look. The edge of a shoe, caught mid-step, half in shadow.

It looks a lot like the photographs Alejandro deleted.

My thumb moves on instinct. I pull up the first image from two years ago. The one from September seventh. Alejandro in the corner of the frame, carpet pattern beneath him, and in the opposite edge, the tip of a man's shoe intruding into the shot like an afterthought.

Then the second. More recent. Someone climbing into a helicopter. Bent knee. White pants. Black shoe. Same angle. Same intrusion.

Different moments. Same ghost.

"Grim," I say, keeping my voice level, "can you enhance this? And the photos Alejandro deleted?"

There's a pause. Then a low sound of understanding. "Ahh. I see where you're going with this. Yeah. Absolutely."

The clicking of his keyboard fills the silence in my ear as I roll the marble between my fingers. It's cool and smooth, almost soothing, which feels wrong considering where I found it.

"These cameras are insane," Grim mutters. "High-end stuff. I can practically see the stitching."

"Send it to me," I say. "And do you have a way to search the feeds for that same shoe?"

A beat. "Nah," he admits. Then, cheerfully, "But I can write one real quick."

I frown. "What?"

Across the theater, a sharp clink of metal against glass pulls my attention away from the phone.

One tap.

Then another.

Then a third.

Slow. Evenly spaced. Deliberate.

I look up.

He's standing alone on the opposite side of the glass, elevated above the chaos, framed perfectly by the city lights behind him. A Stetson sits low on his head, brim casting his eyes into shadow. His posture is relaxed, smug, like he's just wandered into a bar he owns.

Mother. Fucking. Colt Harrington.

He lifts a hand and gives me a lazy little wave, fingers curling in greeting.

One finger is missing.

The bandage wrapped around the stump is fresh.

My grip tightens around the marble.

In my ear, Grim keeps talking, blissfully unaware. "Yeah, shouldn't take me long at all. I'll—"

"Sure," I say slowly, never taking my eyes off Colt.

I let the silence stretch.

"Take your time."

He doesn't move.

Neither do I.

For a suspended beat, we just look at each other through layers of glass and distance, something unspoken passing between us. Not a threat. Not a warning. An acknowledgment. Like we both understand the rules just shifted and the board has been cleared.

Then I move.

The marble disappears into my pocket. The phone follows. I don't slow down long enough to explain myself or pretend this is anything other than instinct taking the wheel.

"Ummm," Grim says in my ear, "I feel like something's happening."

I don't answer.

I launch myself off the stage edge, boots hitting hard, momentum carrying me forward as I shoulder through a service door and burst back into the corridors. People are still clustered in shock, faces pale, voices loud and overlapping. I plow straight through them, apologies useless, urgency sharper than courtesy.

I break into a sprint.

My legs burn, arms pumping as I hit open air again, the night thick with heat and noise and movement. I don't slow. I step onto the edge of a planter, use it for leverage, and grab the high iron fence. My body knows what to do. I scale it in one smooth motion and drop cleanly on the other side, landing in a crouch with my fingers brushing pavement.

The assassins are here.

And this is a city that doesn't sleep.

Dubai's nightlife is just getting started, streets filling with music and light and people who have no idea how close they are to becoming collateral. That won't work. Not for me. Not for what's coming next.

Because I'm going to end this shit. Tonight.

I lift my head and look up.

The tower looms above everything else, a needle of glass and ambition still closed to the public for another two days. Empty. Controlled. Vertical.

The world's newest tallest building.

"Yeah," I murmur to myself, already moving again.

"That'll work."

Saint

I walk with purpose to the curb where a line of cabs idles, engines ticking, drivers half-asleep and dreaming of fares that won't end in therapy.

No time for subtleties now.

I open the driver's door, grab him by the collar, and haul him out in one smooth motion. He yelps. I don't apologize. I toss my book bag onto the passenger seat, slide in, and peel away from the curb.

The tower is only two blocks away, but I need speed.

If all the world's assassins are in this city tonight, they'll have plenty of room to die in there.

I drive the cab straight through the front doors.

Glass explodes inward, a violent bloom of sound and shards and screaming alarms. The cab bucks, then dies, lodged halfway into the marble lobby like it was always meant to be here.

"Grim," I say, already moving.

"You just can't do anything like a normal person, can you?" He crunches on, what has to be five thousand chips.

"Eh," I reply, climbing out. "Where's the fun in that."

I set the bag on the cab's roof and unzip the rear compartment.

"Hello, my babies."

Plastic-wrapped bricks. Detonators. Cord. Enough bad decisions to redraw a skyline.

Outside, engines growl. Not civilian. Not curious. Heavy. Military-adjacent. The kind of vehicles that don't stop unless something makes them.

I check the gun at my back. Loaded.

I pull out a second. Then a third. Slam magazines home, smooth and practiced, and slide them into shoulder holsters beneath my leather jacket.

Multitool. Back pocket. Good.

Flip phone. I hesitate, then tuck it into a side pocket of the bag. Secured.

"Grim," I say, strapping the pack onto my shoulders and clipping it tight across my chest. "I need you to be my eyes. Tell me how many are coming into the building. Keep civilians out."

"Okay. Give me a minute. Almost done with the program."

I pull a piece of gum from my pocket and pop it into my mouth.

"Oh shit. She's getting the gum out. Take cover, Dubai." I can hear the amusement in his voice.

I smirk and add a second piece. Overkill is a lifestyle.

It should be alarming how much he enjoys this. Not that I'm alarmed. But someone should be.

I zip the bag and walk to the center of the lobby as headlights flood the space, harsh and blinding, pouring through the wrecked doors and reflecting off marble and glass.

Men rush in.

Lots of them.

Tactical. Clean. Efficient. Not assassins, but they work for one.

Kade Mercer's people.

Black uniforms. Bulletproof vests. Assault rifles raised, stocks snug to shoulders, muzzles trained on me like I'm a problem they've been paid to erase.

They fan out, professional, disciplined, forming a perfect circle.

I stand there and chew my gum.

I let my gaze drift from face to face. No masks. No flair. Just men who think numbers equal certainty.

"All right, boys," I say.

I roll my shoulders, stretch my neck, feel the familiar hum settle into my bones.

"Let's have some fun."

I move first.

Not forward.

Up.

I throw myself backward into a handspring, boots leaving the floor as rifles crack in surprise. Muzzles jerk. Fingers tighten. Bullets tear through the air where my head used to be, ricocheting off marble and glass and each other's bad decisions.

Men shout.

Someone yells *hold fire* a half-second too late.

I land low and roll, sliding across the lobby floor as rounds punch through pillars and decorative nonsense some architect got paid too much to imagine. Stone explodes.

Shards rain down. Someone screams when friendly fire finds a spine.

Stupid men.

I come up inside the circle before it can close again.

I grab the closest one by his vest and yank him into me, his rifle barking wildly as I turn him into a human shield. Bullets tear through his back. One finds his throat.

I put one more into his neck for good measure.

He drops.

I don't pause.

I pivot, steal his rifle on the way down, and fire from the hip. Two go down. One staggers, clutching his leg, screaming like this wasn't always going to end badly.

They finally realize the problem isn't numbers.

They spread.

Wrong again.

I sprint, slide across a desk, kick off the wall, and send a chair flying. It takes one man in the face hard enough to snap his head back. I shoot him before gravity finishes the job.

Someone throws a grenade.

Bold.

I kick it back.

It detonates behind them, concussive force rattling the lobby and turning confidence into shrapnel. Smoke rolls in thick and gray. Alarms scream louder, desperate now.

"What a dumb fucking asshole."

I move through the haze like it's familiar territory.

A silhouette raises his weapon.

I fire first.

Another tries to flank. I bend down and steal a knife, flicking it at his thigh. His artery didn't stand a chance.

He bleeds out in seconds, eyes wide, mouth working, no sound coming out.

They're panicking now. Shooting at movement. Shooting at shadows. Shooting at each other.

I just guide the chaos.

One last man backs toward the doors, slipping on blood, rifle shaking in his hands. He looks at me like he finally understands the math.

I shoot him center mass.

Silence crashes down hard.

Smoke thins. Alarms keep screaming, but no one's listening anymore.

I step over bodies, adjust my jacket, and walk to the elevator bank.

I press the call button.

Once.

Then I stand there, gum popping quietly in my mouth, breathing steady, waiting like I'm late for a meeting on the fiftieth floor.

Grim's voice is quiet disbelief in my ear. "...Jesus Christ."

"Lobby's clear," I say.

The elevator dings.

I smile and step inside.

Next stop: upstairs.

The elevator hums as it climbs, glass walls flashing past steel and night and blinking city lights. My reflection stares back at me. Blood-speckled. Calm. Chewing gum like I've got nowhere better to be.

Floor numbers tick up.

Twenty-one.

Twenty-two.

Twenty-three.

The doors slide open.

He's standing right there.

Centered. Still. Hands relaxed at his sides like he's waiting for a bus instead of me.

Rajan Gurung.

Nepalese. Gurkha. Knife man. The kind of assassin people argue about on forums like he's a ghost story instead of a breathing problem.

"Hey, Rajan."

My gun is already up and I shoot him dead center in the forehead.

No flinch. No dodge. No drama.

He drops straight back, skull cracking against the floor with a dull, final sound.

I step out of the elevator over his body and don't look back.

The hallway is pristine. Corporate. Quiet in the way only very expensive buildings are. I turn down the corridor toward the core, toward the humming heart where steel and power and ego intersect.

This is what I came for.

I shrug out of my bag, kneel, and unzip the rear compartment.

Explosives greet me like old friends.

I start assembling the first charge. Hands steady. Motions automatic. Gum popping softly in the silence.

"Grim," I say. "How's it looking out there?"

"Program's live. I'm scrubbing backward through today now. I'll find the owner of the shoe."

"Good."

I keep working. Detonator seated. Cord measured. Timer checked. Gum pops again.

"Any new company I should know about?"

There's a pause.

Too long.

"...Actually."

I stop for half a second. Just enough to know I won't like this.

"What?"

"I didn't know they were real. You know? I thought they were just... urban legends."

I finish sealing the charge and set it gently against the column.

"Grim," I say, standing. "Get to the point."

"It's the Onryō."

I still, just for a beat.

Damn.

"Okay," I say finally, clipping my bag back on. "I'm going up. Keep me posted."

I step back toward the elevator, blood crunching under my boots, and press the button.

The doors slide open.

Next stop: higher.

And things are about to get... respectful.

45

Saint

I set the charges on the ninety-second floor, and the quiet is starting to grate at me.

It's the wrong kind of silence. Not calm. Not empty.

Waiting.

"Grim?" I murmur, tightening the final clamp against the building's core.

Nothing.

I pause, fingers stilling. "How many are coming?"

Static answers me, thin and broken, a hiss in my ear that crawls instead of speaks.

"...Grim?"

Nothing.

I straighten slowly and take in the space around me.

The ninety-second floor opens into a massive interior atrium, all glass and air and polished stone. It rises two stories high, the ninety-third floor exposed above it like a balcony in a luxury mall. A wide walkway wraps around all four sides of the upper level, railings gleaming under soft lights. Thick columns anchor the corners, structural and immovable. Tall white banners hang from the ceiling, drifting lazily in the conditioned air, heavy enough to matter if someone decided to use them.

Tables and chairs sit abandoned across the floor, expensive and fragile and very much in the way.

I zip my bag and leave it on the ground near the column. Explosives sealed. Tools stowed. If Grim doesn't come back online, this turns into a very old-fashioned problem.

I try him once more. "Grim. Talk to me."

Silence.

Then—

Ding.

An elevator opens on the floor above.

I look up.

She steps into view and stops at the railing, white against stone and shadow.

Tomoe.

White kimono. Immaculate. White chrysanthemums embroidered so delicately along the fabric they almost disappear unless you know to look for them. A katana rests across her back, wrapped, untouched. She doesn't scan the atrium. Doesn't acknowledge the charge humming behind me.

She looks only at me.

Recognition settles in my gut like a weight.

Leader of the Onryō.

I tilt my head slightly and offer a thin smile.

"I'm honored the Onryō came all this way for me."

Her gaze doesn't waver.

"We will see," Tomoe says calmly, her voice carrying without effort, "if you are honorable enough for the Onryō."

A presence shifts on my level.

One woman steps forward from between the columns. All white. A fitted jumpsuit instead of a kimono, practical and unadorned. Bare feet. Katana already in her hands, blade angled down. She says nothing.

We circle.

The air tightens. Every sound sharpens. I can feel Tomoe watching, measuring every breath, every shift of weight.

The woman moves first.

Fast.

She doesn't slash. She reaches. Hands going for my shoulders, my balance, my throat. Control before death.

I spin with her momentum, shrugging out of my jacket as her grip closes on leather instead of me. My hand snaps to her wrist in the same breath.

Steel flashes.

I wrench the katana free, step inside her reach, and drive the blade straight through her chest.

Her breath leaves her in a sharp, startled sound as the tip punches out between her shoulders. For half a second, discipline cracks.

Then she collapses at my feet, blood blooming vivid against white.

I don't look away.

Above me, Tomoe studies the scene.

Then, just barely, her mouth curves.

"You, Saint James," she says, "are honorable to battle the Onryō."

She inclines her head in a slight bow.

Elevators begin to ding.

One.

Two.

Many.

Doors slide open along both levels of the atrium. Soft footsteps follow. Controlled. Measured. The whisper of fabric, the quiet draw of steel. They arrive without haste, without chaos, flowing into position like something practiced a thousand times.

I glance down at the woman at my feet, then back up.

"I thought that *was* the fight."

Tomoe's faint smile grows, just a fraction.

"Silly assassin."

They finish assembling.

Forty-nine white-clad figures. Blades gleaming. Formation perfect.

I stand alone in the center of the atrium, katana in hand, my bag abandoned behind me, a body cooling at my feet.

"Well," I say, watching them settle, feeling the space close in. "Looks like all forty-nine of you came."

I draw a slow breath, flick the blood from the blade, and settle into a two-handed grip.

"All right," I murmur. "Let's get started."

They move as one.

And the ninety-second floor becomes a killing ground.

My... killing ground.

They surround me.

Not sloppy. Not frantic. A perfect ring of white and steel, blades catching the light as they angle inward. I turn slowly, deliberately, taking them in one by one. Faces calm. Focused. Reflected back at me in the polished curve of the katana I stole from their dead sister.

Then they move.

From everywhere.

Katanas stab and slash in controlled arcs, steel whispering past my throat, my ribs, my spine. I stay light on my feet, cutting as I dodge, dodging as I cut, never letting myself be still long enough to be pinned. An arm comes off at the elbow. A wrist follows. Someone screams as their sword clatters uselessly to the floor.

I keep them moving. Keep the circle unstable.

A blade whistles toward my head from behind.

I drop into a deep backbend, spine arcing impossibly as the katana sweeps through empty air inches above my face. From that position, I swing blind, trusting muscle memory.

Three women behind me open up at once, red blooming across their torsos.

I snap upright and drive my blade forward, burying it in the chest of the woman directly in front of me. She gasps. Falls.

I don't follow her down.

I pivot, grab a silver fork off a nearby table, and turn just as another Onryō rushes me.

I ram the fork straight into her eye.

Wet resistance. Then give.

She screams, high and raw, staggering back as I yank the fork free. Her eyeball comes with it, stretching obscenely before snapping loose.

I don't give her time to process it.

I sweep her ankles out from under her and chase her to the ground. Her head cracks against the marble hard enough to echo through the atrium.

She tries to scream again.

I drive the fork into her mouth as hard as I can, pinning her jaw open, forcing the ruined eye back into her throat.

She chokes.

Convulses.

Dies gagging on herself.

I rise and move on.

Two more rush me. One dies to a clean slice across the neck. The other to a stab under the ribs that punches out her back. I twist the blade free just as something heavy whips toward my face.

Chain.

Kusarigama.

I spin behind a pillar as the weighted end slams into stone with a violent crack. The chain wraps uselessly around the column.

I step out and slash.

Brutal. Efficient.

Her abdomen opens cleanly. Intestines spill out in a slick, steaming mess, hitting the floor with a wet slap. She slips in her own blood, feet flying out from under her, hands clawing uselessly at her stomach as she bleeds out screaming.

I don't watch her die.

I'm already moving.

But something's changed.

They're not rushing anymore.

They tighten their formation. Adjust spacing. Blades angle differently. They're herding now, not chasing.

They're learning me.

Nope.

I kick backward, flip a table, and sprint for the stairs.

They follow immediately.

I take the first three on the steps, blade flashing in tight quarters. One tumbles backward, taking another with her. I vault over their bodies, hit the landing at the top of the stairs, and don't slow.

I plant a foot on a table and hurl myself forward, launching in a clean arc over the banister.

White fabric flares below me.

I land hard on the upper walkway, boots skidding, knees bending to absorb the impact. I spin as soon as my feet settle, blade coming up just as the first of them pours onto the stairs behind me.

I have exactly one second to catch my breath.

I take it.

Then I smile.

Ready for more.

Three of them push me back at once.

Not wild. Not desperate. Precision cuts, staggered timing, blades moving in clean arcs meant to herd me toward the rail. Steel flashes left, right, high. I give ground by inches, parrying just enough to keep my throat attached to my body.

Fine. You want choreography.

I take the opening when it comes, drive forward instead of back, and kill the first with a brutal upward slice that splits collarbone. The second dies a heartbeat later, blade buried under her ribs. The third tries to recover.

She doesn't get the chance.

I run.

A white banner hangs from the ceiling nearby, impossibly long, heavy fabric meant to impress investors. I jump, catch it in both hands, and don't slow.

I hit the banister at a run and vault, swinging out into open air.

For half a second, I'm weightless.

Then I let go.

I slam into the opposite walkway feet-first, using the momentum to kick the first Onryō square in the chest. She flies backward over the rail, arms pinwheeling, and hits a table two stories below with a wet, final crack.

Her neck bends at an angle no living thing survives.

I land, turn, and snap the banner around another woman's throat before she can react. I shove her toward the edge and lean my weight into it, wrapping fabric tight, tighter, until her hands claw uselessly at it.

I push.

She goes over.

The banner jerks violently as she dangles, feet kicking, fingers scrabbling for purchase that isn't there. I hold until her body goes slack, then let the fabric slide free and watch her fall.

I don't wait.

Four more rush me.

I meet them head-on.

Blade flashes. Bone breaks. One goes down screaming with her arm nearly severed. Another takes a thrust through the sternum and collapses into her. A third lands a slice across my side as she passes me.

It's deep.

I feel it immediately. Heat. Wetness. The pull of torn muscle.

Good.

Pain sharpens everything.

I kill her with a backhand slash that takes her throat open, then finish the last with a pommel strike that drops her to her knees before I drive my sword down through her spine.

Silence crashes down around me.

Bodies litter the walkway. Blood slicks the stone. The banner sways gently above, stained now, heavier than before.

I reach down and pick up the katana that cut me, feeling its balance, its bite.

One sword in each hand.

I turn toward the stairs.

They're gathered there now, the remaining Onryō, standing at the top step, blades held low, watching me from below like they're studying an equation they almost understand.

I plant my feet at the edge of the walkway, blood dripping from my side, chest heaving, both swords raised.

"Come on," I murmur. "Let's finish this up."

And I go to meet them.

The final fury comes fast.

They surge up the stairs toward me, and I meet them head-on, blades already moving as I descend back down into them. The fight compresses instantly. No room for wide swings. No room for pretty.

Just bone and steel and momentum.

An arm comes off at the shoulder and skids down the steps, spinning end over end through blood and bodies before disappearing below. I don't track where it lands.

I stab straight down through a woman's throat as she lunges upward, feel cartilage give, feel the vibration as the blade punches through her neck and into the stair beneath. I wrench it free and kick her body aside.

Another rushes me from the left. I pivot and drive my

shoulder into her, knocking her off balance and straight into her sister's blade.

They collide.

I don't hesitate.

I run my sword clean through both their necks, skewering them together. Their eyes go wide in mirrored surprise as I shove them backward, letting gravity take over.

They tumble down the stairs still joined, hitting hard, rolling until they don't move anymore.

Above the chaos, I feel her gaze.

Tomoe stands on the landing below, white and still, watching her Onryō fall one by one. She doesn't intervene. Doesn't speak. Doesn't flinch.

This is the test.

A *whoosh* cuts through the air.

I turn instinctively, shoulder twisting away just as the first axe sails past my head. It doesn't miss its target.

It buries itself in the skull of an Onryō who had worked her way behind me, the impact snapping her head back before she drops bonelessly to the stairs.

Another axe follows immediately, spinning end over end.

I snap my hand out and catch it by the haft.

No pause. No breath.

I hurl it back the way it came.

It hits the thrower square in the face, metal biting deep, and she collapses without a sound.

The last of them hesitates.

Just a fraction.

That's all I need.

I close the distance in two strides and run her through,

blade punching out between her shoulders. I pull it free and let her fall where she stands.

Silence floods the stairwell.

Bodies lie twisted and broken, blood slicking every step between me and the landing below. My breath comes hard now. My side burns. My hands are slick with red.

I turn.

Tomoe waits.

I take one step down.

Then another.

Tomoe finally moves.

She steps onto the stairs with short, measured strides, every motion disciplined, deliberate. No hesitation. No wasted breath. When she reaches the open space at the base of the stairwell, she stops.

The bodies might as well not exist.

She reaches back and draws her katana in one smooth pull, the steel whispering free. She grips it with both hands, blade angled down, posture flawless.

I mirror her.

I adjust my stance, feet sliding slightly on blood-slick stone, and bring my katana up in a two-handed grip. The noise of the building fades. No alarms. No engines. Just us and the echo of breath.

We circle.

No words.

This isn't a fight. It's an ending.

Tomoe moves first.

One precise step. Two hands firm on the hilt as her katana flashes toward me, a perfect cut meant to end this cleanly.

I slip just inside the arc, turning my shoulder as her blade passes where my throat was a heartbeat ago.

And I come around.

One sweeping strike.

Steel bites deep and true.

Tomoe freezes.

Her eyes widen, locked on mine, not in fear but in sudden, absolute understanding. For a moment, it almost looks like she's tilting her head, as if considering something she's never had to consider before.

Then it keeps going.

Her head slides from her shoulders and drops, thumping wetly against the stone. It rolls once. Stops.

Her body remains standing for a breath longer, perfectly upright, as if refusing to accept the truth.

Then it crumples at my feet.

Silence seals the space.

I stand there, chest rising and falling, blood dripping steadily from my side, the weight of the moment settling into my bones. I give a small nod.

Respect.

I let the katana fall from my fingers. It clatters across the floor and skids away.

My jacket lies where I dropped it earlier. I pick it up, take one look at the blood-soaked leather, and curse under my breath.

"Fuck."

I drop it back to the ground.

My multitool snaps open. I slice a long strip of white linen from a shattered tablecloth and wrap it twice around my stomach, pulling it tight over the deep cut. Pain flares sharp enough to make me hiss as I knot it in place.

I breathe through it.

Then I walk back to my abandoned bag and shoulder it on.

I press the elevator button.

The earpiece crackles to life.

"Saint? Can you hear me?" Grim's voice breaks a few times.

I let out a breathless laugh as the doors slide open.

"Oh, now you show up. After I've done the hard part."

"...Did I miss anything good?

I step inside and shake my head.

"Nah."

I press the button to 115.

The doors slide shut, carrying me upward, leaving the ninety-second floor soaked in blood, silence, and the Onryō Forty-Nine massacre behind me.

Saint

I set the charges every twenty-three floors, the entire length of the building's spine.

Twenty-three. Forty-six. Sixty-nine. Ninety-two. One-fifteen. One-thirty-eight. One-sixty-one.

Clean. Even. Fatal.

Now all that's left is to get to the top. Set them off and bring this beast down.

The elevator hums as it climbs, smooth until it isn't.

It stops short. I push the button for the top floor but, no.

ACCESS RESTRICTED.

Of course it is.

The display tells me I've got three floors left to climb, and no amount of glaring is going to convince the system otherwise. I step out and head for the stairwell, boots heavy, side screaming where the bandage is already soaked through.

I start up.

"How many more are coming into the building?" I ask. "Like... a lot?"

Grim exhales. "Define *a lot*."

"More than the Onryō Forty-Nine."

There's a pause. "Whoa. Was there really forty-nine of them?"

"I didn't exactly count."

"That's awesome. But yeah—there's a shit ton more headed your way. Like, actively trying to crawl up your ass."

"What levels?"

"...A lot of them."

I sigh. "You're not helping very much."

"Saint," Grim says in my ear, suddenly sharp. "I think I found who you're looking for."

I keep climbing. "The shoe?"

"Yeah. Sending images over now."

My earpiece crackles as data crawls in like it's coming by carrier pigeon. I stop on the landing and wait.

And wait.

The images finally load, blocky and useless, all pixels and shadows.

I squint at them. "Damn. The service in here sucks." My boot hits the next step and I resume my trek upward.

"Can you get another phone?" Grim asks.

I laugh, breathless. "Yeah. Because there's a fucking T-Mobile up here right next to the manis and pedis."

Right on cue, a door bangs open above me.

Footsteps pound down the stairs, fast and sloppy.

"You're dead, bitch!" a man screams, voice cracking with terror and bravado. "You're fucking dead!"

I don't stop moving.

I reach into my boot, pull my knife, and hurl it up the stairwell without breaking stride.

It hits him right in the eye.

He drops instantly, momentum carrying him forward. His body tumbles down the stairs, thudding and rolling until it comes to rest at my feet, knife buried almost to the hilt in his skull.

"Fucking gross."

I crouch and pat his pockets. Phone. Wallet. Useless gun.

"But hey," I mutter, pulling the phone free. "He has a phone."

"Score!" Grim says. "Can you unlock it?"

I hold it up. Face ID needed. I'm about tired of all these restrictions. Doesn't the universe know I'm trying to exact my revenge?

I grimace. "Let's see if this works."

I tilt the phone toward his face and magically it unlocks.

I blink. "...Wow. Didn't expect that."

"I'm switching you over," Grim says quickly.

"What does that—"

My earpiece clicks, then reconnects with a cleaner tone. The phone in my hand rings.

I answer it automatically. "Hello?"

"Why are you saying hello like you think it could be a telemarketer?" Grim says.

I snort. "Just shut up and send the pictures."

"Fine," he says. "Hitting send now."

At that exact second, the building makes a sound I don't like.

A deep, mechanical *click* reverberates through the stairwell.

The lights die.

The phone in my hand goes black.

Everything goes silent except for my breathing.

"...Grim?" I say.

Nothing.

I stare at the dead phone, then at the darkness pressing in around me.

"Well," I mutter, straightening. "That's bad timing."

Because now the power's out.

And I really, really want to get out of this fucking stairwell.

And that's how I ended up here—at the top of the world's tallest building, a sniper rifle to my head, and a smug bastard who's been living jealous in my shadow for years breathing heavy down my back.

"Even now," Tex says, pressing the barrel harder, "with a gun to your head and every assassin in the world climbing this tower to claim your bounty, you still can't admit you made a mistake."

I smile.

"That's what happens when your balls are bigger than your brain. You forget one simple little detail."

"And what's that?"

"That I'm Saint motherfucking James," I say. "And I don't make mistakes."

I slam the wire.

The building answers with a furious groan, steel screaming as the first detonation blooms far below us. Then another. Then another. The explosions roll upward through the tower like a dying heartbeat, fast and relentless.

Tex swears as the floor shudders beneath our feet, the vibration throwing his balance just enough to matter.

"I've got about twenty seconds to get out of here," I tell him, turning my head just enough to grin.

"But that's plenty of time to kill you."

I kick sideways hard.

The rifle jerks. He fires, missing me by inches as the shot blows out the window beside us. Glass detonates into the night, wind roaring in, ripping at my clothes and dragging smoke toward the open void.

He swings the rifle back up.

I'm already moving.

I crash into him, knock the barrel aside, and wrench the weapon from his hands. It skids across the floor and disappears into the darkness as another explosion rocks the building, closer now. Too close.

We go at each other bare-handed.

He lands a punch. I land two.

My knuckles split his lip. His elbow catches my ribs. I feel something crack but keep moving, driving him back toward the gutted framework as the floor tilts under us.

The building is coming apart.

"If we're dying," he snarls, pulling a knife. "You're going first."

He slashes. I dodge. The blade kisses the strap of my book bag, slicing partway through it.

I growl and slam my forehead into his face.

He swings a wood end table with everything he's got. I make myself smaller and it shatters against the wall next to me. Then, he lunges from behind, looping something rough and fast around my neck—a rope, cable, something scavenged from nearby.

It tightens.

Stars bloom at the edges of my vision as I jam my fingers between the rope and my skin, fighting for space, for air. The tower shudders again, a massive detonation ripping through the levels just below us. The floor drops an inch.

We're out of time.

I rock back into him once.

Twice.

Then plant my feet and shove off a metal cabinet with everything I have.

We go airborne together.

The night explodes around us as we sail out through the shattered window, the screaming skyscraper behind us folding in on itself, finally admitting defeat.

And gravity takes over.

He clings to me as we fall, fingers digging into my jacket, his breath hot and panicked.

"You stupid bitch," he snarls, spittle flying. "I'm going to make sure you die before we hit the ground."

Wind screams around us, ripping the air from my lungs, tearing the city into a blur of lights and glass and rushing death.

I bare my teeth at him. "I've got a better idea."

I grab the cord and loop it around my hips, hands moving fast despite the chaos. Knot tight. No hesitation. Then I swing the loose length up and around his neck once.

Twice.

Three times.

His eyes go wide as realization finally catches up.

"It's about time you fucking died," I growl at him. "Asshole."

I drive my elbow into his face.

Bone cracks. His nose explodes. Blood sprays and vanishes into the wind as I hammer him again, and again, splitting his brow. I dig both thumbs into his eyes, grunting through my teeth, until he's clawing at nothing and I kick.

He falls and I rip the cord to my parachute hard.

My book bag jerks violently as the chute deploys, catching wind with a brutal yank that rips a scream from my throat and wrenches my spine. The rope around my hips goes taut—I scream at the agony in my side—and Tex's neck snaps with a wet, final sound.

He goes limp instantly.

Dead weight.

Too much dead weight.

The strap he sliced earlier starts to tear, fibers screaming under the strain. I reach for my multitool and realize I can't get to it. My bag. My cut arm. The wind won't let me.

"F-f-fuck."

The strap gives another inch.

I start to slide out of the harness, heart slamming into my throat. I grab the remaining strap with both hands and cling to it as the world spins.

Below me, the building finally gives up.

The tower collapses in on itself, folding like a dying animal, floors pancaking in a roar of smoke and fire and screaming steel. I hang there, spinning slowly, watching it fall.

"Holy shit." I pant, watching it in disbelief. Knowing the assassins that ran in there to cash in on the bounty of

Saint James died, knowing it was me that brought them all down in the end.

Then the chute catches a bad current.

I'm yanked sideways, dragged screaming through the Dubai skyline, glass flashing past far too close. Tex's body slams face-first into a building, bounces, then hits it again with a meaty thud.

The wind shifts.

The Kurohana Palace rushes into view.

"Hold on," I mutter to myself. Pulling up and finally fixing the single strap in the crook of my elbow. My second hand, gripping my wrist with everything I have. "Just hold on."

Tex's body bangs into another building, then another, leaving a smeared red trail across pristine glass as he slides along it like the world's worst mural.

"That's fucking disgusting."

We're dropping fast now.

The ground surges up.

My eyes dart, calculating, already bracing for impact. I don't see an immediate way to die.

Which means it's absolutely waiting.

Tex's body slams into an SUV with a crunch of metal and bone, then drags along the asphalt, sparks flying as it slows me just enough to matter.

"Oh. Oh shit."

I lift my legs just in time to clear a massive mound of camel poop.

Tex doesn't.

His corpse slides face-first straight into it, disappearing in a wet, humiliating splatter.

I snort despite myself.

"Now, that is fucking beautiful."

The chute finally collapses enough to dump me hard onto the pavement, rolling, bruising, but alive.

I lie there for a second, staring at the night sky, chest heaving, body screaming, city sirens beginning to rise in the distance.

The building is gone.

Tex is dead.

And for reasons I will laugh about for the rest of my life—

he's also covered in camel shit.

I close my eyes and laugh.

Just a little.

But the itch between my shoulders doesn't fade.

Because this isn't over. Not yet.

I force myself upright, every muscle protesting, and stagger to my feet. My side burns. Blood drips down my hip and soaks my pants.

I don't care.

There's still someone that set this in motion who didn't climb that tower. Didn't bleed for it. Didn't fall screaming through the night.

They're still out there.

And I know they're waiting.

I roll my shoulder, wince, and start moving before anyone can decide I'm a problem they want to contain.

Because I didn't come all this way just to survive.

I came to finish this.

47

Saint

My back pocket buzzes.

I freeze for half a second, then pull out the stolen phone and stare at it like it just grew teeth.

"I'll be damned."

I swipe it open.

Grim's voice hits my ear immediately. "I'm calling about your car's extended warranty."

A laugh punches out of me, short and surprised. "You're an asshole."

"Alive asshole," he says. "Which I'll take as a win."

I flip to the home screen and open the Guild app.

Tex's face is... a mess.

I crouch, grab a fistful of his hair, and wrench his head out of the camel shit. One eye is swollen nearly shut. The other I pry open just enough and hold the phone close.

The app chimes.

Unlocked.

"Grim," I say quietly. "Get in. Take everything. Files. Rosters. Dead drops. Contracts. Payment trails. I want every secret they ever buried."

"Oh hell yes," he says, practically vibrating. "That's right, fools. The Guild is ours now. Well—yours. I can't legally own anything until I'm eighteen."

I glance up at the hotel grounds beyond the wreckage.

Perfectly manicured. Soft lighting. Flowing water. Cherry blossom trees shedding petals into carefully raked gravel.

Calm enough to be insulting.

"It's not mine yet," I murmur.

Pain flares hot along my side. I hiss, straighten, and spit blood onto the pavement.

"But give me a few minutes," I add. "I'm about to fix that."

I slide the phone back into my pocket and dig into the bottom of my book bag, fingers closing around cold metal. My last gun. I load the final clip with practiced ease, lift my shirt, and tuck it against my lower back.

Then I step into the gardens.

The contrast is almost surreal.

Behind me, smoke claws at the sky and sirens wail through the night. Ahead, water trickles softly over stone. Lanterns glow low and warm. Cherry blossoms drift down in lazy spirals, catching in my hair, sticking to the blood on my skin.

The stillness feels staged.

Designed.

Like a set built for something ceremonial.

I move deeper, boots silent on the gravel path, senses stretched tight. Somewhere ahead, someone is breathing easily. Waiting.

A man stands near the water.

Back to me.

Dark hair. Straight posture. Hands clasped loosely behind him like he's admiring the view instead of standing at the end of a very long mistake. He's tall. Broad-shouldered. Calm in a way that used to make me feel safe.

Someone I trusted.

Someone I shouldn't have.

He turns at the sound of my footsteps.

Strong jaw. Familiar face. That gentle smile that used to mean everything was under control. He inclines his head in a small, respectful bow.

I return it without thinking.

The habit lands like a bruise.

"Kenji," I say softly.

The night seems to hold its breath.

Kenji doesn't rush to fill the silence. He lets it stretch, savoring the moment the way men like him always do. The gardens glow softly around us, water murmuring over stone, petals drifting lazily through the air like nothing in the world is about to break.

"You always did have a talent for making an entrance," he says at last. Calm. Almost fond. "I wondered how long it would take you to put the pieces together."

"I didn't come for conversation," I reply. "I came for answers."

His smile deepens. "And you deserve them. You earned that much."

"It would be rude to spill all the secrets before everyone is here." I shift my weight, keeping my hands loose at my sides. "Let's bring out your partner, shall we?"

Something flickers in his eyes. Not fear. Surprise.

I tilt my head toward the shadows beyond the lantern light. "Alejandro?"

The name hangs there before footsteps emerge from the dark.

Slow and unhurried.

He steps into the light with his hands in his pockets, posture easy, expression unreadable. The sight of him lands wrong in my chest, sharp and sour all at once.

Kenji chuckles, genuinely amused. "Well. Isn't that something."

He looks between us, reassessing. "I'll give you this, Saint. You never were predictable."

"Now that we're all here," I say, "let's introduce everyone properly."

My gaze returns to Kenji first. "The Guildmaster, I presume?"

He spreads his hands and bows, elegant and practiced. "At your service. Though I suppose introductions are a bit late for that."

I turn to Alejandro.

The smirk that curves my mouth isn't fond. It isn't amused.

It's disgust.

"Then I suppose that makes you El Fantasma."

He doesn't react.

He doesn't need to.

I already know.

"Saint," he says instead, like it's a greeting and not a verdict.

He slides his hand out of his pocket and tosses something toward me.

I catch it without thinking.

A blue marble.

I snort and laugh, sharp and humorless. "You can keep it." I toss it back. "I've got one of my own. And you're a lousy shot."

He still doesn't move.

"Let's see if I'm any better."

I draw.

The motion is smooth, practiced, inevitable. The shot cracks through the garden, loud and obscene in the quiet.

Alejandro spins as the bullet hits him, surprise finally breaking through his composure. He slams into the stone bench just behind him, then the path, the sound ugly and final.

He doesn't move.

My arm swings back to Kenji, gun steady, sight lined perfectly with his head.

The petals keep falling.

The water keeps flowing.

Kenji studies me the way he always has, like he's already ten moves ahead and mildly disappointed I haven't caught up yet. The gardens remain perfect. Lantern light. Cherry blossoms drifting. A koi breaks the surface and disappears again, blissfully ignorant.

He thinks this is still his room.

"Why?" I ask.

He tilts his head. "You'll have to be more specific."

"All of it." I gesture vaguely at the ruined skyline behind us, the blood, the bodies, the fact that we're standing here pretending this is civilized. "If we're about to have a final showdown and only one of us is walking away, what's the harm in a little reveal?"

He considers that, then nods once. "Very well."

He clasps his hands behind his back and motions with his head. "Let's walk."

I don't move.

"And put your gun away," he adds lightly. "It's disrespectful."

I hold his gaze for a beat longer than necessary, then slide the gun back into my pocket. Not because he asked. Because I want my hands free.

He starts along the koi pond at an unhurried pace. I fall in beside him, a careful distance between us. Close enough to hear him breathe. Far enough to kill him if I have to.

He sighs. "I'm disappointed in you, Saint."

"Get in line."

A faint smile. "It was supposed to be you here with me at the end. Not Tex. Not like this. But... you know what I mean."

"I really don't."

"You had to go and develop a heart." He clicks his tongue softly. "I tried very hard not to teach you that. Perhaps you can't help it, being a woman."

I snort. "Perhaps it's just because I'm not a fucking dickhead."

He chuckles, amused on the surface. I know better. He files the insult away, sharp and precise, for later.

"You wouldn't understand," he continues calmly, "the necessity of this power balance. Someone has to control the superpowers of the world. Checks and balances."

"Oh," I say. "So this is supposed to be some heroic act for all of mankind?"

"There will always be someone sitting at the top, Saint."

He stops walking and turns to face me.

I don't slow. I stop with him. "I'm going to make sure it's not you."

His eyes warm, almost fond. "Your confidence was always one of your best traits."

"And my worst?" I ask.

He turns and resumes walking.

I follow.

"So you've been selling the Guild," I say. "Trading power. Killing for profit and influence. Starting wars so you can be the elite asshole sitting at the top of the pyramid."

"Essentially."

"And this?" I sweep a hand around us. "Why all this?"

He exhales, pleased. "It's time to rebuild the Guild. Launch it fresh. A new creed. New mindsets. The old oaths are limiting. They put the Guild beneath those with power over the contracts."

He looks at me and smiles.

"I'm changing that."

My stomach tightens.

"And you helped me do it."

I stop again. "How so?"

He doesn't.

"You killed every assassin who would have been a problem," he says easily. "The ones who wouldn't bend to the new Guild."

The words land like a dropped blade.

All those bodies. All that blood. The last few days of staying alive by inches.

I had been doing his work for him.

"It's simple," Kenji continues, almost conversational. "Everything needs to be rebalanced. A world war would accomplish that. Killing the presidential hopeful puts someone I control into power. Once America does what it does best—bullies the world into a third war—the Guild will bring it to an end."

He glances at me. "Eventually. For the right price."

I feel something cold settle behind my ribs.

"New assassins," he says. "Ones who understand how the world actually works now. The superpowers indebted to us. Under our thumb."

He pauses.

"Though I had hoped you'd be dead by now."

"Why frame me for this?" I ask quietly.

"You would never bend a knee to the new creed," he replies. "And I needed to clean out the narrow-minded. I assumed Tex would take you out in the chaos." A faint sigh. "I always did put too much stock in his capabilities."

He turns to me then, extending his hand. His other remains in his pocket, and I hear it—the soft clink of marbles rolling together. A habit. Always has been.

"For what it's worth," he says, "I wanted it to be you. I hope that boy's life was worth yours."

I look at his hand.

I don't take it.

"The poison," I say. "Your berries."

He laughs softly through his nose. "Of course."

"And how did you keep track of me for so long?"

He lowers his hand and slips it into his other pocket. "The tea I served you when you came to me for help. Same micro-trackers as the ones in your sigil. Dissolved. Elegant."

He meets my eyes. "I never lost sight of you, Saint."

He turns away.

Takes one step. Then another.

"It's time we part ways."

"I agree."

He stops and turns back, posture shifting. Formal. Familiar. The stance he drilled into me until it lived in my bones.

"Despite it all," he says evenly, "it was my honor to mentor you."

I mirror him without thinking.

"All you did was teach me how to kill you."

Something dark slides into his expression, erasing the warmth. The calculation sharpens into something lethal.

"Well," he says, settling into a fighting stance.

"Let's see if the student can finally best her teacher."

48

Saint

Kenji's gaze drops to my hip.

"Toss it," he says calmly. "We won't disgrace this with gunfire."

For half a second, I consider arguing. Consider just shooting him.

Then I don't.

Because I want to finish this with my hands. Feel every second of his life end at my grip. I'm going to earn every drop of his blood.

I pull the gun free and flick it once in my hand before hurling it into the koi pond. It breaks the surface with a sharp splash, ripples racing outward as orange and white bodies scatter beneath the water.

Kenji nods, satisfied.

We step apart, shoes silent on gravel, cherry blossoms drifting lazily between us. Lantern light catches the lines of his face, familiar and unreadable. The garden seems to shrink, like it knows what's coming.

We take our stances.

And we wait.

The stillness stretches, taut as a drawn bowstring.

Then, we move at the same time.

He comes in fast and low, all economy and intent, striking before my muscles fully register the motion. His elbow slams into my ribs, precise enough to steal my breath, and he pivots immediately, foot sweeping for my ankle.

I jump it—but he's already there.

A palm strike snaps my head sideways. I taste blood. I stagger back into a stone lantern and barely catch myself before he's on me again, driving a knee into my thigh that makes my leg buckle.

"Sloppy," he murmurs, almost kindly.

I snarl and swing anyway, catching his jaw with the heel of my hand. It lands. Solid. He grunts, more surprised than hurt.

I press the advantage for half a heartbeat too long.

He punishes me for it.

Kenji grabs my wrist, twists, and uses my momentum to sling me into the gravel. I roll, coming up just in time to block a kick that would've caved my chest in. The impact rattles my arms to the bone.

We circle again, petals crunching underfoot.

I feint left. He doesn't bite.

I lunge and he steps inside my reach and drives his forearm into my throat, shoving me backward toward the pond. My heel skids on slick stone and I windmill, barely keeping my balance as koi scatter beneath the surface.

He comes at me again, relentless.

A fist to my kidney. An elbow to my shoulder. A knee that slams into my already wounded side hard enough to make my vision spark.

I hit back where I can—an uppercut that snaps his head, a sharp kick to his shin—but he absorbs it, adjusts, and counters. Every move I make, he's already anticipating the next one.

Because he taught me how to fight.

And he taught me where I fail.

And for one stupid, treacherous second, my body remembers something it shouldn't.

His hand at my shoulder years ago, steady and firm, turning me an inch to the left.

"Again," he'd said, not unkindly.

Not a weapon. Not an asset.

A student.

A girl who believed him when he said he was keeping her safe.

I spit blood onto the gravel and laugh breathlessly. "You always did hate when I improvised."

"And you always confused improvisation with strategy," he snaps back, driving me sideways into a wooden bridge railing.

The bridge creaks as we crash into it. Water splashes below. Lanterns sway overhead.

He pins me there for a moment, forearm pressing into my throat, eyes hard now. No fondness left. Just certainty.

"You could have ruled beside me," he says quietly. "Instead, you chose chaos."

I headbutt him. "Rule that. Fucking asshole." I mutter the last two words.

It catches his nose and makes him curse as he stumbles back a step.

Not far.

Never far.

I don't chase him. I reset, stance tight, breathing measured, and he does the same. The moment stretches again, taut, and deliberate.

Then he advances.

One step.

I step back.

Another.

I give him ground inch by inch, letting him think he's herding me, letting him believe he's dictating the terrain. Gravel crunches under my heel, then stone, then smooth tile as the garden gives way to the hotel entrance.

The glass doors loom behind me, reflecting two bloodied figures locked in a familiar geometry. Teacher and student. Predator and prey. It's impossible to tell which is which anymore.

Kenji keeps coming, unhurried, confident, every movement sharp and contained. He wipes blood from his lip with his thumb, eyes bright now, alive in a way that makes my stomach twist.

"Good," he says softly. "Let's finish this properly."

He doesn't wait for an answer.

Kenji explodes forward, speed shocking even now, his palm slamming into my chest hard enough to drive the air from my lungs. I stagger back, barely getting my guard up before his elbow crashes into my shoulder, then my jaw.

I hit him back. A knee. A sharp hook that glances off his cheek. Not enough.

Never enough.

He catches my wrist, twists, and throws me across the patio. I slam into a low stone table, pain flaring white-hot through my back. I barely have time to roll before he's there again, driving a kick into my ribs that lifts me off my feet.

I crash through the glass doors.

They shatter around me in a roar of breaking crystal as my body punches through, fragments exploding inward. I hit the tile hard and slide, skin tearing, glass biting into my arms, my side, my hands. My breath vanishes in a sharp, panicked gasp.

For a second, I can't breathe.

The world narrows to pain and ringing.

I drag myself onto my hands and knees, lungs burning, vision swimming as blood drips onto the floor. Glass crunches under weight behind me.

Kenji steps through the wreckage slowly.

Deliberately.

Each footfall grinds shards into the tile as he circles me, calm as ever, unhurried, like he has all the time in the world. Like he's enjoying this.

"You always struggled when the ground dropped out from under you," he says mildly. "Too much emotion. Not enough patience."

I bow my head, sucking in air, shoulders shaking.

And quietly, I curl my fingers around the glass beneath my palms.

Sharp. Jagged. Perfect.

It's always a mistake to underestimate me. And I'm going to remind my old teacher of that fact.

I push up in one violent motion and sling my hands forward.

The shards tear through the air and into his face.

Kenji shouts, real surprise breaking through as glass cuts

across his cheeks, embeds in his lips, slices into his eyes. One shard catches the inside of his mouth when he inhales, and blood sprays bright and sudden.

I don't wait.

I run.

Boots pounding tile, I sprint across the hall as he roars behind me, half-blind and furious now. I slam through the first open doorway I see and skid to a stop inside—

A showroom with glass cases. Silk-lined walls. Spotlit displays of Japanese weapons arranged with reverent precision. Katana. Wakizashi. Naginata. Yari. Blades old and new, ceremonial, and lethal, all waiting behind pristine panes.

I turn, chest heaving, blood slicking my hands.

Kenji staggers into the doorway moments later, eyes red and streaming, blood smeared across his face. He wipes at it with shaking fingers, rage burning through the pain.

Our gazes lock across the room.

And now I'm done playing with my dinner. It's time to eat.

I move first.

Not at him.

At the space.

I duck behind the nearest display as he charges, his strike shattering glass where my head was a second ago. Blades spill free, clattering across the floor in a sharp metallic rain. I roll, come up with a wakizashi in my hand, and slash low as he pivots.

He blocks, but barely.

The impact jars his arm. I see the flicker of irritation cross his face.

He retreats a step and his hand dips to his pocket where I know his marbles are.

He snaps the sling into place and fires.

The first one cracks past my head like a gunshot and obliterates the display behind me, glass exploding outward. The second shatters a pedestal at my feet, spraying shards up my legs.

Fast. Accurate. Deadly.

I move anyway.

Another marble screams past my ribs, close enough that I feel the pressure of it. I dive behind a case as the fourth punches straight through it, leaving a perfect, fist-sized hole in reinforced glass.

That's why they're deadly.

At distance, Kenji's marbles are faster than bullets and quieter than gunfire—pure kinetic violence guided by muscle memory and calculation. No recoil. No warning. Just precision.

Up close, though, they're useless.

The sling needs space. Arc. Room to breathe.

And I'm not giving him any of that.

I surge forward, collapsing the distance before he can reset, forcing him to abandon the weapon entirely as the fight turns brutal and close.

He curses and backpedals, trying to reset the sling, but the space collapses too fast. I slam into him before he can get another shot off, shoulder-first, driving him into a silk-lined wall.

Our bodies crashing through another display. A naginata skids across the floor. He grabs it one-handed and swings, the long blade whistling past my ribs close enough to kiss skin but only slicing my shirt.

I rip a polearm from the wall and jam it into the haft, redirecting the strike into another case. Glass explodes outward as we slam together again, fragments raining down around us.

He lands a hit to my shoulder.

I answer with a knee to his gut.

He grunts and I don't stop.

I slam the butt of the weapon into his ribs. Once. Twice. The third time something gives. He exhales sharply, the sound wrong, pain finally breaking through discipline.

"There it is."

He comes at me harder now, faster, frustration bleeding into his movements. Precision slips. He overcommits. Just once.

That's all I need.

I step inside his guard and twist, catching his wrist mid-strike and snapping it down hard against the edge of a shattered case.

Bone pops and he shouts, real pain ripping loose as the weapon clatters from his hand.

"Improvising now?" I ask breathlessly.

He snarls and backhands me, but it's sloppy. I take it, then bury the short blade into his side, just beneath the ribs.

Not deep enough to end it.

Deep enough to matter.

Blood blooms dark and fast across his shirt. He stumbles back, breathing ragged now, eyes wild.

The rest of the marbles spill from his pocket and scatter

uselessly across the floor, rolling away between broken glass and silk.

The calm is gone.

The certainty too.

And now he's out of distance weapons.

Exactly where I want him.

Blood slicks his fingers as he staggers back.

Kenji's eyes flick behind him, calculating. Reassessing. For the first time, he's choosing exits instead of angles.

He snatches a handful of throwing knives from a shattered display and hurls the first one without breaking stride.

I tilt my shoulder.

It whistles past and embeds itself in a silk-backed wall.

He throws another.

This one goes wide enough that I don't even bother dodging. It skitters uselessly across the floor, clattering to a stop at my feet.

His jaw tightens.

He keeps backing up, faster now, glancing over his shoulder again—and his heel catches the edge of the first stair.

Kenji stumbles, falling back hard onto the steps. Panic flashes sharp and ugly across his face as he flings another blade on instinct.

That one I have to move for.

I twist sharply, the knife tearing through the space where my throat was and feel the rush of air as it misses by inches.

He uses the moment.

Scrambling. Hands slipping in his own blood. He turns clumsily, finally getting his feet under him, and bolts up the stairs two at a time, breath breaking into something ragged and uneven.

I don't rush. Just follow.

Measured and controlled.

Each step deliberate as I climb after him, listening to his uneven footfalls ahead of me, watching the trail of blood mark his path upward.

Teacher ahead.

Student behind.

And for the first time in his life—

Kenji is running.

Every step he takes leaves more blood behind, a dark, uneven trail marking his retreat. His sling lies abandoned among it, just another thing slipping from his grasp as his strength bleeds out with every heartbeat. By the time I reach the top of the landing, he's slumped against the railing, chest heaving, his face pale beneath the blood and embedded glass.

I stoop and retrieve the leather sling.

It's worn smooth with years of use, softened by habit, balanced perfectly in the hand.

This is the first weapon he ever trusted me with.

I remember the weight of it then. How proud I was when he finally nodded and said my name like I'd earned it.

I tuck it into my pocket beside the single blue marble already waiting there—the one I found on the stage after Hartley died screaming. Just like the ones I've watched Kenji wield with merciless precision for half my life.

Funny how tools outlive the men who believe they own them.

I advance again, steady, and unhurried, forcing him back

one step at a time. There's nowhere left for him to go, and he knows it.

"Men like you never learn," I say quietly. "You build the world to suit yourselves, then act offended when it finally refuses to hold you."

He snarls something unintelligible and lunges, desperation shredding whatever discipline he has left. At this point, I'm running on nothing but pure spite.

I meet him head-on, driving the heel of my hand into his face with everything I have. Bone crunches under the impact, his head snapping back as I follow through, shoulder-checking him with ruthless intent.

Kenji goes over the balcony railing.

He hits an upholstered armchair on the floor below in a slow, surreal collapse—fabric tearing, wood splintering— before spilling onto the tile in a heap. His leg bends at a wrong angle. For a long, suspended moment, he doesn't move at all.

Then finally, he does.

Crawling. Dragging himself forward with shaking arms. Pushing, grunting, trying to stand on a body that's finally betraying him.

I watch him for a second longer than necessary before I turn and descend the stairs.

By the time I reach the bottom, he's upright again— barely. One leg useless. One wrist hanging crooked and discolored. Blood runs freely from his mouth and side as he hauls himself toward the shattered glass doors he threw me through not long ago.

He keeps looking back at me.

Checking to see if I'm coming.

I stop, drawing the sling from my pocket and take the marble between my fingers, feeling its weight, its promise. I load it carefully, watching him drag himself a few more feet across the floor. I'm not giving him mercy.

I'm giving myself space.

When the distance is right, I call his name.

"Kenji?"

He freezes.

Turns.

Blood spills from his mouth in a steady stream, dripping onto the tile. Glass has torn the skin around his eyes, leaving them red and raw, fury and disbelief flickering together there. His chest rises and falls in ragged pulls, his hands trembling as his strength finally gives out.

I don't do this for closure. I do it because he taught me never to leave a threat breathing.

"Goodbye," I say.

I spin smoothly, letting the momentum carry through my shoulders, down my arm, and into the sling. The release is clean. Effortless.

The marble punches through his forehead dead center.

His skull bursts out the back in a wet, violent spray, the sound sharp and final. The marble clatters to the floor a heartbeat before his body does, eyes already rolled back, expression caught somewhere between disbelief and understanding.

Finally, the garden settles into silence once more.

And this time, it stays that way.

Saint

I've looked better.

I've definitely felt better.

The sun is starting to crawl up over the horizon, soft and golden and deeply inappropriate considering I just killed my way through the night. My body is running on adrenaline fumes. I've got a limp in my left leg, one hand pressed to my side to keep everything where it belongs, and my lip is swollen enough that I'm going to sound charmingly concussed for the rest of the day. One eye is already threatening to swell shut. My arm needs stitches. A lot of them.

That's a future-me problem.

Right now, I've got one more body to reckon with.

I limp down the garden path toward Alejandro, who's still face-down where he fell, sprawled like a man who dramatically committed to the bit and maybe committed a little too hard. I let myself smirk for half a second—

Then I notice he hasn't moved.

The smirk drops.

"Alejandro?" I call, and this close to sunrise, after everything, it comes out softer than I expect.

I kneel beside him with a hiss, ignoring the way my knee protests, and check his pulse. Strong. Steady. Of course it is. I didn't shoot him anywhere that would actually kill him. Just his arm. Enough blood to sell it. Enough for Kenji to see the pavement stained and assume the rest.

Still.

I grab his shoulder and heave, trying to roll him over. It's harder than it should be because he's a big fucking bitch and I am *exhausted*. After a moment of undignified effort, he finally flops onto his back, head lolling to the side.

There's a nasty cut on his forehead. A knot already swelling beneath it.

"Jesus," I mutter.

A foot away, a shallow stream winds through the garden, water glinting in the early light. I reach over, scoop up a palmful, and fling it into his face.

The cold does the trick.

Not dramatically. Just enough.

He groans, brow furrowing, blinking slowly like the world is taking its sweet time loading. Confusion gives way to recognition.

"Saint," he murmurs, my name the first thing out of his mouth.

"Hey," I say, and it comes out a whisper whether I want it to or not.

He pushes himself up with a wince that suggests he's going to complain later once the shock wears off. He blinks around, takes in the destruction, then glances down at his arm.

Clarity settles in piece by piece.

I cross my arms carefully. "What the fuck did you do?"

He exhales. "I was being dramatic," he admits. "Wanted to make sure I really sold the *you shot me* thing."

He glances at the stone bench beside him and scowls.

"Fucking knocked myself out on the way down," he adds. "Stupid fucking bench."

Despite myself, I snort.

He gets to his feet first and offers me a hand. I take it, letting him haul me up, and the second I'm standing, his brown eyes are all over me—cataloging injuries, irritation tightening his jaw.

"Kenji?" he asks.

"Dead."

"Tex?"

"Also dead," I say. "Everyone's dead."

He lets out a long breath, relief pouring out of him like he's been holding it since he ran away from that locker room. He steps in close and rests his forehead against mine, careful of the swelling, careful of me.

For the first time all night, the tension drains.

The desert waits and I can finally take a goddamn breath.

And the first thing my brain offers me in the quiet is his face.

Not Kenji's.

Not Tex's.

Owen Liang. The wrong guy. The wrong guy, that I killed.

The man who wasn't supposed to die. Who found something he shouldn't have, tried to do the right thing, and paid for it because I was marked for blackmail.

I swallow hard and shove the thought down.

There's no absolution coming. Just direction.

"You figured it out."

Alejandro says it quietly, his hands coming up to cradle my face with careful fingers, like I'm something that might break if he presses too hard. His eyes are full of something heavy and unguarded, and suddenly this feels less like aftermath and more like confession.

"Of course I figured it out," I tell him.

My hands slide around his sides and up his back, feeling solid muscle under torn fabric, grounding myself in the fact that he's real and standing here.

"You would never miss a shot."

"That's right, baby," he says, voice dropping low.

He leans in and kisses me, slow and deliberate, holding it just long enough to make my knees threaten to fold. When he pulls back, he rests his forehead against mine and exhales.

"But I missed my shot with you, Saint," he murmurs. "For two fucking years."

The words land.

I remember everything all at once, and my hand slides down to his arm, fingers curling carefully around the gunshot wound.

"Why the fuck didn't you tell me you were El Fantasma?"

He hisses, jerking slightly. "Fucking Christ, Saint."

"I'm not squeezing that hard."

He gives me a look. "Debatable."

Then his expression shifts, serious again. "You would've shot me."

"I did shoot you."

"Somewhere fatal."

I lift a brow. "There's still time."

He laughs despite himself and pulls me back into his arms. I let him, resting my head against his chest, listening to his heartbeat slow.

"Come here," he murmurs.

After a moment, he speaks again, quieter now. "I never lied to you, Saint. I've been hunting the Guild since they framed me."

He pulls back just enough to cup my face again, forcing me to look at him.

"There's more at stake than just me, *Picarita*," he says softly. "I needed you to see the truth first."

His eyes search mine, almost pleading.

"But I couldn't risk my family. I had to clear my name and keep them safe. And by some miracle..." His gaze flicks between my eyes, his mouth curving into something vulnerable and real. "...get you back."

We stand there for a moment, neither of us rushing to speak, the quiet settling around us like something earned rather than imposed. The garden is still torn up from the fight, petals crushed into stone, glass catching the early light, but the sky above us is beginning to pale, the first real hint of morning stretching over the desert.

"Where did you go?" I ask finally. "Tonight. Where did you run off to?"

Alejandro exhales slowly, one hand sliding to my lower back as if anchoring himself there. "I had to track down who put the hit out. Whoever contacted Kenji claimed to be El Fantasma. Promised him a partnership. Hartley was the mark. A takeover after."

My brow furrows as the pieces shift again. "Then who was it? Who put the hit out?"

A soft, almost incredulous laugh escapes him. "Hartley."

I blink at him. "He put out a hit on himself?"

He nods. "It wasn't meant to succeed. He told Kenji he had to do it himself, to prove loyalty. Set the location. His guards were supposed to intercept. Take Kenji out, take the Guild in the chaos. A double-cross stacked on top of another."

"The poison," I say quietly.

"Kenji was the waiter," Alejandro replies. "No one ever looks at the staff."

"Not even the staff," I murmur, the memory clicking into place.

"He was at the brunch," Alejandro continues. "Tripped that poor server with one of these." He pulls a marble from his pocket and rolls it between his fingers. "Needed to stop you from warning Hartley. He didn't know Hartley was in on everything. Then later, at happy hour, I saw him again. Martini glass. Hartley was dead the moment he took a sip."

My chest tightens. "You knew that night we went to Kenji's house. The berries. You said they smelled sweet."

"Sweet like the poison," he confirms. "I needed to be sure."

There's regret in his eyes now as he cups my face, thumb brushing gently under my swollen eye, his other arm steady at my waist. "I know how close you were to him. I couldn't accuse him without certainty."

Everything finally settles. The doubt. The anger. The relentless noise of the last few days.

"I'm sorry," I say.

He glances down at his arm. "It's a scratch."

"I'm not sorry I shot you."

He gives me a look that's deeply unimpressed.

"I'm sorry for earlier," I amend, softer now. "For accusing you. For not trusting you."

He kisses me, slow and grounding, and when he pulls back his forehead rests against mine. "Don't apologize. Everything was designed to look wrong. On purpose."

"I should have known," I say. "I should have known *you*."

He studies me for a long moment, then shakes his head slightly. "I understand why you didn't."

And I believe him. After two years of hating him, after days of suspecting him, he understands in a way that doesn't ask to be forgiven but accepts what was.

I pull him in and kiss him again, longer this time, slower, letting the world narrow down to breath and warmth and the fact that neither of us is alone anymore.

Then a voice cuts in.

"Mwah. Mwah. Oh, Alejandro." Grim is making his voice higher like he's mimicking a woman's.

I groan. "Jesus, Grim. You're still here?"

"Unfortunately."

"You should have a bedtime."

"I saved your ass."

"We'll call ourselves even. Goodnight, Grim."

I hang up and toss the phone into the stream without ceremony.

Alejandro watches it disappear beneath the surface, then looks back at me, something thoughtful flickering behind his eyes. "You never explained that" he says gently. "Why Grim?"

I hesitate, just long enough to decide not to lie.

"He was a mark," I say. "A job I was supposed to do years ago. I got cocky and ended up on someone's radar. When I finally found him, he was fourteen."

Alejandro's expression tightens.

"I couldn't kill a kid," I continue. "So, I told him the truth about the Guild. Told him to disappear. He did. Changed his name from Pussy Reaper to Grim Reaper." I roll my eyes. "I made him change it. There was no fucking way I was going to let him keep that."

Alejandro chuckles. "And Kenji found out."

"Which is when he decided to use me to burn the Guild down," I say. "Grim was leverage. Proof. A loose end."

He studies me for a moment, then snorts softly. "So you're the only one who actually broke Guild law between us."

I poke his bullet wound. He winces. "Watch it." We both laugh.

We both look down at our sigils.

Alejandro's is burned and scarred. Dead against his skin. The Guild branded him once, claimed him, then tried to erase him when he complicated their plan. Whatever power it held is gone now—severed, rejected, rendered obsolete.

Mine is different.

The wound is still raw, the lines distorted where the sigil was burned away and reforged by choice instead of obedience. It's healing, slowly, painfully, but it's alive. No longer a mark of ownership. A mark of exile.

Of refusal.

"Grim's inside the Guild systems now," I say. "Every ledger. Every contract. Every name they thought was buried."

Alejandro's expression hardens as the implication settles. "So the Guild's blind."

"And exposed," I add. "For the first time in its history."

I lift my hand slightly, fingers brushing the scar. "This isn't about taking it over. There doesn't get to be another Kenji. Another Tex. Another man deciding who lives and dies from the shadows."

He nods once. No hesitation. No doubt.

"We hunt what's left," he says. "The ones who corrupted it. The ones who hid behind the creed."

"And when we're done," I say quietly, "there won't be a Guild like the old one ever again."

Alejandro studies my face, then gives a slow, dangerous smile. "You're talking about ending a legacy that's lasted centuries."

"I already ended about a dozen tonight."

That earns a low laugh from him.

"I'm in," he says. "All the fucking way, baby."

The desert wind lifts around us as the sky lightens, carrying smoke, dust, and the last remnants of a world that thought it could survive us. Somewhere behind us, bodies cool, and systems collapse. Somewhere ahead, names are already surfacing.

Targets.

I lace my fingers through his and squeeze.

"We don't ride off into the sunrise," I tell him. "We walk straight into the fucking fire."

Alejandro tightens his grip, eyes sharp and unafraid.

"Good," he says. "I was hoping you'd say that."
And together, we leave the garden behind—
not as fugitives,
not as pawns,
but as the reckoning that's been coming for the Guild all along.

Epilogue

Alejandro

I've walked into active war zones with less resistance in my chest than this.

Saint stands beside me, shoulders loose but eyes sharp, popping two pieces of bubble gum into her mouth like she's bracing for impact. She chews once. Twice. Fast.

That's never a good sign.

"You don't need to look like we're about to breach a compound," I tell her quietly, adjusting my grip on the stack of oversized, brightly wrapped boxes in my arms. "It's a birthday party."

She doesn't look at me. Her jaw tightens just a fraction.

"I don't do family."

I glance over, softer now. She's healed. Mostly. Scar lines pink against her dark skin, confidence back where it belongs, but this—this is different. There's no blade for this kind of threat.

"You'll do great," I say. "You've survived worse."

She snorts. "That's not reassuring."

We step out of the car together, all business. She carries the pasta salad like it might explode. I balance the gifts, shifting them higher against my chest as music thumps through the tall wooden gate ahead of us. Laughter. Too much laughter.

I stop her just before we reach it.

"Saint," I say, lowering my voice. "You took on the Onryō Forty-Nine by yourself."

She looks at me now, eyes wide and absolutely unimpressed.

"I would rather fight them again," she says flatly. "Please."

I chuckle and reach for the gate. "It'll be a walk in the park."

The gate swings open and it's chaos.

Dozens of people. Fifty, maybe sixty. Kids running everywhere. A long table covered in food. Balloons. Music blasting. Spanish flying from every direction at once, loud, and fast and alive.

Saint freezes.

Her mouth actually drops open.

She looks at me like I've betrayed her.

"You said it would just be family," she says slowly, chewing her gum like it personally offended her.

I look around, taking inventory of the faces. "Si. This is just the family."

Saint looks like she wants to throw the pasta salad like a grenade and run but it's too late.

My sister spots us instantly. Her face lights up, one hand already resting on her very round belly as she waves wildly and shouts my name. My mother appears beside her, eyes locking onto me like a missile system.

And then they're moving.

Saint barely has time to react before she's swallowed whole.

Hands on her arms. Cheek kisses from both sides. Rapid Spanish questions she is trying to catalog. Someone plucks the pasta salad from her hands. Someone else relieves me of the gifts. An aunt she's never met hugs her like they've known each other for years.

She looks back at me over my mother's shoulder, eyes narrowed, panic sharp and unmistakable.

"If I yell Skippy," she says through clenched teeth, "I need an extraction. Immediately."

I laugh, helpless and fond.

"I'm sure you can handle yourself."

She disappears into the crowd, dragged toward the center of the madness, and I watch her go—this lethal, brilliant woman who has never belonged anywhere like this in her life.

And somehow, against all odds, she's standing in the middle of it anyway.

My brother-in-law shows up at my side with a beer and a grin like nothing in the world has ever gone wrong.

"Brother."

We hug, solid and familiar, the kind that says *you made it back alive.*

"It's good to see you," I say, and I mean far more than tonight.

The party blurs after that. Laughter. Music. Old faces I haven't seen in years pulling me into conversations that feel like they never paused. Stories overlap. Someone presses food into my hands. Someone else claps me on the shoulder like they're checking I'm real.

And through all of it, Saint.

I spot her eventually, still being dragged from group to group by my mother, introduced like a prized discovery. She's laughing now. Really laughing. Talking with my sisters like she belongs there, like she always has. The purple sundress she chose moves when she does, light and dangerous, the color pulling her eyes sharp and bright.

She looks relaxed.

That hits harder than any punch ever has.

I rescue her with a beer and earn a look of mock gratitude that tightens something low in my chest. After that, the night settles into something easy.

Too easy.

I'm halfway through my third hot dog when she appears in front of me, arms crossed, eyes narrowed in judgment.

Not just because it's aggressively processed meat but because it's *land meat.*

Saint's mortal enemy.

She looks at the hot dog. Then at me.

"Hmm, eating your favorite shape again, I see."

I groan. "I'm being attacked in my own family home."

Before she can finish the execution, someone sets down a fresh platter beside the grill. More hot dogs. Raw hamburger patties stacked and ready.

RED RIBBON PROVISION CO.
Quality Meats Since 1949

Same brand.

The thought hits me so fast my stomach drops out from under my ribs.

I freeze with the hot dog halfway to my mouth, jaw hanging open as memory slams into me like a physical blow. Saint's eyes follow my stare to the packaging in the man's hands. I see the exact second it clicks for her too.

That logo.

That red-and-white striping.

The same damned brand stamped across the crates in the hot dog factory that we turned into a war zone.

The one where bodies fell into the processing line, where meat grinders didn't care about tailored suits or polished shoes or the fact that one of those men was already three days dead, bloated, leaking, and dragged halfway across the world before being fed into industrial blades.

Skippy.

Christ.

I look down at the hot dog in my hand like it's suddenly breathing.

Then I look back at the packaging.

Then at Saint.

"I've had three," I say quietly.

She stares at me for half a second before covering her mouth. "I may be sick."

"You?" I gesture at myself, panic finally clawing up my throat. "I'm the one who ate the corpse-meat."

I turn the hot dog over, inspecting it like I might find a button, a cufflink, some horrifying piece of recognition staring back at me.

"Ay, Dios mío," I mutter. "What if I turn into Frank?"

I throw the plate into the trash like it might jump back out.

Saint laughs. Full, unrestrained, delighted laughter. The sound hits me straight in the chest.

She lifts a fork with a piece of pineapple and holds it up.

"See?" she says sweetly. "Pineapple would never betray me like that."

She feeds it to me and walks over to the table, watching the dancing, hips swaying slightly to the music.

I grab another beer mostly to wash down the lingering horror and tell myself repeatedly that it was *just* hot dog.

Probably.

I come up behind her and slide a hand around her waist, grounding myself there. I offer her the beer. She takes a sip and smiles back at me, a faint sheen of it still on her lips.

I want to kiss it away.

I lean in.

She pulls back just enough.

"Do you have Skippy hot dog breath?"

I chuckle low and bend close to her ear, my hand drifting down her hip, slow and intentional.

"I'd much rather have the taste of you in my mouth," I murmur, pressing a kiss to her neck.

She pushes back into me, just slightly.

That's all it takes.

I'm already hard.

She turns her head, teasing. "Not really sure that's family-friendly. Might scare the children."

She kisses me anyway.

My hand keeps moving, sliding along the curve of her hip, hovering dangerously close, my mouth finding that place on her neck I know by instinct now.

"I think," I say softly, voice rough, "I should give you a tour of the house."

Another kiss. Slower.

"A very, very good tour."

I take another drink, then her hand, giving her a look that promises trouble.

"Come on."

And she comes with me.

She slows as soon as she's inside, like the house has weight. Frames line the walls. Birthdays. Holidays. A life documented in proof.

She stops in front of one and stares.

I don't say anything. I can tell she's cataloging something she never had. The way her fingers hover instead of touch, like she's afraid the glass might break if she claims it.

"You were loved," she says quietly.

It's not an accusation. It's not envy. Just fact.

"Still am," I answer, softer than I mean to.

She turns, catches a different frame, and her mouth curves. "Oh my god."

I groan before she even points. "Don't."

She holds it closer. "Please tell me you didn't cut your own hair."

"I was very handsome," I say, dead serious.

She laughs, full and bright. "You look like a mushroom."

"It was very stylish."

She steps into me, still smiling, still holding the picture between us. "Liar."

I take the frame from her, set it aside, and back her up until her shoulders hit my bedroom door. Her smile fades into something darker when I kiss her. Slow at first. Teasing. I want her to feel how badly I want this without rushing it.

The door shuts behind her.

Something about it feels dangerous in the best way. Like being young. Like doing something you're not supposed to.

My hand slides into her hair, tilting her head back as my mouth claims hers again. She kisses me like she's been waiting, like the teasing already lit her up.

"You like being in my room?" I murmur against her mouth.

Her breath hitches. "Feels... illicit."

"Good."

I walk her backward until the backs of her knees hit the bed and she falls onto it with a soft gasp. I follow her down, kiss a path along her throat, her collarbone, lower. My hands slide under her skirt, thumbs hooking into lace.

"Already wet," I say quietly. "You thinking about me doing this all night?"

She bites her lip, nods.

I peel her panties down slow, deliberately, letting my knuckles brush her skin just to make her squirm. When I finally sink between her thighs, she arches up, already needy.

My mouth takes her apart. Tongue slow, then ruthless. I want her breathing broken, hands tangled in my hair, hips lifting helplessly as I keep her right on the edge and then shove her over it.

"Fuck," she whispers. "Alejandro—"

I don't stop until she comes hard, trembling, breathless, wrecked.

She's barely caught her breath before she's pushing me back, crawling up my body with that look—starving, cocky, a little dangerous. She straddles my hips, palms flat on my chest.

I'm still wearing too much. She yanks my shirt up, nails dragging over my abs, smirking when I tense for her. "Still dressed?" she teases. "That's not very accommodating."

I grab her wrist, roll my hips up against her ass. "Take what you want, mi vida. We both know you love my cock."

She peels my shirt off, impatient, biting her lip when she sees the mess of old scars, the cut lines of muscle. She pushes me back, eyes raking over me like she's memorizing the view for later.

She goes for my belt next—fingers clumsy, desperate—finally frees me, and her hand closes around my dick. She hesitates, mouth parted, pupils blown wide. "Jesus. So fucking big?"

She sinks down, and I have to grit my teeth, grip her hips to keep from slamming up into her like an animal. She gasps, a strangled sound that's all satisfaction and disbelief. I slide my hand up her side. Thumb gently caressing over the pink scar of her katana injury, still tender sometimes.

"Fuck," she whimpers, eyes fluttering shut, head thrown back.

I press a hand to her lower back, guiding her. "That's it, Picarita. Every inch is yours."

She rides me slow, hips rolling, tight and so goddamn perfect I nearly see stars. Her nails rake down my chest, marking me as hers, and I let her have the illusion of control —for now.

"Look at you," I growl, voice rough. "On top, thinking you're in charge. You have no idea, baby."

She leans in, lips at my ear. "Pretty sure I've got you exactly where I want you."

I snap, flipping her in one brutal motion, pinning her wrists to the bed. "Not a fucking chance. This is where you belong—right here, under me."

I drive into her hard, deep, every thrust drawing a broken sound from her throat. Our eyes lock, everything hot and desperate and too much to survive.

Her hand flies up, covering her mouth as I thrust deep— her moan caught in her palm. I grin, breath hot against her ear. "What, scared someone might hear you?"

She bites her lip, eyes wide. "You want to get us caught?"

I brush her hair off her neck, press my mouth to the spot just below her ear. "No, mi amor. I want you to try and keep quiet for once in your life."

She laughs—a soft, trembling sound I swallow with a kiss. My hips move slow, relentless, dragging every breath out of her until she's writhing, desperate, thighs trembling beneath my hands.

She tries to muffle another moan. I pin her wrists above her head, lips against hers, catching every gasp and whimper before it escapes. "That's it," I whisper, voice rough. "Let me have all of it. Give it to me, quiet, right here."

She nods, eyes glassy, mouth opening beneath mine as I thrust harder, deeper. The bed creaks—too loud—so I pause, teeth gritted, forehead pressed to hers, both of us panting. I ease my hand between us, thumb circling her clit, mouth hovering over hers to steal the sound.

Her body tenses, legs tightening around my waist as she comes, every muscle straining to stay silent. I catch her cry with my mouth, swallowing it whole, fucking her through the aftershocks while her nails dig into my back.

I don't last—can't. I bury my face in her neck, breath shuddering, muffling my own groan in her skin as I spill inside her.

We collapse, tangled and breathless, heartbeats thundering in the hush of the house just beyond the door.

Perfect? Not even close. It's messy, stolen, risk burning on our skin—but that's what makes it real. And I'd risk it again, every time.

Thank you so much for reading! If you enjoyed this story, please leave a review.

Check out the other books in the Accidental series:
That Time I Accidentally Took Over the Mafia
A **Why-Choose**, **Second Chance** dark romantic comedy.

AND

That Time I Accidentally Became a Serial Killer
A **Legally Blonde** meets **Dexter** dark romantic comedy.

NOTES

Welcome to
The Black Ledger

Where every desire has a price...
and every contract is final.

The Black Ledger
Billionaires

Check Out www.RebekahSinclairWrites.com for more!

www.ingramcontent.com/pod-product-compliance
Lightning Source LLC
Chambersburg PA
CBHW022019300726
48970CB00003B/956